PRAISE FOR DONNA GRANT'S BEST-SELLING
ROMANCE NOVELS

"Grant's ability to quickly convey complicated backstory makes
this jam-packed love story accessible even to new or periodic
readers." –*Publishers' Weekly*

"Donna Grant has given the paranormal genre a burst of fresh
air…" –*San Francisco Book Review*

"The premise is dramatic and heartbreaking; the characters are
colorful and engaging; the romance is spirited and seductive."
–*The Reading Cafe*

"The central romance, fueled by a hostage drama, plays out in
glorious detail against a backdrop of multiple ongoing issues in the
"Dark Kings" books. This seemingly penultimate installment
creates a nice segue to a climactic end." –*Library Journal*

"…intense romance amid the growing war between the Dragons
and the Dark Fae is scorching hot." –*Booklist*

DARK KINGS SERIES

Dark Heat ~ Darkest Flame ~ Fire Rising ~ Burning Desire
Hot Blooded ~ Night's Blaze ~ Soul Scorched ~ Dragon King
Passion Ignites ~ Smoldering Hunger ~ Smoke and Fire
Dragon Fever ~ Firestorm ~ Blaze ~ Dragon Burn
Constantine: A History, Parts 1-3 ~ Heat ~ Torched
Dragon Night ~ Dragonfire ~ Dragon Claimed
Ignite ~ Fever ~ Dragon Lost ~ Flame ~ Inferno
A Dragon's Tale (Whisky and Wishes: *A Holiday Novella*,
Heart of Gold: *A Valentine's Novella*, & Of Fire and Flame)
My Fiery Valentine ~ The Dragon King Coloring Book
Dragon King Special Edition Character Coloring Book: Rhi

DARK WARRIORS SERIES

Midnight's Master ~ Midnight's Lover ~ Midnight's Seduction
Midnight's Warrior ~ Midnight's Kiss ~ Midnight's Captive
Midnight's Temptation ~ Midnight's Promise
Midnight's Surrender ~ A Warrior for Christmas

CHIASSON SERIES

Wild Fever ~ Wild Dream ~ Wild Need
Wild Flame ~ Wild Rapture

LARUE SERIES

Moon Kissed ~ Moon Thrall ~ Moon Struck ~ Moon Bound

WICKED TREASURES

Seized by Passion ~ Enticed by Ecstasy ~ Captured by Desire
Books 1-3: Wicked Treasures Box Set

HISTORICAL PARANORMAL

THE KINDRED SERIES

Everkin ~ Eversong ~ Everwylde ~ Everbound
Evernight ~ Everspell

KINDRED: THE FATED SERIES

Rage ~ Ruin ~ Reign

DARK SWORD SERIES

Dangerous Highlander ~ Forbidden Highlander
Wicked Highlander ~ Untamed Highlander
Shadow Highlander ~ Darkest Highlander

ROGUES OF SCOTLAND SERIES

The Craving ~ The Hunger ~ The Tempted ~ The Seduced
Books 1-4: Rogues of Scotland Box Set

THE SHIELDS SERIES

A Dark Guardian ~ A Kind of Magic ~ A Dark Seduction
A Forbidden Temptation ~ A Warrior's Heart
Mystic Trinity (a series connecting novel)

DRUIDS GLEN SERIES

Highland Mist ~ Highland Nights ~ Highland Dawn
Highland Fires ~ Highland Magic
Mystic Trinity (a series connecting novel)

SISTERS OF MAGIC TRILOGY
Shadow Magic ~ Echoes of Magic ~ Dangerous Magic
Books 1-3: Sisters of Magic Box Set

THE ROYAL CHRONICLES NOVELLA SERIES
Prince of Desire ~ Prince of Seduction
Prince of Love ~ Prince of Passion
Books 1-4: The Royal Chronicles Box Set
Mystic Trinity (a series connecting novel)

DARK BEGINNINGS: A FIRST IN SERIES BOXSET
Chiasson Series, Book 1: Wild Fever
LaRue Series, Book 1: Moon Kissed
The Royal Chronicles Series, Book 1: Prince of Desire

MILITARY ROMANCE / ROMANTIC SUSPENSE

SONS OF TEXAS SERIES
The Hero ~ The Protector ~ The Legend
The Defender ~ The Guardian

COWBOY / CONTEMPORARY

HEART OF TEXAS SERIES

The Christmas Cowboy Hero ~ Cowboy, Cross My Heart
My Favorite Cowboy ~ A Cowboy Like You
Looking for a Cowboy ~ A Cowboy Kind of Love

STAND ALONE BOOKS

That Cowboy of Mine
Home for a Cowboy Christmas
Mutual Desire
Forever Mine
Savage Moon

**Check out Donna Grant's Online Store at
www.DonnaGrant.com/shop
for autographed books, character
themed goodies, and more!**

www.DonnaGrant.com
www.MotherofDragonsBooks.com

ENDLESS SKYE

SKYE DRUIDS

FOUR

NEW YORK TIMES & USA TODAY BESTSELLING AUTHOR

DONNA GRANT

CHAPTER ONE

SKYE DRUIDS

Edinburgh

Her ragged breathing was so loud she could barely hear her shoes slapping against the wet cobblestones. Willa Ryan slipped as she turned a corner and pressed her back against a building to listen and catch her breath. Sweat clung to her, driving away the cool March air and the dampness of the recent rain.

Her hands shook as she lifted her mobile to text her brother a warning, but her fingers wouldn't work properly, and it was one of the rare times when autocorrect didn't do its job. She wanted to scream in frustration as she deleted the message and tried again, only to mess up once more. It would be easier to call Scott. She'd have to keep her voice down, but at least she could warn him. Willa was about to dial when she heard her pursuers. She clutched her mobile as she raced through the city, the streetlamps seeming to reach out with their light to find her.

She needed to hide, rest, and think. And notify Scott.

Willa turned onto another street. She continued to weave around the clusters of people out for dinner or looking for some fun. She kept her attention in front of her, watching where she planted her feet, allowing her to move quickly when someone stepped before her.

"Sorry," she hurriedly muttered when she hit a woman's shoulder.

Willa didn't look back. She knew those chasing her were still there. They were relentless. And they wouldn't stop until they found her. Willa's eyes darted about, scanning faces as she came to another intersection. She glanced at the crosswalk lights and noticed the cars traveling across her path.

When she spotted a group of people crossing the large intersection, she hurried to join them. She hated slowing to a casual walk, but at least she blended for the moment. It allowed her to rest and look back the way she had come. She saw the man and woman who had been trailing her anxiously searching. She wouldn't stay hidden for long. Willa had to make the most of it.

She shoved a long strand of hair that had escaped her ponytail away from her face. Her chest burned, and her lungs ached. Her legs were so fatigued they could barely hold her up. She brought her mobile up again to call Scott. She navigated to her favorites and was about to press his name when someone bumped into her from behind. Magic pooled in her palms as Willa whirled, ready to launch it, only to find two very drunk women.

"Ooh. You're pretty," the blonde said as she wound an arm around Willa's shoulder. "You should come hang with us."

Willa saw they were pulling her toward a nightclub. It would be a good place to hide, but she had no money or ID to get inside. She forced herself to smile, but she wasn't sure it appeared as relaxed as she wanted since both women gave her a funny look. "I don't have my wallet."

"You're not gonna need it," the bleached blonde said with a wink.

Willa continued with the group as the women talked loudly in between whistling at people. She couldn't see behind her, which meant her hunters likely couldn't find her. Then she was at the doors of the club. Someone at the front held up a black credit card and slurred, stating he was paying for the entire group. A bouncer counted them, and then, before she knew it, Willa was through the door.

She quickly maneuvered off by herself. The music was so loud her ears rang. Clusters of people were everywhere, leaving her barely any room to move. She had to shove people aside just to get to the bar and order a water. She gulped it quickly.

Willa wiped her mouth and looked around the dark club. When she spotted some stairs, she made her way to them. She weaved between people as she headed up, hoping she could find a quieter place to call her brother.

The flashing lights bothered her, but she tried to ignore them. There was a second bar upstairs, and she snagged another water. She debated her location. Scott would never be able to hear her over the music. She needed to text him instead. At least now, she could do that without worrying about being found, and maybe her hands wouldn't shake so badly. Once she warned him, she would make her way out of Edinburgh. Her father was probably already on his way to Skye.

Willa found a column near the balcony so she could watch the entrance. She didn't see her pursuers. Still, she kept one eye on the door as she typed out her message. She was on the last sentence when something slammed into her ribs, shoving her painfully into the balcony railing. The impact snapped her head to the side.

She immediately ducked when she spotted a fist coming at her face. Willa recognized the woman as one of her pursuers. How had they found her again? Her only thought was getting away. Willa slid to the right to bolt when a thick forearm connected with her throat. The lights spun above her before vanishing out of sight as she gasped for breath. Then, she was falling. She panicked and reached out for something to grab. Anything. Her fingers latched on to the cool metal of the railing as screams filled the building.

Willa tried to lift her right arm, but pain shot through her. She bit back a cry and looked at her hand on the railing. Her palms were sweating. She wouldn't be able to hold on for long. She then lowered her gaze to see the dance floor cleared, people rushing out and glancing back at someone. No. Not someone. They were looking at *her*.

"What the fuck are you doing?" someone shouted from above her.

She tried to imagine how far she was about to fall. If she landed wrong, she could twist an ankle. Or worse, break something. She glanced at her left hand and then looked back at the floor below. Her only choice was to drop and land as best she could.

Suddenly, someone grabbed her arm. She started to struggle, believing it was her attackers.

"Easy, lass!" a man yelled over the music still blaring. "We've got you. We're going to pull you up."

He and two other men helped get her back on solid ground. She bit back a cry of pain when they yanked at her right shoulder.

"You're safe. The wankers who attacked you are gone," the man told her.

Willa could barely see past the agony blinding her. "Thank you." Something warm and wet soaked her black sweater. She tentatively touched her shoulder and gasped. She licked her lips and glanced around. "I have to get out of here before they come back."

"The police are on their way."

She shook her head. "I need to leave. Now. Please. It's life or death."

One of the other men, a burly redhead, motioned for her to follow him. "I work here. I can show you a way out."

She followed as he led her through a doorway and down a hallway to a set of stairs.

There, he stopped and pointed. "There's a door at the bottom. This comes out at the back of the club."

"Did you see where the two who attacked me went?"

He twisted his lips ruefully. "I was too busy trying to reach you."

"Thank you," she told him and then started down the stairs.

She halted at the bottom to call Scott, but when she looked for her mobile, it was gone. It must have slipped from her grasp during the scuffle. She didn't have money, a phone, or a vehicle. Edinburgh was a big city with lots of places for a person to hide, but that wouldn't do her any good if she couldn't contact her brother.

And if she couldn't get in touch with him, once their father reached Skye and found she wasn't there, the two would come looking for her.

"Can't have you two doing that," she murmured, pushing against the door.

Willa opened it wide enough to look out before slipping through and away from the light. The area was dark—a perfect place for someone to wait for her. It was where she would be if she were the one doing the chasing. One out front and another at the back.

She stood against the building, letting her eyes adjust to the night and studying the shadows. If someone were there, they would've already come at her. Or maybe not. She wasn't sure of anything anymore. It was hard to think at all with the pain throbbing through her.

Something dripped. She looked down as she followed the sound and found blood drops falling from her fingers. Willa brought her injured arm against her, cradling it carefully. Then she crept into the night. She kept to the shadows, moving carefully. She needed a phone. What she really needed was a car. She had never stolen anything before, and she wasn't sure how easy it was to do. Especially wounded. But what choice did she have? If she stayed, they would kill her.

How did one even go about stealing a vehicle? It wasn't as if she could walk to Skye. Well, she *could*, but it would take too long. They were no doubt watching the train. Same with the buses. The only way for her to get out cleanly was in a vehicle.

She had no idea how long she walked before she saw two guys trying to park. They were so piss-drunk that half the car was on the curb. She paused to watch them. Perhaps she could use this to her advantage. The men weren't with it enough to overpower her, and she had her magic if she needed it. They would report the vehicle as stolen, but not until morning if she did things right. She could be in Skye by then.

Willa slowly looked around to see if anyone was watching. It was late, and the lights she saw in the residential buildings were behind closed curtains. She needed some good luck. Maybe this was finally it.

"Please, let this work," she whispered to the Universe.

She made her way to the men, who were laughing hysterically at something. This could be a setup. She didn't trust anything in the city. If she had any other choice, she would keep walking. But this was it. She was sure of it.

The passenger door opened, and a guy fell out onto the sidewalk. He rolled onto his back, laughing as his arm got caught in the seat belt. The driver got out and left his door open as he used the car to hold himself up and then stumbled around the hood, promptly unzipping his pants to urinate. Willa wrinkled her nose in disgust.

The passenger managed to free his arm and began to crawl toward a set of stairs, all while singing at the top of his lungs.

The driver didn't bother zipping up as he weaved toward his friend. "Where ya goin'?"

"Home," the passenger slurred.

"That ain't home, you idjit," the driver stated.

The two looked at each other and busted out laughing again.

The driver then turned and lurched forward, catching himself on the car's bonnet before falling. Willa debated rushing over and getting in right then. They were so drunk she would likely get away with it, but they could also turn belligerent.

"Who left my doors open?" the driver angrily demanded as he stared at the vehicle.

Willa glanced behind her as the driver managed to get to the door and push it closed. He then walked around the back and closed the passenger door his friend had left open. She bit her lip anxiously, debating when to make a run for it. She waited as she watched the driver try to get the passenger on his feet.

They both started singing and lurching haphazardly down the street straight toward her. Willa gathered her magic in her left hand as she remained in the shadows with her back against a building. If this were a ploy, she would be ready.

But the guys walked past without incident. Still, Willa didn't move until they were out of sight. Only then did she make her way to the car, all the while praying that the keys were inside. She furtively looked around before sliding behind the wheel. She slumped against the seat to see the push button start but no key fob.

Tears of frustration and fear filled her eyes. She clenched her jaw and got out of the vehicle. It wouldn't be long before her pursuers found her again. If she didn't take this opportunity, she might never get out of the city. Willa softly shut the door and started after the drunks. She followed their singing and jogged to catch up with them, all the while remaining on high alert for another attack.

When she came upon the two men, she sent out a soft wave of magic directed at their outer sides so the bench caught them as they fell unconscious. A quick check of the driver's pockets yielded the key fob and a mobile. She took a moment to rouse him long enough to unlock his phone and change the password so she could get in.

"Thanks," she told him as his eyes rolled back in his head again. "I'll have your car returned. I promise."

She pocketed the mobile and spun around. Willa wanted to run back to the car, but she made herself walk casually. She didn't want to draw attention to herself. Every shadow she passed held a potential enemy. She kept her magic at the ready, listening behind her as she made her way back to the vehicle. Cars passed, and the world continued as if she weren't fighting for her very life.

Willa sighed when she reached the car. She quickly got inside and started it. Then she maneuvered the vehicle back onto the road and drove away. She didn't breathe easily until she was out of the city. It was about a five-hour drive to Skye, and she didn't plan on stopping unless she had to.

But with each mile, it became harder and harder to stay awake and focused. She found napkins in the glove box and used them to stanch the flow of blood, but they didn't do much good. She started to dose off a couple of times. That made her pull over and get out to walk around. Then she was back on the road. It felt like an eternity before she finally drove over the bridge to the isle.

She had used the last bit of her energy to stay awake long enough to get to Skye. Willa didn't know where Scott lived, and she didn't think she could continue driving. She was surprised she had made it as far as she had. She was so damned tired. She just needed to close her eyes for a moment.

The impact startled her awake. She opened her eyes to find that she had hit a road sign. Willa tried to get the mobile, but her fingers were clumsy. It took her three tries before she held it in her hand and keyed in Scott's number. It rang twice before the line connected.

"Hello?" he asked sleepily.

The sound of his voice brought another round of tears. She had made it. He would find her. "I need help."

"Willa? What is it? What's wrong?"

She heard the urgency in his voice, the worry. "I just crossed the bridge. I'm on Skye, but I'm injured. I need you."

"I'll find you. Stay there. I'm coming, Willa."

She nodded, the phone slipping from her fingers.

CHAPTER TWO

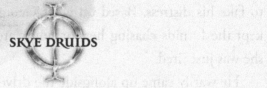

SKYE DRUIDS

"I see her," Jasper said when he caught sight of the black Volkswagen erratically coming over the bridge onto the Isle of Skye.

Georgina Miller, better known as George, made a sound over the phone. "The team following Willa will turn around and come home. The rest is up to you, Jasper. Don't let me down."

"I know what to do."

"A lot is riding on this."

"I know. It's why I'm here."

George sighed loudly. "Don't let your guard down around them. *If* you get in."

"Oh, I'll get in."

"Let's hope so."

The line disconnected. Jasper focused on the car driven by Willa Ryan. He had to admit he was a little impressed that Willa had stolen the vehicle. It wasn't something the Ryans had ever done before. And he should know. Jasper had spent the last few months studying everything about the family. He knew them better than they knew themselves.

He frowned when the vehicle suddenly pitched to the left. George had informed him that Willa was injured, but it was supposed to be minor. He slowed as the Volkswagen did. His concern grew when the car struck a sign.

Jasper pulled up behind the vehicle and got out. He didn't have to fake his distress. Based on what George had shared, Willa had kept the Druids chasing her for hours around Edinburgh. Maybe she was just tired.

He warily came up alongside the driver's door. "Hello? Are you all right?"

There was no answer or even movement from within the car. Jasper leaned close to the window and peered inside. He spotted Willa slumped over, obviously unconscious. He tried the handle, but it was locked.

"Fuck," he muttered and moved to the door behind her.

Jasper broke the window with his magic and hit the unlock button. As soon as he opened the driver's door, he smelled the unmistakable coppery scent of blood. He paused when he saw just how much of it covered the seat and pooled on the floorboard.

"Fuck," he said again. "Minor injury, my arse."

He would have a long talk with George about her idea of *minor*. Jasper gripped Willa's wrist and felt for a pulse. Relief poured through him when he found it. It was faint, but it was there. He gently removed her from the vehicle and laid her on the grass. He felt around on her sleeve, following the blood until he found the source—a wound on her shoulder. He ripped the sweater enough to see better.

"Jesus. Fuck," he declared when he saw how much blood still leaked from it.

Jasper put his hand over the wound, the blood seeping through his fingers. Instantly, his thoughts wrenched him to the past when he'd attempted to stem the bleeding of another injury on a cold, damp night. He shook his head to dislodge the memory. It would take more than his hand to stop the blood.

He tore off his jacket, tossing it aside to get to his button-down beneath. He yanked so hard on the shirt that buttons went flying. After wadding up the material, he pressed it firmly against the wound. His gaze went to Willa's face, but she didn't stir.

Blood soaked the shirt quickly, the scent clinging to the air around him. The memory resurfaced, dragging him back to that dreadful night. He blinked and returned to the present, refusing to be sucked into that long-ago moment. Willa had been driving the entire time while bleeding. He was surprised she had made it as far as she had.

"Come on, Willa," he murmured. "You made it here. Surely, you're no' giving up that easily. Fight, lass."

The sound of a car door closing caught Jasper's attention. He raised his head and yelled, "Help! Call 999, we need an ambulance!"

Footsteps quickened into a run from behind him. "What happened?" a man asked.

Jasper pressed against the wound with both hands, using most of his weight. "I saw her hit the sign. When I approached, I found her unconscious."

The man knelt beside him and felt Willa's pulse at her throat. "How bad is the injury?"

Jasper looked up into the face of Detective Inspector Theo Frasier. "Bad."

"Keep pressure on it. I'm calling som—"

His words halted as lights bounced along the road, and a vehicle pulled up behind Jasper's SUV. Jasper knew without looking that it would be Scott Ryan. A moment later, he had confirmation as Scott came running.

"Willa? Willa!" Scott yelled.

Frasier straightened to face the man. "She's alive."

"What happened?" Scott demanded.

Jasper didn't look up as Frasier repeated what he had said moments earlier. Jasper stared at Willa's pale face in the light of the headlamps. What had gone wrong in Edinburgh? How could George have thought this was a minor wound? They would be lucky if she lived. And only if they got her to the Healers in time.

Though he couldn't say that to anyone.

"Has she said anything?" Scott asked, his voice tight.

Jasper looked up to find Scott's gaze on him. "Nay."

Scott raked a hand through his hair, his fear palpable. A moment later, two other people arrived. The night hid the fact that Jasper looked for Rhona, leader of the Skye Druids, and her mate, Balladyn.

The Reaper strode to him and laid a hand on Jasper's shoulder. "I'll take it from here."

"We need to wait for the ambulance," he said, continuing to play his part.

Frasier shook his head. "It's coming. This man is trained. Let him take over while I get your statement over here."

"My statement?"

Frasier took out his credentials and showed them to Jasper. "Please. This way."

This was how it was supposed to happen—well, except for Willa being unconscious and pale as death. Reluctantly, Jasper let Balladyn take over holding his shirt. He stood and followed Frasier. It didn't go unnoticed how the Detective Inspector carefully turned Jasper so his back was to Willa. Which meant he never saw Balladyn teleport away with Willa.

"What's your name?" Frasier asked as he pulled a notebook from his pocket.

Jasper looked down at his hands, still covered in her blood. It had taken him days to get it off the last time, and there were still occasions when he saw them covered in blood. Just as they were now. Who would he see when it happened again? Would it be the blood from that first time? Or would it be Willa's.

"Sir?" Frasier prompted.

Jasper wiped his forearm across his mouth. "McCabe. Jasper McCabe."

"All right, Mr. McCabe. Tell me the sequence of events again."

Jasper went through it twice more. Cars came and went, and the voices behind him were some he recognized. He wanted to turn and see all of the people, but that wasn't what someone in a normal situation would do. His role required him to act like any other person would—not a Druid spying on those on Skye.

"I think we're done for now. If I need to talk to you again, I know how to get in touch with you," Frasier said.

"You think I hurt that woman?" Jasper asked with just enough shock to be believable. He was used to becoming different people and, thanks to his upbringing, had learned early on to read others.

"I'm piecing everything together. Someone hurt her."

"It wasna me."

"Do me a favor and doona leave the isle."

Jasper wiped his hands on his jeans and undershirt for the tenth time, wishing for soap and water. "I live here."

"Still. Doona leave."

He nodded, and Frasier walked away. Jasper turned then. He saw the DI talking to someone Jasper couldn't make out because of the headlights of a car behind them. With nothing more to do, he returned to his car.

He got into his SUV and drove home. Jasper waited until he was inside before calling George. "What the hell happened in Edinburgh?" he demanded as soon as she answered.

"Excuse me?" she snapped.

"It wasna a minor injury. Willa was barely alive. Most of her blood covered the inside of the car."

A brief pause came over the line. "Did Balladyn show up?"

"Aye," he bit out.

"She's not dead yet, Jasper. They won't let her die. Trust me."

He held out a hand, seeing it shake. This was one of those times he wished he drank. "You need to have a talk with whoever was supposed to wound her because they didna understand your order."

"Let me handle my people. Now, tell me if things played out as you thought they would."

Jasper paced the kitchen in an effort to calm down. "Aye. The only difference was that Frasier arrived before Scott."

"Then you have nothing to worry about. The Healers will save Willa, and we can continue with the plan. Right?"

He closed his eyes. He was used to running his own things. Taking orders from—and answering to—someone else hadn't yet become the norm. He wondered if it ever would. But this was what he wanted, wasn't it? To have others around him, people he could count on. "Right."

George lowered the mobile and looked across the room at Beth and the two female guards that flanked her.

Beth Stewart sighed and rolled her pale brown eyes. "Well? What was all the drama about?"

"I thought your people were going to *mildly* wound Willa."

"They did."

George carefully set the phone on the table and smiled, but it was a cold one full of anger. "They didn't. In fact, had Jasper not gotten to her in time, she'd be dead."

"But he *did* get to her in time."

George was starting to wish she had never allowed Beth and her small group into the organization. But Beth had the book. And it wasn't just any book, either. It was one about Druids and magic with information that had been lost for ages. George wanted that tome, and she would have it. First, however, she had to tolerate Beth. She was another connection to Skye, and one George intended to use.

Beth quirked a brown brow. "They won't let Willa die."

"You took a chance she'd get to Skye in time."

"It paid off, didn't it? Besides, your people were following her. They would've stepped in had it been needed." Beth smoothed her fingers over her pixie cut.

"I make plans for a reason. If you're going to be in my organization, you'll follow *my* rules. Is that clear?"

Beth grinned, not bothering to hide her contempt as she stood. "Crystal."

George watched Beth and her two guards walk out of the room. The only time George had seen the book was when Beth approached her to join. If George hadn't seen it with her own eyes, she never would've believed it existed. But the book was real.

And she would have it. One way or another.

Her people were following Beth. George would find where she'd hidden the book. No one else would steal it. Only *she* would get her hands on it. It was too valuable to let just anyone handle it.

And once she had it, there would be no stopping her from getting her revenge on everyone who had betrayed her.

CHAPTER THREE

SKYE DRUIDS

The whispers pulled her from a dreamless sleep.

"Scott. You *have* to tell her," a woman said.

"Nay, I doona."

"You do. I would if she were my sister."

"Would you, love? I know there's something you've no' told *your* sister. And doona dare say it's different."

The woman sighed. "It *is* different. This happened *to* Willa."

She'd heard enough. Why wouldn't they let her sleep? Willa turned her head toward the voices and cracked open her eyes. She saw her brother with his back to her near the door, talking to a pretty woman with blond hair. "What happened to me?"

Scott immediately whirled around, relief covering his face. His deep blue eyes met hers as he rushed to her side. "You're awake. How do you feel?"

She swallowed and licked her dry lips. She took stock of her body and tried to ease the tense muscles. "I've been better."

"I'll get some water," the woman said and hurried out.

The mattress sagged when Scott sat on the edge and took her left hand in his. "You had us worried. You've been sleeping for some time."

The woman returned with the water. Willa used her right arm and tried to rise. She cried out and fell back as pain instantly shot through her.

"Easy. Easy," her brother soothed. "I should've warned you."

Willa clenched her teeth as the pain crested and finally began to ebb. She reached up and felt the bandage covering her upper arm and shoulder beneath the loose tee she wore. "How bad is the wound?"

"Bad," the woman said.

At the same time, Scott said, "No' that bad."

The two looked at each other, and the woman quirked a brow. Scott sighed. "Fine. It's…no' great."

"I'm Elodie," the woman said with a warm grin.

Willa smiled. "It's good to finally meet you."

"Same."

Willa slid her gaze back to Scott. "Help me sit up." Once she was comfortable, Willa took the water from Elodie. "What doesn't he want me to know?"

"It can wait," Scott said evasively.

Willa shook her head. "Out with it."

She brought the glass to her lips and let the cool water slide down her throat. Nothing had ever tasted so good. She drank and watched her brother fidget as he always did when he didn't want to share something. She gave him until she finished drinking, then she stared, waiting.

"We got you to the Healers, but they found something in the wound," Scott said.

Willa's fingers tightened on the glass. "What?"

"A splinter of ebony wood."

She frowned and shook her head. "I don't know what that means."

"None of us does. Or did," Elodie said with a slight frown. "It's what hindered your healing. It's why you still have pain."

Willa glanced at her arm. "Is it still in there?"

"The Healers got it out," Scott told her. "But it did a lot of damage while in there."

"Can the Healers return?"

Scott shook his head of dark hair. "There was magic attached to the splinter."

Apprehension churned in Willa's stomach. "That did what, exactly?"

"We're not sure," Elodie answered.

"It's being investigated. We'll eventually know more about this ebony wood," Scott added.

Willa looked between them. "Why would someone put a spell on some wood and use it as a weapon? That seems...specific."

"We'll have answers soon," Elodie reiterated.

Scott glanced away briefly. "The Healers removed the wood and closed the wound. But you lost a lot of blood. It was touch and go there for a bit."

Had she been that close to death? She winced when she shifted, and throbbing pain ran through her arm. "And the ache? How long will that last?"

Her brother hesitated for a long moment, a muscle ticking in his jaw. "They couldna say."

"I take it no one knows what the wood will do to me either."

Scott shook his head.

"I got out of Edinburgh with my life. I'm grateful for that. Where's Dad?" Willa asked.

Scott sat on the bed once more. "I was hoping you could tell me."

"He didn't make it out?" she asked, fear choking her.

"Nay. What happened, Willa?" Scott asked in a soft voice filled with concern. "He's no' answering my calls."

She swallowed hard. She had been sure her father had made it out. Had he been chased as she had? Was he injured? "We tried to steal the book from Beth."

"Bloody hell! I knew it," Scott declared angrily as he jumped to his feet to pace.

Elodie held up her hands to stop him. "Let's wait to hear everything before you get upset."

"Too bloody late," Scott bit out.

Willa watched her brother. "Dad and I had a solid plan."

"I never should've asked you to find it," Scott said. "I should've known it'd be too risky."

"We found the book. Beth has it, just as you suspected. And she's joined George's organization."

Scott halted at her words. His brows snapped together. "George still runs things?"

"Of course."

Elodie crossed her arms over her chest and snorted. "I wonder how much longer that'll be true."

Scott ran a hand down his face. "We all know how important —and dangerous—that book is. If only we'd gotten to it before Beth."

"She knew the hiding place. We didn't," Elodie said.

He nodded and let his shoulders drop as he looked at Willa. "Go on. What happened?"

Willa drew in a breath and slowly released it, careful not to move her right arm. "George never asked Dad or me to leave, but they watched us carefully. We were still allowed to attend the meetings, but they weren't as welcoming as before. No one trusted us. But Dad and I knew how important it was for us to remain until we had the book. Rumors about it began to swirl. It was all anyone could talk about. Just a day after you told us about Beth waking, she showed up in Edinburgh with the book in hand. She came to our meeting place and walked directly to George. I don't know what words they exchanged because I was too far away, but George could hardly take her eyes off the book."

"Was Beth alone?" Elodie asked.

"Nay," Willa said, shaking her head. "She had two women with her. And both looked as if they were well used to fighting. Beth and George's conversation didn't last long. George welcomed Beth and her associates into the organization that night. George asked to hold the book, but Beth refused. She did, however, open it to show George something. Whatever it was, it pleased her immensely."

Scott grunted. "I'd love to know what that was."

"George hates my brother, Elias," Elodie said. "She targeted him before. I don't think she'll give up."

Willa twisted her lips. "She won't. Everyone knows about her animosity toward Elias."

"I bet she doesn't like me very much, either." Elodie grinned.

"She feels you've personally slighted her since Scott stayed on Skye."

Scott rolled his eyes and shook his head. "Bloody hell. I can make my own decisions."

"Well, it's you and the fact that Elodie is Elias's sister," Willa explained.

Elodie wrinkled her nose. "Yikes."

"George holds grudges," Willa said with a shrug, wincing slightly. "She takes everything personally. So, when Beth returned without the book, the tension between them started. It's a power struggle thing, and everyone knows it. George has led for a long time. She's amassed a significant number of Druids who are loyal to her."

Scott grinned. "And there are those who doona care for her."

"Exactly. My guess is Beth was counting on something like that. Bringing the book showed everyone she had something that could change everything—at least, that's what everyone is saying. Once Dad and I realized Beth wouldn't bring the book with her, we followed her to figure out where it could be. Given how Beth held the tome, I suspected she wouldn't let anyone near it. That meant we didn't need to concern ourselves with the two guards she had with her. We worked out Beth's routine fairly quickly, and it seemed likely that her hiding place was her flat."

Elodie's brow furrowed deeply. "She would've warded that when she left."

"She did."

Scott closed his eyes for a heartbeat. "Tell me you and Dad didna try to break in."

"We're not idiots," Willa stated dryly. "We waited until we thought she was alone. Two against one."

Elodie's face was pinched. "Which didn't go well."

"It didna." Willa paused as she thought back to when her

moment of elation at getting into the flat turned to terror. "She was waiting for us and wasn't surprised at all. She knew we were coming."

"I would've guessed someone would try something like that," Scott said.

Willa pulled her knees up until her feet were flat on the mattress. "We still should've been able to surprise her, but we didn't. One moment, we had her. The next, the two guards were there. Dad and I agreed that if anything happened, we would split up and meet back here on Skye. We each had a route to get out of the city. We escaped the flat and split up as planned. One of Beth's women came after me, but it wasn't long before a man I'd never seen before joined her. They chased me all over Edinburgh. I stayed just ahead of them and went into a club to contact you when they attacked. That's when this happened," she said, jerking her chin to her arm. "I got away with some help, stole a car and a mobile, and drove to you. Well, I drove to Skye. I remember calling you, but then nothing after. I take it you got to me?"

"A man found you after you ran into a road sign. He got you out of the car and slowed the bleeding. Theo reached you before Scott and I did," Elodie said.

Scott headed toward the doorway. "Dad should be here. If he's no'... I'm going to call him again."

"He might have lost his phone as I did," Willa warned.

The statement was a reminder that everything she had was in Edinburgh. Yes, they were replaceable items, but something about losing those objects was both alarming and upsetting. No doubt George had sent people to her flat and her father's. Would it be ransacked? Would they destroy anything? The mere fact that individuals could have broken in was a violation she didn't want to consider. She certainly couldn't return home.

Though she never wanted to return to Edinburgh at all.

"We can get whatever you need," Elodie said as if reading her mind.

"I'm not sure that's safe."

Elodie grinned. "There are ways we can get in without anyone knowing."

"You're talking about Balladyn." Scott had told her and their father all about his friends on Skye. Willa was excited to meet the Reaper. She had seen Fae, but Balladyn was much more than that.

"Aye. You'll have whatever you need soon. Until then, you can continue wearing your brother's shirts, but you're also welcome to anything in my closet."

Willa smiled. "You're taller, so I'm not sure how much will fit."

"I'm not the only one offering. Bronwyn, Rhona, Ferne, and even Sabryn have dropped some things off for you. You'll get to meet all of them soon."

"I think I understand why Scott never wanted to leave."

Elodie shrugged a shoulder. "There was a time I felt completely alone, but Scott was there with Filip in my darkest hour, along with Rhona and Balladyn. We came together for Elias and Bronwyn. And most recently for Theo and Ferne. I guess you could say we've created a little family. Though, it's not little. It's rather big and growing larger." She grinned.

"I see why Scott fell in love with you."

"He changed my life."

"And you've changed his. I can say I finally have a sister."

Before Elodie could answer, Scott strode back into the room. "Dad isna answering."

"Saber," Elodie replied and looked at Willa. "He's a hacker who works with my brother and the Knights."

Scott nodded and started typing on his mobile. "It's infringing on the Knights, but I doona care. I need to know if Dad's okay."

Willa slid her legs over the side of the bed. Her brother's mobile dinged a moment later.

"Saber's looking," Scott told them.

Willa hoped they wouldn't have to wait too long for an answer.

CHAPTER FOUR

SKYE DRUIDS

It had been three days since Jasper found Willa. Days of waiting to learn if she was alive. Jasper hadn't been thrilled when George sent him to Skye. Not because he feared the Druids there—he didn't care if they were considered the most powerful Druids or not. He hadn't wanted to come because he was a city boy, through and through.

He'd expected life on the isle to be slow and boring. He found it to be much different. There was something about the isle. He'd heard the many reasons Skye was so extraordinary. He'd walked the Fairy Pools. He'd hiked to Old Man Storr. He'd visited Kilt Rock, Mealt Falls, and the Fairy Glen. He'd seen everything that made the isle *special* to tourists, but none of them were what he liked about the place.

It was easy to fit in with those on Skye. George wanted him to use his skills as a grifter to spy on Rhona and her group. He'd had many identities over the years, but when it came time to choose this one, he'd kept it simple. The people on the isle were easygoing. He'd become a regular at several places. People knew his name and welcomed him. He knew them and made sure to chat with them each time. He was good at his job, after all.

Jasper drummed his fingers on the kitchen table as he considered things. George had found him in Edinburgh. He'd expected Rhona to do the same, but he hadn't gotten a visit from the Druid leader. Which meant she either didn't know about him, or she did and was watching him from afar.

He anticipated the latter. It made following them a little more difficult, but not nearly as hard as it should've been. For such powerful Druids, they seemed almost disconnected from the world.

Rhona and Balladyn, in particular. They were the hardest to learn about. Most of the information Jasper had accumulated came from George when she was on Skye. George spoke of Rhona's incompetence as a leader, saying the only reason she was still around was because of Balladyn. Everyone supposedly feared the Reaper—including George. Jasper wasn't quite sure what a Reaper was, but Balladyn was a Fae. And that was enough for him to be wary of the man.

He tugged a leatherbound journal toward him and leafed through it. He had many of them. One was filled exclusively with notes and sketches about Skye and the Druids that called the isle home. His main goal was to find something that could help George prove that Elias was a murderer. George had been stonewalled by those on the isle, even the police. But with Frasier on the force, that was easy to do.

The killing mist had thrown Jasper. He'd glimpsed it firsthand

and wasn't too afraid to admit that it had terrified him. George had wanted him to find out who controlled it, and she hadn't been happy when he'd come up empty-handed. Though, to be honest, he hadn't tried all that hard. He didn't want any part of someone who could do something like that. If George really wanted to know, she could discover that from someone else.

Over the past few weeks, Jasper had had his hands full, trying to keep up with everything. People interacted with Scott, Elodie, and the others in their group that Jasper didn't know. The newest trio concerned him. Especially since the auburn-haired giant of a man had looked right at him.

Those in Elias's group knew of him now, which they'd planned. But everything hinged on whether Willa lived. His gaze dropped to his hands. One moment, there was nothing. The next, they were covered in blood. He blinked and looked away, determined not to wash his hands again.

"There's nothing there," Jasper told himself. "The blood is gone. Washed off that night."

He might deceive people and pretend to be something he wasn't in order to defraud others, but he had never used violence. Ever. Seeing Willa in such a state still bothered him. George had assured him the one responsible had been taken care of, and he had no reason to believe otherwise.

Jasper shut the journal and rose. He'd read over his notes a thousand times. He knew all the players, from Rhona and Balladyn, to the newest member, Ferne Crawford—a London Druid who had taken up with DI Theo Frasier. That had shocked the hell out of him, but it appeared Ferne wasn't going anywhere anytime soon.

What was it about Skye that drew Druids here and made them stay? Jasper might have adjusted, but as soon as he finished his current job, he would return to Edinburgh. Though George wouldn't rest until she'd put a murderer behind bars. If the police in Edinburgh and Skye wouldn't listen to her, she would find another way. And Jasper would help her achieve that.

And figure out how to remove Rhona as leader before she corrupted everything.

That was more proof the powerful Skye Druids had no idea who their leader was. If they did, they would rid themselves of her quickly. But Jasper wasn't here to judge. He was on Skye to gather intel and get close to Willa.

His head snapped up when the doorbell rang. He hid the journal on a bookshelf in the hall and made his way to the front door. When he neared, he made out long, dark hair through the frosted glass. Jasper opened the door and was stunned to find himself looking into Willa Ryan's blue eyes.

He'd seen photos, but they couldn't compare to the woman before him. Her eyes weren't just blue, they were a mesmerizing, tranquil color somewhere between sky and sea, with a band of navy surrounding the irises. She was a classic beauty with high cheekbones, a straight nose, clear skin, and full lips. As arresting as she was, her hair captured his attention. The full, glossy brunette length fell to the middle of her back, and large curls framed her face.

"Hi," she said with a hesitant smile. "Ah…I know showing up on your doorstep is a bit unorthodox, but I understand I have you to thank for being alive."

Jasper briefly ran his gaze down her length to take in her light-colored jeans and navy sweater. And the sling that supported her arm. Had the Healers not done their jobs? He held back a frown. "I was the one who found you. It's good to see you on your feet. Would you like to come in?"

"Just for a moment."

He stepped aside to let her in and closed the door behind her. Jasper led her through the entry to the kitchen. "Would you like anything to drink? I was about to make some tea."

"None for me, thanks."

"Please, sit," he said, motioning to the table.

She pulled out a chair and lowered herself into it as he heated water in the electric kettle.

"I never got a good look at your injury. I was more concerned with stanching the blood flow," he told her. "I take it you're healing well?"

Willa vacillated for only a moment, but he caught it. "I'm healing, aye."

"Glad to hear it."

She nervously looked away from him. The kettle beeped, and he used the time to pour the water over his tea bag before bringing the cup to the table.

"You have a beautiful home," she said.

He grinned as he poured milk into the mug and stirred. "I've no' been here long, but I like it."

"Thank you. For what you did for me."

His gaze jerked up to hers. "I did what anyone would've."

"Maybe. But I owe you a debt."

"You doona."

"I disagree. A simple *thank you* seems far from enough."

He grinned. "It's a good thing this isna ancient times. But I assure you, there is no debt."

"I have to do something. Please," she begged.

Jasper saw his opening and took it. "Dinner."

"You want me to take you to dinner?"

"Why no'?"

She shook her head to move a curl out of her eyes. "Dinner it is, then."

"Good."

"Are you free tonight?"

"I am." This was going much smoother than expected.

She rose to her feet. "Shall I pick you up at seven?"

"How about I drive since you're still recuperating?"

Willa chuckled softly as she glanced at her arm. "That might be better."

He wrote down her address as she gave it to him, even though he already knew it. "I'll be there at seven."

Jasper followed her to the front door. She walked out, turning to wave before making her way to her vehicle. He observed her for a moment before closing the door. Jasper moved to a window to watch her drive away. Then, he called George.

"I hope you have good news," she said by way of answer.

Jasper smiled. "I'm having dinner with Willa tonight."

"I told you she would survive. The Healers did their jobs."

"No' exactly. She's still wounded."

George made a sound over the line. "She doesn't know you're a Druid. She has to pretend to be hurt. Once she knows, she'll show you she's healed. Now, forget all of that. You moved quicker than I anticipated."

"She came to me, and there was an opportunity."

George laughed. "Leave it to Willa to do the unexpected. Let me guess, she said she owes you for saving her."

"Aye." For some reason, George's tone bothered him.

"Perfect. That's exactly where we want her. She'll feel that connection to you, and you'll have an easy way into the group."

Jasper turned away from the window and walked out the back door to the stables. "How are things in the city?"

"Keep your focus there. Willa is your way in. Once you are, we can bring down Rhona from the inside and get justice against Elias."

"I'll do my part."

"But?" she asked testily.

He tightened his lips. "Do I need to repeat that Willa almost died?"

"I told you, things went a tad too far. It's been taken care of."

"I hope so, because I draw the line at violence."

She snorted. "Just because you don't draw blood with your schemes doesn't mean you don't hurt people, Jasper."

"I've never taken everything from my targets. I only take what I need."

"Say whatever you want to appease your conscience. We both know the truth."

He slowly released a breath. "I need to know you have your organization in hand."

"*Our* organization. You're part of us. I want to make that clear. I've lost enough people. You need to understand that you're part of the community."

"I'm no' breaking away. I'm no' the Ryans."

"That's good to know. And don't worry about what's happening here. I've always got things in hand."

Jasper walked to a stall and leaned against it as the bay mare swung her head to him for a scratch. "I'll get you what you need. I always do. But after this, I willna hide in the shadows anymore. If I'm really a part of the organization as you claim, then I want to be seen as a member."

George didn't answer, she merely let the silence lengthen between them.

He paused in petting the horse. "When I'm done, there willna be a need for you to use me like this anymore."

"You're right. Get me what I want, and you can come home to a hero's celebration. It's what you deserve."

"I doona want that."

"Everyone will know what you've done for us. I'll make sure every Druid around the world knows. You've hidden in the shadows for too long."

Jasper went back to petting the mare. "Let me finish the job first."

"Be careful with Scott. He'll be wary of new people and especially suspicious of anyone around his sister," she warned.

"Willa is my way in. She'll convince Scott to let up."

George laughed. "Oh, I hate that I'm going to miss seeing this. I want details. Every juicy one there is to double my enjoyment."

"You'll have them. Talk soon."

Jasper ended the call. The sling Willa wore had alarmed him, but George was right. Willa had to look injured until she learned he was a Druid. There were five Healers on Skye, and from what he'd heard, they were good. He would've liked to see them in action. He'd only ever seen one Healer in his life. With five on Skye, he doubted anyone ever had much more than a scratch.

"How about a ride, beauty?" he asked the bay.

She stared at him with big, dark eyes and bobbed her head. Jasper laughed and went into the tack room to grab the equipment. It didn't take long for him to saddle the mare. Then he was on her back, flying across the grounds. He would miss the horses when he left, but he would enjoy every second while he was here.

CHAPTER FIVE

SKYE DRUIDS

"I doona like this, Willa. No' one bit," Scott grumbled from the door of her room.

She looked at him through the mirror and caught Elodie whispering a warning to him. Willa tossed down the earring she had been trying to put on. "He saved my life. How many times do I have to repeat that? I'm saying thanks."

"Out," Elodie said as she pushed Scott away. Then she came into the room and closed the door. "He's upset and worried that Saber still hasn't found your dad. Unfortunately, he's taking it out on you."

Willa sank onto the side of the bed. "I'm worried, too, but I can't sit around anymore going over what happened in Edinburgh. I've repeated the story for the last time. I'm not going to remember more or see anything differently than I already have."

"I agree."

She looked up into Elodie's light blue eyes. "Scott won't let me help with the work you all are doing. What am I supposed to do? Twiddle my thumbs?"

Elodie sighed as she sat beside her. "We've not known each other long, but I understand the protectiveness of siblings. You might know what we've been through with the mist killing Druids and finally trapping Kerry, the one who controlled it, but there's so much more."

"I understand. The thing in the…what did you call it?" Willa asked as she struggled to find the word. "Oh. That's right. The Grey. No one is going between dimensions again, so it isn't as if I'll be facing that monster thingy that attacked Ferne. Kerry is imprisoned, and the mist is gone."

"But Kerry wasn't working alone. She gained power from the Druids she killed, but someone else was pulling the strings."

"Someone on Skye."

Elodie nodded once. "We don't know Jasper. What if he's mixed up with George? Or worse, Beth?"

"If he were out to do me or any of you harm, wouldn't it have served him better to let me die?"

Elodie looked away, grinning. "That's the same argument I used on your brother." Her smile died as she slid her gaze back to Willa. "Still, someone tried to kill you. Your father is missing, and George and Beth won't give up."

"They'd be stupid to come to Skye."

"There are arguments for both sides of that statement." Elodie blew out a breath. "You're a grown woman. Just be careful."

Willa flashed her a quick smile. "It's only dinner."

"Rhona said he was cute."

Willa shrugged and looked away, her thoughts going to when

Jasper had opened the door, and she'd gotten her first look at him. Tall with broad shoulders and a lean body. Thick hair so dark brown it could be mistaken for black. He kept the overall length short but still long enough that she could run her fingers through it.

A shapely jaw outlined by a beard he kept neatly trimmed. His eyes were as deep a brown as his hair, and at first glance, appeared black. There had been surprise in those dark depths—and interest. She hadn't noticed his mouth until he smiled, but once she did, noticing the bottom lip was slightly larger than the top, she had trouble looking away.

"It certainly won't be a chore to sit across a table from him," Willa said.

Elodie chuckled, her eyes sparkling with laughter. "After what you went through, you could use a good night."

Willa shifted on the bed to face her. "I'm not going to let my guard down."

"Please, don't. I'd like to say you're safer on Skye because George and Beth aren't here, but there's a darkness on the isle that makes everything unsafe."

The sound of male voices reached them. Willa grimaced. She wasn't ready yet. Only being able to use one arm made things difficult.

"Let me help," Elodie offered and got the earring Willa had been trying to put on.

Willa held still until the other woman had fastened it. She stood and looked in the mirror. The jeans had come from Bronwyn, and the lavender sweater from Ferne. Willa ran her hand across the sling holding her arm and wondered if she would ever be able to use it again.

"I can make you a sling from ribbons if you'd prefer," Elodie said.

Willa turned to her with a grin. "Thanks, but this will do."

Scott opened the door and poked his head in long enough to say, "He's here."

Willa nodded but hesitated.

Elodie got to her feet and caught her gaze. "What is it?"

"Maybe Scott's right and I shouldn't go anywhere until we know about Dad."

"Your brother can't do anything except sit around and worry. You've been doing that for days. Saber is working on it, and if anyone can find Luke Ryan, it's him. You deserve a night out. Go have fun."

Willa twisted her lips. "And you and Scott could use a night to yourselves."

"There is that," Elodie said with a wry smile.

"It's just dinner. An hour. Two tops."

"Exactly. I'm curious to see Jasper. Ready?"

Willa took one last look at herself before walking from the room. She found Scott and Jasper standing awkwardly in the kitchen. The minute Jasper's dark eyes landed on her, they crinkled at the corners, an easy smile curving his lips. She found herself grinning in response.

"Hi," Elodie said as she moved around Willa. "I'm Elodie."

Jasper inclined his head, the smile still there but not quite as wide. "Jasper McCabe. A pleasure."

"We all owe you thanks for reaching Willa when you did."

Jasper turned to her. "I'm glad I was there."

Willa's smile grew as she looked away, only to find her gaze clashing with Scott's. He gave her a flat look. She returned it with a glare, hoping it would be enough to make him lose the attitude. He didn't relent until Elodie moved to his side and elbowed him in the ribs.

"Aye," Scott said grudgingly. His face softened as he looked at her. "We're grateful. I doona know what I would do if I lost Willa."

Jasper cleared his throat, drawing her attention. "Ready?"

"I'll see you two later. Enjoy your night," Willa called as she grabbed the purse Elodie lent to her and the new mobile she'd picked up the day before. She had canceled all her credit cards and had new ones on their way to Skye. Until then, she had to use money she'd borrowed from her brother.

"I hope Scott wasn't too, well...Scott," Willa said as they left the house.

Jasper led her to the passenger side of a white Jaguar F-PACE. "He has every right to be protective after how he found you the other night. I'd be the same if I had a sister."

"Not brothers?" she teased as she climbed inside the vehicle.

He grinned. "I'm an only child."

The conversation halted as he closed the door and walked around to the driver's side. She waited until they were driving away before she said, "I can admit, there were times when I was younger that I wished I was an only child. Scott and I would get into the biggest fights over the stupidest things."

"Who would win?"

"He thinks he did, but I held my own."

Jasper laughed at that. "I can well imagine."

There was a lull, and it made Willa nervous. She glanced out the window and finally said what she should've admitted earlier. "I hope you won't be angry at Theo for giving me your address."

"Theo?" he asked, their eyes meeting briefly.

"DI Frasier. He's a friend of my brother's."

"Ah. I'm glad he did. It saved me the trouble of trying to learn your name to find out what happened to you. I'm not sure they would've given it to me at the police station. As I said, I was worried. It isna every day I find someone unconscious and bleeding."

She picked at the hem of her sweater. "Nay, I don't guess it would be."

"How was it that you were attacked in such a way?"

It was an innocent question anyone would ask, yet Elodie's warning came back to Willa.

"You doona have to talk about it if you doona want to," Jasper said when she paused. "I shouldna have asked."

She shrugged her good shoulder. "I don't blame you for being curious. A lone woman in the wee hours of the morning in such a state is bound to raise questions."

"Having Frasier on the case will help find the culprit, I'm guessing?"

She hesitated once more.

"I'm sorry. I've done it again."

She blew out a breath. "It's not you. There's just a lot going on. More than what happened to me."

"Sounds like you need to talk about it."

"That's not what this dinner is about."

He shrugged a shoulder and grinned at her. "It can be about whatever we want. If you want to talk about the weather the entire time, we can do that."

"You must not get out much," she teased.

He threw back his head and laughed. "Is it that obvious?"

She was still grinning when he pulled into a parking area.

"Is this okay?" he asked.

Willa looked at the building, seeing a sign that read: *Old School Restaurant*. "I've never been here. Do you like it?"

"It's one of my favorites."

"Then I'm game."

He turned off the engine. Willa barely got the door open before he was there. She had been so attuned to her brother when she'd first seen Jasper tonight that she hadn't gotten to look him over. He wore dark jeans, boots, and a burgundy dress shirt with a black suit jacket.

"You look nice," she told him.

He held out his arm for her. "So do you. I would've said so in front of your brother, but I thought I should wait."

"Wise man."

They shared another chuckle as they headed into the restaurant. The host seated them toward the back near a corner. Almost immediately, a server appeared to take their drink order. Then, they were alone again.

Willa looked at him over the menu. Jasper held himself with confidence, an air of something enigmatic and commanding about him. His warm gaze met hers, and he slowly lowered the menu.

"Are you up for this? I can take you home anytime. Just say the word," he told her.

Willa shook her head. Danger lurked around every corner. Even on Skye. She should keep her thoughts to herself, but she needed someone to talk to, someone who wouldn't demand details instead of asking her how she was. Scott had done that, of course, but only after grilling her for hours. It wasn't the same.

"Willa?"

She sat back in the chair. "I was attacked. That same night, my father went missing, and we haven't found him yet."

Jasper's brow furrowed. "I can no' imagine how you and your brother must feel. I doona understand why anyone would assault you."

If she was going to talk to him, she needed to know just how much he knew about Skye first. "Tell me what you know about the isle."

He studied her for a long moment. Then he said, "You're no' asking for population or size facts."

"Do you know who first settled on Skye?"

"Aye."

She saw the truth of his answer in his eyes. "I need you to say it."

"Why?"

"You have to admit the truth before I tell you my story."

Jasper drew in a breath and slowly released it. "Druids were the first to settle here."

"What do you know about them?"

"I'm sure as much as you do, if you're asking."

She raised a brow. "Are you one?"

"A Druid?" He nodded. "Aye. You?"

"I am."

"I wasna the one who hurt you, if you're wondering."

"I know. I saw their faces."

"There was more than one?" he asked, his brow furrowing.

She nodded. "At least two."

"Are you and Scott going after them?"

Willa waited until the server set down their drinks before

saying, "We have to locate my father first. He should've checked in by now."

"Checked in?" Jasper repeated. "You make it sound like you were on a mission."

"In a way, we were. Have you ever lived in Edinburgh?"

"I've lived many places."

"Doing what?" she pressed, suddenly wary.

Jasper took a drink of his red wine. "I came into an inheritance and invested in a startup company that took off. I doona need to work. I move around a lot since I get tired of places frequently. My travels included a stay in Edinburgh."

"Did you have any contact with the Druids there?"

He leaned his arms on the table. "I'm sure I did. Druids are everywhere."

"Do you know a woman named Georgina Miller? She goes by George."

"Is she the one who attacked you?"

"She's the one who sent Scott to Skye to convince Elodie to join her organization."

There was a subtle shift in Jasper's body, a tightening. "Why would George do that?"

"Her grand plan is to take the Druids to the next level."

He set aside his menu and leaned forward. "Tell me more."

CHAPTER SIX

SKYE DRUIDS

Jasper had been many things in his life, but this was the first time he'd played spy for someone else. Instead of keeping the information to himself, he shared it. It wasn't a huge leap. Or so he'd initially believed.

But as he sat across from Willa and listened to her side of events while attempting to reconcile it to the things he knew—or the things he *thought* he knew—Jasper got to see things from another perspective. George had never said anything about sending Scott to the isle. She wasn't one to tell anyone everything, but that knowledge could be beneficial in Jasper's endeavor. She'd left it out for a reason. He just couldn't figure out what that was. Yet. He would suss it out eventually.

Jasper hadn't been acting when his unease showed. "What would Elodie have to do with anything?"

"She comes from a powerful line." Willa shrugged one shoulder and sipped her wine. "From what my brother told me, George thought he and Filip could persuade, encourage, or entice

Elodie to come to Edinburgh. Things...didn't exactly go as planned."

There was more to the story, and Jasper wanted to know what it was. He wouldn't push now, though. "I suppose no' since Elodie and Scott are here. How did this George take it?"

"Not well. Both Scott and Filip began questioning her, and she took offense. My family was part of her organization, and her anger was known by all. Most didn't know why, but Dad and I knew, thanks to Scott."

Jasper could imagine what George had said and done. She held on to her authority with an iron fist.

Willa's blue eyes met his. "George came to Skye soon after. Scott told me how she confronted him and Filip about their *desertion*, as she called it."

Willa grew quiet then, her gaze lowering to the table as if deep in thought. Jasper motioned the server over and used that time for them to order. Once they were alone again, he asked, "What happened then?"

"Filip was born on the isle. As was Elodie. They have deep connections here. Filip never intended to come back, but once he did, he said he knew he could never leave again. Elodie's sister still lives here with her family, and their brother, Elias, also returned. Things were looking up for the MacLean family. Then George accused Elias of murder."

Jasper let shock show on his face. He had known that much. It was one of the reasons he was spying. Maybe he could make Willa let something slip. "Surely, George wouldna accuse someone without evidence."

"You would think, wouldn't you? But she did."

Once more, his frown was real. If George had proof, why not show it? "How so?"

"She went to the police on Skye and made her allegations. To add to the insanity of it all, a body was found on the rental property where Elias was staying. The blame, of course, landed on him. He was cleared of everything when a security video outside the home showed another group of people dumping the body. They were eventually arrested and charged with the murder."

Jasper never trusted anyone. How could he, in his line of work? He gave George more trust than anyone else because she had earned it. In the two years since she'd found him in that pub, she had proven time and again that she was honorable. Still, he always double-checked anything she gave him for accuracy and truth.

Someone was lying. Was it George, who had shown him time and again who she really was? She claimed the police were working with the Skye Druids, which made sense, given Frasier. Or was it Willa, who he knew only from studying the information they'd gathered on her? She had every reason to lie.

"George was furious. She told Elias that she would get him one way or another," Willa said.

Jasper slowly turned his wine glass by the stem. "It sounds like she's adamant he did something."

"Theo—Detective Inspector Frasier—said she returned to Edinburgh and gave evidence there. I'm not sure why she didn't do it before."

Jasper wasn't either. "Has anyone from the city contacted Elias?"

Willa shook her head. "Not yet. He swears he's innocent."

"You believe him."

She held his gaze. "You might be a Druid, but you're not a part of anything. You don't understand—or probably don't know—what's been happening to our people all over the globe." Willa briefly closed her eyes. "I'm sorry. What you do isn't my business, and I certainly have no right to lecture you."

"I want to know. How does all of that fit into your attack?" Her words had stung. Mainly because they were true. He hadn't cared about being part of a Druid community until George brought him into hers. Even then, he hadn't truly been a part of it. She'd kept him in the shadows, watching and listening in case she had need of his skills.

"The group charged with the murder Elias was initially blamed for came from Edinburgh. Sydney Russell was the one in charge. He came because he couldn't let go of his ex-girlfriend, Bronwyn Stewart. Elias stepped in to help her, and George colluded with Sydney to frame him."

This wasn't the George Jasper knew. No wonder everyone on Skye hated her. And why she loathed each and every Skye Druid and anyone connected to them. "How do you know that about George and Sydney?"

"There was a battle at Bronwyn's estate. George stood with Sydney and his gang."

"You saw it?" He knew she hadn't been there, but he needed facts.

She tilted her head to the side. "This is my first time on Skye. I heard it from those who were involved in the skirmish. One of which was Rhona, the current leader of the Skye Druids."

"People lie."

"That they do. But none of them have a reason to lie about this. There were seven witnesses in all. George was there, and she specifically went after Elias. If she has the evidence she claims, then why not allow the police to do their job? Why go after him?"

Jasper was asking himself that same question. "She sounds like she wants justice."

"Maybe," Willa said softly. She shifted in her seat. "Sydney had a book with a plethora of Druid information. Having it allowed him access to things he wouldn't normally know. And the stuff he learned from it made him dangerous. He killed many people. Including Bronwyn's father."

Jasper took a large swallow of his wine. George had never said anything about any book. Not until Beth came into the picture, anyway. George had told him she didn't know where it had come from. It was possible she didn't know Sydney had it. Jasper certainly wouldn't have shared that information with anyone.

"Scott told me about the book and everything happening on the isle. Dad and I came up with the plan to find it before George or anyone else could."

Jasper grunted. "It sounds like no one should have it."

"You're probably right. Everyone who thinks they should have it believes everyone else isn't deserving."

"But you still went after it."

She nodded. "Beth, Bronwyn's cousin, had been dating Sydney. She was...detained for a bit, but she soon returned to Edinburgh. Dad and I didn't locate Sydney's flat in time. The next thing we knew, Beth came to a meeting with it in her hands. George couldn't take her eyes off it. That was when the two of them began working together."

"If George considered your brother a defector, I'm surprised you and your father remained in the group."

"We knew our days were numbered, but we were determined to do whatever we could to help."

"Help who?"

Willa didn't hide her look of amusement. "The Druids."

"No' the Skye Druids? No' your own organization?"

"*All* Druids. Someone is targeting our people. Druids are being killed all over the world. Elias is part of a group called the Knights. They've been searching for the killers. They find some and turn them over to the police, but they also help Druids in need. You already know about the deaths on Skye. Those were all Druids."

Murdered horrifically, if the papers could be believed.

Willa released a breath. "Dad and I tracked Beth and those with her for days. We located where she lived and came up with a plan. We went in to get the book when we knew she was alone, but she was waiting for us. We ended up surrounded. Dad went one way, and I went the other."

Her gaze drifted to the side, her breathing rate increasing as she relived that night. Jasper almost told her she didn't need to continue, but he wanted to know the details so he could compare it to what George had told him.

"I couldn't shake them," Willa continued. "They found me wherever I went. I ran for what felt like days. I found a nightclub and got inside. I planned to warn Scott about what had happened, but I never got the chance. Someone hit me and pushed me over a railing on the club's second floor. I couldn't lift my right arm. I'm not even sure how I held on with only one hand. While most of the occupants ran out, a couple of guys stayed behind. They got to me before I fell and helped me up. I ran, then, realizing too late that I'd lost my mobile somewhere. I had nothing. No keys, no wallet, no phone. I couldn't go back to my flat." Her gaze slid back to him. "I did the only thing I could. I stole a car and a mobile and drove straight here."

Jasper leaned his forearms on the table. "That's when I found you."

"This might all sound a bit crazy, but there's a reason my father and I went to such lengths. Besides someone killing Druids, besides George's grudge against Elias, a growing darkness has been on Skye. It'll stretch much farther if someone doesn't stop it."

Jasper thought of the mist. "Are you saying a Skye Druid is responsible?"

"You've seen the mist, haven't you?"

"Aye."

"It attacked Scott and Elodie. It went after Bronwyn and Elias. It even struck Sydney and his gang. The mist is part of it, but there's more. So much more."

Jasper's brow furrowed. "Which means it's a Skye Druid. Maybe they're more powerful than they have a right to be."

"Or," she said, drawing out the word, "it's attacking here first because none of the other factions stand a chance if the Skye Druids are removed."

Jasper slowly sat back and considered her angle—one he hadn't thought about before. It was certainly plausible.

"You don't have to believe me. I'm not sure I would if I were in your shoes. You're hearing my side. If you asked George, she'd likely have her own version that would make her look good and prove that everyone else is on the wrong side. That's how these things always go, don't they?"

"There are always several sides to every story."

"I know what happened to my brother. I trust him and Filip. I might not have been around for the other things that happened, but I'm here now. And I'll stand with them against whatever is coming."

Jasper held her gaze for a long moment. "I've no' felt any kind of darkness—unless you want to call the mist that."

"The mist is gone. It was made up of Druid souls forced to do another's bidding. A new friend—Ferne—released them. She's a Druid from London who sensed the darkness and came to help. As I said, there are a lot of things going on. I owe you, Jasper. Please, take this warning to heart. Even if you don't believe anything I've said, know there's danger here."

CHAPTER SEVEN

SKYE DRUIDS

Willa wanted to ask Jasper what he thought of everything she had shared, but she needed to give him time to take it all in. It was quite a bit, after all, especially for someone who hadn't been a part of any type of Druid society. She just hoped he didn't think her addled. It was meant to be a fun night. She had nearly ruined it by telling him everything her friends were dealing with.

Their food arrived, and the conversation shifted to other, safer topics. Luckily, Jasper was charming and easy to talk to, which would have been treacherous to her heart if this were an actual date. As handsome and amiable as he was, there was no time for any sort of flirtation. The dinner was exactly what she'd said it would be—a *thank you*. Nothing more. Nothing less.

Out of habit, she attempted to put her right elbow on the table. The still-healing muscles from her injury pulled. Willa sucked in a breath and squeezed her eyes closed at the spasm of pain. The throbbing was slow to ebb, and she knew from experience that it would linger for another few minutes.

"Did the Healers no' heal you?"

She opened her eyes to find apprehension clouding Jasper's face. "They did what they could."

"Maybe Skye needs better Healers."

Willa shouldn't like that he seemed to care so much. He was probably just being polite, but regardless of the reason, it was nice. "They're very good. This isn't about their skills."

"Meaning?"

She vacillated. They had moved the conversation away from such things. Should she turn it back? But it was rude not to answer his question. Besides, her enemies knew exactly what they had done. There was no hiding from what had happened. "I wasn't just stabbed with any weapon. It was ebony wood, and some remained inside the wound. Apparently, that made it impossible for the Healers to mend me fully."

"Did you say ebony?" Jasper asked in a soft voice after becoming very still.

"Aye."

He softly set down his fork and leaned back in his chair, his head turned to the side as a muscle tensed in his jaw. He stayed like that for several moments before swinging his head to her. "Many years ago, I heard about such a thing, but I didna believe it was true until I saw it myself."

"I'm here to tell you it is."

"Have you lost the use of your arm for good?"

"No one seems to be able to answer that question."

He glanced at her wound. "I'm guessing the pain is...considerable."

"When I forget and use my arm, aye."

"Was all the wood removed?"

She smiled wryly. "Scott pestered the Healers with that same question, and they told him, in no uncertain terms, that they'd gotten it all. It'll just take some time to heal."

"Most would want revenge for such a tactic."

"Trust me, I've thought about how I'd like to repay those who did this to me, but my focus needs to be on helping my friends end whatever is happening to our people. And finding my father."

"You're a bigger person than most."

She grinned and relaxed a little more as the pain began to subside, lessening to a manageable level. "You wouldn't say that if you knew the kinds of revenge I've pictured in my head."

Jasper chuckled, his eyes dark, and his gaze warm on her face. "You said you've never been to Skye. If you're willing, there's something I'd like to show you before I take you home."

"I should warn you that if you try anything, I won't hesitate to put you on your arse," she teased.

His smile widened, and he relaxed. "I would expect nothing less from such a formidable woman. And I mean that honestly."

They finished their food, and once she'd paid the bill, they walked back to his SUV. After sharing such a lovely meal with Jasper, she was in a good mood. He was just her type, and if things were different, she might pursue him. The night was clear and cool, and the stars blanketing the sky above were brighter than she had ever seen in the city.

"I couldna stop looking up when I first came," Jasper told her as he drove.

"It's easy to forget just how many stars there are when the city lights block them."

"Skye has a few places with a grand view of the stars, planets, and even the Milky Way that can be seen with the naked eye. On a clear night like this, we should get a spectacular view," he told her.

"Is that where you're taking me?"

He glanced at her and nodded. "If you're up for it."

"Definitely."

"Good." His lips curved at the corners as if her agreement pleased him.

Willa sat back and enjoyed the ride and the easy silence that settled between them. It wasn't long before Jasper entered a car park near the water. It seemed they weren't the only ones with the idea. Several other vehicles were already there. Some visitors were laid out on their cars' bonnets or on blankets on the ground. Others were in reclining chairs.

Jasper parked and looked at her. "What do you think?"

"I'm hoping you have a blanket, because I want to lie down."

"You're in luck."

They shared a smile. Willa wondered why a man like Jasper was single. Or maybe he wasn't. She hadn't exactly asked, nor had he said anything. They got out together and walked to the back of the vehicle. Jasper pulled out a tartan throw and motioned for her to follow with his head. He chose their spot, which was in the grass, well away from others. He spread the blanket, and they sat. Willa was careful not to put any weight on her injured arm as she lay back.

She stared in awe at the carpet of stars winking down at her. "This is amazing."

"That it is. If you look just there," he said, pointing to the left, "you can see the Milky Way."

"Wow," she whispered in awe.

She tried to follow along when he pointed out constellations.

She could decipher some, but others were lost to her. She could probably make out more if she looked up at the night sky often enough. Especially with Jasper showing her where they were.

Willa didn't know how long she lay there before she realized Jasper had stopped talking. She turned her head and found him still gazing at the stars. He looked at her, their gazes clashing. She wondered again why she had shared so much of herself that evening. The perils of Edinburgh could just as well find her on the isle. George hadn't hesitated to come once. She could return.

Or send others.

"You shouldna be out with me alone," he said.

She breathed deeply and then slowly exhaled. "Do you plan to hurt me?"

"Nay, but that doesna mean you should trust so easily."

"I don't. And I promise you, we're not alone."

Dark brows snapped together.

"If I know my brother, he got Filip, one of his close friends, to follow us."

"Smart move. It doesna anger you?"

She shook her head. "Does it bother you?"

"Nay. Scott is merely protective of those he loves. That's admirable as long as someone isna confined."

"You say that as if that happened to you."

Jasper returned his gaze to the stars. "There's love, and then there are chains."

"Did you break free?"

"In a manner of speaking."

It was obvious he didn't want to talk about the past, so she didn't push. She stretched her legs out, crossing them at the ankles as she let the beautiful night settle over her. She'd never been one to want to go camping. Something about sleeping in a tent on the ground with rocks and roots just didn't sound appealing when she had a perfectly comfortable bed. But she reconsidered it now. Sleeping under the stars was something she would have to do. Though, perhaps when it was a little warmer. The night would be perfect if she had a blanket covering her. And perhaps a hot cup of tea.

She shifted her gaze to find the half moon, a waning gibbous. Suddenly, Willa thought about her mother. She had tried to get Willa and Scott to do moon rituals with her, but neither had been interested. Willa now wished she had paid more attention before her mother got sick.

Was it Skye itself, or being able to see the world differently away from the city that called to something deep within her? There was no going back to Edinburgh. Willa might not have seen much of Skye yet, but she was smitten with what she had viewed.

"Do you feel it?" she asked.

"Hmm?"

"The isle. It has a certain...." She paused, looking for the right word. "Influence."

He put one hand behind his head. "I was going to say attraction."

"That, too."

"Aye, I feel it. I doona think you can have magic and no' sense it."

She turned her head to look at him again. "Scott said it changed him for the better. I think his exact words were that it opened his eyes to the truth."

"The truth of what?" Jasper asked as he looked at her.

"I never asked. I think maybe what he believed before.

Whether from childhood learning from our parents or being a part of the organization in Edinburgh, I'm not sure."

Jasper's brows rose. "Both of your parents are Druids?"

"Aye," she said with a grin. "I hear that's rare nowadays."

"If you listen to some, Druids are losing their magic because of the dilution of their blood."

She twisted her lips. "Maybe. Or perhaps Druids are forgetting who they are and what it means to have magic. If they don't use it, maybe it disappears."

"That's a curious thought. Where did you come up with that theory?"

"My parents were part of a small group of Druids in Edinburgh who'd been around for decades. George spoke to them and explained that she was looking for other Druids. She had a dream of bringing our culture into the light, so to speak, so we didn't have to hide who we were anymore. But more than that, she wanted to find those who thought they were alone. My parents and others helped her do that. I met many who had no idea there were more of us out there, and still others who could hardly do magic because they had never been taught. George's aspirations made sense, and I wanted to be a part of something grand like that."

One side of Jasper's mouth tilted in a grin. "It sounds like George had a good goal."

"She did. She had a knack for finding Druids and growing her ranks. Though she is a seer, so I've a feeling her power had a hand in that. I have always had a community, so I don't think I really understood how life-changing it could be for those who don't."

"Some need it."

"But not you?"

"I didna say that," he said with a quick grin.

She studied the way the moonlight fell on his face, casting it in a soft, bluish glow. "Who are you, Jasper McCabe?"

"Just a man," he answered.

"I don't believe that for a moment."

His expression grew somber as he stared at her. His gaze dropped to her mouth, and her stomach fluttered in response. He blinked and shuttered whatever had just happened. Jasper got to his feet and reached out his hand for hers. "I should probably get you back before Scott comes looking for you."

His tone was teasing, but there was a thread of something else in his voice that Willa couldn't quite pinpoint. She let him help her up with her left hand. He shook out the blanket, folded it, and they walked back to the vehicle in silence—a quiet that continued on the drive. It was fraught with tension. Willa wasn't sure what she had said to cause it, but the night had been nice. She wouldn't ruin it further by digging deeper.

All too soon, Jasper pulled into the drive of Elodie's house. When Willa got out, Jasper was beside her. He pulled something from her hair and showed her a piece of grass. Once more, their eyes clashed. She felt a pull toward him and wished the night didn't have to end.

"Thank you for dinner," he said.

She stared into his beautiful, dark eyes. "Thank you for a view I'll never forget."

They stared at each other for a long, quiet moment. He leaned toward her slightly, and she thought he might kiss her. She wanted it more than she had wanted any kiss before.

"Be safe, Willa."

"You, too."

She should walk away, but she didn't want to leave, even though the moment had passed. Willa flashed him a smile and forced her feet to move. She didn't look back until she reached the door. He stood in the same spot, watching her. She waved before entering the house. Then she waited to hear him drive away.

Willa poked her head into the living area, thinking Scott and Elodie would be there, but it was empty. She noticed their closed door as she walked to her room. Quietly, she closed her own door and sat on the bed, thinking about the evening. Despite spending hours with Jasper, she knew very little about him. It was too bad she wouldn't have a second chance because she wanted to get to know him. And kiss him. She really wanted to kiss him.

CHAPTER EIGHT

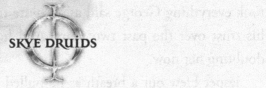

SKYE DRUIDS

Jasper couldn't stop thinking of Willa. He knew her and her family, but only on paper. Tonight, he'd gotten to know her. She was as gutsy as she was beautiful. She was ardent in her beliefs and devoted to her friends and family. She was complex yet straightforward.

And she stirred things within him that took him by surprise.

He was supposed to seduce her, and he'd had a chance to end the night with a kiss. He'd wanted it. He'd been staring at her gorgeous mouth all night, wondering what her lips would taste like. She would've let him do it. So why hadn't he?

That answer wasn't so simple. And it all went back to what Willa had divulged. While George had never promised to tell him everything, there were things she should've shared. Like sending Scott and Filip to Skye for Elodie.

Why had she left that out? Or was it that Scott and Filip lied to everyone? Jasper shook his head. He could well imagine George sending them, which made Jasper very uneasy. And not just because George hadn't communicated that.

He kept coming back to *why?* Why did George want Elodie if she hated Elias? Or maybe that was the reason. To turn the sister against the brother.

As far as Jasper knew, Filip had talked Scott into going with him to Skye, and the two had never returned. It wasn't that Jasper took everything George said as absolute truth, but she had earned his trust over the past two years. And he didn't like that he was doubting her now.

Jasper blew out a breath as he pulled into his garage and shut off the car's engine. He didn't immediately go into the house, instead detouring to the paddock. He whistled, and the horses lifted their heads before galloping to him.

He smiled and braced his arms on the top of the fence, his hands outstretched. The bay reached him first. He gave her a scratch behind her ears, which was her favorite. The white and gray reached him together with the sorrel following, walking sedately, her tail swishing.

"Hello, my beauties," he murmured, giving each of them love.

He unbolted the door to the stables before walking back to the paddock and swinging open that gate. The horses walked into their stalls with him shutting the doors behind them. They had already been fed, but he gave each of them a carrot before closing up everything for the night.

Once in the house, Jasper hung his jacket on the back of a kitchen chair. He made some herbal tea as he retrieved his leather journal. He removed his boots and sat at the table with his mug. Then he opened the book and turned to a blank page. There, he jotted down things Willa had shared. By the time he came to the end, he'd finished his tea.

Jasper made another cup before resuming his seat. He searched through the journal, going back to the pages where he had listed facts George had given him. For the next hour, Jasper compared the two. He highlighted the things that differed and starred the similar ones. And then he double-underlined the one he wanted to question George about.

But he would have to be careful. He couldn't confront her outright because she would become suspicious and question his loyalty. He needed details. The small things could ruin any attempts he made to get close to Willa and those around her.

Jasper took out his mobile and rang George. He put it on speaker, the ringing breaking the silence in the house. The sound grated on his nerves. He was about to hang up when the line connected.

"I take it by the late call the dinner went well," George said, approval in her voice.

"Aye."

"Good. Good. Did you see Scott?"

He leaned back, one arm on the table, his other hand resting on his thigh as he stared at the journal. "I did. I met him and Elodie."

"And?" George prompted when he didn't say more.

"Scott wasna thrilled about the dinner, but Elodie was welcoming enough."

George snorted. "I bet he wasn't. He has always been overprotective of his sister."

"Willa was seriously injured."

"Stop making more of that than it was. I told you. I got it sorted."

He paused as anger spiked. It wouldn't do to let her know just how furious he was with that situation.

"If you have something to say, Jasper, say it."

He drew in a deep breath. "She's no' healed fully."

"Then that's the Healers' fault, not mine."

"There are five Healers here. But you already know that."

"And they're obviously not as good as they think they are."

Jasper realized he'd fisted his hand. He loosened each finger and splayed his palm on his jeans. "It doesna matter how powerful they are when ebony wood is used."

"What?" she barked.

"The Healers pulled a shard of ebony wood out of Willa's injury."

"That...can't be," George murmured.

Jasper wished he could see her face. Few people knew how to hide their emotions well enough, and George wasn't one of them. If he were before her, he'd know if she was lying. "I take it you know what ebony wood does when in the hands of a Druid."

There was a pause before George said, "I've recently learned, yes."

"If you really didna know about it—"

"I didn't know it would be used," she interjected.

"Then someone went behind your back." He didn't need to say Beth's name. They both knew she was involved.

George sighed loudly. "What else happened? Did Willa share anything more?"

"She told me quite a lot."

"I want details. Tell me every word."

Jasper glanced at the journal pages and started with Willa's attempt to get the book from Beth. When he finished, he asked, "How did Beth know Willa and Luke were coming for her?"

"We both suspected Willa and Luke from the moment Scott deserted the organization. I've had my eye on father and daughter ever since. That's how we knew they were following Beth. She and I came up with the plan to trap them."

"But things didna go as you wanted. Both of them got away." Jasper worded it that way because he wanted to know what had happened to Luke Ryan.

George made an imperceptible sound. "We needed Willa to get to Skye so you could worm your way into the group. Things worked out just as planned."

"And Luke?"

"Don't concern yourself with him."

That could mean anything. George didn't confirm having him, but she didn't say Luke had gotten away, either. That wasn't part of Jasper's undertaking, so he put it out of his mind. For the moment.

"Now," George continued, "what else did you talk about?"

Jasper's gaze locked on the section he had underlined twice. "Her family. They're verra close, apparently. She also told me about meeting you."

"Did she? I bet she had some choice words about me," George said with a soft laugh.

"A few. In her mind, there's a valid reason."

"And what reason did she give?"

He tapped his journal pages with the pad of a finger. "The way she tells it, you sent Scott and Filip to Skye for Elodie MacLean."

"Ah."

"Is that true?"

George made another indiscernible sound. "It isn't something everyone needs to know. I made a play to get Elodie, and it failed."

"Why did you need her?"

"It was twofold. One because her family line is formidable, despite her father not being a Druid. Secondly, it would have been a slap against Elias."

Jasper made notes as she spoke. "Instead, Scott fell in love with her."

"It was a minor play, as I said. It didn't work. So what?"

He lowered the pen and sat back. "I know your hatred for Elias runs deep."

"Deeper than you'll ever know."

"No' so deep you would ruin all you've spent years building, I hope."

"You don't need to worry about that," she stated, her voice edged with annoyance.

Jasper scratched the corner of his eye. "Willa told me a story about you. Something about standing with a group led by a man named Sydney who attacked Elias and Bronwyn."

"As I've already told you, Bronwyn and Beth are cousins. Bronwyn tried to separate Beth from Sydney, which led to Beth leaving Skye for good."

"The book Beth has. It was Sydney's."

"Since that wasn't a question, there's no point in answering."

Jasper held on to the last of his patience. "Did you fight alongside Sydney?"

"I was on Skye. I stood against Rhona, and I told the police about Elias. Of course, they would want to show me in a bad light."

It wasn't an admission. Nor was it a denial. Worse, her voice had changed from calm and vaguely irritated to higher-pitched. Some might not have noticed it, but Jasper had been listening for just such an event. George had been there, and she had fought against Elias. Why lie, though? What didn't she want him to know?

"Is there anything else you'd like to ask me about?" George demanded.

"I have to know what's true and what isna if I'm to navigate these tricky waters."

"What does it matter? Go along with whatever Willa says. You're not supposed to know me."

He clenched his jaw. "It's a given that people lie, George. I expect it from most, but I'm putting myself inside the lion's den. I need facts."

"You need to know what I've already told you. You're seducing her, Jasper, not counseling her. Get her into your bed so you can infiltrate her life and report back to me about their plans. You know the players. You've done your homework on all of them. You have all you need. So, get to work."

The line went dead.

Jasper contemplated the call before adding the new details to his journal. Then he closed the book and put it away. He readied for bed but couldn't sleep. He tried to read, but his mind kept going over why George wouldn't admit to fighting alongside Sydney. It darkened her reputation a smidgen to align with a murderer, but that would be the worst of it. And only he would know.

Unless she thought he might tell.

But who would he share that with? Willa and the others already knew. As for the organization in Edinburgh, he wasn't friends with anyone. Though that would change once he completed this job and could leave the shadows behind. Well, not completely. He wasn't sure he could hold down an honest job, but he wanted the other Druids to know who he was. He wanted to truly be a part of something for once.

George was right. He didn't need to know everything. But he *wanted* to know. Her caginess and Willa's truth didn't sit well with him. He shouldn't be doubting George, but that didn't mean everything Willa said in the future would be reliable. Jasper knew he had to weave the truth into the lies to be a successful grifter. Nearly everything he had shared tonight had been true. Maybe Willa was doing the same.

She could suspect him. He'd told George it was risky for him to be the one to find her because anyone suspicious could think he had been waiting for her the night of her accident. George had dismissed his concerns. Rhona's group was so tight-knit and suspicious there wasn't another way for him and Willa to meet that wouldn't have everyone looking at him.

Yet Willa showing up at his house had been a huge surprise. She should be mistrustful of everyone. She probably was. Scott had made it perfectly clear that he didn't trust Jasper. Most likely, everyone around Willa was suspicious. As they should be.

The night with Willa had gone well. Jasper would give it a day or two before he dropped by to check on her. He'd strike up a friendship. If her arm felt better, he'd invite her over for a ride on one of the horses.

The thought of her wound sent him back to brooding. If Beth had resorted to using ebony wood, what else was she capable of? Unfortunately, Jasper already knew the answer.

CHAPTER NINE

SKYE DRUIDS

Willa shuffled into the kitchen in her pajamas and slippers. She had never been much of a morning person, unlike Elodie, who seemed to wake up on the chipper side every day. Even Scott smiled in the mornings now. Willa looked over to see Elodie sitting on Scott's lap as they kissed.

"Bedroom. Please," Willa grumbled as she rolled her eyes and made her way to the electric kettle.

"We were in the bedroom," Scott said, a smile in his voice. "We can no' spend all our time there."

Elodie laughed. "Not that it wouldn't be fun."

They got quiet, and Willa knew without looking they were kissing again. "I need to find my own place."

"Ah, I doona think so."

There was the grumpy brother she knew and loved. Willa ignored him as she searched through the cabinet with its incredible assortment of teas, all from a local shop called Tea Talker. She couldn't wait to finally meet the Druid, Ariah, who created the blends. Every one Willa had tried had been exceptional. She opted for one called Jane's Garden today. The green tea tasted like spring, with hints of rose and cardamom. And right now, she was looking forward to spring, which felt months away.

"Tell me you're joking," Scott said from behind her. "You're wounded. We've still no' located Dad. And I want you here."

Willa poured the hot water over the tea bag and faced her brother. He was on his feet, his face set. Behind him, Elodie had taken his chair and was scrolling through her mobile. "You do realize I've lived on my own for years."

"Aye. But this isna Edinburgh."

She crossed her arms over her chest and immediately regretted it as pain flared. She tried to keep from showing her agony, but she failed.

"That's why you need someone around," Scott said, pointing to her arm.

Willa held it protectively against herself. "It's an injury, I admit, but I can do for myself. I don't need to be coddled."

"There's danger here. You might be out of George's reach, but doona think for a minute she willna send someone after you."

"Please, don't go into the speech again," she begged. "I know things aren't good on the isle, but I have you, Elodie, and all your friends. The fact is, I won't be safe anywhere."

Scott turned away and raked a hand down his face. Filip knocked on the back door as he opened it and came inside. He took one look at Scott before his gaze darted to Willa, his smile fading.

"Uh…mornin'," Filip called.

"It is a good morning," Elodie said as she pushed the chair

beside her out with a foot. "Willa just told Scott she wants to get her own place."

Filip chuckled as he sat. "She tired of seeing the two of you snogging?"

"Aye," Willa answered with a grin.

Elodie smiled, but Scott clearly didn't find any of it humorous if his glare was any indication.

Willa took out her tea bag and added milk before taking a seat at the table. She shouldn't have brought up moving yet. It wasn't the right time. Besides, she didn't have the energy to fight with Scott about it at the moment. It was better to just leave things alone. "We can't leave my and Dad's things in Edinburgh."

"It's only been a few days," Elodie said.

Willa sipped her tea. "We both knew we wouldn't be returning. Though we thought we'd leave on our own. We figured we'd have time to finish packing."

"Finish?" Scott asked with a frown.

"We had already begun. I thought you knew."

He shook his head. "Evidently, I didna."

Willa grimaced as she exchanged a look with Elodie. "I thought Dad told you. I'm not going anywhere today, but I don't plan on staying here forever."

"You're welcome to stay for as long as you'd like," Elodie said.

"I appreciate that."

Filip shrugged. "I have an extra room."

"That's no' happening," Scott declared.

Elodie gave him a warning look that had Scott dropping his chin to his chest.

Willa looked from her brother to Filip. "Thanks, but I'd rather have my own place."

"What are you going to do for work?" Scott asked.

She stopped herself before she shrugged and hurt her arm again. "I'll find something."

"Ariah might have something available," Elodie offered.

Scott blew out a frustrated breath. "Willa, can you just hold up? You're moving a thousand miles an hour."

"I'm sorting out my life. Unless you don't want me on Skye."

His lips flattened. "I never said that. I want you to stay."

"Then what's the problem?"

"I can no' do this now. We've a job to get to." Scott gave Elodie a kiss and stalked from the house.

Filip twisted his lips as he got to his feet. He waved before hurrying after Scott. Willa looked at the door long after her brother had departed.

"He's worried about you and your father," Elodie said.

Willa nodded and put her hands around the mug to warm them. "I know. I'm here and healed as much as I can be. He won't let me help you or any of the others, nor will he allow me to join him and Filip."

Elodie jerked her chin to Willa's arm. "It isn't as if you'd be able to do any construction work with that."

"I could hand them tools. I could run errands. I want to be useful."

"I know, and I'm trying to convince Scott of that. Almost losing you hit him hard. He blames himself for asking you and Luke to get the book."

Willa nodded. "It was our decision. Not his."

"Try telling him that," Elodie replied with a wry smile.

"True. I'm going stir-crazy sitting around doing nothing. I need something to do. And, aye, eventually, I will move out."

Elodie glanced at the table. "Maybe wait until we hear something about your dad. Scott isn't handling not being able to look for Luke well."

"Neither am I, so I understand." Willa blew out a breath as she realized she had been thinking only about herself, and not about what Scott might be thinking or feeling. "You're right. I'll hold off doing anything for the time being."

"Good. As for something to do, I have an idea."

Willa sat up straighter in the chair when she saw Elodie's eyes twinkling. "Oh?"

"Come with me to Carwood Manor."

"Bronwyn's place? Where the group conducts their business?"

Elodie's smiled. "Aye. There. If you're up for it, I'll situate you in our meeting room so you can handle calls that come in and other admin duties."

Willa's smile died as she looked at her wounded arm. "Writing anything will be impossible."

"Not impossible. Maybe more difficult with your other hand, but if I've learned anything about you these past few days, it's that you never quit. Besides, have you seen Theo's handwriting? Anything would be more legible than his scratch."

Willa laughed, feeling a sense of purpose she hadn't since she woke on Skye. "Scott will be pissed."

"I've already run this by him. He'd rather you stay at our place, but even he admits the manor is better protected than here. He also realizes you need something to do."

"It will be fine for now, but I need to bring in some money. I have savings, but I'd rather not dip into that since there isn't much there. It wasn't as if I loved my job in the city. It was just a place to work, but I'd been there for a few years. I'm glad they took my excuse about an injury for missing those days and accepted my last-minute resignation."

Elodie grunted as she stood. "It wasn't an excuse. It was the truth." She rinsed out her cup and faced Willa. "Do you need help getting dressed?"

"I'll manage."

Willa got to her feet and brought her cup with her to her room. She was halfway down the hall when Elodie's voice stopped her.

"Oh, I meant to tell you, I'll speak to Scott about getting your things. You'll feel better with your own clothes."

Willa smiled at her and continued on to her room. She found she did, indeed, need help with her bra, but she dealt with the pain instead of asking for assistance. She wanted to do things for herself, and if she ended up having this trouble forever, she needed to learn how to adjust to it.

She blinked away the tears of discomfort and resentment. The fact that Beth would stoop so low and use ebony wood was outrageous. It proved just what kind of Druid the woman was. And George, for that matter. Willa didn't believe in revenge because it never served a purpose. But if they had hurt her father, she *would* get retribution.

Willa finished dressing in her borrowed clothes. She stopped in the bathroom to brush her teeth, which seemed to take twice as long with her left arm. It amazed her that her non-dominant arm couldn't work as efficiently as her dominant one, even though it knew exactly what to do. She was working to get the brush through her hair when Elodie passed by and stopped.

"Need a hand?"

Willa closed her eyes and nodded.

"Just brushing?"

"I'd like it out of my face, please." She opened her eyes and met Elodie's in the mirror.

"High or low ponytail?"

Willa knew how heavy her hair could get, and she didn't want a headache. "Low, please."

Elodie made quick work of Willa's hair, and before long, they were in Elodie's car and headed to the manor.

"I did a search on ebony wood yesterday," Willa said. "I didn't find much about it on the Druid forums."

Elodie glanced at her. "Rhona's been doing some investigating on that, too. Saber found a few things. I asked Elias to print them out for you. It isn't much, but it's more than any of us knew before."

"Makes you wonder what else we don't know."

"I get the feeling it's a lot."

"Beth knows, though, doesn't she? Because of the book. I bet that's how she knew about the ebony wood in the first place."

Elodie shrugged as she drove. "It's likely. Scott and Filip are livid with George, but it doesn't compare to Rhona's rage at the moment. God help George if she comes back to Skye. And Bronwyn is beside herself with what her cousin has done."

"It's not Bronwyn's fault."

"She's as stubborn as your brother. You'll never convince her otherwise."

Willa watched the passing scenery. "I'd feel the same."

She let her mind drift, and it found its way to Jasper. For long hours after she'd gotten home, she lay on the floor with the blinds open just so she could see the stars. She wondered what he was doing and if their paths would cross on the isle.

"Can I ask how the dinner went?"

She swung her head to Elodie. "It went well. He took me to stargaze after."

"That's different. Did you like it?"

"I loved it," she said, looking back out the window.

Elodie was quiet for a moment before she asked, "You want to see him again, don't you?"

"He was easy to talk to and very charming."

"Those don't sound like reasons *not* to see him."

She looked at Elodie again. "He's a Druid."

"Do you think he's working with George?"

Willa shrugged when Elodie glanced her way. "I didn't get that impression. He's a loner, as far as any groups go. He asked what'd happened to me, and I told him."

"All of it?" Elodie asked in shock.

Willa nodded. "All of it. I shared some other stories. The one about George sending Scott and Filip here for you. We got to talking about her then."

"Did he ask about her?"

"Not really. He seemed interested in all of it."

"But?" Elodie asked, her brows raised.

Willa shook her head and frowned. "Why pull someone into this mess if they're not already involved?"

"It is quite a mess, isn't it?"

"The biggest. And it seems to keep growing."

Elodie gave her a sad smile. "I wouldn't bring anyone into it either."

"I had a lovely night, but that's all it can be. One night."

CHAPTER TEN

SKYE DRUIDS

A magical fire at the center lit the cavern. Rhona stood next to the blaze and looked across to one of the six smaller, unused grottos. Inside was a woman Rhona had once considered a friend. Someone her predecessor had thought highly enough of that Kerry had been made one of only five deputies.

When Corann died, everything changed. Rhona was thrust into a position she had never considered nor wanted. But someone had to lead the Druids on Skye. It fell to her, so she reluctantly took the role. The weight of it was sometimes too much to bear. So many lives depended on her decisions and actions.

She stood within one of the Red Cuillin mountains, or the Red Hills as most locals called them, in a place created to serve one purpose—to detain and confine. The cavern was a prison for Druids. And within one of the smaller cells was the person who had controlled the mist that had so ruthlessly murdered Druids.

Rhona ran her gaze over Kerry. The older woman sat on the cold, hard floor. Her arms were wrapped around her bulk in an effort to stay warm. She had never married or bore children, but she had been loved and admired by those in her sector. What had happened to turn Kerry from that Druid into a killer?

"Why did you target those particular Druids?" Rhona asked. "What about them made you want to take their lives?"

Kerry didn't bother looking at Rhona as she moved a thin, chin-length strand of graying-brown hair away from her face.

Rhona didn't give up. She had been here every day for over a week, and would continue coming until Kerry talked. "Who are you working with?"

"You can keep asking the same stupid questions I won't answer," Kerry stated.

Rhona hid her smile. It was the first time Kerry had spoken. It wasn't an answer, but it was something. "You might have been powerful enough to secure a position as a deputy, but there's no way you had enough magic to gather Druid souls to create the mist."

Kerry turned her head to Rhona, her eyes blazing with hatred.

"Ah. You didn't create it. Someone else did."

"You think you're so clever. You've no idea what you're up against."

"Tell me. I'm all ears," Rhona said.

Kerry rolled her eyes and turned her head away. "Enjoy your reign while it lasts."

"So, you wanted my position. If Corann had thought you were capable, he would've tapped you."

She didn't respond.

Rhona tried again. "You've lost everyone's confidence. You turned against your own. I want to know why. You had a good life, Kerry."

That didn't get a reaction, either.

Rhona lowered her gaze to the floor for a moment. "You're going to spend the rest of your life in this prison. Think about that until I return tomorrow."

With a snap of her fingers, she extinguished the fire. Rhona walked down the long, winding tunnel until she came to the entrance. She stepped out into the sun, lifting her face to it. A warm hand slid against hers, their fingers twining. She looked to the side and stared into Balladyn's red-ringed silver eyes.

"She spoke. That's an improvement."

Rhona nodded, loving the sound of his Irish accent. "Am I doing the right thing?"

"What other choice do you have? A regular jail would never hold her."

"Some will question her rights."

Balladyn tightened his fingers around hers and stepped closer. "She's dangerous. She's killed, and she'd do it again. If we send her away, we're responsible for any other lives she takes. I don't want that, and I know you don't either."

"What I want are answers."

"She won't give them up easily."

Rhona nodded glumly. "And the longer it takes for us to get information, the more danger everyone is in."

"You found out she didn't create the mist."

She loved that he could veil himself to others. It allowed him to watch her back without anyone knowing he was there. "We had already guessed that."

"Her reaction said a lot."

"She doesn't like being thought of as less than."

Balladyn raised a black brow, the breeze lifting the long locks of his silver-streaked midnight hair. "She craves power. Maybe that's why she killed."

"Maybe, but I think it's more. She could've come after me with the mist. She hates me enough. Why didn't she?"

"I'm here."

Rhona shrugged and faced him. "She could've sent it after you, too. We're missing something."

"Saber has already compared all the murdered to find any links between them. There aren't any."

"There is one. They're Skye Druids."

"Other than that."

"Maybe that's the only link needed."

Balladyn studied her. "Meaning?"

"I don't know. I'm tossing out ideas that probably mean nothing."

"Or something."

She sighed. "We might have caught Kerry, and Ferne may have released the souls in the mist, but that's all we've done. We haven't zeroed in on anyone who might have been working with Kerry."

"They're here. We'll find them."

"Let's hope it's soon. Druids are losing their magic, there's a growing darkness over the isle, and who knows what else is coming."

Balladyn gently cupped her face and tilted it upward. "We'll handle it."

"I know."

His lips curled into a seductive grin before he placed his mouth on hers.

Edie sat on her bed, staring off into nothing. She pulled up the picture of her husband, Trevor, kissing another woman. She didn't know who had sent it to her. At first, she was shocked and hurt. Then, the anger set in.

But she didn't ask Trevor about it.

She still didn't know why. Every day, she told herself she would show him and ask him to explain it, and each day passed without her doing it. She muddled through the hours, keeping to her normal routine and getting all the things done she usually did. But she felt separated from herself. As if she were out of her body.

No one seemed to notice, either. Not the kids, not Trevor. She didn't expect her sister and brother, Elodie and Elias, to notice because they were always off doing whatever they did. The other parents she saw at pickup and after-school activities didn't notice, either. Maybe she looked normal, even if she didn't feel it.

She checked her call log and then her texts. There had been nothing from Kerry. Edie had waited for days before she drove past Kerry's house. Her car was there, but she didn't come to the door. Edie had even looked through the windows in case the Druid had an accident and couldn't get to the door.

Kerry had spent a lot of time convincing Edie to join her in remaking the Druids into the group they should've always been. At first, Edie had refused, but the idea had grown on her. Now that she was ready, Kerry had disappeared.

Edie supposed Kerry could've left the isle, but she didn't think that had happened. Kerry had used the mist to kill. Why leave a place where she had such power? Though the mist hadn't been seen in days. Maybe Kerry had left *with* the mist. She had told Edie to be ready. Well, she was more than ready.

She wanted to talk to Kerry about more than just the Druids' new direction. She wanted to know if Kerry had sent the photo of Trevor. While Kerry hadn't come out and said Trevor was cheating, she had hinted at it. Edie's marriage had been rocky, but that was because she had let her rage and bitterness for her siblings get in the way.

Edie rose and went to the closet. For the third time in a week, she shuffled through every item of clothing, looking for anything that might confirm Trevor was having an affair. She moved to the dresser and the bedside table before searching the bathroom. She looked through every room in the house, including the kids' rooms, but she didn't find anything. Edie ended in the garage, empty-handed.

The only places she hadn't looked were Trevor's car and office. She could search the vehicle tonight while he slept. The office was another matter. There was no way she could get inside without his secretary notifying him.

Edie walked into the house and glanced at the monitor in the kitchen that displayed the security feed from around the house. She remembered that all of their rental properties had the same cameras. Edie hurried into the office and sat behind the desk. She moved the mouse to wake the computer and clicked on the security software. After she'd keyed in her password, she began clicking through each property.

There were hours of video to watch, with no way to zero in on any specific time or place to see if he was using one of the houses. She plopped back into the chair and closed her eyes. Every time she thought she had a way to find out, it slipped through her fingers. That left her one avenue—she'd have to ask him.

Edie's stomach clenched every time she thought about it. Of course, she shied away from the truth because it would destroy her world. What kind of person stayed with someone who had affairs?

"I knowingly have for the last week," she answered.

Edie sat up and put her elbows on the desk before dropping her head into her hands. She didn't want to believe the picture. It was why she had been searching for proof. While things with Trevor weren't as good as they had been, they *had* gotten better. All that would fall apart if she asked him if he was having an affair.

But didn't she want to know the truth?

The not-knowing was hard, but divorce would be harder. There would be lawyers and bickering over custody of the kids. Not to mention the property they had amassed over the years. It wasn't just her life that would be shaken. The kids' lives would be upended drastically. She knew all too well what kind of effect that had. She'd experienced it after her father's death and her mother being convicted of the crime. Edie went from having a family to losing both parents in one day. Her mother was still alive but locked away—at least for another few months.

Or...Edie could leave things the way they were. Not rock the boat, so to speak. She could become the wife she'd once been and make Trevor fall in love with her all over again. If he was having an affair, he'd end it. She'd have her family back. And she'd never let anything like this happen again.

Ever.

That meant she needed to confront her siblings. She'd ignored them for a few days, but now that she had a course of action for her marriage, she could shift some of her focus back to them.

Edie rose, showered, and changed to look her best before heading out to pick up the kids and stopping by the store. She would cook Trevor his favorite meal and dessert tonight. She strode into the bathroom and pulled out the massage oil to set on his bedside table. Trevor could never turn down a massage. And that always led to sex.

She wouldn't give up on her marriage or her husband. It was time Trevor knew that. A person needed to know they were loved and wanted. Tonight was a turning point. For her. For him.

For both of them and their future.

CHAPTER ELEVEN

SKYE DRUIDS

Jasper leaned low over the horse's neck as they raced across the land. He had a smile on his face when the mare effortlessly jumped over a low stone fence, never breaking stride. The white wanted to run, and Jasper let her.

Having such a magnificent creature carrying him at such speeds was exhilarating. In another life, he would've devoted himself to horses. Even rescuing them when they needed it. Because everyone needed saving at some point in their lives.

This pretend life he lived would be tough to give up. But he would do it. He had walked away from all the different people he'd become over the years. He didn't have a choice. It wasn't as if this would be the first time he'd found a place he wanted to stay and couldn't. Good or bad. It was what it was.

When he saw they neared the next pasture, Jasper sat up and gently slowed the mare to a gallop and then to a walk. Both he and the horse were breathing hard after such exercise. He'd found it was an excellent way to start the day, and the horses seemed to agree.

He patted the white's neck. "Good lass."

Jasper tugged on the reins to stop her when they reached the gate. He dismounted and looped the reins over the mare's head before opening the gate to walk her back to the stables. His phone dinged with a text as he removed the saddle. He didn't bother looking. George disagreed with his planned course of action regarding Willa and was letting him know in no uncertain terms. He'd had to remind her twice already that he knew what he was doing and she needed to trust him. The fact that she continued trying to contact him said just how little she did. He tried not to take it personally.

So far, it wasn't working.

Jasper hung the saddle before removing the white's bridle and putting that away, as well. He returned with a brush and an apple. The mare happily munched on the treat as Jasper brushed her down. It was as much for the horse as himself. Many times, he'd turn to find the animals staring at him. He wished he knew what they were thinking. At the very least, he hoped they knew how much he enjoyed them.

When the white had cooled down, Jasper let her into the paddock with the others and then went to the house. He removed his boots by the back door and made his way into the kitchen. He toasted a couple of slices of cinnamon bread and heated water for tea. Then he turned to the table.

Scattered atop it were pages he had printed from the internet as he searched for anything to do with ebony wood being used in magic. He'd been shocked at how much he uncovered. Some of it was nonsense and took hours to sort through to find pertinent information to match what little he knew from experience. Once he did, he'd fallen into a rabbit hole of material. Not much of it was good news for Willa.

He rubbed his eyes as he yawned. The toast popped up, and he spread butter over the warm slices before biting into one. He had a big mug of tea in one hand and the cinnamon bread in the other while he stared down at the papers on the table.

When he pressed George to get the name of the individual who had used the ebony wood on Willa, she had shut him down quickly. He'd find out one way or another. It would be easier and quicker if George gave up the individual, but Jasper didn't mind weeding them out of the organization. Though he wasn't sure what he would do when he found them.

George's shocked reaction to hearing that ebony wood had been used on Willa seemed genuine, which turned Jasper's attention to Beth and her two female guards. Yet Willa had said a man and a woman had been after her. Not two women. Either Beth had others following Willa that George didn't know about—which was highly possible—or Beth had garnered some of George's people. Also, highly probable.

As far as he knew, George hadn't done anything to those responsible for using such a deadly instrument. That also made Jasper lean toward Beth and her people. If George wasn't taking action, it was because she knew she'd lose. And that meant she'd already lost her position of power. She just didn't know it yet.

But all of that was speculation. Jasper wasn't in Edinburgh. All he had to go on were his instincts and whatever George shared with him—which wasn't much.

His phone dinged again. Jasper set down his mug and checked it to find that George had sent multiple texts demanding to know when he would see Willa next. He finished off the piece of bread and wiped his fingers on his jeans before replying with one word: TODAY.

It had been two days since he had dropped her off after their dinner. He'd spent that time researching in hopes of finding something to take to Willa. He had, but it wasn't what he'd wanted. Still, it was a start. And it gave him a reason to talk to her.

An alert popped up on his laptop screen notifying him of a response to his query on one of the Druid boards. Jasper grabbed the second slice of toast and pulled out a chair to navigate to the right board. There were about a dozen really active forums where Druids willingly shared information. And misinformation. There were always arseholes who got off on fucking with others.

Jasper found the thread he'd begun and clicked on it, going to the last message. He read it twice to be sure he understood it. Then he printed it and put it in the stack with the other pages to show Willa. All the while, an unpleasant feeling settled over him. He'd always known ebony wood in the hands of a Druid was dangerous, but it could be disastrous wielded by someone like Beth.

After finishing his breakfast, he cleared the table and went to shower. Within thirty minutes, he was in his vehicle and headed to Willa's. Except she wasn't there. No one was. What Jasper had to say couldn't wait. He knew of someone else who could help him— Theo Frasier.

Jasper had never willingly gone to a police station before. He'd never been forced there, either. Which said something about how good he was at getting away from his marks. Yet he walked into the building without hesitation. He told himself it was what his character would do, but it was more than that. He was disturbed by Willa's attack and how easily George seemed to have lost control of the organization.

"Is DI Frasier in?" Jasper asked the officer behind the front desk.

"Just a moment," the woman said.

Jasper took the time to look around. The entrance had a few empty chairs, a locked door only accessible by a code, and a wall of plexiglass that separated him from the officer. He found it amusing that the police were so worried about people wanting to get in when few ever *wanted* to be there. Criminals, especially.

The door opened. Jasper turned to find Frasier standing with a brow raised.

"Mr. McCabe?" Frasier asked.

"Jasper, please," he said as he walked to the door. "I wondered if you had a few moments. There's something I'd like to discuss with you."

Frasier paused as he looked behind him. Then he stepped out into the lobby and nodded at the female officer. "Follow me," he told Jasper.

Jasper trailed him outside and through the car park until no one was around. Jasper understood his secrecy. Frasier was a Druid, which no one in the force probably knew. Whether he liked it or not, he and Frasier both lived with secrets. The only difference was that Frasier could get him thrown in jail.

Frasier stopped and faced him. "What is it?"

"I wanted to give this to Willa, but she's no' home. I'd be most grateful if you could relay this information to her."

Frasier studied him, his face blank. "Let me see what you have."

"It's some research I've done on ebony wood," Jasper said as he pulled the papers from his back pocket and handed them over. "I've highlighted the parts I think are important. The last page, specifically."

Frasier leafed through them to the last one and read over the message Jasper had gotten that morning. Frasier's gaze jerked to him. "I'm sure you'll understand if I question why you're looking into this."

"Having someone's blood covering you as they lay dying from something another Druid did tends to stick with a person."

"You could've put that shard in her when you found her."

Jasper held his gaze. "I could've, but I didna. I'm no' in the business of violence, Detective Inspector. What happened to Willa is unconscionable."

"I agree. We may no' know Willa well, but she's Scott's sister, which means she's one of us."

Jasper inclined his head as he got Frasier's meaning. "I'm trying to help. That's all."

"I hope so. We're doing our own investigating into ebony wood, but I'll admit, you found things we have no'."

"I'll keep digging. If I find anything else, I'll give it to—"

"Me," Frasier stated.

Jasper shifted his weight to his other foot. "Right. I'll give it to you."

"I'm glad we're clear on that."

Jasper inclined his head again and walked away. He got two steps before Frasier called his name. He halted and pivoted to look over his shoulder.

"You have our gratitude for finding Willa. But if we learn you put the ebony inside her or had anything to do with her injury, we'll bring the full force of our fury down on you."

Jasper turned to face him head-on. "You talk like a man who has many enemies."

"We're Skye Druids. We always have enemies. Those who doona understand our roots or take the time to learn who we are fear us. And those who fear blindly strike out. You may be all you say you are, or you could be someone else entirely. Either way, it'd be better if you kept your distance from Willa."

"Is that what she wants? Or is that what Scott wants?"

"It doesna matter." Frasier lifted the papers. "Thanks for this. Have a good day."

Jasper held his gaze for a long minute before turning and walking away. He wasn't entirely surprised by Frasier's reaction. Jasper wasn't a Skye native, which made him an outsider and a potential problem. No doubt Frasier had run a background check on him, but Jasper had expected that and had paid a hacker to set up a cover that would pacify the police no matter how much they dug. It had cost a fortune, but it was worth it. If Frasier had found anything, he would've come for Jasper already.

Jasper drove away, irritated at being told to stay away from Willa. She was a grown woman and could make her own decisions. But they were right to be wary of him. He knew men like Frasier and Scott. They would make it impossible to get close to Willa, thereby ending his job before it even really began.

He'd had a good in with Willa, but that had been blown to bits by her injury, which was excessive any way he looked at it. There weren't many jobs he didn't complete. In fact, there were only three others. It rankled him that he wouldn't be able to finish this one. That also meant he'd be leaving Skye. And the horses.

Unless he stayed on to continue his surveillance. That was precisely what he would do. Besides, he'd heard Willa—and now Frasier—mention other enemies. He wanted to know who else was after the Skye Druids. That intel could be beneficial to George and allow her to get the upper hand against Beth.

CHAPTER TWELVE

SKYE DRUIDS

Willa rolled her head from one side to the other to stretch her neck. She arched her back in her seat after sitting for hours, reading over reports from Saber on the computer. She'd yet to actually talk to the man. Everyone said the hacker was male, but she wondered if it might actually be a woman. It made sense with Saber going to such pains to only talk through text and emails.

Once Willa had that thought in her head, she couldn't let it go. Not that she would ever ask Saber. He—or she—had a reason for going to such lengths. And that was all she needed to know.

Willa bit back a yawn. Her eyes were crossing, which meant it was time to get up and walk around. Maybe get some tea. Herbal this time. Bronwyn had an even larger variety than Elodie. It was as if the two of them had at least one of every option Ariah sold. Plus, the blends the Druid only sold to her kind. Willa couldn't wait to meet the tea maker.

After snagging her cup, Willa made her way downstairs and

saw Theo talking in low tones to Scott in the entryway. She hadn't known her brother was at the manor. Whatever the reason, it must be important for him to leave his remodeling job.

"Hey," she called out. "What brings you here?"

Scott looked up, a frown marring his face. "Nothing."

She knew that expression. It was the one he got when he was trying to hide something. "Elodie is out with Sabryn at the moment."

"Aye." Scott shifted from one foot to the other.

Frasier wouldn't even look her way.

Willa continued to them and spotted Scott quickly folding papers to put them on the other side of his body as if to hide them. "Theo," she said when she reached them.

He nodded, briefly meeting her gaze. Then he looked at Scott. "We'll talk later."

"Thank you," Scott said.

"Anytime." Frasier pivoted and walked away.

Willa swung her attention to her brother. "That was awkward."

"What are you talking about?"

"You know exactly what I'm talking about."

Scott cleared his throat. "There's a lot going on. You'll need to be more specific."

"You want specific?" She jerked her chin to the hand he tried to keep out of her view. "Whatever Theo gave you that you're trying very hard to pretend doesn't exist. Oh, and the way Theo wouldn't look at me and couldn't get away fast enough. You know. How you're acting right now."

Scott looked at the floor and blew out a breath. Then he met her gaze. "It's nothing."

"If what you're hiding has to do with me, then tell me right now."

"I will. As soon as I finish with it."

Willa tucked her empty cup into the crook of her injured arm and held out her left hand. "We can look at it together. I don't need protecting."

"That's exactly what you need."

"Scott," she stated firmly. "Hand it over."

"Why can you no' let me be your brother and protect you?"

"I need you to be my brother, and I'm fine with you protecting me. What I'm not good with is you trying to rule my life as if I'm a child."

He shook his head but finally put the papers in her hand. "Why do you have to be so stubborn?"

"Because it's the only way I can deal with you and Dad."

"We taught you to be careful."

She frowned because she knew he was referring to Jasper. Which didn't make sense because she hadn't seen or spoken to the Druid since their dinner. Why would Scott be reminding her to be cautious? Unless the papers were from Jasper. It was difficult, but she managed to open the documents with one hand. She skimmed the first to find links and a short description about each pertaining to ebony wood.

Her head snapped up. "Who did this come from?"

"Frasier."

Willa held back a sarcastic reply, knowing it wouldn't get her anywhere. "Who gave it to him? And don't even think about lying."

"McCabe."

Her suspicions were right. It was from Jasper. "What is it about him that rubs you so wrong?"

"The way he found you is too convenient."

"I'm happy he was there, no matter the reason. You should try to see it that way, too, since I wouldn't be here otherwise."

Scott ran a hand down his face and sighed. "I do, Willa."

"Then act like it."

She walked around him toward the kitchen. Once there, she set the papers on the counter, intending to ignore them as she made her tea, but she couldn't. There were five pages in all, each filled with information that Jasper must have found himself. He had done that for her. Had he gone to the house looking for her? Had he run into Theo and asked him to deliver them? That was possible, but obviously, Theo was as skeptical as Scott since the Detective Inspector hadn't given them directly to her.

But she had them now.

With a freshly brewed cup of tea in hand, Willa made her way to the second-floor room the team used as their meeting place. She took a seat in a comfy chair to do a thorough read of what Jasper had sent.

A small portion of it was what she and the others had already found, but there was much more that showed Jasper had dug deeper. As far as she could tell, the only use for ebony wood was to harm someone. She wanted to think there were other uses for it, but the more she read, the more she began to doubt. Then she came to the last page.

Her heart skipped a beat as she read…*if ebony wood penetrates the body, there could be lifelong effects. Worse, if even the tiniest piece remains, it can corrupt the person.*

Willa's hand shook as she pulled up her ongoing chat with

Saber. It took her twice as long to type with one hand. She explained what she had and then took photos with her mobile to forward them.

Saber always seemed to be around to answer, no matter what time of day. Today was no exception. Maybe it wasn't one person. Perhaps it was two or more. He promised to look into it. She knew it wasn't fair to add to his already crammed workload, but he was the only one with the wherewithal to know if what Jasper found was true. She could spend weeks—months, even—learning the same things Saber could find in a day or two.

She gathered the papers and folded them to put into her purse. After leaving a note on one of the blank whiteboards, she grabbed Elodie's keys and walked from the house. Willa had to see Jasper. She wouldn't be long. She'd probably be back before any of the others returned.

The entire drive to Jasper's, she couldn't stop wondering if there was still wood in her wound. Wood that could corrupt her. The knowledge that something could force her to change made her sick to her stomach. Should she go back to the Healers and ask them to look again? Should she find other Healers?

Anger mixed with her misery. She understood why Scott had wanted to keep the papers from her, but that didn't lessen her annoyance. If anything, it made it worse. Because she would trust him enough to make his own decisions. Clearly, he didn't think she was capable of that.

Before she knew it, she had pulled into Jasper's drive. She stared at the two-story house. Its sleek, modern design was simple on the outside, with the real beauty and charm within. Her gaze ran along the many windows that showcased the impressive landscape all around him. Rolling hills spread on three sides, with mountains in the distance on one side and water on the other.

She spotted horses grazing that she had missed the first time she'd visited when she was too impressed with the house to see anything else. He had mentioned horseback riding. She wasn't much of a rider, but she had always loved horses. She couldn't imagine what it would be like to see Skye on horseback. The jarring motion would no doubt be unbearable with her arm, though.

Another reminder of what had been done to her.

Willa grabbed her purse and got out of the vehicle. She rang the bell and waited. After a few moments, she tried again. When Jasper didn't come to the door, she decided he wasn't there. Just as she turned away, she heard male laughter. She followed it around the house to see Jasper at the fence with the horses. They were all vying to get to him. He held his hand out to each one, offering some treat, she guessed.

He laughed again when one of the horses tried to shove another out of the way. She smiled as she watched him. The shadow of a cloud passed over the sun, briefly blanketing the area. Jasper put one foot on the bottom rung of the wooden fence and scratched a white horse's neck.

Another took notice of her and pricked its ears. Then the others followed suit. Suddenly, Jasper turned, their eyes meeting. She started across the yard, unable to look anywhere but at his dark gaze.

His surprise was evident. She wanted to know what Theo might have said to him, but that might anger her. Whatever the Detective Inspector had done, he'd done it out of friendship for

Scott. She needed to remember that. And have a word with him—with all of them, evidently.

"This is a surprise," Jasper said.

She glanced at the ground. "A welcome one?"

"Verra much so. Does that mean you got what I sent?"

"I did."

He blew out a breath and swung his head to the gray, who nudged him. "Good."

She watched the way he reverently stroked the horse's huge head. Given how they hung around him, it was clear the animals loved him, too.

"Would you like to meet them?" Jasper asked.

Her gaze darted to him, and she felt embarrassment for having been caught staring. "I would."

"Come," he beckoned. When she reached the fence, he held out some small carrots. "Enticing them is always the way to go," he said with a smile.

Willa grinned as she held out her hand.

"Do you know horses?"

She wrinkled her nose. "I've been around a few."

"You're no' scared of them, are you?"

"Nay," she said and turned to the bay, which was closest. "They're too beautiful to be afraid of."

"That they are. Be sure to keep your hand flat. We doona want them to mistake your fingers for carrots."

Willa offered her palm to the bay. The horse's nostrils flared as it smelled her. Then the bay's top lip brushed across her hand, seeking the carrot. Once it had it, it quickly chomped. Jasper handed her another, and Willa moved to the next horse, the sorrel. Then the gray, and finally, the white.

"What are their names?" she asked.

Jasper's smile slipped just a fraction. "I never name anything."

"Whyever not?"

He shrugged and focused on the horses. "It's just no' something I do."

"What do you call them then?"

"White, Gray, Bay, and Sorrel," Jasper said as he pointed to each one.

She laughed and smoothed her hand down the bay's nose. "That might be difficult if you had two of the same color."

"Notice, I doona," he replied with a warm grin.

She got lost in his eyes again. For a moment, she forgot why she'd come. It was easy with his smile and the horses, but this wasn't a social visit. Though, a part of her wished it was. "I wanted to thank you."

"I'm sure all your friends have dug up the same material, but just in case I found something different, I wanted to get it to you."

"I appreciate it. Truly."

He glanced at the house. "Would you like to come inside?"

"Sure."

She gave the bay one last pat and turned with Scott. They walked side by side to the house. When they reached the back door, she paused and looked behind her. "Wow."

"The view is something," he murmured.

She swung her head to find him right beside her. The wind tugged her hair into her eyes, and he quickly lifted his hand to pull it free of her lashes. She became all too aware of how close they were, and how handsome he was.

Of how much she liked being around him.

He tucked the hair behind her ear, then trailed his fingers

down the length to a large curl over her shoulder. His eyes followed his hand until he came to the end of the strand, and then he lifted his eyes to hers.

Her ear tingled where the pad of his finger had touched, and it traveled all through her body, prickling her skin and causing her stomach to quiver unexpectedly. He dropped his hand to his side as he stepped away, breaking the spell.

CHAPTER THIRTEEN

SKYE DRUIDS

Jasper's fingers tingled from touching Willa's hair. He'd been entranced with it from the moment he saw her picture. He'd never seen hair like hers, and his need to touch it, to feel its weight, overrode everything else.

He was playing his part perfectly if the desire flaring in her blue eyes was any indication. The thing was, he hadn't been pretending. That meant trouble for him. He would have to be careful. She was a job. Nothing more. And he couldn't forget that. Not for one second.

Jasper opened the door and motioned for her to enter. He leaned forward slightly as she passed to get another whiff of her scent. Jasmine. It lingered softly in her wake. He shut the door behind him and followed her inside.

"Can I get you anything?" he asked.

She shook her head as they entered the kitchen. "You spent a lot of time researching, I imagine."

"I have a penchant for it. After our dinner, I got curious and started investigating. The ebony wood is treacherous to wield, and even more perilous when used on someone. I doona like the idea of any Druid having it."

"And that's why you went to all this trouble?" she asked, pulling the papers from her purse.

Jasper looked at them as she laid the stack on the table. "I wanted to know if you would ever regain the use of your arm."

"Because you found me that night? Because you saved me?"

He couldn't exactly tell her that he had been part of the reason she had been injured in the first place or that he was attempting to fix what had been done. But he could tell her some of the truth. "I've seen ebony wood used once before."

"You've seen it?" she asked, her brows raised in surprise. "Did you use it?"

Jasper tried not to take offense to her suggesting he would stoop to such levels. "I didna. I witnessed it. Many years ago."

"Do you mind if I ask what happened?"

He looked down at his hands, remembering the blood and screams of torment. "The Druid who used it died. As did the Druid they used it on. Both of them horrifically."

"I'm sorry."

Jasper blinked and inwardly shook himself, hating that he'd delved into those memories, even briefly. "It was long ago."

"It obviously left an impression."

"What it did was show me that anyone who resorts to using ebony wood has reached a place of no return. They'll go to any lengths."

Willa set her purse on the table and sank into a chair. "How do you stop someone like that?"

"I'm no' sure anyone can. Ebony wood might be rare and

expensive, but that willna stop someone from getting their hands on a piece if they really want it."

"That's just what we need," she mumbled.

Jasper studied her face as she stared down at the pages. "Have you learned anything about your father?"

"Nay." She lifted her gaze to his. "And it's not making things easier for me or Scott. If Dad were able, he would've gotten in touch with us. He was supposed to come here."

"Are there others you could ask for help?"

"Not any I know of. My friends are doing their best."

"Your friends are distrustful of outsiders."

Her lips twisted wryly. "With good reason. I wasn't jesting the other night when I said there are other enemies."

"You make it sound as if you're at war."

"We are. Evil managed to get a foothold on the isle, and my friends stopped it. We're trying to see what things are connected."

"What kind of evil? What things?" he asked, eager to learn about her friends and their enemies.

"The mist, George, the darkness over Skye, Druids losing their magic, and the Ancients being silenced."

Jasper frowned. This was the first he'd heard about the Ancients being silenced or Druids losing their magic. He'd never heard the Ancients personally, but the news still shook him. "How do you know the Ancients have been silenced?"

"They spoke through Ferne. And nearly killed her in the process."

He took a second to digest that. "You're serious."

"I am."

"Shite."

She gave him a wry smile. "I wasn't kidding when I said there's a lot going on. You can understand why Scott and the others are hesitant to welcome new people."

He most certainly did. They had a right to be wary of him. Even if it didn't serve his purposes. "I'd think the more people willing to help, the better."

"Are you offering?"

"I didna say that."

"Hmm," she said and looked down at the table.

Jasper suspected there was more Willa wasn't telling him, but he didn't blame her. She might treat him better than her friends did, but that didn't mean she welcomed his involvement any more than her brother or Frasier.

What this showed him was that those on Skye had their attention divided and diverted in several places. That made it a prime opportunity for things to be disrupted. Yet, he hesitated. If even a tenth of what Willa spoke about was true, then toppling the Skye Druids might only make things worse. It seemed the best course of action was to let them fight the battles, and then George could make her move.

"Because I doona believe my help would be welcomed," Jasper added.

Willa's blue eyes slowly lifted to his. "I didn't think you wanted to be a part of anything."

"That was before I found you bleeding to death on the side of the road because of ebony wood."

"We've researched the wood and didn't come up with nearly as much as you did. I think you could prove useful. The others don't need to know."

Jasper shook his head. "Hiding anything from your family and friends would only make them more distrustful of me. If I do help, it'll be with their agreement. I'd also need to earn your brother's trust."

"I've skimmed over a lot that's happened. It's a jumbled mess that we're still sorting through, trying to connect things and people. I think we need others to join us. The more Druids we have, the better chance we have."

He crossed his arms over his chest and did the unthinkable. He said exactly what he planned to do. "Unless someone infiltrates your group from the inside to destroy it."

"They could try," she said with a grin. "They'd soon learn how strong we are. I just arrived, but I've always considered myself a part of things. I might not have experienced it with them, but Scott has. They've saved him, and he's been there for them. That kind of bond isn't easily broken."

No, it certainly wasn't. Jasper wouldn't be breaking it, though. His job was only to gather intel.

"I think you should know just how dangerous things are," Willa said. "If you really want to join us, that is."

"I'm seriously considering it."

She licked her lips. "It's a lot. We should probably get comfortable."

"This way." Jasper led her to the living room and let her choose her seat.

She sat in the corner of the sofa, leaning her uninjured side against the arm. He took his favorite chair. Then he waited.

"It began when someone tried to kill Rhona," she said.

Jasper was rocked by the news. "What?"

"Balladyn saved her."

"Were they already a couple?"

"That's how they came together. He found her after the attack and brought her to Skye. I don't know all the specifics, but somehow, during all of that, he became the Warden of the isle."

"What does that mean?"

"It means they're a formidable couple. They can mix their Druid and Reaper magic, and when they do, I hear it's something to see. And nearly impossible to beat. Rhona is a powerful Druid in her own right, but with Balladyn as the Warden, the isle is guarded carefully."

Jasper's research on Reapers hadn't yielded much, and George had given her biased opinion. He wanted Willa's. "What is a Reaper? I've heard a few things."

"I only got the basics from Scott. Reapers are Light and Dark Fae chosen by Death for their warrior abilities and magic. They're stronger and faster than other Fae and keep the balance between their factions. They also do exactly as their name implies—they reap Fae souls."

In other words, George was right to fear Balladyn. Jasper would have to be extra careful around the Reaper.

"A group of Druid Others tried to kill Rhona because she didn't want to form such a faction. They lured her away from Skye and attacked. She very nearly died. Rhona and Balladyn sussed out the group responsible but not the individuals because they communicated online. All of them except a Druid on the isle. Kerry. She was one of Rhona's deputies."

Jasper interrupted to ask, "What's a deputy?"

"The isle is divided into five sections, each with a Druid overseeing it. Druids go to their deputies instead of Rhona. The deputies handle many of the smaller issues and only take the larger ones to Rhona. It frees up Rhona's time."

Jasper nodded in understanding.

Willa then continued. "Kerry swore magic had been used on her and that she never meant Rhona any harm. Rhona removed her as deputy but allowed her to remain on Skye."

"Wow," Jasper said in astonishment.

"Not far on the heels of that, the mist came. It tried to kill Elias after it attacked Scott, Elodie, and Filip. It did kill several other Druids."

"The news left off the part that they were Druids."

"Right around the time the mist first showed up, some Druids started having issues with their magic. Rhona's been searching for a cause. After what happened to Elias and Bronwyn, Ferne came to Skye. She's a seer and has some amazing abilities."

Jasper hadn't realized Ferne was a seer. George likely wouldn't enjoy hearing that since she was one, too. "What kind of abilities?"

"Well, she can talk to people in their minds. It takes a lot out of her when she does it, but that's how she found Kirsi. She saw Kirsi in a vision and knew she was the one who could defeat the growing evil."

Kirsi. Jasper searched his mind for memories of her but couldn't come up with an image. "Who is Kirsi?"

"Another Skye Druid. Ferne came from the London Druids, who are apparently the founders of those kicked off Skye long, long ago for some misdeed. One of their rules is their members can have absolutely no contact with anyone from Skye, and they can never, under any circumstances, come to the isle."

Jasper quirked a brow. "Ferne did."

"Aye, because she knew if the Druids on the isle fell, then all the others around the world would, too. She decided to join the fight here. By coming to Skye, she discovered she is a conduit the

Ancients can use to speak. They forcibly took control of her body to let my friends know they were being silenced."

"Did they say who was doing it?"

"They only mentioned the Ageless One. When they finished, Ferne's body was a shell. The Healers called her brain dead."

Jasper frowned, wishing he was writing all of this down. "The Healers were able to save her?"

"Nay."

He raised his brows, waiting for her to finish.

Willa paused, apprehension lining her face. "This is where things will start to sound weird."

"I can take it. Go on."

"Ferne's body was here, but her soul was in The Grey."

"The what?" he asked, unsure if he'd heard her right.

Willa softly rubbed her right arm as if it pained her. "The Grey. It's the place between dimensions. I left out the part where Bronwyn can open portals between dimensions. That's where she put her cousin, Beth, to keep her away from Sydney's slimy clutches."

Jasper hid his grin at her use of *slimy*.

"When they retrieved Beth, they saw something trying to cut through the veil to get to them. They got Beth out in time. Unfortunately, that was also where Ferne's soul went."

"How did they know that?"

Willa tapped her temple. "Ferne was able to reach both Kirsi and Theo to describe where she was."

"Frasier?"

"Aye," she said with a soft smile. "Feelings developed there. Anyway, once Theo learned where he had to go, he convinced Bronwyn to open the portal. The creature attacked Ferne, Theo, and Finn. But we think it was scared of Kirsi because it vanished when she got near. She was the one who brought Ferne's soul back to our dimension and melded her soul with her body again."

Jasper blew out a breath, shocked to his core. "Bloody hell."

"As a conduit, Ferne could hear the mist and was able to free the Druid souls. Kerry, the one who controlled the mist, has been dealt with."

"The same Kerry?"

"The same."

"I bet Rhona regrets allowing her to stay. Was Kerry killed?"

Willa jerked back as if hit. "Never. Though they couldn't turn her over to the police because she would get loose. She's in a Druid prison."

He'd had no idea there was such a place. Though it made sense. Only Druids could hold another Druid.

"We don't know who the Ageless One is. We don't know who helped Kerry because she didn't have the magic to create the mist herself and isn't talking. We don't know what this darkness is surrounding the isle. We don't know why Druids are losing their magic."

"And George?"

Willa rolled her eyes. "Everyone knows what she wants."

"Which is?" he pressed.

"She wants revenge against Elias, and she wants power. I believe she had good intentions to begin with, but things changed once Druids learned about the Others. You know about them, right?"

He nodded once. "I'm on Druid forums, and it is heavily discussed."

"The Fae Others didn't survive attacking Skye. Druid Others

won't either. Not even George's group, though she believes differently. Though I suppose anything is possible with Beth and that book."

Jasper had known there'd been a Fae battle on Skye recently. It had been shared on the forums by some Skye Druids themselves. But he hadn't realized they were Fae Others. George needed that information. It could change everything. Because he agreed with Willa. If even the Fae couldn't stop them, George didn't have what it took to topple Rhona and Balladyn.

"Well? Is that too much for you?"

He stared into her blue eyes and spoke the truth. "Nay."

CHAPTER FOURTEEN

SKYE DRUIDS

Relief poured through Willa. Perhaps she was wrong about Jasper, but it felt right for him to be involved. "There are a couple of other things I should tell you about," she added.

He quirked a brow, a crooked smile on his lips. "There's more?"

"More involved. Most are Druids. Besides Balladyn, there are...other...allies."

"You didna hesitate to tell me about The Grey and the monsters within it, but you falter at allies?"

She lifted her left shoulder in a shrug. She was getting better at remembering not to move her right side. "Because I was a wee bit shell-shocked when Scott told me about them."

"Doona keep me in suspense. Who is it?"

"I don't suppose you've heard of the Dragon Kings?"

His expression froze for a moment before his brows slowly drew together. "There has been a mention or two of them, but people quickly rebuke it. Are you telling me they're real?"

"They are. They live in Scotland. Dreagan, actually."

"As in…the whiskey?"

"The very one," she said with a smile. "Earth was the dragons' home until humans came. There's a long story I've still not heard, but what I do know is that the dragons are on another realm. However, the Kings remain here. They can shift from dragon to human at will, and they protect the planet. Scott and Elodie actually saw one of them shift. They still talk about how exciting and terrifying it was to witness such a huge creature. I hate that I missed it."

"And the Dragon Kings are allies? You're sure?"

She grinned at his dismay. "Positive. They defeated the original Others."

"Why no' have the Kings come and dispose of whatever is happening on Skye then?"

"Rhona will if it comes to it, but Skye is being attacked because Druids are here. The Kings are aware. Nikolai is on the isle and will step in if needed."

"A Dragon King is here?"

Was it her imagination or was there a thread of fear in Jasper's words? Not that she blamed him. She'd been intimidated when she first learned of it herself. "Aye. He's mated to Esther. Which brings me to the next allies. Brother and sister, Henry and Esther. Long ago, our kind had a pair who regulated Druids."

"The TruthSeeker and the JusticeBringer."

"You know about them?" she asked enthusiastically.

Jasper ran a hand over his jaw. "I read about them doing some research, but I heard they were killed off."

"They were hidden. The line never died out. Henry and Esther are here, and wherever Esther goes, Nikolai goes."

"Those are impressive allies."

She started to tell him about the Warriors and Druids from MacLeod Castle, but she decided to wait on that. No need to inundate him with everything at once. It might be better to do a little at a time.

Jasper swallowed and shook his head. "Sounds like the Skye Druids have all the help they need to defeat any enemy."

"That isn't true. Look at me."

"Can none of your friends help?"

She twisted her lips. "Possibly."

"Did you read the papers I sent?"

The urgency in his voice caught her unawares. "Aye. The last page especially. I admit, I'm sickened to think I willingly followed George once. I agreed with her wish of unifying Druids, but to take such drastic measures to kill Elias and then attack me? Not to mention whatever she's done to my father. She's lost her way."

"If she knew about your allies, she might back off."

"Maybe. If she didn't have Beth and the book. Though I'm wondering how long George will remain leader before Beth takes over."

Jasper grunted. "Probably no' long. Makes you wonder, does it no'? Who used the ebony wood? Was it done on George's order? Or Beth's?"

"We've asked that, as well. We know they're working together, so I'm not sure the delineation matters."

"It always matters. Especially in a power dynamic like that."

Willa shifted without thinking and moved her right arm. She grimaced and tried to hold it in, but the shooting pain was too much.

Jasper was beside her in a second. His large hands lightly

wrapped around her wrists. "Easy," he murmured. "Doona hold your breath. You need to breathe through the discomfort."

"Easier said than done," she stated through clenched teeth.

He caught her eyes. "Breathe with me."

His face was so close she could make out the flecks of onyx in his eyes. When he took a breath, so did she. And when he slowly released it, she followed suit. Again and again, they did it until the pain ebbed to a more manageable level.

"Thank you," she said.

"How often does that happen in a day?"

She shook her head. "I lose count. I try not to move it, but I forget sometimes."

"I wonder if no' moving it is causing it to worsen."

"There's less pain that way."

His Adam's apple bobbed as he swallowed. "Can I...feel?"

Anytime someone touched her arm, it was excruciating. She made sure to stay out of others' way. So why then, did she find herself nodding in agreement? Was it his deep, soothing voice? Was it the trepidation she spotted in his dark eyes? Or was it because she desperately wanted his hands on her? Maybe it was all of it because there was no denying something was developing between them. And no amount of ignoring it was working.

His touch was light as his hands slowly moved upward to her elbow. He paused for a heartbeat before proceeding to her shoulder. She sucked in a breath as he neared, the nerves tingling in expectation—and dread of more pain.

"Breathe," he reminded her.

She stared into his dark eyes, unable to look away. Her breaths remained even and calm. Any anxiety she might have had faded to nothing. She couldn't tell if it was magic or Jasper. His hands gently and tenderly cupped her shoulder. It wasn't pain she felt but a soft, beautiful warmth. Jasper jerked away suddenly. He stood and took a few steps back, his face tight. The heat she'd felt left with him.

"I doona know why I did that," he said absently, staring at her shoulder. "I doona know why I wanted to touch the wound."

"You didn't hurt me," she hurried to assure him. "In fact, it felt quite good."

His brows snapped together. "How? I didna do anything."

"I don't know. There was warmth, and it felt amazing. Did you feel anything?" Surely, he must have felt it, too.

"Nothing."

It was difficult to hide her disappointment. She glanced at the time to realize she had been gone far longer than expected. She needed to return to the manor. Willa got to her feet. "I'm going back to ask the Healers to take another look. I don't want anyone or anything trying to change who I am. I'll leave Skye if that happens."

"And go where?"

"Far from where I could be used against my brother and the others. They're good people trying to do what's right. George can't see that, or perhaps she doesn't want to. She's driven by revenge and blinded by power."

Jasper asked, "So you doona believe Elias is guilty?"

"I do not."

"You know him that well?"

"I know my brother, and if he trusts him, then so do I. Elias admits to being in Edinburgh when George says he was—he and the other Knights. They were tracking a killer and helping some Druids. He didn't murder anyone."

Jasper stared at her for a long moment. "Everyone lies, Willa."

"That may be true, and I suppose there's an argument that Elias isn't who he says he is. But until I see irrefutable proof that Elias murdered someone, I'll side with him. I don't mean taking someone's life in a fight. I mean actual murder. If George had that evidence, she would've gone to the police with it so they could investigate and, at the very least, question Elias. No one has. That tells me a lot."

Jasper rubbed his hands on his jeans. "You're right. I shouldna question that."

"You don't know my friends. Not yet. I'd hoped to be in the fray with them when the time came." She glanced down at her arm. "I'm sidelined, but I'm still aiding them where I can."

"When are you going to the Healers?"

She hesitated. "I don't actually know them. I was unconscious when they tended to me. I'd need to find out who they are."

"If you doona want to go alone, I can take you."

His offer surprised her. "I'll think on it."

"Wait," he said when she started to turn away. He wrote something on a pad of paper and tore it off before handing it to her. "My mobile."

Willa accepted the paper and tucked it into her purse. Then she gathered the other pages she'd come with and returned them to her bag, as well. "Thank you again for all the research."

"There are always counters to things like ebony wood. I've no' found anything yet, but it's out there. I'll keep looking."

She forced herself to look away from his gorgeous eyes before she got lost in them again. "I hope you're right."

Willa felt his gaze on her as she walked outside. She looked back when she reached the vehicle and found him standing in the open doorway. Jasper raised a hand in farewell. She returned the wave and climbed into the car.

One way or another, she would convince Scott to give Jasper a chance. Why would someone go to so much trouble to help her if they couldn't be trusted? Her brother just needed convincing. Her plan to do that fell apart when she arrived at the manor to find Scott leaning against his truck, waiting for her.

"Willa," he began.

She held up a finger. "Don't. I understand you're suspicious, but he's done nothing but help. I need you to give him a chance."

"You like him that much?"

"I...think we could use him. He's good at research. Look what he found for me. We turn to Saber for everything. Wouldn't it be nice if we had someone else who could help? Someone who is good at the very thing we need?"

Scott pushed away from the vehicle and carefully wrapped an arm around her. "Then I'll give him a chance."

CHAPTER FIFTEEN

SKYE DRUIDS

Jasper started at the sound of his phone ringing. He pushed up from the chair and walked from the living room into the kitchen, where he'd left his mobile. As soon as he saw the number on the screen, he tensed. He glanced at the clock to see it had been hours since Willa left. Time that he had sat and thought about her.

And his job.

"Aye?" he answered.

"How are things, Jasper?" George asked.

He wasn't fooled by her sugary tone. "Proceeding."

"Are they? That's good to hear."

He frowned. Something was off. "What is it?"

"Oh, I'm wondering when you planned to tell me that Willa came to see you today."

It shouldn't come as a shock that she had someone watching him, but it did. He'd never let her down before. Cold ire swept through him. "Are you worried I willna do my job?"

"I've lost two very good Druids to Skye. I'm not going to have anyone else defect," George countered.

"If you're so concerned about that, then maybe you should come yourself. I doona appreciate being spied on, George. I'm here to do a job for *you*."

"Don't get your knickers in a twist. My people aren't watching you. They're keeping an eye on specific individuals."

Which meant Willa, Scott, and Elias. Probably Rhona, as well. "Since you have someone watching, I doona need to report in."

"Don't get cheeky, Jasper. It doesn't suit you."

"What doesna suit me is your lack of trust. I've put myself in a powder keg, and I'm trying to figure out how much you know and didna share."

"What are you talking about?" she snapped.

Jasper walked to a window and looked out over the pasture where the horses grazed. "The mist."

"You knew about it. You even saw it."

"Do you know what it was?"

"It was mist, Jasper. That happened to be controlled by a Druid."

He clenched his jaw. "It was far more than that. It was made up of Druid souls that someone bound to them."

"Interesting," she said after a brief pause.

Jasper closed his eyes. "Ferne freed them."

"She's more powerful than I thought. Too bad she's already aligned herself with Skye. She would've made our community even better."

"Take a look at the number of formidable Druids on Skye. They're gathering for something." He didn't know why he didn't tell her about the Dragon Kings or the JusticeBringer and

TruthSeeker. Maybe it was the other spies on Skye. Perhaps it was the fact that she hadn't shared everything with him. Whatever the reason, he kept it to himself.

"Find out what it is. Not that it matters. We'll be ready."

He braced a hand on the edge of the window. "You and Beth, you mean?"

"Aye."

"I want a name, George. I want to know who used the ebony wood on Willa."

She sighed loudly, her frustration evident. "I thought we were past this."

"No' hardly."

"It was done. She's alive. There's nothing more to say."

The anger that swelled nearly choked him. "Have you seen what ebony wood can do to someone? Have you heard their screams?"

"You have?"

"Aye," he said in a low voice edged with fury. "You've no idea what you're messing with. Stop it now. Before it's too late."

"Let me worry about things here. You focus on Willa. And work faster. You should have already taken her as your lover by now."

The line disconnected. Jasper turned and hurled the mobile across the room. It smashed into the wall before dropping to the floor. He braced his arms on either side of the window and dropped his chin to his chest.

There had been a moment during Willa's visit when he could've leaned in and kissed her. He'd wanted to know her taste, her body. The longing that consumed him made him pause. It was too profound, too intense. He feared what he might feel if he gave in to the desire. Before he did anything, he had to get his emotions under control.

There was also her injury to consider. Plus, it would be better to take things slowly. Those around her were already suspicious. If he moved too quickly, it would raise their hackles even more. Caution was the only way to proceed if he were to be successful. But Willa was the problem. There was an effortlessness between them that made being around her easy.

Maybe a little *too* easy.

That was the only simple thing about this job. He'd been rattled by the stories she'd shared. The Grey, the Ageless One, the silenced Ancients, and portals between dimensions. George knew none of that. At least, he didn't think she did. But what if she knew? Hypothetically, what if she had told him all of it? Would he still have agreed to the job?

Jasper pushed away from the window and stared at the spot Willa had sat hours before. He slowly closed his hands into fists. No matter how many times he asked himself why he had touched her shoulder, he didn't have an answer. That confounded him, but it was nothing compared to what he had felt.

And had seen in his mind's eye.

Even now, he couldn't reconcile any of it. He wasn't sure he *wanted* to understand it. And he sure as hell didn't want to touch her wound again. He hoped she returned to the Healers because they hadn't finished the job. If he had to drive her himself, he'd get Willa to them before it was too late.

A soft evening sea breeze wafted around Callum, pulling his hair into his face. He shoved it back as he walked along the footpath. It had been another breathtaking sunset. He meandered through town, not paying attention to where he was going or who might be around. The night was always his favorite time. The shadows hid him, fading him from the eyes of those on Skye who looked down upon him and his family.

He stopped and faced the sea. One day, he'd be able to leave. And when he did, he'd never return. He anxiously awaited that day, longed for it. Prayed for it. He feared it would take decades before he was free. Would the poison of his family's blood infect him by then? Would he be like his father, grandfather, and great-grandfather? Would he become the very thing he reviled?

Callum squeezed his eyes closed as the choking dread took hold. He hurriedly fumbled for his one earbud. Music was the only thing that kept the panic at bay. He had to get somewhere quiet, somewhere hidden. His safe space was too far away to reach in time. He got the lone earbud into his ear and took out his mobile to play his music.

Before he could, he heard someone singing. Callum searched the area, continuing to walk until he reached the co-op. His gaze lifted to the flat above the store. There, standing near an open window with her headphones over her ears, singing with everything she had, was Kirsi.

Callum stood entranced, watching her through the upstairs window as she hung string lights. She had on a magenta-colored sweatshirt with a cut-out collar. It hung off one bare shoulder. Gray sweatpants covered her legs. Her light brown hair was pulled back in a ponytail with a few strands hanging loose. She shoved them away with her shoulder as she reached up to hang the lights.

Then she ascended the stepstool and rearranged it to repeat the movements.

He listened to the words she sang. Then he looked them up on his phone. Callum did a double-take at the singer's name.

"Who's Juice Newton?"

Then he read the lyrics for *Queen of Hearts*. He was about to listen to the music when he realized Kirsi was singing something different. He saved the song to listen to later, and promptly looked up the new lyrics. This one was *Amarillo by Morning* by George Strait.

"Eighties country, Kirsi?" he mused with a grin.

Callum added it to the new playlist and hit play. As the first poignant strings began to swell, he lifted his gaze to her. He hadn't stopped thinking about what he had seen with her. The Grey haunted his dreams. He'd heard the creature's growl, felt its breath on him. The fabric separating the dimensions was paper-thin. If that thing ever got loose...

That day had only gotten weirder with a battle that featured a Dragon King standing alongside Balladyn and the Druids. But Kirsi's withdrawal into herself after coming out of The Grey took most of his attention. He hadn't seen or spoken to her since returning home that night. He had no business being around her. She came from a good, upstanding family. And he...didn't.

Callum turned away from Kirsi. She had been kind to him. The nicest thing he could do was to stay far, far away. He had taken only a few steps when he heard his name. As soon as he saw Sarah with her friends, he stopped and removed his earbud, putting it and his mobile into his pocket. There was no use pretending he hadn't heard them. Sarah would chase him down.

She considered herself the *It Girl* of Skye, which was laughable.

Sarah might be passably pretty, but her attitude was as sour as his father's. She only sought out Callum to anger her dad. It had been amusing when they were in school, but Callum was long past it. Unfortunately, Sarah wasn't.

"I was hoping to find some entertainment tonight," Sarah said with a big smile as she walked up, swaying her hips.

He tried to move away when she put her arms around him. He could smell alcohol on her breath. "I'm on my way home."

"Just one drink," she begged in a high-pitched voice. "I'll buy."

Callum glanced at Sarah's friend, Lizzie, who eyed them with a secretive smile. He leaned away when Sarah tried to kiss him. "What are you doing?"

"I told you. I want to have some fun."

"You're getting married next month."

Sarah shrugged and exchanged a look with Lizzie before pressing her ample breasts against him. "So? I'm not married yet."

"Find someone else."

She winked. "I've chosen you. And Lizzie is going to join us."

Callum turned his head to the side to drag in a breath of fresh air. "I'll drive you both home before you do something stupid."

"I knew you'd come home with me," Sarah said.

Callum soon had a girl on each side of him. He didn't bother arguing anymore. They wouldn't hear anything he said. He had to hold the girls up as they stumbled, but eventually, he made it to Sarah's car. With any luck, they'd both be passed out by the time he reached Sarah's house.

Kirsi slowly lowered her arm as she watched Callum leave with Sarah and Lizzie. She had caught sight of him and was about to call out when he turned away. Then Sarah arrived. Kirsi knew she shouldn't watch them, but she couldn't look away.

She was disgusted by how Sarah threw herself at Callum. Kirsi thought he might refuse them, but then he left with both women. She descended the stepladder and closed the windows since the night air was getting cooler.

She had been occupied all week with setting up her place in hopes of forgetting what had happened at Carwood Manor—and her involvement. She still didn't know how Callum had known she'd lied to the others about what she remembered about The Grey.

He hadn't come into the store since. At least, not when she worked. It wasn't that she stayed away from him exactly, but she had been trying to figure things out. First, Ferne told her she was the only one who could stop the darkness and that Kirsi had already in past lives. And if that weren't enough to freak someone out, Kirsi had known to go into The Grey and get Ferne's soul.

How?

Her parents knew something was wrong. She had stopped sharing things with them, and they were growing more worried by the day. But she couldn't talk to them yet. She had to sort things out, and she was doing a poor job of it. She was heading in a direction that scared her. One she feared she wouldn't come back from.

CHAPTER SIXTEEN

SKYE DRUIDS

"Are you sure you feel up for a visit to Ariah's?" Elodie asked as she parked the car in front of the Tea Talker store.

Willa smiled and nodded with great effort. Ever since she had returned from Jasper's, her shoulder had begun to ache continuously. It had gotten so bad that she hadn't been able to sleep. Nothing she did helped with the pain.

Elodie had planned to take her to Ariah's, but when Willa came out of her room, Elodie and Scott immediately knew something was wrong. Scott wanted her back in bed, but Willa couldn't spend another moment there. She had tossed and turned all night without any relief. It took some doing, but she'd finally convinced both Scott and Elodie that a trip might be just what she needed.

"A short visit," Elodie stated, her brow creased in concern. "Ariah will have some tea to help with the pain."

"There's one more stop after this."

"I don't think we should," Elodie began.

Willa met her gaze. "To the Healers. Something is wrong. I can feel it."

Elodie was silent for a moment, then she nodded. "I agree. I'll call Scott and have him meet us there."

"Don't. Please. He's already behind, and he can't do anything but stand there. That's why I didn't say anything about it this morning."

Elodie blew out a breath. "He's not sleeping either. He spends all night chatting online with Saber, going over routes your dad could've taken. Scott is convinced George has him."

"I thought if I got away, then Dad would, too. But the longer we go without hearing from him, the more I think Scott's right."

Elodie looked forward. "Scott and Filip plan to leave tonight to look for Luke."

"I was expecting that."

"I want him to find Luke, but I don't want Scott to go."

Willa shot Elodie a sad smile. "I'm just as conflicted. If George gets her hands on Scott or Filip, I'm afraid of what the outcome might be. But we can't sit and wait any longer. If I were able, I'd be right there with them."

"I know." Elodie swallowed. "Come. Let's go drink some fabulous tea and chat with Ariah."

Willa hadn't bothered with a jacket that morning. The light fever had begun sometime during the night, and she hadn't told anyone. The cool air offered some relief. She carefully placed one foot in front of the other and followed Elodie to the shop. The sign above the door said *Tea Talker*. A black-and-white-striped canopy with climbing roses ran up the sides and across the top of the building. A glass-paneled door painted a beautiful deep forest green stood out against the stone edifice.

Elodie walked in first and held the door. The instant Willa stepped inside, she felt an easiness settle over her. The narrow-planked wood floor ran in diagonals. There were six tables of various sizes, with an eclectic mishmash of chairs. The ceiling was paned glass, allowing filtered sunlight to serve the ivy that grew along the rafters and across the connecting boards.

Along with the ivy were huge baskets of ferns, all hanging from metal hooks on the ceiling. There were also large pots housing different tall plants, and shelves of even more plants on the walls—some flowering, some not. It was almost as if Willa had stepped into a greenhouse.

Then she looked to the back and saw the simple wooden counter with a cash register that looked like it had come out of the 1800s. Behind it stood a woman taking down jars from shelves behind her. Once she had the ones she wanted, she opened each and began mixing something.

"That's Ariah," Elodie said with a smile.

Ariah's dark hair was wrapped in a vibrant scarf with tendrils framing her face. She wore a deep brown flowy shirt that matched the green, beige, and brown design of her long, billowy skirt. She had several bracelets on each wrist, some beaded, others silver and gold bangles. Elodie drew closer, and Willa could make out the crescent moon-shaped earrings that dangled to Ariah's shoulders.

Willa watched as Ariah moved gracefully from jar to jar, knowing exactly what she was getting and how much to put into a small pouch she sealed and handed to a customer.

Then it was finally their turn. Ariah greeted them with a warm smile. Willa soon found herself staring into Ariah's golden-brown eyes and feeling a kinship she couldn't explain. It was as if she

knew Ariah, but that was impossible. This was the first time she
had met the Druid. Maybe the fever was making her hallucinate.

"Bring her to the back," Ariah said.

Willa blinked, wondering who the Druid spoke to. Then
Elodie took Willa's good arm and steered her around the counter
and past a beaded curtain hanging from the doorway. Willa liked
how they clinked together after they'd passed through. She found
herself sitting, and then a mug was put in her hands.

"Drink this," a voice said.

Willa did as she was told. The cool, slightly sweet concoction
helped to clear her head and temper the fever. There was a bitter
aftertaste, but Willa suddenly found herself parched and drank the
entire cup. Soon, she felt much more herself.

"There you are," Ariah said with a smile. "Better?"

Willa nodded. "Much. What did you give me?"

"An herbal brew."

"I knew you weren't feeling well," Elodie said worriedly from
beside her. "I never should've brought you."

Willa gave her a quick smile. "I insisted."

"It's fortuitous you did. Otherwise, the fever would've really
taken hold." Ariah sat back in her chair and crossed one leg over
the other. "How bad is the pain?"

Willa glanced down, knowing her answer would alarm Elodie.
"Significant."

"I can help manage it, but my skills stop there. You'll need to
return to the Healers," Ariah told her.

Elodie nodded once. "We're headed there after this. I don't
know what they can do, though. They said all the slivers were out."

"They're not." Willa glanced at Elodie. "Something remains."

Ariah inclined her head. "I'm in agreement. I had hoped our

first meeting would be under better circumstances. I've heard a great deal about you from Elodie and your brother."

"Don't worry. I'm a fan of your teas. You'll have me as a customer for life," Willa said.

Ariah smiled and then elegantly got to her feet. "Let me get a few things together for you. Elodie? Is there anything in particular you or Scott need?"

"To find his father."

Ariah's face pinched with worry. "If only I could help with that."

Willa and Elodie followed Ariah back through the beaded curtain to the front of the store. Willa could breathe easier now, and the agony of her shoulder had diminished enough that it didn't consume her. Her fever had loosened its hold, too. Whatever Ariah had given her was amazing, and Willa wanted more.

"Hello, Emilie," Ariah called to an impeccably dressed middle-aged woman, her dark hair cut in a cute bob. "How are you today?"

"Hi, Ariah. I'm better. I'm going to browse for a bit," Emilie answered.

Willa met Emilie's eyes and then exchanged smiles. After watching Ariah mix up a few things, Willa walked around the store, looking at all the plants. She could stay here all day relaxing amid the greenery and drinking Ariah's wonderful brews. It seemed she wasn't the only one who felt that way as people doing just that occupied most of the tables. Some read, others had laptops, and a few just sat and talked.

"This place is amazing."

Willa didn't realize she'd spoken aloud until Emilie said, "It certainly is."

Willa walked to Emilie, who stood at an antique hutch that held hand-painted teapots, teacups, and saucers. "This is my first time in the shop, but it won't be my last."

"I haven't met anyone yet who hasn't fallen in love with the Tea Talker and Ariah. New to the isle, are you?"

"I am. I'm Willa Ryan."

"Any relation to Scott?"

Willa grinned. "He's my brother."

"Well, welcome, Willa. I'm Emilie. He and Filip did a small job for me. Excellent work."

"I'll be sure to tell him."

"Ah," Ariah said as she and Elodie walked up. "I see you two have already met. I was going to introduce you."

Willa saw Emilie's smile tighten slightly.

"This is *the* Emilie?" Elodie asked.

Ariah nodded and motioned to Willa. "Emilie, could you take a look at her shoulder?"

"I don't do that anymore. I haven't in…years. You know that," Emilie replied, her words clipped.

Willa hastened to say, "It's fine. We're going to the Healers now."

"Ebony wood was used," Ariah continued as Emilie started to turn away.

The other woman paused, her shoulders drooping as she released a breath. She turned her head and pinned Ariah with a look. "I can't."

"The Healers said they got it all but didn't." Ariah continued talking. "Willa was feverish when she came in today."

Emilie's brown gaze slid to Willa. "I'm sorry. I wish I could help, but I can't."

Willa watched the woman leave. Then she swung her head to Ariah. "What just happened?"

"Emilie's a Healer," Ariah said as she looked at the now-closed door. "She was one of the best on Skye. But…she suffered a tragedy and turned away from her skills. She can help. I know it."

Elodie twisted her lips as she and Willa shared a look. "I'm not sure we should push it. She seemed upset by the request."

Ariah turned to both of them. "Take Willa to the Healers. If they can't do anything, let me know. I'll talk to Emilie again."

"You've been a great help, as always," Elodie told her. "Thank you."

Willa thanked Ariah and walked to the car with Elodie.

They drove several minutes in silence before Elodie said, "We're going to Lucy's. She's the top Healer on the isle."

"What if she can't help? Or won't?"

"Then we'll find someone who will," Elodie replied.

Willa stared out through the windscreen. "You saw the printouts Jasper gave me. This could change me."

"That information hasn't been substantiated."

"But what if it's true? What if it happens?"

Elodie shook her head of long blond hair and glanced at Willa. "We're not going to let it." She slowed and turned onto a road. "You should've told us how sick you were."

"I know. I didn't want Scott to worry. He's already consumed by Dad's disappearance. I didn't want to add to that."

"You're dealing with all of that, too, you know."

Willa wrinkled her nose. "It's always different for us, isn't it?"

"It is," Elodie admitted. "You need to be honest with Scott, though. I speak from experience. Elias and I are keeping something from Edie. We're doing it out of love, but it kills both of us to stay silent. She's the only one who doesn't have the trauma, and we don't wish that for her."

Willa nodded and looked at Elodie. "I'll be more open with Scott. With both of you."

"Here we are," Elodie said as she pulled to a stop on a residential street. She turned off the engine and looked at Willa. "Ready?"

"Aye. I want this thing out now."

"They'll have to reopen the wound."

"I don't care."

They walked up to the door. Lucy, an older Black woman answered the door, her eyes going straight to Willa.

"I need your help," she told the Healer. "There's still some wood in my wound."

Lucy's brows snapped together. "We triple-checked. There's nothing there."

"I can feel it," Willa insisted.

Lucy stepped aside and opened the door wider. "Come in. I'll call the others, and we'll look again."

"Thank you." Willa sighed in relief. It was finally going to be over.

CHAPTER SEVENTEEN

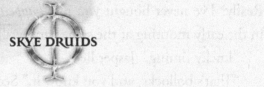

SKYE DRUIDS

No matter how much he tried, Jasper couldn't stop thinking about Willa. He hoped she went to the Healers. He wished he could have gone with her, not only to watch but also to make sure they found the last bit of ebony wood within her. It was there. And it had to come out immediately.

The morning was a blur. He went for a ride on Sorrel, but it did nothing to ease the churning in his stomach. A part of that was because he couldn't stop reflecting about his hands over her injured shoulder. He shouldn't have felt anything. He most certainly shouldn't have *seen* anything in his mind's eye.

But he had.

After lunch, Jasper gave up wondering and drove to see Willa. She probably wasn't at Scott and Elodie's, but he had to try. To his surprise, he saw two vehicles in the drive when he parked. Concern furrowed his brow as he made his way to the door and rapped his knuckles on the wood. A moment later, it swung open. Scott's displeasure at finding Jasper standing there was clear.

"Now isna a good time," Scott stated.

Jasper tried to look around him for a glimpse of Willa. "Did she go to the Healers?"

"Aye."

When he didn't say more, Jasper asked, "Well? What happened?"

Scott's nostrils flared as his eyes narrowed. "Why do you care? Really? I've never bought you just *happening* to be driving around in the early morning at the same time Willa crashed."

"Lucky timing," Jasper lied.

"That's bollocks, and you know it," Scott stated, his tone low.

"Scott," Elodie admonished as she came up behind him. She looked from him to Jasper and back again. She gently moved Scott aside and opened the door. "Please, come in, Jasper. I'll take you to Willa."

He followed her to the living area, where Willa was curled up in the corner of the sofa with a blanket over her legs and a cup of something hot in her left hand. He made his way to her. Jasper's gut clenched when he saw the dark circles under her eyes. He had hoped to find her hale and hearty. Instead, she looked as if just sitting up cost her a great deal.

"This is a surprise," Willa said, her lips softening into a smile.

Jasper glanced at Scott to see the deep worry lines on his face. "I wanted to see how things went with the Healers."

"Not good, I'm afraid," Elodie answered. "Have a seat."

Jasper sat on the opposite end of the couch. "You had them look again, aye?"

"We did. All five of them stood around me," Willa explained. "But they told us once again that they'd retrieved all the ebony wood from the wound."

Elodie's face was pinched as she sank into the stuffed chair. "I told them about Willa's fever and how she'd nearly passed out at Ariah's, but they couldn't find a reason for any of it."

Fever? Things were bad, then. Jasper knew the reason the Healers couldn't sense it. He should speak up, alert Willa. But they would ask questions, and he couldn't answer them. Yet he couldn't let Willa continue to be harmed either.

"The fever is gone," Willa hastened to add.

Scott ran a hand through his hair. "For now. You scared the hell out of Elodie. I doona want to even think about what could've happened had you no' been at Ariah's."

"I'm sorry. I've apologized numerous times. I didn't think the fever was that bad," Willa said as she looked into her cup.

Elodie leaned over and put a hand on Willa's arm. "You're better now. That's all that matters."

"But for how long?" Willa murmured.

Scott leaned a shoulder against the wall. "I doona understand how the Healers can believe your no' sick."

"Are there any other Healers you can contact?" Jasper asked.

Scott and Elodie shared a look. Then Elodie said, "There is someone we could call."

"We owe them already for helping you," Scott said.

Elodie shrugged. "Then we'll owe them more."

"Whoever it is, call them," Jasper urged.

Willa watched the exchange. "Who are you two talking about?"

"The MacLeod Druids," Elodie said when Scott didn't answer.

Jasper's gaze slid to Scott. Could they really know those Druids? "What are you waiting for? Call them."

Scott walked out of the room with his mobile in hand. Jasper turned back to find Willa's blue eyes on him. He wanted to scoot closer and wrap his hands around her wounded shoulder again, but he didn't dare. He swallowed and looked away, only to discover Elodie watching him.

"I'm sorry about Scott," Willa said. "He's just upset."

Jasper inclined his head. "It's understandable."

"We thought we'd located Dad last night, but it turned out to be someone else." Willa sipped from the mug.

Elodie forced a smile as she got to her feet. "We'll find Luke and get you better. I'm going to see if Scott got ahold of anyone."

Jasper waited until Elodie was out of the room before turning his head to Willa. "Are you really okay?"

"I feel better than I did this morning. It's all so strange because I felt amazing when I left your place yesterday. The pain started around midnight, and it made it impossible to sleep." She twisted her lips. "If I had told either of them,"—she gestured to where Scott and Elodie had gone—"they would've kept me in bed, and I had to get to the Healers. Something's wrong, Jasper. I know it."

So did he. Scott had a lifeline, though. Whispers of the MacLeod Druids could be found all around Skye. He had heard rumors all his life, but it wasn't until he'd come to the isle that he discovered the tales were true. Research had given him little facts. Instead, he had to take whatever he heard from others.

It said something that Scott and Elodie not only knew of the MacLeod Druids but were acquainted with them enough to be able to call in a favor. If the MacLeod Druids were as powerful as everyone claimed, they could help Willa.

"Your brother is finding help."

Willa set the mug on the end table beside her. She looked at him with her large, blue eyes, enthralling him. "Will you put your hands on my shoulder again?"

"I doona think that's wise. I might hurt you."

"You took the pain away."

He frowned as he shook his head. "And, apparently, made you worse in the process."

"You admit it then?" she asked with a smile. "You did something."

"I—" he began, but the words locked in his throat. He cleared it twice before he could say, "I doona know what happened. I can no' explain why I did what I did. I'm no' a Healer in any sense of the word."

She untucked her legs and turned toward him. "I don't care. If the constant ache lets up for even a moment, I'll take it."

His palms tingled in response to her words, as if they were eager and willing to do as she asked. But he couldn't get past the knowledge of how sick she had been that morning. It might have nothing to do with him.

Or it could have everything to do with him.

He couldn't take that chance. "I doona think it wise."

Scott rushed into the room, his relief palpable. "They're coming. They'll be here in just a—"

A knock on the door interrupted him.

Scott and Elodie answered it. Jasper slowly stood when he heard voices. Out of the corner of his eye, he saw Willa getting to her feet. He glanced her way as a woman and two men walked in. The female had long, curly red hair. She looked at Jasper with amber eyes before shifting her attention to Willa.

"You must be Willa," she said. She stopped before Willa. "I'm Sonya. I'm here to see what can be done about your injury."

The already small room became cramped when the two other men entered. The tall, blond one kept most of his focus on Sonya. The dark-haired man spoke to Scott in low tones, his deep green gaze sweeping over everyone in one glance. Jasper knew in an instant the two men were Warriors from MacLeod Castle.

There were many folklore stories about them, and they usually had a grain of truth to them somewhere. Based on rumors around the isle, the Warriors held primeval gods inside them that made them immortal.

"Hello."

Jasper was startled to find Sonya standing before him. She had her head tilted slightly as she studied him. "Hi. Thank you for coming to help Willa."

"That still remains to be seen. And you are?"

"McCabe. Jasper McCabe," he introduced himself.

Sonya smiled. "The handsome one is my husband, Broc MacLaughlin."

Jasper nodded at the blond.

"Behind him is Fallon MacLeod."

Jasper met Fallon's green eyes and inclined his head in greeting.

"Now," Sonya said as she turned back to Willa, "Scott told us what happened. I'd like to analyze your shoulder myself."

Jasper moved to allow Sonya to sit with Willa on the sofa. He should probably leave, but how could he when he was in the same room with Warriors and a Druid from MacLeod Castle? Besides, he wanted to see Willa healed. What better way to do that than with his own eyes? He moved to a wall out of the way so Scott had no reason to notice him and force him to leave.

The room became silent as Sonya rubbed her hands together and then held them over Willa's shoulder about an inch away. To his surprise, Willa met his gaze. He gave her an encouraging nod. Her lips curved slightly before she grimaced and shut her eyes. Jasper was rooted to the spot, his eyes moving from Willa to Sonya in an effort to discern what was happening.

Seconds turned to minutes before Sonya lowered her hands to her lap, her expression grave. "I don't feel anything."

"It's there," Willa insisted.

Sonya nodded. "I think something is. We know little about the use of ebony wood on others. Whoever did this wanted you to suffer. What concerns me is the fever and the pain. That hints at an infection."

"You couldna feel anything?" Scott pressed.

Sonya shook her head of curls. "Nothing. Which is disturbing since something is obviously wrong."

"Could it be a spell?" Broc asked.

Sonya drew in a breath and slowly released it as she looked at him. "I don't sense anything. But that doesn't mean it isn't there."

"Are you telling me nothing can stop this?" Willa demanded.

Sonya got to her feet. "I'm saying I can't do this on my own. We need more Druids."

"I can call others," Elodie said.

Fallon stopped her before she could begin calling. "Sonya means from the castle. I'll be back as soon as I can."

And then he was gone. Just vanished. Jasper blinked to make sure he hadn't been seeing things.

"His god gives him the power of teleportation," Broc explained.

Had he just confirmed that the Warriors actually *did* have primeval gods inside them? It certainly appeared so. "What's yours?" Jasper asked, unable to contain his curiosity.

"I can track anything."

"Like my father?" Willa asked.

Broc quirked a brow. "Your father is missing?"

"We've no' heard from him since he and Willa escaped Edinburgh," Scott explained.

Broc faced him. "I need something of his. A picture of him, a shirt. Anything."

"I have a photo," Scott said, scrolling through his mobile until he found it. He handed the phone over.

"Give me some time," Broc said before striding out of the house.

Jasper was stunned at how readily the Warriors and Sonya helped others without bargaining for something in exchange. Scott had called, and they had come. Just like that. Willa had asked for help with Luke, and Broc was going to assist. Jasper was still reconciling that when Fallon arrived with more Druids.

CHAPTER EIGHTEEN

SKYE DRUIDS

Willa had been in the company of many Druids before, but something about the Druids from MacLeod Castle was altogether different. Whether it was because of their formidable magic or because she knew they were several hundred years old, she couldn't say.

Sonya made quick introductions of the other women, but Willa was so enamored by them she didn't remember a single name —though she was too embarrassed to admit that or ask Sonya to repeat any.

The Druids didn't waste any time either. Sonya quickly detailed the situation, and then the six stood around Willa, their hands outstretched. She couldn't see or feel their magic, but she didn't need to. It charged the air.

Willa tried not to fidget with everyone's attention on her. This had to work. It was the MacLeod Druids, after all. If they couldn't help her, no one could. She didn't want to lose who she was. She might not have figured everything out about herself yet, but she liked her life. She wanted to keep living it the way she was, not be corrupted and turned into the very thing she fought against.

She lowered her gaze to the floor, but it wasn't enough. She needed something more. She scanned the room, quickly passing over faces until she met deep brown eyes. The instant her gaze collided with Jasper's, she paused. He gave another barely perceptible nod, never looking away. She inhaled deeply and felt her tense muscles loosen.

Something about him was reassuring, steadying. Scott thought she felt that way because Jasper had found her the night of her accident, but she felt it was more than that. Not that her brother would listen to her. Everyone was a suspect to Scott. And with what the group had been fighting, she understood that.

But that didn't mean she had to like it.

Now that Broc was helping to locate her father so they could bring him to Skye, it left her the option of tracking down those responsible for using the ebony wood on her once she was healed.

"I'm sorry."

Willa was so deep in thought it took her a moment to realize someone had spoken. She blinked and saw the worry in Jasper's gaze. Willa then shifted her attention to the Druids surrounding her. They'd lowered their hands, and no one would meet her eyes. No one except Sonya.

"I'm so sorry," Sonya said again. "We still can't find anything."

Jasper stepped forward. "Try again. Please."

Sonya gazed at him for a moment before looking at Fallon and asking, "Can you bring the others? *If* we can do this, it will take all of us."

Fallon left without responding, which Willa realized was a reply in itself.

Willa wrapped her left hand around her right elbow, holding her injured arm more securely. "None of you felt anything?"

"If we didn't know about the ebony wood, your pain, or the fever, I wouldn't think anything was wrong," Sonya answered.

A Druid with long, straight black hair and ice-blue eyes flattened her lips. "Something's at work here, that's for sure."

Willa thought her name was Isla, but she couldn't be sure. She didn't look at Scott. She couldn't. She didn't want to see his distress because she knew it would mirror hers.

"The book. It has to be the book," Elodie said into the silence.

Willa reached for her now-cold tea. She took a drink anyway because it held herbs from Ariah to combat the pain that wouldn't diminish. When Fallon returned with the rest of the Druids, Willa barely listened as Scott and Elodie filled everyone in on what had happened on Skye. The room was so cramped that Willa began to fidget and sweat from all the people.

She spotted movement out of the corner of her eye and turned in time to see Jasper winding through the bodies to get to the window near her. He opened it wide, letting in air that instantly cooled her.

"*Thank you,*" she mouthed.

He gave her a quick smile and looked up. His grin vanished as he returned to his place across the room. Willa swung her head around to find Scott glaring at Jasper. So much for her brother giving him a chance.

"Get comfortable," Sonya told her. "This might take a while."

Willa leaned back against the cushion. She tried to find Jasper through the crowd, but there were too many around her. So, she closed her eyes. The only sound was the soft ruffling of the curtains from the wind.

Five seconds or five hours could've passed before Willa felt a hand on her good arm. She didn't need to look at the Druids to know their magic hadn't healed her. The pain told her that much. Willa opened her eyes, but she didn't see faces. Their voices reached her ears, but she didn't hear any words. They had been her last hope, and now, that was gone.

Finally, she was alone. Or so she thought until Jasper squatted in front of her.

"They're no' giving up. You shouldna."

She tried to smile but wasn't sure she succeeded. "They're the MacLeod Druids. If they can't do it, no one can."

"They're going to do some investigating."

"Has Broc found my dad?"

Jasper shook his head. "I've no' seen him." He straightened to his full height. "I've overstayed my welcome. I should be going."

"I need to get out of here for a wee bit. Would you take me for a ride?"

"Of course. Scott—"

She got to her feet. "I'll talk to him. Give me a sec."

Willa left Jasper to go in search of her brother. She found him outside with Elodie. They stopped talking as soon as they saw her. "Anything from Broc?"

"He thinks he found something," Scott said. "He's going to check it out."

Elodie linked her fingers with his. "Your brother's upset that Broc wouldn't take him along."

"It's right for me to stay here with you," Scott said.

Willa knew it was unfair to be irritated with him, but she couldn't help it. "I'm not a child who needs looking after."

"You're no' a child, but you do need looking after," Scott snapped.

Elodie moved between them, a hand on Scott's chest. "Let's not do this, guys. Scott, you'd be just as disappointed if you were in Willa's shoes. So, ease up on her."

Scott blew out a breath. "Aye."

Elodie then turned to Willa. "You would be acting just as overbearing if Scott were the one hurt. Right?"

"Aye," Willa admitted begrudgingly. "How did you figure us out so easily?"

Scott pulled Elodie to his side. "I keep asking her that."

"And I keep saying that it's what siblings do," Elodie answered with a grin.

Willa waited until Scott looked her way. "I am frustrated. Greatly so. I appreciate what everyone has done. And I'm sorry for not telling you how bad I felt this morning. It won't happen again."

"But?" Scott asked, his face impassive.

"It's not a *but*. It's an *and*. I need to get out and do something."

Scott shrugged. "Tell us where you want to go. We'll take you."

"Honey," Elodie said gently. "She wants to be with someone else."

Scott's gaze hardened. "Why him?"

"I don't know," Willa answered honestly. "Maybe it's because I feel in his debt for saving me. Maybe it's something else."

"I doona trust him," her brother said in a low voice.

Willa took Scott's hand in her left. "You trust me, don't you?"

"You know I do."

"Then trust I know what I'm doing."

Scott turned away, looking at the water in the distance. After a few moments, he turned back. "He better no' make me regret this."

"I won't be gone long. I just need to clear my head. And the moment I start feeling bad, I'll come home," Willa told them.

Within minutes, Willa was in Jasper's Jaguar. She stared out her window, watching the blur of the outside world as he drove. "I bet you wish you hadn't stopped for me that night."

"On the contrary," he replied.

She turned her head toward him. "It's funny. A few hours ago, I reconciled myself to the fact that I couldn't be healed. Then the Druids from the castle arrived, and I just knew they could do something."

"There's an answer out there. The world is a big place. We'll find it."

"We?" she asked, brows raised.

Jasper glanced at her and nodded. "Aye."

"Skye's powerful Healers have assured me nothing was left behind, but I can't shake the feeling there was. Otherwise, why the pain and fever?"

Jasper had one hand on the wheel and his other elbow on the console. "I think you're right. So do Sonya and the others. They agree something isna right, which is why they're going to do some digging to see what they can find."

"How long do I have before the wood inside corrupts me?"

He was silent for a long minute. "I can no' say. That information came from a source on a message board. Everything they have given me in the past has been accurate, but I can no' find anything to refute or verify the claim. No' yet anyway."

"I can't become the thing my family and friends are fighting."

She looked out her window again. "That would destroy Scott and Dad."

"You willna."

He sounded so sure that Willa wanted to believe him.

"You spoke of powerful allies, but I didna realize that included the Warriors and MacLeod Druids. Until I moved to Skye and began hearing all the rumors circulating, I thought the stories about them were just folktales."

Willa grinned at him. "When Scott first told me, I could hardly believe any of it. And I didn't tell you the other day because I'd already given you so much information. I didn't want to overwhelm you."

"Oh, you overwhelmed me, all right," he teased.

Willa chuckled. "I guess I did. With a story so big, it's difficult to know what to keep for another time. Everything's connected."

"So it would seem. You'd think your enemies would run away in terror."

"At the very least George and Beth, but I don't think we'll get that lucky," she mused.

Jasper pulled onto a road. She looked where they were going and saw his house up ahead.

"I can keep driving if you'd rather," he offered.

She shook her head as she spotted the horses in the distance. "This is perfect."

He parked, and they made their way inside the house. She immediately went to a window to look out at the pasture.

"I don't think I'd ever get tired of this view," she said.

"I certainly doona. Do you want anything? How's your pain level?"

She looked at him over her shoulder. "Elodie gave you some of Ariah's tea, didn't she?"

Jasper pulled a baggie out of his back pocket and shook it. "Yep."

"I'm okay now."

"How about we keep it that way? We can take our tea down to the horses if you'd like."

"That sounds divine. I'm tired of sitting."

He heated water, but her attention shifted from the horses to Jasper. She watched the way his green shirt tightened over the back of his shoulders as he moved. She especially liked how his jeans fit around his trim hips—not too tight but not baggy. A perfect mix that gently hugged his firm ass and tapered slightly at his ankles.

Her brother wanted to know what she liked about Jasper. It was everything.

Absolutely every detail.

CHAPTER NINETEEN

SKYE DRUIDS

Edinburgh

George strode through the dark warehouse on the edge of the city toward the back room she used as her office. She didn't need a light. She knew this building as well as her home. Her community of Druids had helped to attain the building when she otherwise couldn't. That was just one of the many ways her organization propelled themselves far above any other Druids.

The echo of her boot heels on the concrete was as loud as a shot. But she wasn't scared. This building was her domain. Her Druids stood guard around its perimeter, as well as on the roof. Some were meant to be seen, while others stayed hidden. She'd always taken that precaution because George knew the bigger the group became, the more of a target she'd become.

She had a few hours before the Druids arrived for their next meeting. It was her tradition to spend that time in her office, delving into her seer abilities and reviewing what her spies had passed on.

George paused when she rounded the corner and saw her office light on. The door was shut. Only one person would dare to venture where others wouldn't. Beth. She was becoming a thorn in George's side. Unfortunately, she needed the Druid. Actually, she needed the book, which meant she had to deal with Beth, at least for the time being. Soon, the tome would be hers, and Beth would be a distant memory.

It was on the tip of George's tongue to call in her guards, but that would make Beth believe she was afraid. George feared few things, and Beth wasn't one of them. She would go in alone. But she would keep at least two guards with her in the future. Beth needed to be reminded of her place.

George walked to the door and opened it. She didn't throw it open in anger. Nor did she allow any emotion to touch her face. That would give Beth too much satisfaction. George stopped and stared at Beth, who sat in her chair, feet up on the desk with the large tome open and resting on her legs.

"You're in my seat," George stated.

Beth didn't even look her way as she flipped a page. "This is a very uncomfortable chair."

"Get up."

"I find something new every time I read through these pages. At first, I thought to call it a grimoire. It does give recipes, rituals, and the like. Yet there is much about spells and the practice of Druidry, which some would say means this is a spellbook." Beth's light brown eyes lifted to hers. "There's also the…" She trailed off with a secretive smile. "There's a little of everything in here. And I do mean *everything*."

George coveted the book so badly she could practically feel it in her hands. Beth wanted her to make a move to grab it. George wouldn't be so crass. There were ways to get it that Beth would never see coming. "It's lucky it didn't fall into the hands of someone from Skye."

Beth softly closed the book. She laid her hands on top of the scuffed leather worn smooth in places. "Isn't it just?"

George held Beth's gaze, waiting to see what the Druid would do. Beth wasn't subtle in the fact that she wished to usurp George's mantle. But George wouldn't give it up without a fight. Beth thought she had the upper hand with the book, and that would be her downfall.

"I've been waiting to hear a thank you."

George raised a brow. "Have you?"

"Come now," Beth said with a too-confident smile. "Why play coy with me?"

"This isn't a game. This is my life. It's the future of all Druids."

Beth rolled her eyes and set her feet on the floor before standing, the book tucked against her chest. "You're so serious. You remind me of my cousin. Bronwyn forgot the meaning of fun. Don't follow in her footsteps."

"Oh, aye. Because you've delivered such a retaliatory blow."

Beth's eyes narrowed. "Careful. You wouldn't want me as an enemy."

"I could warn you of the same," George said as she took a step toward her.

Beth shoved her long brown bangs from her eyes and smiled once more. "Willa and Luke thought to betray us. They're a lesson for everyone."

"By using ebony wood."

"I wish I would've used it on Willa myself, but knowing she's suffering is enough. I thought you'd rejoice in her impending demise."

George looked Beth up and down. "Messing with ebony wood is dangerous."

"I'm not afraid. Then again, I have the book." She patted the leather lovingly.

"We agreed on a plan. You changed it without talking to me."

Beth shrugged, her lips twisting. "I seized an opportunity. The Ryans have become a problem you should've taken care of weeks ago. So, I dealt with them."

"And I was doing that. You've complicated matters."

"No, I've simplified them. I know for a fact you don't mind killing."

George's stomach clenched with dread. "Don't forget your place. I'm the leader. Plans don't get changed until I alter them. Is that understood?"

"Completely."

George watched Beth walk out of her office. She didn't relax until several minutes later. That's when George realized Beth's two female guards hadn't been with her. And Beth didn't go anywhere without them. George might be able to get the book sooner than planned.

"That can't be right," Rhona said as she braced her elbow on her knee and dropped her forehead into her hand.

Ariah gently set the teacup and saucer on the coffee table from her seat across from Rhona in the Tea Talker. "I wish I had better news. Willa's time is running short."

"We've done all we can," Lucy added. "We can't find anything to heal."

Rhona squeezed her eyes shut. They burned from lack of sleep. She went to rub them but stopped herself in time before she made them hurt worse. She wished Balladyn were there, but Death had called him away for Reaper business. That was the agreement between them. Balladyn was part of both the Druid and Reaper worlds. She knew it was tough on him sometimes, but he never complained. Neither would she.

She blew out a breath and looked at the Druids filling the room. Sonya and Isla from MacLeod Castle, the five Skye Healers, and Ariah. Her perusal stopped when her gaze landed on Sonya. "Have you found any other way of healing Willa?"

"We have not," Sonya replied, her face grim. "We think her attackers used a spell."

Lucy glanced at the other Healers on either side of her. "We didn't sense anything."

Rhona rubbed her hands on her thighs, her chest squeezing with dread. "What other options do we have?"

"There's always Con," Isla offered.

The King of Dragon Kings could heal anyone of anything, but he was currently on another realm. "Do we have time to get him here?"

"Maybe. It depends on what's happening with the Kings," Sonya said.

Ariah played with the moon pendant at her neck. "There might be someone closer to home."

Rhona raised her brows. "Who?"

"Emilie Wilson."

Lucy scoffed at the idea. "Emilie stopped being a Healer nearly thirty years ago. If none of us in this room can help Willa, how can she?"

"Emilie can," Ariah replied.

Rhona held up a hand when Lucy intended to keep arguing. Rhona swung her gaze to Ariah. "Do you think Emilie would try?"

"It will take some convincing—by you."

"Then we'd better get to it." Rhona got to her feet. She looked at Lucy and the other Skye Healers. "Thank you for coming. Be ready in case we need to call you in."

They filed out with Lucy in the lead.

Rhona then turned to the MacLeod Druids. "Thank you for the assistance. I'd like to think we can handle the rest on our own, but I'm not so sure of that."

Isla shook her head of long, black hair. "We're all Druids. It isn't our group and yours. It's us. Together."

"Exactly," Sonya said with a nod. "Don't hesitate to contact us. We're always willing to help."

Rhona smiled in gratitude. "You have no idea how much that means to me."

"We do. Trust me," Isla said with a wry smile.

Sonya grinned. "We're going to stay on Skye until Broc and Fallon return."

"You're welcome to remain in the shop," Ariah offered.

Isla rubbed her hands together. "I was hoping you'd suggest that."

"Help yourself to whatever you want."

Rhona was so used to having Balladyn teleport her everywhere that she was irritated at having to drive. Ariah climbed into the passenger side while she got behind the wheel. Then Rhona navigated the roads to Emilie's.

"I should've thought about Emilie," Rhona said after a few minutes of driving.

Ariah shook her head, her moon earrings clinking with the motion. "You're too hard on yourself. You can't expect to think of everything."

"Corann did."

Ariah snorted and looked in her direction. "He did not. He relied on his deputies a lot. Something you might try. If you continue as you are, you'll run yourself into the ground."

"You sound like Balladyn."

"Because he's right."

Rhona sighed, wishing the knotted muscle in her shoulder blade would loosen up. "I've already been betrayed by one deputy."

"If you think the others will do that, then replace them."

"I didn't say I thought that."

"Didn't you?"

Rhona glanced at Ariah to find the Druid's slim brow arched. "I'm bombarded on all sides. One wrong decision could cause someone to lose their life. Or worse, the Druids could be wiped out."

"One thing at a time. The mist is gone."

"Thanks to Ferne."

Ariah smiled and looked out the windscreen. "Someone you trusted helped not just you but everyone on the isle."

"She did." And Rhona would be eternally grateful.

"Let's not forget you caught Kerry. She's no longer a threat."

Rhona wrinkled her nose at the mention of the Druid. "We don't know who she's working with."

"Not yet. But you will. Take the wins. That will allow you to give attention to what's needed now."

"Willa."

Ariah nodded slowly. "And those responsible for her injury."

"George and Beth. I never should've let either leave the isle."

"Did you know Beth would get the book?"

Rhona cut her gaze to her friend. "You know I didn't."

"Then why beat yourself up about it?"

"Stop being so practical. It makes punishing myself that much harder."

Ariah's laugh filled the car. "You always were good at that."

Some of the tension eased out of Rhona as they continued to chuckle. All too soon, they pulled up to Emilie's house. The cottage sat at the base of a mountain next to a loch. It was a picturesque scene straight out of a book.

They got out and walked to the front door. It opened before they even reached it, revealing a middle-aged woman with straight dark hair streaked with a few grey strands and cut into a chin-length bob. Emilie Wilson had youthful skin that barely showed any wrinkles, making her look ten years younger.

"The answer is still nay," Emilie stated.

Ariah clasped her hands together. "Ebony wood was used. Willa needs your help."

"We wouldn't have come if it weren't important. The Healers have tried. The MacLeod Druids were called in. None of them can find anything," Rhona said.

Emilie looked between them and wrapped her cardigan tighter around herself. "The last time I helped someone with ebony wood, I lost my family."

"Willa will lose her life if you don't," Rhona said.

CHAPTER TWENTY

SKYE DRUIDS

Jasper walked out of the feed room and stopped. Willa was on her second cup of tea. It was balanced on the top board of the fence as she stood with all four horses gathered near her. She was talking low and petting them, all while giving each of them equal attention.

She looked as if she belonged there with her faded jeans and navy sweatshirt, her long, full curls hanging down her back. He could watch her all day. Despite her predicament and pain, she had a smile for the horses. He grinned when he saw White trying to nudge Bay out of the way to get closer to Willa. She laughed at the antics.

She turned her head to look over her shoulder. Their gazes met. Her smile widened, and he found himself responding in kind. Jasper wondered if she had any idea how alluring she was, how she could twist a man up with just a look.

Not him, of course. Not with the role he played—one blurring every moment he spent near her.

"They love you," Jasper said as he made his way to her.

She lovingly looked at the animals. "And I adore them. I wish I could ride."

"You will." He patted White's neck.

"This place suits you."

He chuckled. "You barely know me."

"True, but you look good here. Like you belong."

"So do you." The truth of it struck him like a sucker punch to the kidneys.

She turned to face him and reached for her tea. "How long have you lived here?"

"About three months." There was no reason to lie. Anyone could find that information.

"Really? I would've thought it was much longer. How did you find the house?"

He leaned against the fence as the horses moved off to graze. "I found a couple of places, but none really called to me. Until I spotted this house and the land and was instantly taken by it. But it wasn't for sale. When I heard the owner was going through a nasty, expensive divorce, I reached out to her. She was having some money problems, so I offered to rent it for a few months, allowing me to live here and also help her keep it."

"That was fortuitous for both of you. Did it come with all the furniture?"

"Her ex took most of it. She took a couple of pieces that were family heirlooms. I filled in what was needed from there."

Willa looked at the horses. "Did they come with the house, too?"

"Bay did. I came across Gray by accident, but I figured Bay could use a friend."

"And the other two?"

He chuckled and turned to rest his arms on the fence's top rail. "There's a rescue center near Glencoe. Sorrel and White were seized from owners who hadn't taken care of them. The rescue saw to their medical issues and put them up for adoption once they were healthy. They have been together since they were foals. I wanted to keep them that way."

"Aren't you a softie?"

Jasper heard the smile in her voice. She wouldn't say that if she knew the real him, the person behind the dozens of masks he wore. He wasn't even sure he knew himself anymore. He had played one part after another until it was all he knew. It was all he had ever known.

"And your family?"

He paused. Everything he'd told her about the house and horses was true. Knowing how many lies to add to that was what made him so good at what he did. It never bothered him to lie. People did it all the time. Sometimes, they were wee white lies. Other times, they were enormous falsehoods. He dealt with the ones in the middle.

Jasper looked into her striking blue eyes and found his tongue wouldn't work. The words were jumbled in his head, unable to escape.

She glanced away. "I'm sorry. I shouldn't have pried."

He gripped the fence, unsure what was happening to him. He hadn't tripped up like this since he was a kid. Why now? Why with Willa? He worked his jaw, but it wasn't until he decided on a truth that he could finally speak. "I doona talk about them. They're gone."

Her brow furrowed. "As in...dead?"

"Aye."

"I'm sorry."

On the few occasions Jasper had shared that, he always waved away people's condolences. But not this time. Because he knew Willa meant it. "Thank you."

"Was it recent?"

He tried not to wince when the image of his hands covered in blood popped into his mind. "I lost my father twelve years ago. I never knew my mother."

"Jasper, that's horrible," she said as she moved closer. She set down the mug and rested her hand on his. "No one should have to go through that."

Why had he mentioned his mother? He never did that. With anyone. "I didna know a difference."

Her hand tightened on his. Jasper was all too aware of how close they were. He could see the navy outline of her irises. His eyes dropped to her mouth. She had the most amazing lips. He was desperate to feel them moving against his. Jasper realized he was lowering his head toward her to do just that.

It was exactly why he was on Skye. This was his chance to seduce her, get close, and learn all the secrets of those around her. Instead, he stopped, unable to go through with it.

He blinked and looked up, his gaze scanning the area. Where were George's spies? They could be in the house up on the hill above him or even in the cottage near the shore on the opposite side of the road. They could be anywhere.

"It's ironic that any day could be our last day," Willa said, drawing his attention. "Yet we don't live like it is until we learn that it actually will be."

He frowned, not understanding. "What?"

She answered by rising on tiptoe and placing her mouth on his. A current rushed through Jasper, singeing him at the same time it sparked something primal that had been locked tightly away. The kiss was all too brief. When she leaned back, their gazes met.

There was no going back for him now.

He gently cupped her face, running his thumb over her full lips. Then he kissed her. Leisurely, deliberately taking his time to learn the feel of her soft lips and the intoxicating glide of her tongue against his.

She moaned softly, her body melting into him. He skimmed his palms down her neck and over her shoulders to her back. He pressed her against him tightly, needing her there. Unfortunately, her arm in the sling was in the way.

Gone were the unhurried, lingering kisses. They had turned heated, fiery. Impassioned. Need consumed him. It made him forget reason and logic. All that mattered was claiming Willa. She saw *him*. The man he kept securely locked away from everyone— even himself. She'd thrown open those doors and let the light inside. It terrified him.

But he didn't let his thoughts linger on that. Not when she was against him. Not when he was finally kissing her. He never wanted to stop. She tasted and felt as wonderful as he knew she would.

He reached for the arm between them, skimming her shoulder. As he did, he felt her inflamed muscles and jerked away at the contact. Jasper looked down at a dazed Willa, her kiss-swollen lips begging him to return for more.

"You feel it. Admit it," she said in a voice hoarse with desire.

Jasper thought she referred to his need until she looked at her right arm. Where his hand lay. He stared at his fingers that curled gently around her shoulder.

"Admit it," she said again.

He couldn't look away from his hand. "Admit what?"

"The warmth passing from you into me."

Was that him? He'd thought she had done it. "I-I…"

"The pain is gone."

Jasper dragged his gaze to her face.

"You didn't tell me you're a Healer."

"I'm no'," he replied.

She gave him a flat look. "What I'm experiencing says otherwise."

"I'm really no'."

"Then how are you doing this?"

"I wish I knew." He wanted to pull his hand away, but how could he if the pain returned to her? "Is this what it feels like with the Healers?"

Willa shook her head. "I don't feel anything with them. Just you."

"That means I'm no' a Healer then."

She covered his hand to keep it in place and moved her arm. Jasper didn't have time to stop her.

"Look what I can do. I've not been able to do that since Edinburgh. You're doing that. You're healing me."

Jasper shook his head, but even as he did, he saw in his mind's eye exactly where the tiniest sliver of wood remained in her tendon. He might see it, but he couldn't do anything about it. Moving it might cause more damage to the muscles and other connective tissue. But he couldn't leave it in either.

"I shouldna be able to do this," he said, more to himself than to her.

Willa grinned up at him. "But you are."

"What happens when I let go? You got sick last time?"

"That might not have been you."

He quirked a brow. "It was. If your brother knew, he'd never let me around you again."

"Scott doesn't need to know."

"He's your brother, Willa. He's worried about you and your father."

She winced. "I'm an awful daughter that I forgot about Dad."

"You're allowed to enjoy life. You doona have to carry the weight of things with you all the time."

"You may be right, but I feel even worse when all I want to do is kiss you again instead of checking in with Scott."

Jasper took a deep breath. "I'm going to move my hand away. Slowly, this time. Then we're going back to the house where I'll fix a fresh cup of tea. While I'm doing that, call your brother. Ready?"

"Nay."

He tried to move away, but his body wouldn't obey. He wanted her, ached for her. His gaze lingered on her mouth, and his balls tightened with need. Before he knew it, he had leaned down and taken her mouth once more. He kissed her deeply, pouring all his desire into it as he caressed down her sides to rest his hands on her hips.

She moaned softly. The sound heightened his craving until stripping her of her clothes and laying her down on the grass was all he could think about. It took everything in him to end the kiss. Even then, he couldn't open his eyes. The outside world awaited. One where he lied and conned others.

A world he was beginning to question.

One he wished was his.

Jasper pressed his forehead against Willa's to let them both catch their breath. He opened his eyes and studied her face, watching for any signs the pain had returned.

Her lids lifted, and she looked at him. "No one has ever kissed me like that before."

"Me either." He wished it was a falsehood to go along with his role, but it was as far from a lie as it could be. He took her left hand and grabbed her cup with the other as he led her to the house. There were no words. They didn't need them. The passion and hunger still simmered between them.

Somehow, he released her when they entered the back door. She went to the living area to call Scott, leaving Jasper alone in the kitchen. He braced his hands on the counter and closed his eyes. What had he done? He'd never sunk so deeply into a role that he had lost himself, but that was happening now. He had to get control of things.

Of himself.

He could still help Willa and do what he'd promised George. But he couldn't allow his emotions to get in the way. That would be disastrous for everyone, but most certainly for him. It was just a kiss.

It didn't mean anything.

It *couldn't* mean anything.

Jasper straightened and blew out a breath. If he told himself the lie often enough, maybe he'd believe it.

CHAPTER TWENTY-ONE

SKYE DRUIDS

Willa didn't hear the ringing through her mobile as she held it to her ear. All she could think about was the kiss. The earth-shattering, mind-boggling kiss. She could still feel Jasper's lips against hers, his incredibly hard body, his strong hands. The delicious stroke of his tongue against hers, sending her spiraling into desire so heady and intoxicating she never wanted it to end.

Then it had. Her stomach quivered when she recalled the longing in his eyes as he looked down at her. Passion had hung between them like a tangible force. It was a moment she would remember for the rest of her days.

"Willa!"

She started at the shouting in her ear. "I'm here," she answered hurriedly. Then, in a calmer voice, said, "I'm here."

"I've been yelling your name. Why did you no' answer? Are you hurting?" Scott demanded.

"I was lost in thought." She hoped he didn't ask what about

because Scott didn't need to know what kind of thoughts they were. "Have you heard anything from Broc?"

There was a long pause before Scott finally answered. "Aye."

"You do that when you don't want to tell me something. You might as well spit it out because I'm not letting it go."

In the background, she heard Elodie say, "Tell her."

"Fine," her brother said with a sigh. "Broc might have found Dad."

"That's great news. I'll come back so we can leave."

"Uh…well, that's the thing. We already have."

Willa sat forward, hoping she hadn't just heard what she thought she heard. "What?"

"Broc is having a harder time than normal locating Dad. He thinks some kind of spell is shielding him."

She digested that bit of news. "I don't like that he can't be found. When did you go?"

"About an hour ago."

"For someone so adamant about me not being alone, you didn't hesitate to leave."

"It wasna like that."

"It's exactly like that," she retorted. She heard another voice, one she couldn't quite place. "Who else is in the car?"

Scott sighed again. "We didna drive. Balladyn jumped us to Dad's flat. We thought we might find something here. We're boxing up some things. We've already been to yours and grabbed a big haul."

"I wanted to be there to look for him."

"We need you to heal. Speaking of, I spoke to Rhona. She should ring you soon."

Willa didn't mention his quick change of subject. "About what?"

Voices in the background took Scott's attention. "She'll tell you everything. I've got to go. I'll call when I know something."

"Scott," she said, but the line was already dead.

Willa sat with her irritation until she got it under some semblance of control. Then she went looking for Jasper. She walked through the spacious house. The few pieces of furniture and decorations were on the sparse side, but the minimalist style worked. The soft gray contemporary sofa and chairs had simple, elegant lines with deep seating. The thick, oval rug was an off-white and softened the room, bringing together the entire look against the light gray plank tiles and black granite surrounding the fireplace. Simplicity seemed to be how Jasper lived, and she liked it.

She found him in the kitchen. He stood with his hands braced on the edge of the sink as he stared out the window. She wondered if he was thinking about their kiss. Was he going over it again and again in his head as she was? Or maybe he regretted it. She didn't think someone could fake that kind of passion. She knew she couldn't.

A timer beeped, drawing him out of his musings. He removed the tea strainer from the cup and set it in the sink. He turned with the mug in his hand and drew up short when he saw her.

"Scott and Elodie are in Edinburgh," she said.

His brow furrowed. "Is that wise?"

She shook her head, at a loss. "Broc might have found Dad. It seems my brother is very happy I wasn't there when they left, so he didn't have to bring me."

"You're upset." Jasper walked over and handed her the mug.

Willa's right arm still felt good, but she was leery about using it too much. She kept it in the sling, just in case. Jasper turned the cup so she could grab the handle. "Thanks. I'm angry. And hurt. I wanted to be there."

"I doona think that wise with your injury."

"I was the last to see Dad." Her gaze skated away as she thought about that night. "I can still see the panic in his eyes when we looked at each other. He shoved me out a window and told me to go. I didn't," she said with a brief smile as her gaze returned to Jasper. "I blocked a round of magic meant for him. It gave him time to climb onto the balcony and down the fire escape with me. Then we went in separate directions."

Jasper guided her back to the living area. Once she was seated, he went to a basket she hadn't noticed and pulled out a blanket, draping it over her legs. Then he sat on the stool in front of the chair. "You shouldna blame yourself for anything that happens to your father. He loves you and Scott verra much, and he would do anything to keep you both safe."

"You sound as if you know him."

"That's what parents do, right?"

She set the mug on top of her thigh. "For most, it is."

"Is that your father?"

"Aye."

Jasper gave her a soft smile. "There you go."

"Did you have a good relationship with your dad?"

"It had its ups and downs. He wanted things done his way without any deviation, and I liked to try different things. We argued a lot."

She wished he wasn't sitting so far away. Only a few feet

separated them, but it felt like miles when she wanted him beside her. "Do you miss him?"

"Would you think less of me if I said nay?"

"I wouldn't," she answered with a shake of her head.

Jasper shrugged. "We had a complicated relationship. He was a hard man."

"I'm sure you have things to do. I've taken up enough of your time today."

"It's nothing that can no' wait." His gaze met hers. "How is your arm?"

She almost moved it to show him. "The pain has returned, but it's minimal. Like a soft, dull ache. You didn't believe me the first time, but you must now. Because you felt it, too."

"Maybe. I might have only made things worse."

Willa opened her mouth to speak when her mobile rang. Jasper was up in a flash and took her mug so she could get her mobile out of her back pocket. "Hello?" she answered.

"Hey, Willa, it's Rhona. There's someone I'd like you to talk to. She might be able to help with your shoulder. I can come get you."

Jasper caught her gaze. "I'll take you."

"Tell me where. I have a ride." Willa memorized the address. "I'll be there shortly."

Jasper put the mug in front of her face. "First, drink."

She took the still-hot cup and sipped on it until she had drunk half the tea. Willa stood as Jasper brought the mug to the kitchen. She met him at the inside garage door. Once in the SUV, she gave him the address to put into the navigation system. Then, they were off.

"Do you know where we're going?" he asked.

She tempered her excitement since her hope had been snatched away before. "I've no idea."

They drove in comfortable silence. Her thoughts weren't on who she might be seeing or even her shoulder. They were firmly locked on Jasper and their kisses. She fought not to touch her lips as she replayed those moments. The desire had been tempestuous, but not once had he tried to dominate. He had held it in, his body tense and tight, while his hands were gentle, holding her as if she might shatter at any moment. And his mouth. Dear Lord, his mouth...

She bit back a moan, thinking about the hungry way he had kissed her. No. Not hungrily. *Ravenously.*

Her breath caught on that thought.

"We're here."

His announcement brought her to the present in a snap. She swallowed and looked around to see he had parked outside a white, two-story, terraced cottage with a black roof and trim. Willa looked at the numbers on the door. "It's the middle one."

"Great view of the seafront," Jasper said as he looked out his window. He swung his head to her. "Shall we? Unless you wish to go in alone."

"I'd like for you to be there."

He nodded and opened the door. She took a breath and did the same. The moment she stepped out, a steady breeze off the water buffeted her. She glanced at the water in time to see a dolphin breaking the surface. Willa met Jasper at the front of the Jaguar, and they made their way to the door. He knocked and took a half-step back to settle behind her.

The black door opened to reveal Rhona. Her red hair was

pulled away from her face in a ponytail. She smiled at Willa before moving her gaze past her to Jasper.

"Rhona, this is Jasper McCabe. Jasper, Rhona," Willa said.

Jasper inclined his head in greeting. "It's good to meet you."

"Same. I've heard a lot about you," Rhona replied. Then she moved out of the way. "Please, come in."

The inside of the terraced home was as lovely as the outside. The entryway and kitchen had dark tile and wooden trim contrasting nicely with the white walls, ceiling, and doors. Exposed wooden beams added even more charm. Willa spotted a small, updated kitchen with a round, four-chair dining table.

Rhona took them around the corner to the sitting room where Ariah waited. The floor was covered with plush carpet, and she saw a love seat and two overstuffed chairs, all of which had several pillows and blankets over the arms. A television was tucked on a stand in the corner. Behind one chair was a bookcase built into the wall, overflowing with books. Colored stones bracketed the fireplace, while the stone wall it stood on had been painted white to match the rest of the room. Four light fixtures on two walls made to look like candles aided the one window in supplying light.

"Not bad for a two-hundred-year-old house."

Willa recognized the voice and turned to see Emilie standing in the doorway behind her with a tray of tea. "It's beautiful."

"It's mine, so of course I think so," she answered with a brief smile. "Sit, everyone. Please."

Emilie elegantly placed the tray on the coffee table and straightened. She jerked at the sight of Jasper, who stood silently in the corner.

"Forgive the intrusion," he told her. "I'm Jasper."

"He drove me," Willa added.

When Emilie said nothing, Ariah inclined her head toward Jasper, her smile warm and welcoming. "Nice to see you again. I have a fresh batch of the mint tea you like."

"I'll be in to get it soon," Jasper answered.

"I need to get another cup," Emilie said. "I'll be right back."

Willa glanced at Jasper to see if any of that had troubled him. He gave her a nod to let her know he was fine. Emilie returned and poured tea for all. She handed each of them a cup and saucer and took the chair in the farthest corner near the bookcase. Since Ariah had the other chair, Willa and Rhona sat on the loveseat.

Then everyone fell quiet. Willa sipped her tea, wondering who would speak first. She didn't have to wait long.

"Tell me everything that happened," Emilie urged Willa. "Every detail. No matter how small."

Willa set the tea aside and folded her hands in her lap. She took a deep breath and began her tale. No one interrupted her with questions or comments, but it still took a while to get through her story. She ended with the MacLeod Druids and Healers of Skye attempting to help her. Though he hadn't asked her not to, she'd left out what Jasper had done. He had been so skeptical of it that she thought it would be better not to say anything.

Emilie set her cup and saucer on the side table next to her. "Do you know why there is so little information on ebony wood out there? Because my ancestors did everything in their power to wipe away any record of it being used by or on Druids."

"All record?" Rhona asked in a soft voice.

"Aye. They took lives, and they did it because they had no choice. Ebony wood doesn't just harm the one who wields it. The one who uses it will feel its backlash soon enough. As will anyone else who comes into contact with it."

"Why didn't you say something sooner?" Rhona demanded angrily.

Emilie cut her gaze to Rhona. "I've already contacted Lucy. She's taking precautions."

"What will it do to her?" Ariah asked calmly.

Emilie's gaze went distant as she looked at the floor. "It's different for everyone. The user and the one wounded usually get the worst of things because ebony wood is used with intent and magic, but it is only dangerous to someone else if they touch it directly. The fact that someone has begun using ebony wood again tells me they either don't know about the repercussions, or they don't believe it'll happen to them."

"But someone did use it no' that long ago," Jasper pointed out. "If it was so secret, how is it continuing to be used?"

"My ancestors didn't get everyone. Or perhaps someone accidentally stumbled on knowledge of its uses. I didn't ask thirty years ago. Maybe I should have, but I was trying to save a life."

"And after?"

Emilie's chin lifted. "I was too busy dealing with the loss of my family. The consequences of helping that night."

"I won't have anyone else affected by this," Willa announced. She stood and bowed her head to Emilie. "Thank you for your time."

"Willa," Rhona called.

But she was done with all of this. If Emilie's ancestors had killed Druids to keep ebony wood a secret because of its power to destroy, she wouldn't be party to it hurting others. Willa strode from the house and started down the road. A nice, long walk was just what she needed.

A strong hand took hers and drew her to a halt.

Jasper turned her to face him. "Emilie can help."

"At the expense of her life? Or maybe a friend's? What about you? You've done whatever it is you do twice now. Will you feel the backlash of the wood? What about the MacLeod Druids? Emilie said someone has to touch it directly, but what if she's wrong? Everyone could be harmed by this. And why? Because I want to live? That isn't a reason."

His dark eyes were earnest as they met hers. "Everyone who has helped has done so of their own volition."

"Without knowing the risks. That isn't the same, and you know it."

"I know the risks now, and I'd still do whatever I could."

Willa shook her head. "I wouldn't let you."

His fingers tightened on hers. "This is one woman's venture. There are others. We'll find something. Let me take you back to my place. We'll eat and see what we can find."

She wanted that more than anything, but she needed some time to think. "I need some time alone."

CHAPTER TWENTY-TWO

SKYE DRUIDS

"I don't feel right about this," Finn said from the vehicle's passenger seat.

Carlyle propped his elbow on the car door and leaned his head against his fist. "Neither do I, but we have to do it. The sooner we clear Edie, the better it'll be for everyone. But especially Elias and Elodie."

Finn turned his brown eyes to Carlyle and quirked a brow. "It's fekked up."

"Fucked. Why can't you just say fuck? Why do the Irish have to change everything?"

Finn snorted. "Why do the English have to take everything? Feel free to give back the part of Ireland you've laid claim to."

They shared a smile at the words they had said to each other the first day they'd met—and whenever things got too difficult. It always eased their tensions, even if for just a moment.

"It is fucked up that we're following Edie," Carlyle admitted, growing serious once more. "We should've had her marked off the list weeks ago. It seems particularly cruel to leave Elodie and Elias wondering."

"I don't think they are. Both believe Edie doesn't have anything to do with Kerry."

Carlyle scratched his cheek and shrugged. "Maybe she doesn't. But being seen with Kerry put a big question mark beside Edie's name."

"Do you think she's part of things?"

"I'm the wrong person to ask. I think anyone is capable of such deeds in the right situation."

Finn raised both brows. "Anyone?"

"Yep."

"Hmm." Finn returned his attention to Edie's house, then took out the binoculars for a closer look. "That's the fourth time she's looked at something on her mobile in the past thirty minutes."

Carlyle made a note of it on the sheet. "It could be anything. How many times a day do you look at your phone?"

"She's not checking a text." Finn leaned forward. "She doesn't spend much time looking at whatever it is, but once she does, she stares off into space for a long time."

"Well, there's one way to figure out what it is."

Finn lowered the binoculars and looked his way. "That's invading her privacy. It's probably nothing."

"People were killed. Souls were held against their will. I want to find everyone responsible and make sure they can't hurt anyone else."

Finn's lips flattened. "You're right. Clear it through Theo."

Carlyle sent the information to Theo, as well as the idea of having Sabertooth, the fifth member of the Knights and their hacker extraordinaire, see if he can uncover what had Edie's attention.

He lowered his mobile, only to have it vibrate. Carlyle was about to answer the call without looking, thinking it was Theo, but he glanced at the screen at the last minute and saw Mason Crawford's name. He stared at the phone as it continued to vibrate in his hand.

"How long are you going to ignore him?" Finn asked.

Carlyle declined the call. "After what he did to Ferne, a long time."

"There's more to the story. There has to be."

"Maybe."

Finn shook his head and went back to watching Edie through the binoculars. "He's her brother. He wouldn't just write her off if they're as close as you say they are. Have you considered the London Druids might be responsible?"

"I have."

"There you go."

Carlyle saw the notification of yet another voicemail from his former friend. "He would've told Ferne if that were the case."

"Unless he couldn't. Both you and Ferne talked about how dangerous that group is. If they did kill Ferne and Mason's parents, it would give me pause if I were in Mason's shoes. They could've threatened Ferne."

"I thought of that. The London Druids couldn't get to her here, so threatening her would be futile."

Finn pulled the binoculars away for a heartbeat, his face scrunched up. "Is Mason the type to be frightened off easily?"

"He was looking into the elders for his parents' murders, so no.

They could've tried to coerce him, but he never would've caved. There's only one explanation."

Finn sat back and lowered the binoculars to his lap. He met Carlyle's gaze. "Which is?"

"Mason is one of them now."

"He believes they caused the plane crash that killed his parents. I don't buy that."

Carlyle twisted his lips. "You don't understand the London Druids. They want as many Druids as possible in their community, but they hand-pick those they want to lead, the ones who will eventually become elders. Mason was such a Druid. When I say he's one of them, I'm telling you, he stopped putting them off. He's *one* of them."

"Fek me. Does Ferne know?"

"I'm sure she suspects."

"What do we do?"

Carlyle shook his head. "I'm not sure there's anything we *can* do."

Once Finn went back to watching Edie, Carlyle looked through his phone. He scrolled to his father's name and noted it had been almost two weeks since his last text. Usually, his dad was trying to get him home so Carlyle could take over the title and estates one day. Carlyle had never wanted any of that, but especially not after…

The fact that his father hadn't responded was proof the London Druids had told Thomas that Carlyle was on Skye. The London Druids forbade communication with anyone from Skye, and absolutely no visiting the isle was allowed. If either edict was broken, a Druid was kicked out of the group and exiled from their family.

Carlyle had hoped his father would care more about his son than some stupid rule put into place generations ago by angry, bitter Druids kicked off Skye.

His phone dinged with a message from Theo. Carlyle elbowed Finn. "We got the all-clear. Sending Saber the request now."

Edie had to stop looking at the picture of Trevor and the woman. She might have decided not to ask Trevor about it, but it was always there. Fake or not, it had gotten into her brain and taken hold.

"I'm home!" Trevor shouted as he walked in the door.

Edie rose from the bed and checked herself in the mirror. She hurried down the stairs and greeted Trevor as he pulled two wine glasses from the cabinet.

"You're home early," she said.

He shrugged one shoulder. "I thought I'd spend some time with my family. Have you started cooking?"

"Not yet."

"Good. We're having takeaway."

The kids shouted with joy from the living room, where they played a video game.

Edie took a sip of wine. "Anything else planned for the evening?"

"I'm open to suggestions," he said with a slow smile.

She sidled closer. He wound an arm around her and lowered his head for a kiss. She couldn't believe she had almost lost everything, but she had gotten a handle on her resentment toward her siblings. They would never upset her world again. Because they didn't matter. Not like her family did.

"The kids will be busy for a while. How about a soak in the hot tub?" she suggested.

Trevor grinned. "I'll get it heated while you change."

Edie raced up the stairs to find her swimsuit. She opened a drawer and snagged some trunks for Trevor. She changed quickly and grabbed some towels. On her way out back, she saw Trevor on the phone. It wasn't until she drew closer that she picked up part of the conversation.

"She doesn't have a clue," Trevor said. "Leave everything to me. I promise I've got things in hand. It won't be much longer."

Edie immediately thought about the picture. She hated the jealousy that sprang up. All because of that stupid photo. Trevor had never cheated. He wouldn't. Though the thought didn't have the same conviction it once had, not after seeing the picture.

The call ended, and she walked outside as if she hadn't heard anything. She wanted to know who it was, but she didn't want to ask outright. "Tell me you aren't going to be taking work calls tonight."

"Nay. I earned a break."

She tried again to get the caller's name. "Maybe you should turn off the mobile, so work won't call back."

"No one will call. Promise," he said as he walked inside to change.

Edie couldn't let her mind go off on this tangent and spoil the night. She set the towels down before going to get their wine and some snacks. It was rare for Trevor to be home early. He always worked late. He'd begun it early in their marriage. He was driven to be a top lawyer. His work dedication had given them the life they had now.

But he'd also always made time for her and the family. As he was doing now. He wouldn't do anything to jeopardize what they had. She was the one who had done that. She saw the error of her ways now. It wouldn't happen again.

She was walking out of the kitchen with the wine and snacks when she spotted his phone on the island. He was still changing. She could look at it, confirm who he had spoken to. That would ease her suspicions.

The image of the picture filled her mind again.

"Nay," she whispered. "I'm done with that. If he wanted to leave, he would've."

Edie wouldn't let the doubt fester. She pushed it all aside as she set up everything around the hot tub within easy reach and put her feet in. The water was still cool, but she didn't want to wait to enjoy this time with her husband. The roar of the bubbles filled her senses. She smiled and closed her eyes.

"Edie," a voice said in her head. *"You've been chosen."*

CHAPTER TWENTY-THREE

SKYE DRUIDS

It had been years since Jasper's thoughts were this chaotic and muddled. He didn't like it. He was used to an orderly life, one where his choices were clear and straightforward. Nothing had been simple since he'd found Willa near death.

Especially not since they'd kissed.

Jasper squeezed his eyes closed as he sat on the sofa, staring across the room at nothing. If only he could forget how good she tasted. Or how much he liked the feel of her body against his. All of it was seared into his brain, the memories flashing in his mind at the most inopportune moments. He knew better than to let his emotions get involved on a job. It was tantamount to suicide.

He could give himself a million different reasons why he shouldn't feel anything toward Willa, but it didn't make any difference. Desire had been kindled. It burned fiercely, intensely. How much longer did he have before he crossed that invisible line and forgot the job, forgot who he was supposed to be? The best thing he could do was leave. Right now. George would be furious, but she'd find another way.

Jasper grabbed his mobile. He hadn't checked in with her all day. He found her contact information and pressed it to call her. The line rang twice before she answered.

"Tell me you have something," she said.

He looked out the windows to the land beyond. "Scott and Elodie think they've found Luke."

"Do they now? Where are they looking?"

Jasper knew Balladyn was with them. Hopefully, so was the Warrior, Broc. Those two could hold off George and probably Beth. "Edinburgh."

"They're here?" George asked excitedly.

"They are, but they're no' alone."

She chuckled. "Balladyn sticking his nose where it doesn't belong again?"

Jasper parted his lips to tell her about Broc, but he hesitated. "You best no' be around when they find Luke."

"You think I have him?"

He frowned at the surprise in her voice. "Aye."

"Sorry to disappoint. How I wish I did, though."

"Does Beth?"

"She would've told me."

He sat forward. "Are you sure about that?"

"What other news do you have?" she asked tersely.

Jasper slowly sat back. He'd pissed her off. "I took Willa to see a woman today who might help her wound."

"Might? What does that mean?"

"It isna only those who have the ebony wood used on them who are harmed. The one using it gets affected, as well."

George's laughter was so loud he jerked the mobile away from his ear. He had expected worry, even scorn. But not amusement.

"Anything else?" she asked between chuckles.

He hesitated. He should tell her he was leaving. Instead, he said, "Nay."

The line went dead. Jasper scrubbed a hand down his face and shoved to his feet. He debated whether to check in on Willa but realized she wasn't the one he really wanted to talk to. He grabbed his keys and stalked out of the house.

He didn't care if he was being watched. Nor did it matter that returning to Emilie was the last place he should probably be. He had to get answers, and she might be the only one who could give them to him.

He drove straight to the Healer's house. Even as Jasper knocked on the door, he looked around, wondering how many spies George had out there keeping an eye on him. He told himself he was only doing his job. He had to get closer to Willa, and helping heal her was part of that. If he couldn't leave, then he would do whatever he could to free Willa from the influence of the ebony wood.

The door opened, and he looked into brown eyes.

"I thought you might be back," Emilie said.

He was taken aback by that. "Why?"

"I saw the way you watched Willa." Emilie stepped aside. "Come in."

Jasper stepped over the threshold and felt cocooned by the quaint interior. He followed Emilie into the sitting room. He sat on the loveseat this time as she sank into the chair near the bookcase.

"Tell me," she urged.

"What do you mean?"

"It wasn't just your gaze on Willa. She glanced your way when I mentioned the ebony wood harming anyone who has touched it. Tell me what you did."

Jasper swallowed. "I...I can no' explain it. I'm no' a Healer. I've never done anything like it before."

"And what did you do?"

"I had to touch the wound." When Emilie didn't seem surprised by his confession, he continued. "I...sensed the ebony wood. There's a wee splinter in her tendon near the shoulder ball joint, but I didna touch the wood itself."

Emilie took a deep breath as she crossed one leg over the other and covered her knee with her hands. "Who else have you told about this?"

"No one."

"Not even Willa?"

He shook his head. "She says she feels warmth from my hands around the injury."

"Do you feel it?"

"Aye, but I've no' told her that."

Emilie's expression was unreadable as she studied him for so long that it was all Jasper could do to sit still. Finally, she said, "This isn't the first time you've encountered ebony wood, is it?"

It was reflex for him to curl his hands into fists. He told himself not to look down. He knew he'd see blood there if he did.

"Did you use it?"

Jasper recoiled as if struck. "Nay. Never."

"Who did?"

"I didna know the bloke. He and my father were working a job, but things went south. I'm no' sure what happened." Jasper was hurtled back to that terrible day: his father lying on the sidewalk, gasping for breath, his eyes wide as he reached for him. Jasper kneeling beside him, frantic to stop the bleeding. "The man used it on my father. There was so much blood." He looked down at his hands, but it wasn't his father's blood he saw this time. It was Willa's. "I couldna save him."

"You want to save Willa."

He lifted his eyes to Emilie. "Aye. I'm already involved. No' only did I find her that night and try to halt the bleeding, but I've also sensed the wood twice. If what you say is true, then I could already be marked."

"And you want me to help you reverse that," she asked, her slim brows raised.

"I want you to tell me how to get the sliver out."

She pressed her lips together and looked out the window at the day fading to night. "What makes you think you can do anything?"

"If I can feel it and determine where it's located, then I can do something."

"Even if it means your death or losing everything you have?"

It wasn't as if Jasper wanted to die, but things had gotten out of control. He might not be perfect, but he never took another's life or was physically violent with anyone. Ever. George knew his rule about that. It didn't matter if she was aware of what Beth had planned or not. They had involved him. And he would correct that. "Even if."

"The thing is, it'll strike others around you. Ebony wood is beautiful, but Druid magic twists it until it's something altogether different. Something that can't be measured or contained. It takes lives easily, almost exuberantly. I didn't just lose my husband and child, I also lost my unborn baby. All within weeks of each other. I thought I had prepared for any kind of backlash that might come my way. Had I known what would happen or had even an inkling of what the ebony wood would take from me, I never would've helped."

Jasper didn't blame Emilie for wanting nothing to do with ebony wood again. But he didn't have that luxury. Willa had been targeted and used, and he was complicit in all of it. All because George and Beth wanted to destroy the Skye Druids. And he had agreed with George. At least about the things she had told him. He'd never had reason to doubt her. But now…

"You knew there could be repercussions from the wood?" he asked.

She gave him a single nod. "Not that it did me any good."

"I have to do this." He shrugged. "I'm going to do it. I doona want to cause Willa any more pain than I have to. Please, tell me what I need to do."

Emilie rose to her feet. "Tea?"

"That sounds nice." He didn't want anything, but at least she wasn't demanding he leave. The longer he stayed, the more he might be able to wear her down. She knew a lot about ebony wood she hadn't shared yet. He was sure of it.

After Emilie left the room, he stood to stretch his legs. Jasper walked to the mantel and the two picture frames there. He stared into the face of a much younger Emilie, her belly swollen with child and a bright smile on her face as she turned toward a tall man next to her. The man's face was turned to Emilie and mostly blocked by the toddler he held, who had leaned to the side. He stared at the picture for a long time. Emilie and her husband appeared happy and very much in love. How soon after the picture was taken had she lost him?

Jasper slid his gaze to the second frame. This one was of the toddler walking away from the camera into the sea with Emilie holding the child's hand and a beautiful sunset as the backdrop.

He turned at a sound behind him to see Emilie carrying in a tray. He returned to the sofa. Watching her pour tea out of the pot into the cups was comforting.

She caught him eyeing the hand-painted set. "This service has been passed down through my family for five generations," she said.

He met her gaze, knowing it would end with her. "It's beautiful."

"Thank you." She remained beside him, sitting sideways on the edge of the cushion as she daintily lifted the cup from the saucer to drink. "Does Willa know?"

"That I'm here? Nay," Jasper said and shook his head.

Emilie tilted her head to the side, her gaze steady and direct. "That you love her."

He froze, the words barreling into him. Love? He knew it existed. He had even seen it a time or two. But it wasn't for him.

"You can attempt to deny it, but it's there for anyone who looks," Emilie stated matter-of-factly and took another sip.

Jasper's heart thudded in his chest. He felt trapped, cornered. "I care about her, but I barely know her."

"Love doesn't require you to know a person inside and out."

"You're mistaken."

She gently set aside the cup and saucer, then speared him with a look. "There are only two reasons you would come to me for help. The first is that you love her and will do anything for her. The second is that you're responsible for her injury and wish to right the wrong."

The delicate cup looked out of place in his hand as he brought it to his lips for a drink. The brew was delicious, and he went back for a second sip.

"Ariah's calming teas are some of my favorites," Emilie said. "I had a feeling you would need it."

Jasper couldn't look at her. He locked his gaze on the carpet and drank the tea until nothing was left. Emilie refilled the empty cup before placing it back on the saucer and handing it to him. He accepted it without question.

"When you begin, you can't stop. You'll need to be quick and smooth," she said.

He lifted his gaze to her, shocked that she was giving him exactly what he had requested.

"I suggest reopening the wound to make it easier to remove," Emilie continued. "Otherwise, you take the chance of the splinter doing more harm. It will cause her a tremendous amount of pain. That alone will make you want to quit. You can't. You've got to keep going. You will only have one chance at this."

Jasper nodded slowly. "I'll follow your instructions to the letter."

CHAPTER TWENTY-FOUR

SKYE DRUIDS

The clouds attempted to blanket her view. Willa lay on a lounger on the back deck, swaddled in blankets as she watched the stars. No matter how many layers she put around her, she felt numb—from the inside out.

She hadn't even mustered much of a farewell to Jasper when he dropped her off. Her mind kept tripping over the part about there not being a way to fix her problem. Well, there was, but she wasn't about to ask Emilie to do it. Not after what she had endured. Nor would Willa ask anyone else. It was enough that Jasper, the Healers, and the MacLeod Druids might be affected in some way.

It would be easy to hate George and her community, as well as Beth. And Willa held a lot of anger. But there was no use despising anyone. What was done was done. If it hadn't been for Jasper, the Healers wouldn't have gotten to her in time, and she wouldn't have had these last days with everyone.

If only she could see her father.

Willa didn't know how long she had. She shouldn't be wasting them thinking about what had happened. She should be out living her best life and doing the things she had put off. That's what people did when they knew they were dying, wasn't it? Why, then, couldn't she? She had accepted her fate. Maybe *accepted* was pushing it. She had acknowledged it. Aye. That sounded better.

Her phone beeped with a text. Scott had diligently kept her informed regarding what they were doing in Edinburgh. She knew she'd been wrong in not telling him about the visit with Emilie, but she didn't want to pull his focus from finding their father. If only she could help. She wished she was in the city with them, combing through flats and searching for clues.

The tightness in her chest loosened some when she read that Broc had found where their father had holed up for a few days at the edge of the city. Unfortunately, Luke Ryan had been gone by the time they discovered it. Still, there was hope that he had gotten out and away from George. That didn't explain why he wasn't on Skye yet, though.

"Willa."

She started at the sound of Jasper's deep voice. Her head jerked to the side as she sat up.

"I didna mean to surprise you," he said as he stepped from the shadows into the glow of the small lights hanging from the cottage's eaves.

She shook her head. "It's fine. Come sit."

He shifted his shoulders in his black coat as he did as she requested. "The stars are difficult to see tonight."

"True, but the clouds are pretty drifting past. I love how they move across the moon."

"Aye."

Willa lay back and crossed her ankles. "They found the place where Dad was. He's not there anymore, but Broc found it. He'll find my father. If George has him, or worse, if George... Scott will tear them to pieces."

"You want to be with them."

"Wouldn't you? After what they've done to me, and what they could've done to him? Aye. I want to be there. Yet I'm much too aware that battling violence with more violence isn't the answer. However, sometimes, it's the only way. George won't stop. She'll keep coming for Dad, Elias, Scott, and Filip."

"And you."

Willa met Jasper's dark gaze, his face now in shadow. "We both know my days are numbered."

"That's actually why I'm here." He cleared his throat. "I just came from Emilie's. She told me what I need to do to get the last bit of wood out."

Willa let her eyes roam over Jasper's rugged features. Earlier that day, she had begged for something like this from him. But that was before she knew what it would cost him—or anyone. "I can't let you do that."

"It's my choice."

"Actually, it's mine."

"You would rather die?" he demanded, his voice rising as his brow furrowed.

She sat up and swung her legs over the side of the lounger. "It isn't just about me, is it? It's about you. It's about everyone who has helped. The Healers. The MacLeod Druids. Every time I think about all of you, I get sick to my stomach, wondering what the repercussions will be from the ebony wood—even if not all of you touched it."

"They've all talked with Emilie. The Healers are doing

protection spells, and Rhona is with them. The Druids are doing something. Emilie didna tell me exactly what, but she seemed confident they would be okay."

"None of it may work. A lot of people could be harmed because of me. And what of you?"

He leaned his forearms on his thighs, clasping his hands together. "I've taken precautions."

"Emilie knew a way to keep the backlash away from you?"

Jasper nodded, his gaze never leaving hers. "Let me help you."

"What is it?"

"I said I've taken precautions."

Which meant he hadn't done anything. He was trying to make her feel better. Why, though? "Your involvement has been minimal. I'd like to keep it that way."

He suddenly stood and walked to the edge of the deck, his back to her. "I can do this. And few can."

"Why are you so sure *you* can?"

"I…just know I can."

She studied his back, wondering what he wasn't telling her. "How are you able to help me?"

"I have a history with ebony wood," he said in a tight voice. "My father was killed with it."

Willa dropped her chin to her chest. "Oh, Jasper."

"Emilie says that's how I can sense it within you." He turned to her. "Let me do this for you."

She shook her head. "I don't think I could live with myself if something happened to you."

"It willna. Please," he beseeched, his eyes pleading. "Let me fix this. I can do it."

"This isn't on you to fix."

"You were right. I could feel the warmth. I doona know why I didna tell you. Nothing like that has ever happened before, and I wasna sure what it meant." He worked his jaw. "There's more. I can...see the sliver."

Willa frowned. "See it?"

"Inside my mind. It's why I urged you to return to the Healers." He took a step closer. "Emilie told me everything I need to do to remove the wood. I wouldna be here if I didna think I could help you."

There it was, that bud of hope again. It had been dashed so many times it was slower to sprout this time, but it was there. Did she dare take this chance? What if Jasper could remove it? She might have a normal life. She could help fight against Skye's many enemies. Maybe even have a future with Jasper. But only if the ebony wood didn't hurt or affect him. That gave her pause. She had to be sure he would be fine. "Are you sure there won't be any ramifications?"

"It's taken care of."

"What does that mean, exactly?"

Jasper dropped to one knee to look her in the eye. "It means that it's taken care of."

"If you did something to protect yourself, you'd tell me. The fact that you're being evasive says you're leaving things to chance."

He lowered his gaze for a heartbeat. "I stanched my father's wound when he was injured. When that didna help, I pulled out the shard. I even dug inside his chest to make sure there wasna more. Nothing ever happened to me."

"That you're aware of."

"Nothing happened then. Nothing will happen now."

Willa shook her head. "I'm sorry. I can't take that chance."

"Fine. I'll do a protection spell. I'll cast every one I know. Will that make you feel better?"

"Better than you leaving things to chance."

"Then you agree to my proposal?"

Willa looked away from his probing gaze. She wanted to say yes. Who wouldn't? It wasn't just the pain or the fact that she couldn't move her arm. It was the idea that she would change and become tainted. Turn into something her family and friends would fight against. She desperately wanted to allow Jasper to help.

His fingers rested against her chin and gently turned her face to him. "I'll do whatever spell you want me to do, but please, Willa, *please* let me get the wood out."

The last of her resistance faltered and shattered. Hope shot upward, blossoming. "I'd better not regret this."

His face broke into a huge smile. "You willna. I give you my word." His happiness dimmed. "I should warn you that Emilie said the pain will be immense. No' only do I need to reopen your wound, but removing the last of the ebony wood will be agonizing."

"It can't be worse than what I've already endured."

"How is your pain now?"

"It's been minimal since you touched it earlier."

He nodded and looked around. "Good. That's good. Where should we do this? Outside?"

"Inside. I'd rather not be shivering."

"Right. Come, then," he beckoned.

She rose. Trailing the blankets behind her, she entered the cottage, Jasper on her heels. Willa didn't stop until she was in her bedroom. She removed her shoes and turned around. Jasper was in the doorway, his brow wrinkled in concentration.

"You can back out," she said. "I wouldn't hold it against you."

Jasper flattened his lips. "I'm thinking about cleaning up. There will be blood. I also need a knife."

"Hmm. Maybe we should do this in the kitchen. The table isn't big enough. I can put some bin bags on the floor and lay on them for easy cleanup."

"Sounds good. Is there rubbing alcohol? First-aid supplies?"

"I'll get those while you start the protection spells for yourself."

His lips softened into a smile. He closed the distance between them and softly pressed his lips to hers. Then he left. She heard him chanting as she gathered first-aid supplies and towels. Then she laid out the bin bags. She quietly returned to her room to mentally prepare for what was about to happen. There was a chance it wouldn't work, but it was possible it would. She took out her phone and left a voice message for Scott since she couldn't write anything out. When she returned to the kitchen, she found Jasper holding a large kitchen knife as he dumped rubbing alcohol over the blade to sterilize it.

"We should call the Healers to mend the cut," he said without looking at her.

She wished her hair was up, but she only had one hand. Jasper was scrubbing his hands. She would just have to do her best to keep it out of his way. "That could put them in danger again. We can call them afterward if they're needed."

His dark eyes met hers briefly. Willa carefully removed the sling and then her sweater, leaving her standing in just her socks, jeans, and a white tank top. She lowered to the floor and lay back. Jasper kneeled beside her.

"I wish I didna have to reopen the wound," he said.

She shot him a quick smile. "I'm not keen on that part, either."

"I can do this."

"I wouldn't be here now if I didn't think you could. Are all the spells in place?"

"I'm as protected as I can get," he mused.

She gave him a nod. "Then proceed."

He placed his left hand on her shoulder to hold her still as the tip of the knife touched her skin. "I just need a small opening."

"I need something to bite down on."

Jasper rose and grabbed a wooden spoon.

"Thanks," she said and took it from him. "If things go wrong, I won't blame you."

"Everything will go right," he insisted.

She wanted to kiss him again. "Just in case. Also, I left a voicemail for Scott on my phone."

"It'll be fine. I promise. Ready?"

Willa put the spoon between her teeth and took a deep breath before nodding again. He didn't waste a second. In the next moment, her arm was on fire. She stiffened, and the pain of her skin being cut made her squeeze her eyes shut as tears raced down her face. She tried to breathe, but even that caused too much pain.

As much as the knife piercing her skin hurt, it was nothing compared to the debilitating, ravaging anguish that cut through her as Jasper worked to get the remaining piece of ebony wood out of her body. The agony froze her limbs, locking them into rigid, unmovable appendages. Her body was on fire, razed by blinding pain.

She fought against the scream for as long as she could but eventually lost the battle. It was too much. She couldn't handle it. She had to get away, needed to make Jasper stop.

The sight of Willa writhing, her screams ringing in his ears, nearly broke Jasper. He recalled Emilie's words of warning, that he would only have one chance. He tuned Willa out and concentrated on the sliver. It was so small, one teeny-tiny shard nearly too trifling to see. But it was slowly killing her.

He locked on it and called it to him once he had a good grasp. It was buried deep in Willa's tendon. Sweat ran down Jasper's face and dripped into his eyes, stinging them as he slowly, methodically extracted the piece until it hung in the air before him.

Jasper jumped up and turned on the stove burner. The instant the flames ignited, he put the splinter into it, ridding them of it forever. He shut off the burner and returned to Willa's side. She was quiet now. He felt her neck for a pulse. It was strong but rapid. She was just unconscious, which was a blessing for them both.

The cut he'd made was small but deep. Blood ran thick and red as it covered his hands, the bags, and her shirt. He had to close the wound to stop the bleeding. He doused the cut with hydrogen peroxide and hurriedly wiped away the excess blood. He used a butterfly bandage to hold it closed before wrapping her arm with gauze.

Jasper took a second to sit back and release a long breath. His gaze went to her blood-soaked shirt. He cut it off her before gathering her in his arms. He then carried her to bed and covered her. He stepped back, watching her for a moment before cleaning the kitchen. All the while, her screams reverberated in his head. George or Beth—or both of them—would continue using ebony wood on their enemies. How many more Druids would be hurt or killed by it?

He hadn't signed up for this. He couldn't do it anymore. He wouldn't.

Jasper stood in the kitchen with no remnants of what he had done anywhere. He had succeeded in freeing Willa of the hold the ebony wood had on her. Jasper looked in on Willa one more time. He wanted to say so much to her, and even more he never would. She was free. That's what mattered. The only thing that would be better was if he had never come into her life at all.

He wanted to go to her, to kiss her once more. Instead, he turned as he sent off a text. He locked the house as he walked out. The drive to his place was long and silent. He was doing the right thing. He knew that because he felt like shite.

Jasper didn't go inside once he reached his house. He went to the one place that always gave him comfort. The horses each stuck their heads over their doors when he walked into the stables. They watched him with their large, solemn eyes, ears turned toward him.

"I wish I could take all of you with me," he told them. "It wouldna be fair to you, though. You need a steady home, not one where we're moving all the time. I'd be too easy to track. Besides, my time in the UK is over. I'll find you a good home together. I promise."

He wanted to pet them, give them treats. But he was already too attached. Letting them go would be the second hardest thing he'd ever done. The first had been walking away from Willa.

Jasper turned off the lights, shut the barn door, and walked to the house. He'd come to like this version of himself on Skye. Here, he was a good, decent man. He would miss the land and the horses. He would miss the endless sky that gave him spectacular views day or night.

But mostly, he would miss Willa.

It was the wrong time, the wrong place, and the wrong circumstances. If he were lucky and if he earned it, he'd get another chance in a future life with her.

CHAPTER TWENTY-FIVE

SKYE DRUIDS

Edinburgh

George stood in the shadows of the street and looked up at the windows of Luke Ryan's flat. Lights were on, proving the information Jasper had given her was accurate. She spotted three people inside. How confident, how certain the Reaper was that he could get his friends in and out without being discovered.

Druids had stood on the back line for too long. It was time everyone on the planet understood they were here—and powerful.

George searched for Beth. She had waited long enough for the Druid to arrive. It wasn't George's fault she hadn't shown up in time. She motioned for the three teams to go into the building. The surprise attack would give them the time they needed to capture at least one of those inside. The Reaper would likely get away, but it wasn't him George wanted.

Her people knew what was at stake and understood that every decision and action counted. The first group went in through the front, a second through the back, and the third from the roof. There would be no escape for Scott Ryan this night. He would answer for his desertion and betrayal in front of the entire assembly.

With Willa handled, and Scott about to be captured, it was only a matter of time before George had Luke. And then she could turn her full attention to Elias.

Her Druids entered the building without mishap. A stone reader was on his knees at her side, his hands on the ground to connect to the huge network of stones that made up the city. She cut her gaze to him, watching his expression for anything.

"Well?" she prompted when she grew tired of waiting.

He turned his face to her, his eyes still closed. "There's nothing."

"Good."

"I'm no' so sure."

George looked back at the windows. "Why?"

"The stones are no' saying anything."

"Then make them."

His eyes opened, and he pinned her with a look. "That isna how it works."

George's stomach tightened, and her breathing quickened. There was only one way to salvage this. "We're going in."

Balladyn stood veiled atop the roof across from Luke's flat and watched the Druids creeping toward the door. He didn't glance back at the four lookouts he had knocked unconscious before teleporting to the front door of the building.

They had expected an attack might come. It was why Fallon suggested they bring his mate, Larena. The only female Warrior had the ability to become invisible. Larena watched the back while Balladyn took the front.

Rhona hadn't wanted a battle on the streets. She'd said it would only make George hate them more. She was right, of course. The best way to end this was to take George and the Druid Others in Edinburgh out. For good. Rhona wouldn't do that unless George returned to Skye. While Balladyn understood his mate's thinking, he had been around long enough to know how this would turn out.

Still, he did as she asked. He would only take lives if he had no other choice. Though he did have his eye out for George. And he wasn't the only one. Everyone who had come to Edinburgh wanted a piece of her for different reasons.

Balladyn used his magic to seal the front door. Larena would do the same with the back. Broc would handle the roof. Balladyn had already done what he could to keep the building's occupants within their homes until the skirmish was over. Including George, there were over twenty Druids in the building, headed straight for Luke's place.

Balladyn jumped inside the flat and dropped his veil. "They're coming. George is with them."

"She's going to tell me where my father is," Scott said and turned to the door, his eyes blazing with anger.

Filip flexed his fingers and moved to the side. "She certainly is."

"We have to find her first." Elodie slowly rubbed her hands together, her eyes locked on the door.

Fallon nodded to Balladyn and jumped out the window to join Larena.

This clash was needless and unnecessary, but George would never listen to reason. There was only one way to stop her, and Balladyn hoped that task wouldn't fall to Rhona. He wouldn't let it. She had gotten a taste of war, but nothing like he had experienced in his long, long years. War chipped away at a person's soul, hardened them.

But not his Rhona. Never her.

He would carry the weight of those he had slain for an eternity. What was one more if it prevented Rhona from learning all the ways it could destroy her? The Druids on Skye looked to her. They needed her, just as he did. He had known from the moment he found her that stormy night bleeding to death that he would do anything to save her.

Balladyn's enhanced hearing picked up the tread of footsteps coming toward them from above and below. He looked at the three Druids, letting them know their adversaries were approaching quickly.

They each got into battle stances, their hands out and magic ready. Balladyn veiled himself and flattened his back to the wall near the door. Tension mounted in the flat as the group drew near, their footsteps loud. And then they were there.

Balladyn took a deep breath. The Reapers could end this within seconds, but this didn't involve the Fae. It was about humans. He was only mixed up in it because of Rhona and being the Warden of Skye. He was defending the residents of the isle.

The door flew open, smashing into the opposite wall and

bouncing back to hit the three Druids who streamed into the room. Scott, Elodie, and Filip quickly defended themselves. Three more rushed into the flat, but Balladyn remained where he was. They were expecting him. George thought she knew him, and that was her first mistake. They might know of him, they might even know he was a Reaper, but they had never been in battle with him. A part of Balladyn felt sorry for anyone he came in contact with, but they were the ones who attacked.

And they would pay for the oversight.

The room shook with the impact of magic striking the walls. More Druids entered, while others shouted from the hallway, anxiously awaiting their turn to fight. Filip took down an opponent. Scott took another. Elodie removed two. Balladyn was impressed by the way they worked together. They knew their strengths and their weaknesses. Elodie had the stronger magic out of the three, but Scott and Filip held their own.

Balladyn spotted a Druid slinking up behind Filip. Just as he was about to stop him—and give away his position—Scott saw the attack and dropped to a knee, sending a blast of magic that toppled the Druid out the open window. Elodie and Filip killed the two new attackers who ran at Scott when his back was turned.

The shouts of a skirmish in the hallway made Balladyn smile. Fallon and Larena had joined the fray, pushing the Druids up the stairs. Right where he wanted them.

Balladyn looked around the corner and spotted George. She glared down the stairs as her people scrambled to get away from the Warriors. Both Larena and Fallon had let the primeval gods within them loose. Larena's iridescent skin and claws were mesmerizing as she swiped at an enemy.

Fallon let out a war cry and launched himself up the steps into a group of Druids. His lips were pulled back, showing his razor-sharp teeth. His eyes were as black as his skin and claws. The Druids were so shocked at the sight of the Warriors that most were in flight mode, their shouts for death turning to shrieks of fear.

Balladyn forced himself to wait. It wasn't time for his move yet. He wasn't the only one. Broc was outside, hiding in the shadows so innocents wouldn't see his blue skin or wings. One of them would get to George. Hopefully, by dawn, George would more clearly understand the enemies she had made.

Elodie, Scott, and Filip backed up as more Druids crowded into the flat. They were cramming themselves into the doorway, getting stuck as they screamed to get away from the Warriors. Balladyn tried to keep his gaze on George, but he lost her in the crowd. That was when he decided to step in.

He dropped his veil and grabbed Druids, hauling them into the flat and knocking them out. It stopped being a battle as Druids dove for the windows, wanting to chance death on the drop down versus facing him and the Warriors.

Scott, Elodie, and Filip attempted to stop people from falling out the window, but there was nothing they could do. It was over quickly.

Balladyn rushed to the window in time to see Broc grabbing as many as he could to set safely on the ground. Larena and Fallon joined him after tamping down their gods to look like ordinary people once more.

"What the hell happened?" Filip asked breathlessly.

Balladyn looked at the bodies around them. Some were unconscious, but many more were dead—and not all in the fight. They'd been trampled in the others' surge to get away. But there was one he *didn't* find.

"Where's George?" he asked.

Scott turned around with an angry growl. "There's no way she could've gotten away."

Balladyn pointed to Filip and Elodie. "You two check here. Scott, with me."

They ran out of the flat to search the floor. When they didn't find her, Balladyn ran down the stairs as Scott ran up. No matter where they looked, they didn't find her.

"Balladyn!"

He teleported back to Luke's flat, where everyone had gathered. The anger in the room was palpable. "What is it?" he asked.

"She got out. I found a window open on the floor below," Broc said.

Scott shook his head. "We had her. Fuck!"

"Those who lived understand who they're fighting now," Elodie said. "That will make a difference."

Balladyn wanted to say she was right, but she wasn't. Some would run and refuse to fight for George again, but for every one of those, more were waiting and willing to take their places. Those who believed they fought for what was right, just as everyone in the room now did.

"She saw us," Larena said into the silence that followed. "George knows we're involved."

Fallon crossed his arms over his chest, his face grim. "We wanted her to know."

"What are we going to do about all of this?" Broc asked, jerking his chin to the bodies.

Filip shrugged. "What can we do?"

"We got what we needed from here and Willa's flat. I think it's time you three returned to Skye," Balladyn said to the Druids.

Scott's blue eyes met his. "I've no' found my dad. I can no' leave until I do."

"I'll keep looking," Broc promised. "The instant I know something, I'll contact you."

But Scott refused to budge. "Nay. I put both him and Willa in danger. I could lose my sister. I have to find Dad."

"We will. And none of us are giving up on finding a way to help Willa either," Larena said.

Balladyn caught Scott's gaze. "Return to your sister. We'll keep at it. No one is giving up on Luke or Willa. Besides, Rhona needs an update. Theo will, too. Can you three fill them in on what happened while I clean this up?"

"Broc and I will help," Larena added.

Scott blew out a breath. "Aye. I should check on Willa anyway."

Balladyn waited until Fallon teleported the Druids away before dropping his chin to his chest. "We should've had George."

"We did," Broc said.

Balladyn jerked his head up to look at the Warrior. "What do you mean?"

"She had help getting out."

"Beth?" Larena suggested.

Broc shrugged. "I can no' say. I never saw who it was."

"Neither did I," Balladyn added.

Larena shook her head. "Me, neither. What does that mean if Beth wasn't here?"

"It means trouble." Balladyn needed to return to Skye immediately.

CHAPTER TWENTY-SIX

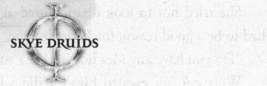

SKYE DRUIDS

Willa came to slowly. Every muscle in her body ached. She licked dry lips, desperate for a drink. The comfort of a bed held her as she blinked open her eyes. The lamp on the bedside table was on. She rolled her head toward it, expecting to find Jasper. Instead, her gaze met Theo's.

His brow was furrowed as he studied her. "How do you feel?"

Her left hand immediately lifted to her right shoulder and met skin.

"Lucy left about thirty minutes ago. She healed the cut," Theo explained. "It'll take a day or two for the last of the pain to diminish."

Willa waited to feel agony in her shoulder, but there was only a slight pull. She sat up, the sheet falling to reveal her bra.

Theo hastily turned away as he got to his feet. "I'll be in the kitchen."

"Where's Jasper?"

Theo paused in the hallway but didn't turn around. "I'll be in the kitchen," he repeated.

Willa threw back the covers and rose to put on her sweater from earlier. She couldn't believe she could move her arm. She hurried from her room into the kitchen, her gaze scanning for Jasper.

"It's just me."

She tried not to look disappointed at Theo's statement. There had to be a good reason for Jasper leaving. "Where is he?"

"Do you have any idea how reckless you were?"

Willa cut her eyes to him. "I did what I had to do. Where is he?"

"I doona know. He told me what he did and asked that I wait with you until you woke."

She looked around the kitchen, but everything had been cleaned and put away. As if he hadn't pulled the sliver from her at all. As if he hadn't done the impossible. Why had he left? It didn't make any sense.

"Willa," Theo began, but the sudden arrival of Fallon with Scott, Elodie, and Filip interrupted him.

She looked at the four of them in the middle of the kitchen and frowned when she saw the condition of their clothes, as well as their disheveled hair. "Tell me you weren't in a battle."

"Wish I could," Filip said as he walked to the cabinet and took out a bottle of Dreagan whiskey.

Before his words were fully out, Fallon was gone.

Willa looked at Scott, who strode toward Filip and took the bottle from him to pour his own glass. Willa then turned to Elodie. "Is someone going to tell me what happened?"

"George attacked," Elodie answered. She pulled out a chair and sank heavily into it.

Filip downed his whiskey. "We thought she might, and we planned for it."

"We went to the manor looking for you," Scott told Theo. "We've already filled in Rhona and the others."

Theo leaned a shoulder against the wall. "I'm all ears."

Willa sat as she listened to the story, shocked at George's audacity. "Dad wasn't there?"

"Broc has his trail. He has to keep breaking through whatever is shielding your dad from him, but he'll keep looking," Scott said.

"I hope so," she murmured.

Elodie closed her eyes and dropped her head back against the chair. "Were things quiet here, at least?"

Theo's gaze bore into Willa. She stared back, waiting for him to say something.

"Willa?" Scott asked as he looked between them. "What is it? What happened?"

Theo pushed away from the wall. "I need to get back to Ferne. We'll talk later."

She waited until Theo was gone before looking at her brother. "I'm healed."

"What?" Elodie asked in surprise as she jerked upright. "That's awesome."

But Scott's face remained impassive. "It can no' be that great if Theo looked that troubled. What did it cost Emilie?"

"Nothing," Willa answered.

Elodie's brows slowly drew together. "I don't understand. She told you there was a price."

"Please tell me she isna dead," Filip murmured.

Willa glared in his direction for a heartbeat. "Emilie is fine and well. She's not harmed."

"Because she didn't heal you," Scott stated.

Leave it to her brother to put the pieces together. "She didn't."

"Then...who did?" Elodie asked as she looked at Scott in confusion.

The look in Scott's blue eyes intensified as he stared at her. "Willa. Who?"

"Jasper."

Scott didn't bellow in anger or jump up in shock. He simply continued to stare. And somehow, that was so much worse.

Willa glanced at the table. "He went to Emilie to ask her how to do it."

"Why would he even try?" Filip asked cynically.

It wasn't her story to tell, but Willa knew they wouldn't relent until she told them. "His father was killed with ebony wood. Emilie said that was how he could feel mine."

"Why didn't you tell us sooner?" Elodie asked her.

A muscle ticked in Scott's temple. "Why did he no' try sooner? Why make you sit in pain?"

Willa shrugged, still amazed the pain was gone and that Jasper had succeeded. "It isn't like that. I just found out he could feel the ebony. He touched my shoulder the other day, and my pain was gone. But it came back."

"When you got sick with the fever."

Willa slid her gaze to Scott and nodded. "Aye."

"And you let him do it again?" her brother asked, his voice wobbling with fury.

"Before we knew there were repercussions, aye."

Elodie rested her arms on the table, confusion clouding her eyes. "Why would you do it after you knew?"

"I shouldn't have. I know that, but I wanted to live. Jasper took precautions against any backlash from the wood. Emilie told him what to do, and I trusted he could." Willa moved her arm. "And he did. Look."

Scott stood, rage rolling off him. "Where is he?"

Willa had hoped Scott wouldn't ask that question. She wanted to speak to Jasper before anyone else. She looked her brother in the eye and lied. "He'll be back in a couple of hours. He needed to rest."

"You should've waited for me," Scott said. "If anything had gone wrong... Do you know what I...?" Scott shook his head and stalked from the room.

Elodie's expression was bleak as she got to her feet. She said nothing before following Scott into their bedroom, the door closing behind her.

"Well," Filip said as he put the whiskey back into the cabinet. "That's my cue to go home." He paused beside the table on his way out. "That wasna well done of you, Willa. No' when we're still looking for Luke. You should've waited for Scott."

She raised a brow and lifted her chin. "We'll see how well you do if your life is ever hanging in the balance."

Willa stood and put her back to him. She didn't move until she heard Filip drive away. Willa showered and quietly dressed while listening to the soft voices coming from down the hall. She couldn't make out their words but could guess the topic.

She turned off all the lights and sat in the dark. Willa didn't have long to wait before the cottage grew quiet. She took Scott's keys and slipped out of the house. It was after two in the morning when she pulled into Jasper's driveway. The lights were on, but she didn't see movement in the house.

Willa walked up the path and knocked on the door. She waited before knocking a second time. A shadow from within came toward the door, and she was able to make out Jasper's silhouette. He was slow to unlock the door and even slower to open it. Even then, it was only a crack. He had changed into jeans and a T-shirt.

"Why did you leave?" she asked.

He wouldn't meet her gaze. "You should go back."

"Are you hurt? Were there repercussions? Tell me. I'll help."

"I'm fine."

She tried—and failed—not to let his words hurt her. "Then why didn't you stay? I expected to see you when I woke."

"It's better this way."

"Nay."

He sighed, finally lifting his gaze to meet hers. "You need to rest. So did I."

"We could've rested together. Unless you don't want to be with me."

A muscle ticked in his jaw. "I never said that."

"You left. That says quite a lot."

He exhaled. "You should go."

She moved closer to the door. "Tell me why. I need to know what you're doing after our kiss. Because it wasn't just any kiss. It was so much more."

He was silent.

"Let me in, Jasper. I want to make sure you're okay. I'll never forgive myself if you're hurt because of me."

He looked away again. "I'm the last person you should worry about."

"Too bad. I'm here because I want to be. Don't push me away."

Seconds ticked by before he held open the door for her to enter. Willa walked past him, knowing she had just won a huge battle, but she wasn't quite sure about what. All she knew was that if she didn't get inside the house, she might never see him again. And that simply wouldn't do.

"How is your arm?" he asked as he walked barefoot around her.

She followed him into the living room. He didn't sit, so neither did she. "Better. But you already knew that." When he didn't say more, she said, "Tell me why you left."

He blew out a breath and looked away. "I told you. I needed rest."

"That's shite. The truth, Jasper. I think I deserve that. You asked me to trust you. I put my life in your hands. Why can't you treat me as if I've earned your trust?"

He stared at the floor before his gaze slid back to her. "It's better this way."

"Better for you or me?"

"Both of us."

He was lying, but she didn't know why. The easy, relaxed demeanor she had come to know and expect had been replaced by rigidity and strain. He was shutting her out. But why? "Did I do something?"

"Nay," he answered, shaking his head.

"Then it has to be backlash from the ebony wood." She moved toward him.

He put up his hands and turned away. "Stop." Jasper took a couple of steps, his hand running through his hair. His voice was tight as he said, "I'm no' harmed. I'm hale and hearty."

Another lie. She walked to him and softly laid her palm on his back. He jerked at the contact, his muscles tensing beneath her hand, but he didn't pull away. She watched his face reflected in the windows. The longing she saw pierced her straight through the heart.

"You've saved me twice. That is a debt I can never repay." Willa walked around him, trailing her hand after her. She stopped before him and let her arms drop. Then she stepped back until she met the windows. "I can't stop thinking about our kiss. I can't stop thinking about *you*. Or how you make me feel. Do you want me to tell you? I ache to feel your hands on my skin. I crave your hard body pressing into mine."

"Willa. Doona," he begged.

She saw the muscles in his jaw tighten. He didn't want her to say more, but she had to. For the passion she felt, for the possibilities.

"My blood heats whenever I think of you. I get wet when I think of your hard cock sliding inside me."

He shook his head, his hands fisting. His voice was ragged as he whispered, "Stop."

"Tell me you don't think about me. Tell me you don't think of me naked." She cupped her breasts. "That you haven't imagined teasing my nipples with your hands until I'm begging to feel your mouth on me."

His breathing quickened. His dark eyes glinted with yearning as he stared.

"Tell me you don't think about the kiss. Tell me you don't want me, and I'll leave," she pushed.

His nostrils flared. "I can think of nothing but you."

A thrill shot through her. She swallowed as her stomach

quivered in anticipation. She hadn't come here for this. Or perhaps she had. "What do you feel?"

"Feel?" he repeated as he closed the distance between them.

She found it difficult to breathe when he placed one hand on the glass by her head and ran the backs of his fingers of his other down her cheek. Then he leaned toward her.

"Aye," she said, her voice cracking with exhilaration.

His cheek brushed hers. "I feel…"

"What? What do you feel?" She had to know.

"A need to touch every inch of your body," he whispered. His lips brushed her forehead. "A yearning to hold you." His breath fanned her other cheek. "A craving to be inside you."

Her knees trembled so badly she didn't think they would hold her much longer. She put her hands on his chest as his fingers caressed her throat and jaw. "What do you want?"

"I want it all." His thumb brushed her lower lip as their gazes met. "I want you."

"I'm yours."

CHAPTER TWENTY-SEVEN

SKYE DRUIDS

Two words. That was all it took to break the last of Jasper's restraint. Willa was the very air he breathed, the woman he craved above all else. And she wanted him.

She was offering herself to him.

All the reasons to push her away, to get as far from her as he could, went up in the flames of desire. He stared into her blue eyes. He'd been such a fool to think he could guard his heart against her. She had seen him, had shown him the sun. Emilie had been right. He loved Willa. He wished it wasn't true, but he could no longer deny it. He knew better than to get tangled with his mark. It had never happened before. Then again, no one had ever been Willa.

Beautiful, dazzling, spirited Willa.

Jasper drew in a shaky breath, his eyes closing briefly as he fought not to take her lips. He reached up and tugged the tie holding her hair. The gorgeous, thick curls tumbled free. He dropped his hands to her waist and returned his gaze to hers. Then he slowly caressed upward, lifting her arms until he had them held over her head.

Her pulse beat rapidly at her throat. Her lips were parted, her breaths coming fast. Jasper moved a leg between hers, pushing her more fully against the window. She sighed softly. How many times had he envisioned taking her? Making her cry out with pleasure?

He held her wrists with one hand and gradually moved his other down her arm and along the side of her breast toward her leg. He bent slightly to hook his hand under her knee and drew it up. His eyes dropped to her mouth, begging for a kiss. He ground his aching rod against her. Her eyes slid shut as she moaned, her head dropping back against the glass. His hand tightened on her leg while he bent and kissed her exposed neck.

"Jasper," she whispered seductively.

He kissed her throat and along her jaw, then looked down at her. Her lids lifted, and she stared at him. He couldn't believe someone like Willa existed. She looked at him with such trust and conviction she made *him* believe it. She made him want to be a better man, the kind she believed he was.

And as long as he was with her, he *was* that man.

He had been given this one night, and he wouldn't let it pass him by. He didn't deserve her, but he wasn't capable of turning her away. He'd face whatever the morning brought. But tonight was theirs.

Jasper groaned when she rubbed against him. He took her lips, pouring all of his longing and the desire coursing through him into it. A storm of yearning and need swept him away. If he only had one night, he would make it one neither of them would ever forget.

He released her hands and lifted her as he turned from the

window. Her arms immediately came around his neck. He didn't stop kissing her as he made his way through the house and up the stairs to his room. When he reached the bed, he stopped and slowly released her legs, lowering her until she stood. He leaned back long enough to reach behind him and tug off his shirt before tossing it aside.

"Oh," Willa murmured, placing her hands on his chest, her eyes roaming over his upper body.

Jasper closed his eyes and fisted his hands at his sides. Her touch was exquisite. Everywhere her fingers traced left a trail of heat that burned straight through his flesh and into his soul. She smoothed her hands over his shoulders, along the backs of his arms, up to his chest, and down his stomach. Then she stopped.

His eyes flew open to find her removing her sweatshirt. His gaze lingered on the purple bra with black lace that covered her breasts. His balls tightened at the sight of the ample swells. Before he could reach for her, she bent to take off her shoes. She calmly set them aside and straightened.

Their gazes clashed. A small smile turned up her lips. Then her hands were at the waistband of her jeans. Jasper's lungs locked as he watched her extract her shapely limbs from the garment until she stood in only her matching bra and panties.

He practically tore his jeans to get out of them. He was about to remove his boxer briefs when she shook her head. He frowned, but she smiled. Jasper quickly forgot about them as he ran his eyes over her body.

No words could describe her loveliness. He closed the distance between them and gently ran a finger from her shoulder to her elbow. He saw goose bumps rise in the wake of his movements. He shifted his attention to her hair, wrapping a large curl around his finger before releasing it. Only then did he place his hands on her sides and stroked down to the indent of her waist and over her hips.

She gripped his arms, her head rolling back to expose her neck. He splayed a hand across her lower back to hold her firmly. Then, he kissed her. Deeply, fervently. Completely. The fire licking at him roared, devouring him.

He reached to unhook her bra when she ended the kiss to look at him.

Nothing had ever felt so right as it did right now with Jasper. The passion between them was too great to be ignored. He was the only thing she wanted. He had been there in her darkest days and never wavered. Jasper had been a constant, giving her hope when all was lost.

And in his arms, she would find paradise.

She couldn't stop touching him. His body was perfection. All hard sinew she would learn every inch of. She caressed the rippling muscles of his arms, chest, and washboard stomach.

Willa looked up to find him observing her. The desire in his eyes made her stomach tremble with eagerness. She slipped a finger into the waistband of his boxers. His chest expanded as he sucked in a breath. She slid a digit from her other hand into the other side and then slowly pulled the fabric down over his trim hips.

His arousal sprang free. Her lips parted as she stared at his hard length and squatted to take his boxers down to his feet. She slowly straightened, running her hands up his legs and pausing right before touching his cock. His breathing was harsh, matching the pounding of her heart. Then she wrapped her fingers around him. A low groan rumbled through his body. This man was like a drug. The more she had of him, the more she wanted.

The more she *needed*.

She rubbed her fingers up and down him, relishing the smooth feel of his warm skin against the steel beneath. Until his hands gripped her arms. Her eyes flew open just as his mouth crashed into hers. Passion erupted in a blaze of need and hunger. The kiss was fierce and scorching. She soon turned to putty in his hands, her body throbbing for his touch. For all of him.

The kiss ended as abruptly as it had begun. She blinked open her eyes to find she now faced the bed. Jasper sat on the corner of it, his hands holding her hips. She could barely stand, but he didn't seem as affected by the kiss. She licked her lips and tasted him there. She watched his face, half in moonlight, half in shadow.

Then his hands moved over her skin. His touch was light, but it only made her crave more of him. He drew her between his legs until her body met his chest. He tilted his face up to her. She placed her hands on his cheeks. The bristles of his beard rubbed against her palms. It shocked her how easily and quickly her life had become intertwined with his. This was the start of something —the first step down a long road.

Her bra loosened. His lips curved into a sexy smile as she let the straps fall from her shoulders before she tossed the garment to the side. Her already-hard nipples tightened even more under his heated gaze. She moaned when he cupped her breasts. A shiver ran through her as his thumbs grazed her tightened buds.

Then his lips were on her. He suckled, each pull sending desire straight to her center. She clutched at him, her legs shaking, her sex throbbing. It felt so good. She wouldn't be able to wait much longer. She needed him inside her—every wonderful, thick inch of him.

She rocked against his chest. His fingers tightened on her hips briefly, and then he tugged her panties down. She stepped out of them, only to find him hauling her onto his lap. She straddled him, their bodies finally skin to skin with nothing in between. Their gazes met, each seemingly lost in desire and its siren's song. His large hands tangled in her hair, holding her head as he kissed her into oblivion.

Willa would be the death of him, but Jasper couldn't think of a better way to exit the world than in her arms. He couldn't get enough of her kisses or her hands on him. He burned for her, for the bliss that awaited them both.

He held her tightly as he flipped them so she lay on the mattress. He settled between her legs but didn't enter her. Not yet. He wanted her screams of pleasure first. Jasper tore his lips from hers and trailed kisses down her chest to her breasts. He flicked his tongue across a turgid peak before continuing down her chest and belly until he knelt on the floor.

She lifted her head to watch him. He spread her legs wider, holding her gaze as he lowered his mouth to her.

Willa arched her back at the first swipe of his tongue against her center. A cry ripped from her lips when he found her clit, circling it again and again. The pleasure was almost more than she could bear. It moved through her, hot and thick. All while her center ached with need.

His tongue was magic, knowing just how much pressure to use and how to lick to bring her to the pinnacle and keep her hovering on the edge. She wanted it to end. She wanted it to last forever. Nothing could feel this good.

Then he thrust a finger inside her. The friction nearly sent her over the edge. She jerked, her body stiffening, but the orgasm stayed just out of reach. He slid his digit in and out, still. Dancing his tongue around her swollen clit. So close. She was so close. Willa sought the release, but it eluded her.

Until Jasper added a second finger. Two pumps of his hand were all it took for her to shatter. The climax swept over her in a wash of white-hot bliss. Waves of ecstasy rolled through her, bringing her higher and higher.

Jasper couldn't take his eyes off Willa as he watched the euphoria sweep through her. Her body convulsed around his fingers before it gradually subsided. Her breaths were harsh and rapid, her body limp.

He rose over her and moved her higher onto the bed. Her eyes were locked on him, desire reflected in her blue depths. She pulled his head down for a slow, hungry kiss, then wrapped a leg around him. He knew what she wanted. He wanted it, too. And he couldn't wait any longer.

Jasper grabbed a condom from the bedside table. He'd never torn open a wrapper or gotten a rubber on so quick. He brought his arousal to her entrance and slowly rubbed himself against her wet, swollen flesh. She moaned, her leg tugging him toward her. He rubbed his finger around her clit just to hear her moan. Her eyes rolled back in her head, and her hands fisted the covers. Fuck, she was beautiful.

His balls tightened, and his cock jumped. His control snapped. He gradually pushed inside her. Her gaze was locked on his face. She felt so damn good. Hot and wet. He moaned, fighting to keep from burying himself in her with one thrust. He gave her body time to adjust to him, moving inch by agonizing inch. With one final push, she took all of him.

Her groan mixed with his. Their bodies were slick with sweat and easily slid against each other when he began moving. She locked both legs around him, and his tempo quickly increased until he drove into her soft body over and over. He braced his hands on either side of her head and thrust hard and deep, each drive bringing him closer to release.

Every nerve ending was awash with ecstasy. There was no him, no her. Their bodies were joined, their souls locked, fused. Thoughts scattered as the pleasure built quickly. There was no holding back now. He was too far gone. He thrust deep once more and shouted as he climaxed. Her body contracted around him, milking him as another orgasm rocked her. The rapture was so intense, so pure, that it took his breath away.

As they lay entwined in each other's arms, all he could think about was how bereft his world would be without Willa in it.

CHAPTER TWENTY-EIGHT

SKYE DRUIDS

Willa woke on her stomach with Jasper placing kisses down her spine. She sighed as his mouth made its way to her neck before he nipped at her earlobe and settled his weight atop her. His hard length rested against her, making her moan with need.

"Och, woman, you've no idea what you do to me," he whispered.

She had some idea. He did the same to her.

His long fingers slid against her face as she turned her head toward him. "I burn for you," he said between kisses along her jaw.

Willa turned in his arms until they were on their sides facing each other. She touched his cheek, her heart tripping over itself as she looked into his fathomless dark eyes. "Then we'll burn together."

Their lips met in a fiery kiss wrought with passion and a longing so vast there was no stopping it. Not that she ever would. There was a man in her arms she hadn't believed existed, one she hadn't even dared to dream about. But he was real—flesh and blood.

He rolled her onto her back and fondled her breasts. She sank her fingernails into his back when he tweaked a nipple between his thumb and forefinger. As good as it felt, she wanted her turn at his body. If Willa didn't stop him now, she wouldn't be able to. She pushed at Jasper's shoulder, but he didn't move.

She shoved harder, rolling them both until he was on his back. He smiled up at her, excitement flashing in his eyes. She splayed her hands on his chest as she straddled his hips. Then she slowly straightened to look down at him. His smile faded as yearning darkened his expression. His hands settled on her hips and caressed up her body to cup her breasts. She dropped her head back when he thumbed her nipples.

Willa began rocking her hips over his shaft. His groan was low and long. She covered his hands with hers. Her head lifted, and she caught his gaze. She recognized the hunger reflected in his eyes because it thrummed feverishly through her.

She bent over him, her hair falling like a curtain on either side of his face. He sank his fingers into her curls. She brushed her lips over his, then took his bottom lip between her teeth. She grinned and lightly pulled. He moaned and rocked his length against her. Willa kissed him then. His hands moved from her hair to her head, holding her tightly as he deepened the kiss.

He stole her breath and commanded her body with merely a look. His touch could turn her to mush, and his kisses consumed her. If she had the power, they would stay locked like this for eternity—just the two of them sheltered from the world.

Willa tore her mouth from his. There were other parts of him she wanted to kiss. She briefly met his gaze before sliding down his body. Everywhere her hands touched, her lips and tongue followed —his broad shoulders, brawny arms, muscular chest, and defined stomach. He didn't stop her explorations, but he never took his eyes off her. By the time she reached his hips, his breaths were hard and shallow.

She kneeled between his legs and smoothed her hands down his powerful thighs. His hard cock lay against his stomach, jumping as if urging her to touch it. She leaned over him, her eyes lifting to his face as she let her breath rush over his arousal. His stomach tightened in response.

His entire body went rigid, his hands fisting the covers when she licked from base to tip. Willa took him in hand, holding him gently as she wrapped her lips around him. Jasper's eyes slid closed as he whispered her name in a voice raw with passion. It made her stomach quiver and her sex clench greedily.

She moved her mouth up and down his length and ran her tongue across the tip to tease him as ruthlessly as he had her earlier. He moaned, urging her on. Willa focused everything on bringing him the kind of pleasure he had wrung from her. She took him deep into her mouth and cupped his ball sac with her other hand.

"Fuck, Willa," he ground out, his body so rigid she thought he might snap in two.

Suddenly, he pulled her up to straddle him once more. She didn't know how he had gotten the condom out of the wrapper and on in that time. Then he lowered her onto his thick length, and she didn't care. It was her turn to sigh at the feeling of him filling her.

He had one hand splayed on her back while the other tangled

in her hair. He waited until their gazes clashed. Then he began moving. Their need, their craving, engulfed them. She matched his rhythm. Their bodies slid against each other, and their lips soon connected. Tongues moved in time with their bodies, sending her spiraling effortlessly toward a climax.

It came swiftly, rushing through her. She tore her lips from Jasper's and cried out. His arms tightened around her, his hands almost too tight as he threw his head back and shouted her name.

Willa was slow to come down. Tremors continued racking her body, even as Jasper pulled out of her. She fell back to sleep almost immediately, waking only long enough to move her head onto his chest when he returned to bed, his arm around her.

Jasper had never been so sated. But there would be no sleep for him. Willa rested comfortably against him. She felt good there. He wanted to remember every detail of their night because this glorious, extraordinary time would be over in a few hours.

He was done. With Skye. With George. With the life he'd led up to this point. He could no longer look at himself in the mirror because what he saw sickened him. If he had been someone different, he could've had a life with Willa. A real one. Not merely pretending as he had been. Though he'd realized too late that he hadn't been faking at all with Willa. His life of trickery and deception was finished. He didn't know what he would do, but he'd figure it out. Somehow.

The minutes ticked by too speedily. Jasper didn't want to think about his past, but he couldn't contemplate his future, either. It would be bleak, utterly desolate, without Willa. He wasn't sure how he would get through each day without her. But once she knew the truth, she wouldn't want him in her life. And he wouldn't blame her for that. She deserved so much more than him. She deserved the best of everything.

He kissed the top of her head and lightly ran his fingers down her back. If he hadn't loved her before, he did now. Completely. Undeniably. It didn't matter when his heart had gotten tripped up. It had, and there was no changing it, even if he wanted to. All he could do was tell her everything. He wasn't sure what would be more difficult: telling her who he really was or leaving.

But he owed her both for his part in all of it.

Jasper squeezed his eyes closed, his throat clogging with emotion. He wasn't worthy of her. He never should've let tonight happen, but he'd been too weak to refuse her. *One night*, he'd told himself. It was just one night to hold in his memories to look back on.

Instead, it would haunt him for the rest of his days. Because he knew what it was to hold Willa, to love her. To *be* loved by her. Nothing could torture him more than knowing he could never be with her and that she would loathe him. He deserved it. He'd earned whatever she said and did. He would make it as right as he could. It wouldn't erase the bad, but perhaps she might not hate him quite as much.

As for George, there would be repercussions for abandoning her. She would send someone after him, just as she had with Scott and the others. The difference was, he would be expecting the attack. And she'd have to find him first.

Jasper wasn't sure if anyone on Skye would retaliate. They had bigger troubles, but that didn't mean one of them wouldn't go looking to exact revenge. He could imagine that person being Scott. He'd never liked Jasper, and with good reason. Willa should've listened to her brother.

The one who really concerned him was Beth. She had her own plans, and he didn't know her well enough to guess what they might be. She hated those on Skye just as much as George did. Maybe even more. Beth would come for vengeance. As long as she had the book, she posed a serious threat to anyone on the isle.

Jasper was good at blending in when the need called for it. He could find Beth and follow her. She'd never even know he was there. He might even be able to stop her. Or, at the very least, slow her down. When her sights turned to Skye, he'd warn those here. He just hoped someone on the isle would listen when he did. He hadn't exactly earned their trust.

All too soon, he saw the sky lightening, signaling the approaching dawn. He willed it to stop, but no one had the power to do that. And with the sunrise came a new day. He looked down at Willa and felt his eyes well with tears. He might not have been a good man when he arrived, but he would be when he departed Skye. And it was all because of her.

The first rays of the sun hit his window, and with them came birdsong. He used to look forward to their tunes each morning, but not today. His few months on Skye hadn't nearly been enough. He wanted more. That was usually the way, though, wasn't it? He kissed Willa's head again and slowly extracted himself from her. She curled into herself. He covered her and stood as a tear fell down his cheek.

Jasper swiped it away and left the room. He had much to do before Willa woke. He dressed and grabbed his phone. He saw

four missed calls from George and six texts. He ignored them all
and walked outside.

"You're up early," Ferne said as she walked into the kitchen. When
Theo didn't say anything, she finished tying off her robe and
turned to the table where he sat with his laptop. "Honey?"

He ran a hand through his hair and shook his head. "Saber
texted."

"About?" If Saber had sent something this early, it couldn't be
good.

Theo turned to her, his brown eyes troubled. "Jasper McCabe."

"What about him?" she asked as she walked to the table and
sat in the chair beside him.

"I asked Saber to look into Jasper a few days ago. My search
through the police computers brought up nothing, but I had a
nagging feeling something wasn't right."

"Saber found something, I take it?"

Theo's face was bleak as he shook his head. "Saber dug up a
mountain of info. Jasper is a grifter. Saber found over forty aliases
for him."

Ferne sat back in the chair, deflated. "You're kidding."

"I wish I were. I've been going through each of them. He's
good, Ferne. I never found anything because he's never been
arrested."

"Who do you think he's here for?"

Theo's lips flattened as he met her gaze. "Willa."

"Then he's connected to George."

"He is. Saber found that, too."

Ferne's stomach clenched in dread. "Bloody hell."

"That's not the worst."

"What could be worse?"

Theo turned the computer screen toward her.

"Oh, God," she murmured as she read the page.

"Get dressed. We need to talk to everyone immediately."

CHAPTER TWENTY-NINE

SKYE DRUIDS

Willa rolled onto her back to stretch. She opened her eyes, a grin forming when she saw where she was. She reached for Jasper, but his spot was cold. She stretched again, wincing at the soreness in her body. She didn't mind it, though. Who would after the night she'd had?

She pushed aside the covers and stood. Willa found her clothes and took them into the bathroom. She dressed, splashed her face with water, and tried to do something with her wild hair. She finally gave up and knotted it atop her head before going to find Jasper. Her stomach growled. She hoped he was making breakfast. It had been a fantasy of hers. After all the times she'd seen a lover making breakfast in movies and shows, she'd dreamed of it happening to her. Jasper definitely seemed the type.

Her smile slipped when she reached the kitchen, only to find it empty.

"Jasper," she called.

She searched the downstairs before realizing he was probably with the horses. Looking out the window, she saw a horse trailer near the stables. She found Jasper standing off to the side as a man led White from the stables to the trailer. Willa hurried from the house, but she didn't make it in time. The horse trailer drove away as she reached Jasper.

"Where is White going?" she asked.

He stared after the trailer. "To her new home."

"What?" She couldn't have heard him right.

Willa blinked when Jasper started toward the house. She glanced at the paddock where the other horses should be. They weren't there. She swung her head to Jasper before running to the stables. It was empty. She checked the other pasture, but the horses weren't there either. All of them were gone.

Her heart thumped wildly as she raced to the house. Jasper stood in the kitchen, leaning against the counter in a corner, vacantly staring at the floor. Was she dreaming? Surely, this nightmare couldn't be real.

"Why are the horses gone?" she asked.

He shrugged. "I couldna leave them here."

Her gut twisted. She told herself not to ask, but the word was already past her lips. "Meaning?"

"I'm leaving."

It *was* a nightmare. She couldn't have had the best night of her life, only to wake to this the following day.

"You should sit," Jasper said.

She shook her head. "Tell me what's going on."

He lifted his gaze to her. "I'm going to tell you. But you should sit."

"Say whatever you need to say."

A muscle bunched in his jaw. He looked away, and she saw his eyes closing. When he looked back at her, resolve had settled over him. "I'm no' who you think I am. It wasna an accident that I found you when you reached Skye. I was waiting."

Willa started shaking. Her eyes blurred with tears. This had to be some cruel joke. Even as she thought it, she knew it wasn't. She wanted to deny it, to cover her ears with her hands and run away, but her feet were rooted to the spot. There was no escape here.

"I was told you'd have a minor wound," Jasper continued. "There was nothing minor about what they did to you."

Realization dawned. Her throat was so tight she had to force her words out. "You're working with George."

"I was. She sent me to spy for her. Things changed when you and Luke went after Beth's book. George asked me to get close to you and get your brother and their group to trust me."

Willa was going to be sick. She tried to pull out the chair to sit, but it wouldn't budge. Jasper started to help, but she held up a hand. She couldn't have him close to her. Not now. "Nay. Stay back." She finally got the chair out and dropped heavily into it. This couldn't be happening.

"You've no reason to believe me, Willa, but I need you to know that I had no idea they would use ebony wood. I never would've been party to that."

"But everything else you are involved in?" she demanded angrily.

He glanced away. "I'm a grifter. I con people out of money. I'm particularly skilled at getting close to people."

"And making them trust you," she bit out.

"Aye."

This couldn't be happening. It just couldn't. She never would've fallen for that. She would've seen right through such a trick. Willa squeezed her eyes shut when she thought about how she had practically thrown herself at Jasper. She had been the one to push things between them from the very beginning. She had made it so easy for him. God, what a fool she was. How he must have laughed at her.

"I never took money from anyone who couldna afford it. And I never took all they had."

She shook her head. She didn't want to hear any of it. Hot tears ran down her face. She couldn't breathe, couldn't think. "What's your real name?"

"Jasper. We had so many different surnames growing up that I doona know if any of them were real. My father never told me."

Willa could no longer look at him. To think that she had given herself to him the night before, that she had thought they had a future.

"I'm sorry, Willa. I've done some bad things but being a part of taking another's life was never one of them. I had to free you of the ebony wood."

She swiped at tears that wouldn't stop falling. "Was anything you told me true?"

"More of it than I've ever told anyone, actually."

"As if I can believe that."

He blew out a breath. "Nay. I doona suppose you can. My father did die from ebony wood. It's why I was so angry at George for using it on you. It's why I wouldna rest until you were free of it."

"And get close to me in the process." She cut him a look. If only the regret lining his face could be believed.

He licked his lips. "I could've left without telling you anything.

I chose to stay. I chose to reveal all of this so you and your friends can prepare yourselves for George."

"I'm going to fucking kill him," Scott said as he paced the room at Carwood Manor.

Elodie blocked the door so he couldn't walk away. "You aren't going to do anything. That's up to Willa."

"The hell it is!" Scott shouted.

Rhona held up her hands. "I understand you're upset. We all are at this news."

"That's my sister," Scott stated. "And she's over there right now."

Filip twisted his lips. "Then we take this to her and show her. We confront Jasper."

"I'm not sure that's a good idea," Sabryn said.

Finn grunted from his position against the wall. "I agree. If we gang up on him, things will likely get ugly."

"He needs to be held accountable for his involvement," Elias said.

Elodie glared at her brother when his words spurred Scott. She blocked Scott once more. "I don't disagree with that, but we need to be careful how we handle this."

"He got the ebony wood out of Willa," Carlyle pointed out.

Bronwyn shrugged a shoulder. "But he was part of those who inflicted that damage on her."

"What if he isn't?" Theo asked as he leaned his hands on the table.

Elodie's head was beginning to pound. She looked at Esther, Nikolai, and Henry, who stood together but hadn't spoken yet. "Theo, you and Saber brought this to us. Are you saying you don't think Jasper is guilty?"

"Of course, that isna what he's saying," Scott muttered.

Theo exchanged a look with Ferne. "What I'm saying is that I heard the worry in Jasper's voice when he called for me to stay with Willa."

"Not to mention him risking his life to help her," Balladyn pointed out.

Esther nodded in agreement. "That could've gone very badly for him."

"All right," Rhona said. "Let's say Theo's right. What do we do?"

Theo straightened. "We do what governments do. We flip him to our side."

The sight of Willa's tears was like a knife twisting in Jasper's heart. It was worse knowing he was the cause. He'd never wanted to hurt her, but that was all he had done. Maybe he should've just left. He could've written her a letter detailing everything. Why had he thought that saying it would be better? He must be a masochist.

"I didna have the strength to turn you away last night. I should've. I know that, but I couldna."

Revulsion contorted her face. "Stop."

He hid his wince. He deserved her hatred. "I'm leaving. You'll never see me again."

"Then go. The sooner, the better."

He pushed away from the counter and started past Willa. He paused at the table and looked at her, but she kept her face averted. It was pointless to say more. She wouldn't believe him. He had shattered everything. He'd earned her reproach. Jasper nodded and walked toward the garage just as someone banged on the front door.

He glanced at Willa, but her face was in her hands. He pivoted and went to the front. He opened it to find Scott glaring at him angrily with Theo beside him. There was a sea of faces behind them, but it didn't matter who all had come. He should've expected this. Jasper stepped aside and let them all enter. As soon as they saw Willa, they'd turn on him. He could slip out while they were occupied with her. She could tell them everything. But he wouldn't. He'd face whatever they doled out.

A tall, auburn-haired man paused beside Jasper. His gaze was as hard as steel, giving nothing away.

"Nikolai," the woman beside him called.

So, he was now face-to-face with a Dragon King. He was as imposing as Jasper expected him to be. Nikolai nodded and followed his mate.

Balladyn was the last one inside. The Reaper's red-ringed silver eyes were cool when they landed on Jasper. That's when Jasper realized they already knew who he was. He shut the door behind Balladyn and took a deep breath. Better get things over with. Jasper found everyone in the kitchen. Elodie spoke quietly to Willa while everyone else stared—or glared—at him. Curiosity and outright anger filled the room.

"Willa, you need to know who he is," Scott said, tossing a file on the table.

Pictures scattered from the folder. Jasper's heart clutched when he saw himself. Willa slowly stood as she opened the file folder and began moving photos around as she looked them over. Jasper didn't think he could feel any worse than he already did, but he was wrong.

"We know all about you," Theo said.

Jasper could see that. He wasn't sure how they had achieved it. It would've taken someone with special skills to go back as far in his life as they clearly had.

"The aliases, the fraud. What kind of psycho are you?" Scott demanded as he stalked to him.

Jasper did nothing when Scott poked him hard in the chest. Why should he? Everything was true. He'd always known he would eventually have to pay for his sins. Jasper just hadn't thought it would be in front of the woman he loved. Theo drew Scott away.

Jasper met the DI's gaze. "How did you find out about me?"

"Saber is a Knight," Sabryn said. "He can dig up anything that's out there."

A hacker. It was too bad Jasper hadn't known about this Saber before. "He's good, then. Because so am I."

Scott snorted. "You want to crow about being a con man who didn't get arrested?"

"Enough," Rhona said. She turned her green eyes to Jasper. "Why choose that kind of life?"

He shrugged. "It's what my father did. After my mother died, he took me with him on his jobs. It's all I've ever known."

"How young are we talking?" Finn asked, his brow furrowed.

Jasper released a breath. "Always. My mother died in childbirth."

"Sweet Jesus," Sabryn murmured.

Scott grabbed pictures from the table and flung them at Jasper. "You stole from people. You conned them out of money. What kind of person does that?"

Jasper could defend himself, but he didn't. The truth lay scattered all around him. The fact was, there was no excuse. So what if he only went after the rich? So what if he only took a little so they would be too embarrassed to call the police? It was still a crime. He still deceived people.

Unwittingly, his gaze moved to Willa. Her beautiful blue eyes were trained on him, new tears falling onto her cheeks. It gutted him all over again. He had told her who he was, but the photos showed everything his words had omitted in vivid Technicolor. He didn't want to look at the pictures, but he forced himself to view his life as the others were. And he didn't like what he saw.

Jasper slid his gaze to Scott. "If this was to keep Willa from me, you're too late. I already told her."

"Right," Scott said with a snort.

Balladyn asked, "Why did you tell her?"

Jasper drew in a breath and tried to ease the tightness knotting his shoulders. "Because I needed her to know the truth. About me and my involvement with George."

"At least you admit it," Filip stated.

Jasper ignored him and kept his gaze on Balladyn. "George sent me here to spy on all of you. Getting close to Willa came later, but things changed as soon as I saw they had used ebony wood. I intend to leave today. None of you will ever see me again. However, that plan was before you showed up. I'm no' working with George anymore. That said, I doona need to tell you to be careful. Especially of Beth."

"I have a proposition I'd like you to consider before you leave," Rhona said.

Jasper tensed. This was where they would tell him he wasn't leaving. That they had their own plans for him. No doubt Scott would have the first go at him. It wasn't as if Jasper could escape them now.

"Stay and work with us," Rhona continued. "Help us bring down George and Beth."

CHAPTER THIRTY

SKYE DRUIDS

Willa teetered on the edge of oblivion. The morning had exploded into a chaotic, frenzied whirlwind that didn't seem to have an ending in sight. She could barely grasp what Jasper had told her when the others arrived, throwing the storm into even more turmoil. She was getting bashed from all sides, scarcely able to hold herself together.

And now they wanted him to stay?

Jasper looked around the room in dismay. "You can no' be serious."

"Oh, they are," Scott replied indignantly. "I'm wholly against it, by the way."

Elias walked around the table. "You've seen for yourself what kind of leader George is. If she and Beth can go after Willa as they did, they'll do anything."

"I didna think George capable of that before." A muscle jumped in Jasper's jaw. "Beth, aye. I doona know about George anymore."

Scott threw up his hands before letting them fall to his sides. "Why are we even listening to this shite?" He spun on Jasper, grabbing him by the collar and slamming him into a cabinet. "Where's my father? What did they do with him?"

To her horror, Willa jumped to her feet as if she might defend Jasper. Then she remembered who he was.

The others pulled Scott from Jasper. His dark eyes swung to her. "I've asked. George says she doesna know."

"As if I can believe you." She raked her gaze over him, then turned to Rhona. "If you want to trust him, do so at your peril. I won't be a part of it."

"You have to," Jasper stated.

His words were like a slap. Willa slowly faced him. The shock was fading. Replaced by cold fury. "I don't *have* to do anything when it comes to you."

"I'm no' the only spy here," Jasper told the room. "There are others."

Scott crossed his arms over his chest. "Can you prove it?"

"Anytime Willa and I were together, and I didna call George immediately after, she contacted me. She knew where we had been and what we did. And she told me there were others here."

Nikolai leaned his hands on the back of a chair. "Looks like you and Willa need to keep up appearances."

"Nay," Willa stated.

Elodie touched her arm. "Think about bringing down George. Think about getting payback for what they did to you."

"I won't do it." And they couldn't make her.

Elias grunted. "I get it. I'd feel the same way. But think about your father. About finding him."

"Broc is on that," Scott said.

Esther's lips twisted. "There's no guarantee he can locate Luke, even with his powers. Our best course of action is through George and Beth."

Willa had been so mired in her emotions that she had forgotten about her father. She would do anything for her family—even work with the enemy. "Fine."

"It has to be believable. George and Beth can't know there's any dissent," Rhona said.

Willa lifted her chin. "I'll play my part. In public."

"I doona want Willa alone with him. Ever," Scott stated.

She turned to her brother and smiled tightly. "Don't worry. I won't be."

"Jasper, is this agreeable to you?" Rhona asked.

Willa refused to look at him. Scott walked to her and put a comforting arm around her. She just had to keep herself together until she was alone.

"Aye," Jasper answered.

Willa turned away and stalked out of the house. Everyone else could hammer out the details. She had to get out of there. She wanted a long, hot shower to scrub him off her. If only she could extract him from her memories as easily.

She fought against a wave of tears and accidentally bumped into Henry. She mumbled an apology and walked out of the house. She didn't stop until she reached Scott's vehicle. Willa yanked on the car door, but it was locked. She tried again in a desperate bid to get away.

"You forgot these."

She stilled at the sound of Sabryn's voice. Willa placed her hands on the window and lowered her forehead to the metal door. "What?"

"Keys. I'm not sure they'll do you much good since you're blocked in."

Willa turned her head to the side and saw the other cars. Could anything go right?

"You're not in the right frame of mind to drive anyway. Let me take you home," Sabryn offered.

"If you can get me out of here now, then fine."

"Give me a sec."

More tears threatened. It felt as if her entire chest had caved in. As if someone had ripped her open and viciously yanked out her heart. She'd had her fair share of sorrow, but this was something entirely new. And to think she had basked in things the night before.

"Come on," Sabryn said when she returned.

Willa blindly followed her to a vehicle and climbed inside. Then Sabryn was driving her away. If only it could be for the last time.

"I've been where you are," Sabryn told her after a few minutes of silence.

Willa stared out the window without seeing anything. "I doubt it."

"Close enough that I know what you're going through."

Willa turned her head to the American. "How did you get through it?"

"I didn't handle it well. I did stupid things. Don't turn the people who love you away. You'll need them eventually." Sabryn's deep blue eyes briefly met hers. "It'll be a long road."

"Are you past it?"

Sabryn was silent for several seconds. "I tell myself I am, and there are days I believe it."

"He told me to leave last night. I kept pushing. I didn't want to let what I felt for him go."

"We've all been there. Don't beat yourself up over it."

Willa snorted. "It was the best night of my life. And today is the worst."

"I'm not sure there's anything I can say that will make it better, but he did tell you himself."

Willa rolled her eyes, her anger spiking as she glared at Sabryn. "Why would he do that? He could've just left. I'd never have known."

"Guilt. Or…"

"Or what?"

"He cares."

Willa covered her face with her hands and shook her head. She lifted her head, dropping her arms to her lap. "That's crazy."

"He didn't fight any of us when we arrived. How many times did Scott get in his face? Jasper didn't retaliate. He didn't even move to defend himself."

"Why are you defending him?" Willa demanded.

Sabryn glanced her way. "I'm merely pointing out things I saw. Think about it. He was confronted with every bad thing he's done in his life by a group of people he'd been sent to spy on, along with the woman he spent the night with. How many people do you know who wouldn't have spewed a hundred different reasons or excuses to make themselves look good?"

"I don't know or care."

"You don't now because you're hurting. No one likes being confronted by every bad thing they've ever done, but he stood there and took it. Look, I'm not saying how he lived is right, but he owned up to what he's done. I'm not sure I would've done the same in his shoes."

Willa rubbed her temples to try and ease the throbbing headache. "He can't be trusted."

"He saved your life. Twice, I might add."

Unbidden, an image of Jasper leaning over her on the kitchen floor with determination and calm flashed in her mind. "For all we know, it could've all been part of the plan."

"Maybe."

"How am I going to walk around and act as if nothing happened?"

Sabryn met her gaze. "You'll do it for your father."

"Aye."

Sabryn put on her blinker and slowed the vehicle before turning. "Besides, we have Saber and a plan."

"A plan?"

"We all met at the manor and went over what Saber dug up before coming here. Scott and Filip are the only ones not completely on board. They'll be going over it now with Jasper. Saber will clone Jasper's phone so we'll know who he's talking to and what the conversation is about. We're also going to put a tracker on his vehicle. Cameras are being installed both inside and outside his home, as well as at Scott and Elodie's."

Willa leaned her head against the backrest. "You honestly think someone will come for us at the houses?"

"Nope. We're just being cautious."

Willa raised her brows and rolled her head to look at Sabryn. "Then how are we to be watched?"

"Scott wants Balladyn with you at all times. Veiled, of course."

"Ugh...I don't think so."

"Those were pretty much Balladyn's words." Sabryn shot Willa a grin. "Rhona's, too. Come to think of it, all of us thought that. But Scott's protective."

Willa nodded. "He always has been. Older brother and all that."

"You're lucky. The other option is to put a tracker on you and Jasper. If either of you are taken, we'll know where to find you."

"Tracker? Like electronic?"

Sabryn wrinkled her nose. "Actually, it'd be on the magical side."

"Such a spell exists?"

"We're trying to find one."

Willa shook her head. "What if we can't?"

"Then you might have a Reaper glued to your ass."

Willa glanced at Sabryn to see her smiling. She couldn't help returning it. "We have crazy lives."

"I wouldn't want it any other way. Could you see me working in an office cubicle somewhere? Naw. I've seen more of the world than most people dream about. Granted, it was hunting the vilest of our kind, but someone has to do it."

Willa needed to take a long, hard look at her life. "You don't mind living on the road?"

"I could say you get used to it, but you really don't. We don't have anywhere to put down real roots. Well, Elias does. And he and Bronwyn have opened the manor for us anytime we want it. Right now, we're needed here. It's nice to have some semblance of home. We always have each other, though. We're family. We argue like siblings, but we'd do anything for the others. They've saved my hide more times than I like to admit." Sabryn turned onto another road and glanced at Willa. "The job is dangerous, Willa. We go up against some really bad people. Sometimes, we get to save innocents, but other times, we get there too late. We rarely come out of a job uninjured. We all have numerous scars and body aches that will impair us sooner rather than later. In all likelihood, we'll die out there."

"Sounds like you're trying to talk me out of joining the Knights."

She shook her head of chin-length, black hair. "I'm not saying we wouldn't welcome additional help, but we know how each other works. We know one another's moves and thoughts. That comes from years of working together. But yeah, I don't want to romanticize what we do. It's dirty, hazardous, thankless work."

"Have you ever thought about giving it up?" Willa asked.

"This is my life. I've accepted that. The boys have shore leave, as I like to call it, and find a companion for a night or two."

"But not you?"

Sabryn's shoulders lifted as she inhaled. "Nope."

"What if you find someone like Elias did?"

Sabryn chuckled dryly. "That won't happen. As for the boys? Maybe. Finn has the absolute worst taste in women. I honestly don't know how he does it. Carlyle is all about sowing his wild oats."

"What about Saber?"

"I don't ask. He does his thing wherever he's at, and that's good enough for me."

"You mean you don't know where he lives?"

Sabryn pulled into the driveway and turned off the engine. "I couldn't even tell you what he looks like. And I don't care. My life doesn't look so grand now, does it?"

Willa met her gaze. "You have a family. I think that's something to celebrate."

"Agreed."

CHAPTER THIRTY-ONE

SKYE DRUIDS

Kirsi was breathing hard when she reached the summit. She bent over, bracing her hands on her knees as she sucked in air. Nothing had been the same since she'd come out of The Grey. Sleep was a thing of the past. Something in the shadows haunted her dreams—something that hunted her.

Something *she* should be pursuing.

She straightened and looked out over the land. Stormy clouds drifted above her while wisps of mist hung around the top of the mountain. Her parents kept asking her to talk to them, but she couldn't. She couldn't even face the truth herself. Besides, how would she tell them she wasn't just losing sleep? She couldn't eat, either. And worse, she was hallucinating.

Kirsi had thought about going to Rhona but quickly nixed the idea. A visit to Ariah's for some tea to help her sleep had been pointless. Not even Ariah's magic could help her now. Kirsi was afraid the only thing that would end her suffering was going back into The Grey. And that petrified her.

She sank to the ground and leaned against a rock. Maybe she should talk to someone. She hadn't been the only one to enter the realm between dimensions. Perhaps one of the others was having similar issues. It was wishful thinking, of course, but she needed something to grasp onto. Because she feared she was losing her mind.

Ferne had told her about her destiny. Perhaps she could help Kirsi. The woman had tried to talk to her before, and Kirsi had pushed her away, refusing to believe any of it. She had ignored and denied it. Maybe it was time she acknowledged the truth.

A low, rumbling growl came from behind her. The icy hand of fear wrapped around Kirsi's heart, squeezing it. She moved to her hands and knees and spun around. Then, she slowly stood to look over the rock.

Her stomach dropped to her feet when she found the day had turned to dusk. Mist hung lifeless and heavy, restricting her vision, but the eerie stillness made her tremble with stark terror. It was The Grey. Kirsi knew it was an illusion, but that didn't calm her racing heart.

She took a step back, only to halt at the next growl. It was here. The beast or creature or whatever it was that walked The Grey. It had tried to kill her friends. It would try to kill her unless she got to it first. But the thought of returning to the in-between world left her reeling.

However, she might make all this stop if she confronted the hallucination now. It wasn't real. She knew that.

Deep and malicious laughter rang out. "Oh, I'm very real. I've waited a long time for this. There's no running from me. Not when I've finally found you."

Kirsi whirled around and started running as fast as she could. She wasn't a warrior. She certainly couldn't save anyone. Her fear overrode common sense. The descent down the mountain was slick, and she was too intent on getting away to watch where she ran. She tripped, twisting her ankle and pitching forward. A cry tore from her when she landed heavily on her side and began to roll down the mountain.

Callum looked at his busted knuckles. There would be hell to pay later. For now, he would go somewhere no one thought to look for him. The approaching storm kept most off the hiking path. It should probably keep him away, too, but the best place for him was far away from others.

His head jerked up when he heard a shout. He spotted someone tumbling toward him, their body flung about like a rag doll. Callum hurriedly moved to intercept them. It was a crazy idea, but if he didn't, they would go off the side and fall twenty feet to the bottom.

He planted his feet, digging the toes of his boots into the rocky soil, and looked up, gauging the distance. They were coming at him fast. He leaned forward, praying he kept his footing. If he didn't, they would both go over the edge.

Callum reached out as the person drew nearer. He got a hold of their jacket and yanked them to a stop. There was another shriek, and he nearly lost his grip but somehow managed to keep his footing. Once he knew the person wasn't going anywhere, he went to see to their injuries.

His mouth fell open in shock when he looked into familiar eyes. "Kirsi?"

Her expression crumpled as she flung herself at him, her arms wrapping tightly around his neck. Callum stiffened. He wasn't sure what to do. Did he hug her? Pat her on the back? The sobs racking her body made his decision to wrap an arm around her loosely. No doubt the fall had terrified her, but he needed to see what kind of injuries she had sustained.

"It's okay," he told her. "You're safe."

She sniffed and loosened her arms before letting them fall away. He immediately dropped his from around her. She kept her face averted as she wiped at her cheeks. He picked some grass from her hair to give her time to calm herself. Finally, she turned her gaze to him.

"Thank you," she said softly.

"What hurts? Is there anything we have to tend to now? Do I need to carry you down?"

She shook her head, then winced. "I hurt everywhere, but I don't think anything is broken."

"Let's sit for a moment and let the adrenaline wear off." He sat beside her while eyeing her for blood. The silence was awkward, and he found he needed to fill it. "It's slippery out here. Anyone could've fallen."

Kirsi plucked more grass from her hair that had come out of her ponytail. "I wasn't paying attention. I shouldn't have come. I knew better, but I thought..."

"Thought what?" he pushed when she didn't finish.

She turned her head to meet his gaze. "Do you...do you dream about The Grey?"

Callum searched her face. He'd assumed her ashen pallor was

due to the fall, but what if it was because of something else? "Do you?"

"I asked first."

"I had a nightmare that first night."

"But none since?" she asked.

He shook his head. "None. You?"

"I can't sleep. It's there every time I close my eyes."

"It? You mean the creature?" They hadn't seen it, but he'd heard it. And that had been enough for him.

She nodded, looking away.

"Ariah—"

"Already tried," she interrupted. "Her tea does nothing."

Callum bent his knees to rest his arms on them. "Shite."

"Aye."

"Anything else?"

She cut her eyes to him but didn't turn her head. "Maybe."

He should press her about it, but he wouldn't. If she wanted to tell him, she would. "Have you spoken to the others?"

"Nay. I figured if I ignored it, things would get better."

He fought a grin at her sarcastic tone. "Has it?"

"I nearly fell to my death. What do you think?"

"Point taken."

She blew out a breath, rubbing her hands together. Then she shifted to him, her face creasing in pain. "Just some bruising," she said before he could ask. "I don't know why I'm going to tell you this, but I am. I have to talk to someone, and I'm just not ready to go to the others. Plus...you were with me then, and, well...now."

Callum wasn't the kind of person people trusted with things like this—whatever this was. He almost told her that but decided it might be better to just listen. If things were really bad, he'd go to Rhona himself. "All right."

"I'm seeing The Grey when awake."

He frowned and shifted to face her. "What do you mean you see it?"

"Like, I'm still in it. The dim light, the mist. The stillness."

A shiver ran down his back as he recalled those exact things from his short time there. It had been the stuff of nightmares. "How often?"

"It was sporadic at first, but I've seen it the last three days."

"When did it start?"

"The day after we got out of The Grey."

Callum ran a hand over his jaw. Then he saw her anxious look. "What else?"

"It happened before I fell, but there was more this time. The creature spoke to me."

"What?" he demanded.

She swallowed loudly. "I-I thought they were illusions, some kind of hallucination because of how freaked out I was about it. Then it said, '*Oh, I'm very real. I've waited a long time for this. There's no running from me. Not when I've finally found you.*'"

"Fuck me." Callum was terrified *for* her. "You need to tell the others. They'll know what to do."

She sighed. "I don't think they will."

"You shouldn't go through this alone."

"Actually, I'm very much on my own with this."

Callum glanced up the mountain where she had been. "I doona believe that."

"Did you know Ferne contacted me?" Kirsi slid her gaze to him. "In my head. While she was in London. She told me I was meant to find and destroy whatever was happening here. That I'd done it in past lives."

He opened his mouth, but the words stuck. Finally, he got out, "That thing in The Grey?"

"I don't know. Maybe. It might be something else. I know the being in The Grey wants me dead."

Callum ran a hand over his jaw.

She nodded. "Exactly. I had all of that in my head when she reached out to me mentally again."

"When she was trapped in The Grey."

"All I thought I needed to do was tell Theo where she was so he could find her. But as soon as we walked into Carwood Manor, something came over me."

He was there. He remembered it vividly. It had been Kirsi, but it also hadn't been her. "Someone else in your head?"

"More like I knew what I had to do. I didn't want to do it, but it had to be me."

He looked down as he thought about his decision to follow her up the stairs in the manor that day and then through the portal Bronwyn opened that led to a pocket of space between dimensions.

"You came with me," Kirsi said. "Why?"

Callum hesitated before lifting his head. "I doona know. I didna want to be there, either, but it…" He trailed off, trying to find the words.

"Felt right?" she supplied.

He nodded once. "Aye. But as we walked through The Grey, it became harder for me to lift my feet. It was like something was holding them down. Then you grabbed Ferne's soul and brought it out when no one else could. The closer I got to coming back here, the easier it was to walk."

"Really?" she asked with a frown.

"What about the fact that the being didna come near us?"

Her lips twisted. "I'm not going to think about that too much."

"You should. Especially since it's the thing you heard, right? If it wants you so badly, why did it no' do anything while we were there?"

"Something must have stopped it."

"Maybe it can no' harm you in The Grey."

She wrinkled her brow in confusion. "And it can here?"

"You're right, that doesna make sense."

"It didn't attack us, and it had plenty of chances." She carefully lifted her left ankle and gingerly touched it. "I have been wanting to ask you something."

He raised his brows, waiting.

"Did you know you could close the cut in the wall that separated the dimensions?"

"Nay."

"It seems we were both needed that night."

He got to his feet and held out his hand. "Right now, I'm more concerned about getting you off the mountain and that ankle seen to."

"I can walk on it."

Callum helped her stand, but the moment she put weight on her foot, she winced. There was only one way to get her down. He lifted her into his arms.

CHAPTER THIRTY-TWO

SKYE DRUIDS

Jasper stared out the window in the living room as he waited for the call to connect. The pastures looked wrong without the horses. The ringing finally stopped.

"Jasper," George's voice said through the speaker.

"George."

"Tell me you have good news. I really need some."

He didn't like the thread of apprehension he heard in her voice. "Why? What happened?"

"We tried to get Scott when he was at Luke's flat. I planned for Balladyn but not the others. Why didn't you tell me about the Warriors?"

Jasper pinched the bridge of his nose with his thumb and forefinger. "I'm still building trust with Willa. How was I to know they'd bring Warriors along? Besides, the Warriors were nothing but rumors. Are you sure it was them?"

"Well, I can attest that the Warriors are very real. Everything we've seen in the chat rooms since the big Fae battle on Skye just might be true. Warriors." She made an indistinct sound. "Do you have any idea how many people I lost?"

Jasper dropped his hand to his side. He could imagine, but that was on her for even thinking she could go up against a Reaper. "You always knew the Skye Druids were powerful. Looks like they have powerful friends. That changes things."

"It changes nothing."

"You can no' be serious. We're talking Warriors, George. Those Highlanders are immortal."

"Unless you remove their heads."

Jasper frowned. "You assume someone will get close enough to do that. We doona know enough about them to go up against them. How much of the myth is true?"

"Their skin changes colors. Each of them is different."

"How many are there?"

"You're going to find out. After all, Willa spent the night with you. You're making great progress."

He'd expected that. "I need to be invited into their exclusive group, remember?"

"You will be. Make sure of it."

"I have to take things slow. I can no' ask too many questions too quickly. It'll look suspicious."

"Do whatever you need to do but work fast. We have to strike when they least expect it."

"You just went after them in Edinburgh. They'll be on alert. Not to mention, if the Warriors were there, they might be here."

"Let me worry about that. By the way, why did you load up your horses this morning? I hope you're not planning to do anything stupid like run off."

"Why would I do something like that? I'm committed," he lied.

"See that you remain that way. Go continue your seduction of Willa."

The line disconnected. Jasper turned to find Elias and Balladyn watching him. "Did it work?"

Elias gave him a thumbs-up. "Saber got a clean link to George's mobile."

"Then you can go after her."

Balladyn shook his head. "Not yet."

"She's watching you, Jasper," Elias said as he got to his feet. "We have to be careful."

Balladyn crossed his arms over his chest and bowed his head to Jasper. "Good call getting everyone to leave after Willa."

"Luckily, you can teleport, or none of this would've worked," Jasper added.

Balladyn quirked a brow. "Why haven't you warded the house?"

"If someone wants in, they're going to get in regardless of what locks or wards I have," Jasper said.

Elias looked at Jasper. "Ready for the next step?"

He was well aware that no one trusted him. They wanted George, and they were willing to use him to get to her and Beth. Jasper could respect them for that. Balladyn and the Warriors had enough power to make him do whatever they wanted, but they had asked instead of forcing. No matter how he looked at it, the situation wouldn't turn out well for him.

Jasper's thoughts turned to Willa as they had throughout the day. He almost hadn't been strong enough to tell her when she came out of the house this morning. She would never again look at him with anything but disdain.

"You good, mate?" Elias asked.

Jasper walked past them to the bookshelf. He pushed aside some volumes and found the journals he had hidden. He turned and handed them to Elias. "This is all the research I've done."

"Research?" Balladyn asked.

Jasper shrugged one shoulder. "I study people and places. Always have. I take notes. Those contain everything I've learned about Skye. Most of my focus was on your group, but I did note other things. Also, there's a notebook dedicated to George and her organization."

Elias opened one of them and slowly flipped through the pages. "This is a lot of detail."

"I like to know my targets and the area."

Elias snapped the journal closed. "This will come in handy. You didna have to tell us about these. Why did you?"

"You would've found them eventually."

Balladyn walked over and put a hand on Jasper's shoulder. "It's time."

"Bend your knees," Elias cautioned.

Jasper opened his mouth to ask what he meant, but the next instant, he was in another room. He weaved as he attempted to adjust to the teleportation. It would've been nice if someone had warned him ahead of time what would happen.

"Welcome to Carwood Manor. Deep breaths. It'll pass soon," Elias said in a low voice.

Jasper nodded his thanks, but Elias had already walked away. Thankfully, the dizziness wore off quickly. Jasper was then able to look around the room. It was large, with two windows and three doors. One was open to a hallway where Theo spoke with Rhona.

Jasper scanned the room. Three whiteboards were at the back. One held a picture of a woman with a litany of crimes, including controlling the mist. The second board had *CLEARED* marked at the top with a list of names beneath it. The third board was empty. There were a few tables with seats and some chairs pulled off to the side. Within the room was the very group George had wanted him to infiltrate. Only one of the fourteen was missing—Saber.

Jasper caught sight of Willa sitting at one of the tables with Elodie. She had changed clothes. Her thick hair was down and hung in such a way as to prevent him from seeing her face. Had she done that on purpose? Probably.

"Okay, everybody," Theo said as he walked to the whiteboards.

Everyone's attention turned to the DI. Some took seats, others stood. Jasper remained standing at the back of the room, out of sight of most.

Theo tapped the second whiteboard with his knuckles. "As you can see, we've cleared all five of Rhona's deputies."

"What a relief," Rhona said.

Theo nodded his head. "For all of us. I'm also pleased to report that thirteen names will be added to this list. Between Saber's deep dives and the past two weeks of our surveillance, we're slowly making progress."

"With only thousands left to go," Filip said as Theo began writing names on the board.

Sabryn shrugged. "We had to start somewhere."

"It's better than what we had before." Theo snapped the cap back on the marker and set it down. "Elodie, Elias, you'll see that Edie's name is on the board."

Elodie exchanged a look with Elias. "We knew our sister wasn't involved."

Theo's gaze then turned to him. Jasper's journals were passed from Elias to Theo. There were pages of notes about everyone in that room. They could turn on him at any time. It's what George would do. It's what his father would've done. He half-expected these people to do it.

"Jasper has turned over the notes he made on us, Skye, and George," Theo told the room.

Elias leaned his chair back on two legs. "From what I read, he's thorough."

"I'd like to take a look," Finn said.

Theo handed the Irishman the notebooks. "Everyone will get a chance to look through them. Saber has cloned Jasper's phone. The cameras are up at Jasper's and will soon be finished at all our respective homes. Thanks to Jasper's call to George a little while ago, Saber uncovered her location and locked onto her mobile."

"Scott, Filip, and I already told you about the warehouse," Willa said.

Jasper slid his gaze to her. She sat stiffly as if being in the same room with him was tantamount to death. He had done that to her. Nothing he could ever say or do would erase the damage he'd inflicted. He'd done the same to countless others and never batted an eye. But he hadn't fallen in love with them.

"We did," Scott said. "But this will track her wherever she goes."

Balladyn spoke up then. "We need to figure out who is watching Jasper."

"I agree, but other things take priority. Getting Kerry to talk is high on the list. So is determining what the evil is over Skye," Rhona said.

Sabryn stretched out her long, black-clad legs and crossed them at the ankles. "Don't forget us clearing more names. We can't do it all."

"We can't ignore any of the enemies," Balladyn warned. "That will give them time to attack."

Carlyle tossed a pen onto the table and leaned forward in his seat. "We've got enemies coming at us from every direction. If we spread too thin, we leave ourselves open to attack."

"The mist is gone. Kerry is locked away. We've got that contained for the moment," Ferne said.

Theo's lips twisted as he shrugged. "Aye, but for how much longer? I've got a feeling it's only a matter of time before something strikes again. And harder and faster next time."

"Then we handle George and Beth," Bronwyn stated.

Elias blew out a breath. "We have an advantage we didna have before."

All eyes turned to Jasper. All but Willa's. He looked back at the others. "George will do anything to bring Elias to justice. She feels betrayed by Scott, Filip, Willa, and Luke. George knows about the Warriors now, but that isna stopping her."

"No' by a long shot," Elias said with a snort.

"Beth, on the other hand, keeps her intentions close to the vest. I wasna around her. My research on her is secondhand, based on what George shared, and Beth's actions. I think she intends to take George's position. The only reason the two of them are working together now is because of their mutual hatred for all of you," Jasper said.

Filip shrugged. "We already guessed that."

"Beth will come for me," Bronwyn said.

Rhona shoved aside her red hair. "She's coming for all of us."

"With the book. If only we could get our hands on that," Filip added.

Scott shook his head. "We'll be lucky to get it."

"So," Theo said, raising his voice slightly to get everyone's attention, "we've still got an isle of people who could've worked with Kerry, a growing evil, a beast in The Grey who wants to do whatever it wants to do, all of which could be individual problems or connected and lead us to the enemy we need to take down."

Sabryn chuckled. "If we're lucky."

"No' to mention George and Beth. We know who they are. We know their intentions—or at least most of them." Theo nodded toward Jasper. "And now have help in that regard. The being in The Grey is contained. Kerry is put away. The mist is gone. And while the evil continues to grow, we doona even know where to start with that."

Ferne blew out a breath. "That isn't up to us. It falls to Kirsi."

"Let's not forget that Druids are losing their magic," Rhona said.

Jasper frowned. They should be more worried about that since it could eventually affect them.

Theo's gaze slowly moved around the room. "Let's do what we can. George and Beth will be our focus while we continue clearing names. That will fall mainly on Jasper's and Willa's shoulders. Are you two ready?"

"Aye," Jasper answered.

Willa's voice was hard as nails when she said, "I'll play my part in public."

"George is looking for a reason to attack," Jasper warned.

Rhona's smile was slow as it spread across her face. "Then let's give her one."

"First, we have to make sure she sees that Jasper earned his way into our unit. It has to be believable," Theo said.

Jasper nodded at the DI. "It will be."

CHAPTER THIRTY-THREE

SKYE DRUIDS

"Are you okay?" Elodie whispered.

It was habitual for Willa to say she was, but she couldn't this time. "Define okay."

Elodie gave her a sad smile. "If you can't do this, you need to tell us now."

"I'll do it." She would just bitch about it the entire time.

Willa could feel Jasper's eyes on her. She shifted her hair with her hand to make sure she couldn't see him. It was important to stop George and Beth. No one knew that better than she did, but could she act as if she were still enamored with Jasper after...well, after this morning? She'd told the others she could, which meant she had to. Yet everything in her rebelled at the idea.

"They shouldna tarry, then," Theo said. His dark gaze swung to her. "Thoughts on today?"

It was on the tip of her tongue to say that Jasper should be roasted over an open pit, but she managed to hold it back. If it were another relationship, she'd want to spend the entire day—and night—with him. However, that was out of the question. "Lunch."

"That's agreeable," Jasper said.

Willa rolled her eyes. "I'll be busy after that."

"Then perhaps dinner," Theo suggested.

Finn nodded. "She could stay overnight again."

"Are you two that dim-witted?" Ferne asked.

Theo looked blankly at her. "What? We need a connection."

"And she just found out who he is. You can't expect her to jump in with both feet," Elodie said.

Elias plunked the front legs of his chair down as he sat forward. "That's exactly what we need. It's also what she agreed to."

"Willa gets to decide that," Scott replied tightly.

Carlyle shook his head. "I'm afraid not, mate."

Willa winced as the argument escalated. She had brought it on by acting the way she was. She jumped to her feet and let out a shrill whistle that quieted everyone immediately. Her gaze locked on Scott's. "I'll get this done to find Dad and stop George once and for all."

"Willa," Scott began.

She shook her head. "Don't. This falls to me. I wanted to help, and now I get to." She drew in a breath and, without looking at Jasper, said, "It'll be lunch. That's it for the day. Pick me up in an hour."

Somehow, her legs held her as she walked from the room. She hurried down the stairs and outside, only to remember that she didn't have a car. Scott had gotten most of her possessions but not her vehicle. That meant she was still dependent on someone driving her or having to ask to borrow a car.

The air was brisk as it rushed past her, and the sky looked as angry as she felt. It would rain soon. If only she could release the tears inside her. But she was afraid if she let even one out, she would never be able to stop. There was only one way she could get through this. She had to stop thinking about herself. Instead, she'd turn all her focus on her father. He was out there somewhere, possibly hurt.

Willa refused to believe he was dead. George had plans for her. No doubt she had one for her dad, as well. She clung to that. Luke Ryan was strong. Each minute she wasted on herself was one missed in locating him. She had already lost so much time with her injury, but she was healed now.

"Take my car," Elodie said and held out the keys. "I'll ride back with Scott and Filip."

Willa accepted the ring. "Thanks."

"We've got your back. If you change your mind, all you have to do is tell us. We'll end the charade immediately."

Willa turned to Elodie. "I can't. I need to find Dad. And we could stop George and Beth."

"George, maybe. Beth is an entirely different animal."

"What would you do if you were me?"

Elodie shrugged, her lips twisting. "I don't know. I've known betrayal, but nothing like yours. It's easy for me to say I'd push my feelings aside and do the job, but then again, I didn't fall for Jasper."

"I was the foolish one to do that."

"He targeted you. Don't be so hard on yourself."

"I kept going to him, not the other way around."

Elodie glanced up at the sky. "We'll find Luke. Broc is looking, and we'll keep doing what we can."

"So will I." Willa squared her shoulders. "I need to get ready for my lunch date."

"Good luck."

Willa was happy to be alone. She drove back to Elodie and Scott's in silence. When she walked into the house, she stood in the middle of her room, soaking in the quiet. She kept her promise to herself and focused on her father. Every word, every movement going forward would be about him. She would find him and let the others bring down George and Beth.

Once that was done, Jasper could get out of her life once and for all.

It was an hour on the dot when a knock sounded on the door. Willa didn't know if her brother and Elodie had stayed away on purpose, but she was glad they weren't here. She stood at the door and took one last breath before opening it, plastering a rigid smile on her face.

Jasper stood on the other side in a wheat-colored sweater and dark denim jeans. His lips curved into a grin. "Hey."

"Shall we go?"

"Sure." He stood aside so she could grab her purse and lock up the house. "Anywhere in particular?"

She kept the smile in place as she walked past him to the Jaguar. "I don't care."

He opened her door and helped her in before walking to the driver's side. Jasper climbed behind the wheel and started the engine. "Willa."

"I don't want to hear anything you have to say unless it's you telling me where my father is. Keep your excuses and explanations to yourself."

There was a moment of silence before he said, "Understood."

She kept her gaze out the windscreen as he drove. He didn't try to speak again, and neither did she. It was the most uncomfortable, awkward car ride of her life. She was grateful when he finally parked in front of a sandwich shop. They both exited the SUV. His hand rested on her lower back as they entered the restaurant. She stiffened at the contact but was proud of herself for not jerking away. That wouldn't be the right reaction after spending the night with someone.

The host took them to a table near the window. Jasper gave her the seat with the view, which she happily accepted. Then she became absorbed in the menu—anything so she didn't have to look across the table at him.

All too soon, the young server came for their order. Then she took the menus, leaving Willa with the option to either look at Jasper or the view. She chose the water and mountains.

"I hate to point out the obvious, but we're being watched, remember?" Jasper said.

She laughed, the sound harsh to her ears, then glanced his way. "I'm aware. What they'll see is someone who has never been to this place before, taking in the view. Which is oh so gorgeous."

"The sandwiches are pretty good, too."

"Hey, Jasper," an older man called out with a wave as he strode to their table. "Back again, aye?"

Jasper's smile was easy as he nodded in greeting. "Afternoon, Billy. I can no' seem to stay away."

"And who have you brought today?" Billy asked as his faded blue eyes swung to her.

Willa shot him a real grin, noting his weathered and wrinkled face. He had a neatly trimmed gray beard and a thick head of gray and brown hair. "Hi. I'm Willa."

Billy bowed his head to her. "Nice to meet you, Willa."

"Likewise." She liked Billy immediately.

He looked between the two of them before looking at her. "I know what he sees in you, but what in the world do you see in him?"

"I couldn't tell you," Willa answered honestly.

Billy busted out laughing. "I like her, Jasper. Keep her around."

"I'll do my best," Jasper replied.

Billy walked away then, and the genuine smile faltered on Willa's lips. She went back to staring at the view. "You seem to charm everyone, don't you?"

"I like Billy. I love his sandwiches. I come here often, and he noticed. He stops to chat for a bit each time. That's it."

Unlike what Jasper had done with her.

Jasper leaned back in his chair. "We're no' going to be able to do this, are we?"

"I'll do whatever I have to."

"You willna fool anyone. No' like this. You can no' even look at me. You willna have a landscape to stare at everywhere we go."

She gazed at the table for a long moment, then lifted her eyes to him, instantly sucked into his dark brown eyes. "Better?"

"I'm sorry, Willa."

"Don't you dare," she bit out as anger rose so swiftly it nearly choked her.

His eyes beseeched her to believe him, and damn her heart, but she wanted to do just that.

Jasper looked away and carefully fixed a smile in place. "I've told the others, but you should be aware that George wants to make an example out of your family for leaving."

"Hasn't she done enough?"

"You'd think."

Willa studied his profile and made herself relax. He was right. This had to look real, or all of it would be for naught. This was about her father, after all. "How long have you known her?"

"Two years."

"Two?" she repeated in shock. "I never saw you at the meetings."

He shrugged and looked at her. "She wanted me hidden."

"Why?"

There was a long pause before Jasper said, "George found me, as she seems to find so many of our kind. I'd never been a part of such a community before. It took her some time to talk me into it, but she wore me down enough to have me take a look for myself."

"Did she know what you did?"

"Aye," he said with a slow nod.

Willa raised her brows. "And? What happened?"

"I joined."

"Just like that?"

Jasper lowered his gaze to the table. "What do you want to hear? That I was tired of being on my own? That I longed to be a part of something?" He shrugged and looked into her eyes. "George had a plan. She spoke about the decline of the Druids. Said there was a way to stop it. Over the years, I'd run into others of our kind here and there, but those times were few and far between. I believed her. I wanted to believe her. And I also wanted to help."

"And what about her crusade to remove the Skye Druids?"

"I was sent to watch."

"To spy."

He inclined his head. "To spy. I listened to what she had to say, but I make my own decisions."

"But you still carried out her orders."

"There are things you told me that no amount of research could've uncovered," he said, his expression hardening slightly. "Things only those in the midst of it would be aware of."

"And it changed your opinion."

A muscle jumped in his jaw. "That was part of it, aye."

"Do you really expect me to believe that?"

"The only thing I ever lied to you about was what I did for a living and if I knew George. Everything else was the truth."

She shrugged as the server delivered their food. "Sure, it was."

CHAPTER THIRTY-FOUR

SKYE DRUIDS

Jasper walked into his house and dropped his keys in the glass bowl on the entry table. He turned into the living room, his gaze going to the window where he'd held Willa against it just hours before, the place where he had battled himself to let her go.

And lost.

He slowly turned, looking at the perfectly ordered room. It was an extension of the perfectly ordered life he had curated for himself on Skye. One he hadn't expected to like. Maybe it wasn't the life he enjoyed. Perhaps it was the people, the isle itself.

Jasper found himself facing the window again. He couldn't look at it without seeing Willa. He could still picture how her vibrant blue eyes had watched him with so much desire and longing. It had taken his breath away. She had been something special, something precious, and he'd ruined it. He'd ruined *her*.

Somehow, he'd even managed to fuck up trying to fix things.

Jasper shook his head, turning away. He hadn't been trying to mend anything. He'd wanted to soothe his conscience, to extract himself from a situation because it was the easiest thing to do. He hadn't dared to stay and fight for her, for them, because it would've been a lost cause. It had never entered his mind to spy on George, either. The Skye Druids had, however. He wasn't naïve. They didn't trust him. But he was a means to an end, and they were taking it. He'd do the same in their place. There was only one problem—Willa. She was caught in the middle.

The painful lunch ran through his mind. She could barely tolerate him. Couldn't even bear to talk to him, much less act as if she cared. There was no way she could carry out the plan, and it was wrong to ask it of her. She had suffered enough. If it were up to him, he'd get her as far from Skye as possible.

His head swung back to the window. He'd lost his heart to Willa. Strong, courageous, beautiful Willa. The way she had kissed him, touched him...*loved* him...was more than he had ever hoped for. Certainly, more than he deserved. He had no right to sully her with his stained past. No number of apologies or regrets could take back what he had done.

Jasper fisted his hand and drew it back. He let out a bellow as he threw magic at the window. Shards of glass exploded outward, but he still saw Willa there, her arms above her head and her lips parted as she waited for his kiss. He destroyed another window and another. Then he turned to the room.

All the rage, all the regret and shame, all the self-loathing inside him welled up into a thick, black ball that threatened to suffocate him. He lashed out at the house and its contents since he couldn't take it out on himself. Jasper went from room to room, eviscerating everything. He didn't stop until the house was in shambles.

And then he found himself outside in the stables, staring at the empty stalls. He missed the horses. They hadn't cared about his past, his name, or who he was connected to. They only wanted his love and attention, granting it in return. He'd never had a pet before. They were a burden he couldn't afford. Just like friends.

Jasper put a hand on Bay's stall door and imagined her head hanging over the side as she sniffed his hands and pockets for treats. He would make sure they had a good life. It was the least he could do.

Tears welled. For the horses, for Willa.

For what could've been.

Jasper stiffened when the air around him changed. He didn't turn around. There was no need. He knew it was the Reaper. Was Balladyn here to talk...or exact revenge? "I've been expecting a visit."

"Were you attacked?" Balladyn asked.

"Nay."

"Then who destroyed the house?"

Jasper dropped his hand from the stall. "I did."

"I know what you're feeling."

"I doubt it."

Balladyn blew out a breath and came to stand beside him. "A very long time ago, I was captain of the Queen's Guard. Usaeil and our people were mine to protect. I took that job to heart. Until one day, after a clash with the Dark, I was wounded and left on the battlefield. I expected a certain friend to find me. But she didn't. Instead, the Dark found me and took me to their king."

Jasper turned his head to the Reaper, but he didn't interrupt.

"I was thrown into their prison and tortured around the clock," Balladyn said as he met Jasper's gaze. "They wanted me to turn. It's a choice a Fae makes, you see. We're all born Light. A Dark chooses to kill, to do evil."

Jasper shifted to face the Reaper as he noted the silver streaks in Balladyn's hair, a sign of a Dark.

Balladyn shrugged. "Everyone has a breaking point. I became Dark. I let my hatred for the Light and the friend I expected to find me fester until it did the job my torturers couldn't. I then dedicated myself to the Dark, working my way up the ranks until I became the king's right hand. I killed any Light I could find. All the while, I hunted that friend to make her pay. I eventually caught her. And I tortured her." Balladyn's throat bobbed as he swallowed. "She didn't succumb, though. She was stronger than I. Stronger than anyone. She broke her bindings, chains that were supposed to be unbreakable."

Jasper didn't know why Balladyn was telling him all of this.

"It wasn't long after that I learned the Light Queen, the one I had pledged to protect with my life, had betrayed me. Usaeil made sure I was wounded for the Dark. She also ensured my friend wouldn't find me. The king, however, had promised to kill me. I still don't know why Taraeth didn't. It was to his detriment. Because I took his life and the throne."

"Fuck me," Jasper murmured. "You're King of the Dark?"

Balladyn shot him a quick grin. "I was for a short time. I joined forces with my friend and the Dragon Kings to bring down Usaeil. She betrayed me a second time by stabbing me in the back. That's when Death found me. She held me in that place between life and death and gave me a choice. I could die, or I could become one of her Reapers. I didn't think I was worthy. I knew I wasn't, but I wanted to right some of my wrongs."

"I appreciate what you're trying to do, but our lives don't mirror each other's. No' even a little."

"Oh, I don't know. I think they do." Balladyn shifted to the side and rested his arm on the edge of a stall door. "You accepted Rhona's offer because you want to right your wrong."

"I did. I do. But it willna work."

"Why?"

Jasper briefly closed his eyes. "Willa can no' do it. I willna continue to hurt her. We need to find another way."

"There isn't one."

"Then we make one."

Balladyn stared at him for a long minute. "Does she know you love her?"

"Does everyone on this bloody isle know that?" Jasper bit out, not hiding his irritation.

Balladyn's brow furrowed. "Who else knows?"

"Emilie. She asked me the same thing. The answer is nay. Willa doesna know. No' that it would matter if she did."

"What is it you want, Jasper?"

He met Balladyn's red-ringed silver eyes. "I want to fix what I've done. I want George, Beth, and anyone who was willingly involved in using ebony wood to be brought to justice. I want George and Beth to be stopped before they hurt more people."

"You want much more, but we'll focus on what you've mentioned. You have the chance to do all of that. You knew it the moment you agreed to spy on George for us. Just as you knew it would be the most difficult thing you've ever done. Not because George was a friend, but because you would have to do it with Willa, who you wronged."

"Can you read people's minds?"

Balladyn chuckled softly. "I've been alive for a very, very long time. You watch others long enough, you pick up on things."

"Willa and I barely got through lunch. I can handle her revulsion, but those watching us will pick up on it. George will never believe things are going well enough that the Knights brought me into the fold."

"It's our one shot. Make it work. However you need to do it."

Jasper knew the Reaper was right. It didn't make it any easier, though. "And when it's over? When we succeed? What happens to me then?"

"You can do whatever you want."

"You expect me to believe that?"

Balladyn straightened to his full height. "I give you my word. If you want to leave, then you leave. We don't turn on our allies."

Jasper ran a hand over his jaw. "I think I screwed up. If they see what I did to the house, then George will know something is wrong."

"There's nothing wrong with your home."

He frowned at Balladyn. "Ah...there is."

"I...righted things."

"Thank you," he said after a small pause.

Balladyn inclined his head. "Now. Let's think about this. George put you in place to be there when Willa came to Skye. You ended up saving her life. You did it a second time by removing the ebony wood."

"No thanks to George and Beth. That was never part of the plan."

"It doesn't matter. To an outsider, you've just cemented your place in Willa's life. And she spent the night with you. We must keep this ball rolling. You know what needs to happen next."

"Willa needs to spend the night again."

Balladyn nodded. "Draw the shades so no one can see in. We need the watchers to think you're having a second night together."

"That will be up to Willa."

"It's being taken care of."

Jasper glanced through the barn doors to the house. Another night with Willa sounded sublime. It would also be pure agony. "I'll do it."

"There's one more thing."

He slid his gaze back to the Reaper. "What's that?"

"Why did you side with George?"

Jasper looked at the ground and shrugged before raising his eyes to Balladyn. "My dad always told me we couldna do the job if we had attachments. He moved us so many times I stopped trying to make friends at school. I spent time studying people, learning my marks. But I wanted more. I needed more. George found me at a low time. She accepted me for who I was while offering what I sought."

"Family."

Jasper nodded. "A place to fit in. Except she kept me in the shadows, waiting to use my skills. She promised once I completed my job here that I would be a welcome member of the community. No more hiding in the shadows."

"Then she changed your mission."

"Honestly, it was the use of ebony wood that made me take a step back and reconsider."

Balladyn quirked a brow. "Just that?"

"And Willa. How she spoke of how each of you, having put your lives on the line for the others. It made me realize that what

George offered wasn't real. She's lost, and she doesna even know it."

Balladyn glanced at the stables. "If you find yourself in a tight spot, say my name. A Fae can hear their name being called from anywhere."

Jasper couldn't believe he would offer such a thing.

"You might want to go answer your door," Balladyn told him. "Willa just arrived."

In the next blink, the Reaper was gone.

CHAPTER THIRTY-FIVE

SKYE DRUIDS

Beth strolled into the mental hospital with sure strides. They had once kept her away from her beloved Sydney. But no longer. The book had changed so very much for her. Now, very little stood in her way. Especially not those who didn't have magic.

The man behind the plexiglass smiled as she approached. "Hello, Ms. Stewart. Sydney is in his room."

"Thank you," Beth said.

The door buzzed as he let her inside. The two orderlies nodded in greeting but didn't stop her. No one would stop her again. Ever. Beth barely contained the shiver that ran through her as she marched through the halls. Sydney was on the third floor. She didn't look into any of the other rooms. She'd made that mistake once. It only took once. She didn't understand how anyone could work in such a place.

There was a shriek down the hall in front of her. A short, slender, middle-aged man ran naked out of his room with wild eyes. Tall, muscular orderlies poured out of every doorway. Beth flattened herself against the wall and watched as it took six hospital attendants to get the man to the floor. It took another two to hold him while a nurse plunged a needle into his arm. Almost immediately, the man's screams faded away. The attendants climbed to their feet, exchanging weary glances before carting the man back to his room.

Beth shrugged off the scene and kept walking. She chose the stairs instead of the elevator since she preferred to be alone. She hated when others tried to talk to her. She reached the third floor and turned right. Sydney's room was halfway down the hall on the left.

She paused at the open door. He sat on his bed in pajama pants, a white T-shirt, and a bathrobe, staring out the window. Beth closed the door behind her as she entered. The rain lashing the window was loud in the quiet room. She walked to the bed and slid her fingers into his brown hair. It was getting long. Almost time for a trim.

"Hello, baby," she said as she sat beside him.

He didn't seem to hear. He never did. They kept him so drugged that he wasn't really here.

She ran her hand down his back and rested her head on his shoulder. "It's almost time. Do you remember how we used to spend hours planning? I miss those nights, baby."

Beth put one hand on his arm and laced the fingers of the other with his. She smiled when he rested his head on hers. Sydney was still in there. He showed her each time she came to see him. He never should've gotten this bad, and if they had allowed her to see him to begin with, she would've made sure they didn't fill him so full of medication that he didn't know his own name. He was strong of will and mind.

She might not know exactly what had happened on Skye that made the authorities send Sydney to this place, but she knew who was responsible—Bronwyn. And her cousin would pay dearly for everything she had done.

"B...B..."

She rubbed her hand up and down his arm. "That's right, baby. It's me. Beth. I'm here. They tried to keep us apart, but no one can keep soulmates from each other. Not the doctors or authorities, and certainly not Bronwyn."

"B...B..."

Beth moved to stand before him. She took his face in her hands and looked into his brown eyes. "I never left you. I never will. Our hearts are bound for eternity."

He blinked, and drool ran out of the corner of his mouth.

She wiped it away. "I've gotten through more of the book. We will own the world when I'm done, baby. It's all there on the pages. You would've known had you been more focused on it, but that doesn't matter now. I'm going to fix everything. Like getting you out of here. You want revenge on Bronwyn, don't you?"

"B...B..."

"Shh," she said, putting a finger to his lips. "Things are in the works, baby. I've got it handled. It won't be long now before I come to get you out of this horrid place." She caressed his face. "The fire is gone from your eyes, but it'll be back soon. I can't wait to show you everything I've learned. There is so much to teach you. Together, we'll set the world on fire."

He blinked repeatedly as if trying to bring her into focus.

Beth took his hand and placed it on her breast. "I miss your touch, baby. When I think of the months we lost because of Bronwyn, I imagine a hundred ways to take my revenge." She took his hand and kissed his palm before settling it on her hip. "There's someone else I need to take care of before I spring you from this joint. Just a little longer, baby."

Sydney's lips moved, but he couldn't voice any words.

She moved closer, grinning. "That's right. It's George. She doesn't trust me, and she's right not to. Remember what we talked about the last time I was here? Things have progressed better than I ever could've hoped. She believes she's setting things up to keep me in my place." Beth ran her hands over his shoulders. "George can't compete. Not with me. But she'll learn that soon enough."

Beth sighed and eyed her lover. "Things would be so much better if you were by my side, baby. Soon, though. I need another couple of days to finish setting up our new home. I've got a list of all the medications they've been giving you, and the detox will be rough. But I'll be with you. And we'll get you through it together, baby."

His mouth softened into a smile.

"I love you, too. You brought me out of the shadows, but I'll be the one to shatter the sun. And it's going to be epic." She leaned down and pressed her lips to his, lingering for a moment. "I'll be back soon."

Panic contorted Sydney's face.

"Shhh," she whispered, placing tiny kisses on his cheeks. "We're bound, remember? We're soulmates, baby. Together for eternity."

Beth stepped back and smiled. She blew him a kiss and walked out of the room. The trip out of the hospital wasn't nearly as noisy as it had been coming in. No skinny, naked men were running the halls, though screams from other floors did drift into the stairwell.

She pushed the door wide and walked out of the hospital. The rain beat a steady rhythm on the concrete as she made her way to the car, uncaring that it drenched her. She climbed into the back seat of the silver Jaguar sedan and adjusted her trench coat.

"Drive," she told the man behind the wheel.

He started the engine without question and pulled out of the car park. She grinned as he did as she commanded. She was getting better at the spell. Soon, she'd be able to take control of dozens at a time.

Unlike George, who was building her army by convincing Druids to help her, Beth was doing it the old-fashioned way. With magic. When she finished, no one would dare stand in her way.

All because of a book.

Beth leaned her head back on the seat and closed her eyes. The countdown had begun.

George grabbed hold of the desk to stay upright. She put a hand on her chest in an effort to calm her racing heart. The vision had been clear. Her legs still shook as she plopped down into the chair. Hot fury ran through her. Someone was going to betray her, but she hadn't seen the face of the person who would do it. It was pointless to try and force the vision to return. It had shown her all it would. It was up to her to figure out the rest.

Her phone beeped with a text. She flipped her mobile face up on her desk and scanned the message from her spy. Beth had paid another visit to her incapacitated lover. A fat lot of good Sydney would do for her now. George had to give Beth props for remaining by his side even though his mind was gone.

The squeak of the door opening pulled her attention from her phone. Her gaze landed on Felix as he strode toward her with purposeful steps, a smile on his face. He was always impeccably attired in a suit, dress shirt, bow tie, vest, and Christian Louboutin dress shoes. Today, he wore a spruce blue windowpane-check suit with coral accents paired with a pink shirt and a coral-pink bow tie and matching pocket square.

"Good news, then?" she asked when he reached her.

His gray eyes crinkled at the corners, showing deep lines in his round face. "Willa has returned to Jasper's. She brought an overnight bag this time."

"He's good." George tapped the desk with her finger. "It's just a matter of time before he's inside the group. Anything on the others?"

Felix put his hands in his front trouser pockets. "They continue to meet at Carwood Manor. They keep whatever they're doing under wraps. Do you really think Jasper can pull this off?"

She rocked back in her office chair. "I wouldn't have tapped him for the job if I didn't. Why? Don't you think he can?"

Felix shook his head of blond hair cut in the latest style and shrugged. "A lot rides on him. Then there's the fact that he has grilled you on the ebony wood."

"He needs me, and I've made sure he knows what I can offer. He hasn't wavered. He won't."

"If he does?"

George sat forward. "Scott will kill him. Of all the people who might betray me, it isn't Jasper."

Felix hesitated. "Unfortunately, I do bring a bit of bad news. We've still no' located Luke Ryan."

"Any more sightings of the Warriors?"

"None. If they're in the city, someone will see them and alert us."

George was pleased with how Felix was handling things. "I don't want anyone attacking them. They'll lead us to Luke. He's who I want."

"Dead or alive?"

"Either."

Felix bowed his head. "I'll get the word out."

"Have my spies located where Beth hid the book?"

"I'm afraid no', sadly."

George had feared as much. "Push them harder. The sooner I have the tome, the better."

Felix's gaze intensified. "You had a vision."

"Aye."

"About Beth?"

"About someone betraying me."

Felix's forehead creased with his frown. "Did you see a face?"

"A partial one," she lied. She trusted Felix, but only so far.

"Then you can stop them."

She put a smile on her face that she didn't feel. "Exactly."

"I'll get back with you as soon as I have new information."

George waited until Felix was gone before relaxing in the chair. With the book, Beth was a concern. She had done things George hadn't known were possible. If Beth wanted her position, she could've taken it already. Since she hadn't, maybe she didn't want it. Or perhaps she was waiting for the right moment.

The Ryans and Elias were thorns in her side. Willa was in her grasp without even knowing it. Soon, she'd have Luke's son and daughter. If they hadn't found him by then, she would use his children to draw him out.

Then there was her ultimate target. Elias. She would take extreme pleasure in causing him as much pain as he had caused her. She wouldn't let him die, though. After she'd finished with him, she'd hand him to the authorities. He'd beg to confess everything by then. It wouldn't matter what evidence they did or didn't have with his confession.

The Skye Druids and their allies were a kink in her plans. Everything hinged on Jasper. If he betrayed her, everything could go up in smoke. He had never been caught. Had never been arrested or charged with any crimes. That told her more than if she'd known him his entire life. Jasper was a professional. He knew the stakes, and he would get the job done.

Having an insider in Rhona's group was a huge coup. George could hardly wait for the day when Jasper began passing along all the information he gathered. When she returned to Skye, no one would be expecting it—least of all Rhona and her hulking Reaper.

CHAPTER THIRTY-SIX

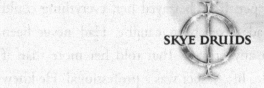

SKYE DRUIDS

This was the last place Willa wanted to be. But it was the only place she *could* be. She walked up to Jasper's house with her heart thumping against her ribs. A different kind of nervousness assaulted her. She'd been giddy before. Now, she was tense and edgy. Her steps faltered, but she managed to keep moving forward. How could she do anything else now?

Her hand trembled as she lifted it to ring the doorbell. Willa shook out her hand. "Keep your shite together," she murmured to herself.

This time, her finger was steadier as she pushed the bell. Then, she waited. She tried not to look around to see if anyone watched. They could be anywhere.

The door opened, and Jasper was there with a warm, if hesitant, smile. For a heartbeat, she was transported to the night before when numerous possibilities had awaited them. It faded as reality set in.

His gaze searched hers, but his smile never slipped. "Let me get that."

Willa relinquished her overnight bag. Their fingers brushed. She hated that she wanted his touch him at the same time she couldn't stand to be near him.

"Come in," Jasper beckoned.

She looked inside before cautiously stepping over the threshold. It felt as if a lifetime had passed since she had been here. She heard a soft click as the door closed behind her, shutting her in with Jasper. Her traitorous body heated, craving him, but she pushed those thoughts away. It didn't matter how much pleasure he could give after he'd stomped on her heart.

"Take any room you want," Jasper said as he walked around her.

Willa watched as he made his way to the stairs and took them two at a time. A few moments later, he returned.

"I set your bag at the top." He put his hands in the front pockets of his jeans. "I'll stay out of your way. I've already closed the blinds and shutters. No one can see inside."

She swallowed and carefully set her purse on the entry table. "That's good."

"I need to get back to dinner before it burns."

Willa briefly met his dark eyes before looking away. She waited until he'd walked into the kitchen before going upstairs. Her bag was just where he'd said it would be. She looped her hand around the handles and looked to the left, catching a glimpse of his bed through the doorway. She turned to the right and took the room farthest from him.

Since she wouldn't be able to turn on any lights once night fell, she went ahead and set things up for her stay. She piled pillows on the floor and checked to make sure the book light she had worked. She then set out her toiletries. All too soon, the simple chore was finished. She didn't have anything else to do, so she sat on the corner of the bed, trying not to think about the last time she had been in the house.

It would be a long night.

Willa clasped her hands together and twiddled her thumbs. She knew Balladyn had visited Jasper. What had the two of them talked about? She desperately wanted to know, but she wouldn't ask either of them. Balladyn wouldn't tell her, and she couldn't trust anything Jasper said.

She fell back onto the mattress and looked up. Her mind made images out of spots on the ceiling as her thoughts drifted from one thing to another. She didn't know how long she lay there before a soft knock sounded on the door, followed by Jasper's muffled voice on the other side.

"Dinner is ready, if you're hungry."

Willa sat up and scowled. She wouldn't call herself a picky eater, but he hadn't asked what she might want to eat. What if she didn't like what he cooked? It wasn't as if she had to be nice and lie now. She would just return to the bedroom and the pile of snacks she had brought for just such an instance.

She stood and made her way to the door. When she opened it, the hall was empty. She looked both ways just to be sure Jasper wasn't waiting. At least they were fast-tracking their *relationship* to get Jasper invited into the group. It had to look official for anyone watching. But that meant this would be the last time she had to be seen with him.

The mere thought of people spying on her every move made Willa want to lash out. And she had, much to her regret. Scott had gotten the brunt of it. Even poor Elodie had taken some heat. Same with Filip and even Theo. The only one who had stopped her cold was Rhona. She'd been calm, never raising her voice when they had their chat. Rhona was the reason Willa was even here.

Willa's stomach rumbled, reminding her she was hungry. She hadn't gotten much of the sandwich down from lunch. Too much had happened for her to want to eat much of anything. Elodie had shoved a bag of nuts at her. At first, Willa had refused them, but she'd eventually given in and ate a handful. That was hours ago.

She descended the stairs and smelled something good, which only pissed her off. Why did everything Jasper did have to be perfect? Couldn't he mess something up? She made her way to the kitchen, ready to take her plate and leave so he'd eat alone, except Jasper wasn't in the room. A covered plate sat on the counter.

Her feet brought her to it, even as she tried to tell herself she didn't want it. She lifted the lid to see spaghetti. Her mouth watered as she inhaled the delicious smell of marinara sauce and noodles. She had the plate in hand before she knew it. Willa took the first bite and sighed. Then she began shoveling the spaghetti into her mouth as fast as she could, uncaring if it got on her face. She was ravenous, and the food was delicious.

Finally, she made her way to the table and sat. There, she found grated parmesan that she liberally sprinkled over the noodles. It wasn't long before she finished and went back for a second helping. When she cleared the second plate, she sat back with a sigh of satisfaction.

Willa didn't stay in the kitchen long. She didn't want to run into Jasper. So, she cleaned up after herself and slipped back upstairs before they bumped into each other. She didn't know where he was in the house, which suited her just fine. It was the only way she'd agreed to this overnight stay. They would make nice for anyone watching, but otherwise, they would stay far from each other.

Once she'd shut herself in the bedroom once more, she went back to wondering how to occupy herself. She had brought a book, but she knew she wouldn't be able to concentrate on it. She'd been waiting months for the release, and she wanted to give it the attention it deserved. However, it might take her mind off her current situation. Willa walked to the pile of pillows and made herself comfortable. Then she opened the book.

It took her a few tries before it sucked her in, but once the author caught her, she was a part of the story. Willa stayed there until her neck started to ache, and she had to turn on her book light. She set aside the novel to get up and stretch. She wanted to peek out the blinds, but she didn't. Everything relied on their charade working.

Worries about her father soon took hold. Willa texted Scott for an update, but he had nothing new to report. She resettled on the pillows, adjusting them for a more comfortable recline, and happily dove back into the book. She stayed that way until a loud pounding startled her. She sat up and listened. It came again.

Willa closed the book and jumped to her feet. She cracked open her door and listened as more pounding commenced. She didn't hear Jasper. Had he left? Quietly, she walked down the hall and then descended the stairs. When she reached the main floor, she spotted Jasper standing in the entryway.

"Who is it?" she whispered.

He shook his head, his gaze locked on the front door. "I doona know."

"Are you going to find out?"

"I doona think I should."

Willa jumped as the pounding came again. The person outside rattled the door handle and shouted for help.

"Bollocks," Jasper muttered. He swung his head to her. "Stay back."

He didn't need to tell her twice.

Willa flattened herself against the wall and peered around the corner. Jasper nodded before making his way to the door.

"Who is it?" he called out.

"I need help. Please!" a man shouted from the other side.

The sound of locks turning reached her a moment before Jasper turned the knob. All she could see was his back and broad shoulders in the partially open door.

"You have to help me," the visitor said breathlessly.

Jasper opened the door a little more. "What's wrong?"

"Can you no' see it?! The pain! Help me!"

Willa winced at the man's howl. He was in agony. Why wasn't Jasper doing anything?

"Tell me where you're hurt," Jasper shouted over the man's wails.

"It's in my chest. Right here!" the man bellowed.

Willa stepped out from behind the wall. What was it Jasper couldn't see?

"Hey, mate. Mate!" Jasper barked to get the man's attention. "I need you to calm down."

"Calm down? That's not possible with a piece of black wood stuck in your chest!"

Willa gasped and started toward Jasper.

He must have heard her because he looked back, his hand out, halting her. "Nay."

The man jerked Jasper forward before she could reply. She hesitated a heartbeat before rushing to the door. The man, a twenty-something who looked more inebriated than wounded, had a hold of Jasper's T-shirt.

"Get it out! Everyone else is at Emilie's, but I know you can help me. Do it. Now!" the man demanded.

Willa looked at him, searching his upper body for signs of an injury, but she couldn't find anything. She slid her gaze to Jasper, but his dark eyes were filled with uncertainty. A sound from the street drew their attention. Three more people were making their way to them, screaming in pain.

"Balladyn. Get Balladyn," Jasper whispered as he pushed her back inside.

"Jasper," she screamed when he slammed the door shut, putting her safely inside with him outside.

Willa turned in a circle to figure out what to do. Then she realized there was only one thing to do. "Balladyn!"

She probably didn't need to scream, but that's what came out. Willa waited, the seconds ticking by. When the Reaper didn't show, she called his name again, this time in a more sedate, calm manner. But he still didn't appear.

Willa rushed to a window to look outside, thinking maybe Balladyn had already arrived. Jasper knelt by the man who now lay on the ground, rocking back and forth in obvious pain. Jasper kept trying to talk to him, but there seemed to be no getting through to the man. She looked up to see the three others getting closer.

"Balladyn, please," Willa begged.

She couldn't wait for the Reaper. She dashed upstairs, her toe catching the edge of a stair, which caused her to pitch forward. She caught herself, then jumped back up. Willa ran to her room and grabbed her mobile. She dialed Rhona, but the call never connected. She then called Scott. Willa knew something was wrong when her brother didn't pick up. She tried Elodie, then Theo, and then Sabryn. No one answered. That couldn't be good.

Willa rushed from her room and down the stairs to the front door. She threw it open as two of the three others reached Jasper, their screams of pain piercing the night. They were clawing at him, each trying to pull him toward them.

"Help."

Willa spun, but it was too late. Strong hands caught her and dragged her to the ground.

CHAPTER THIRTY-SEVEN

SKYE DRUIDS

Jasper's head snapped up when he heard Willa's shout of surprise. The instant he saw a woman dragging her down, Jasper jerked away from those around him and rushed to Willa. He couldn't get there fast enough. His heart leaped into his throat when he saw the terror flash on her face.

He disentangled Willa from the woman, shoving the stranger away hard until Willa was free. Willa wound her arms around him as he pressed her body to his and turned away. Jasper didn't take offense when she released him a moment later. Reluctantly, he did the same, moving her behind him. He kept a hand against her to make sure she remained there.

"Run to the door and get inside," he told her after spotting more people coming from every direction.

"What's going on?" she asked in a tight whisper.

He shook his head. "I'm no' sure."

Jasper didn't leave her side until they reached the door and he knew she was safely in the house. He met her gaze as she closed the door. They didn't have time for words, but at least she was safe. Jasper turned and raised his hands, walking toward the wailing individuals. He didn't know if Willa had called for Balladyn or if the Reaper just hadn't responded yet. Hopefully, he would get there soon.

Jasper scanned those around him. "Balladyn," he said aloud. "Willa needs you."

The group pressed in on him. The pain on their faces and in their screams left him reeling. He didn't know how to help them. No matter how hard he looked, he couldn't find any wounds or blood. Could it all be in their heads? There were too many of them for it to be a coincidence. And they had mentioned Emilie. Maybe Balladyn was with her.

The people started pulling and yanking on him again, each pleading for help. Jasper debated using magic to get them off him, but if they were indeed hurt, he didn't want to make things worse. The squeal of tires had him swinging his head toward the road. He spotted headlights coming at him fast. Just as he was about to dive out of the way, the vehicle jerked to the side and came to a rocking stop as someone threw the passenger door open. Finn stepped out.

"Get down," he shouted.

Jasper dropped. A heartbeat later, the screaming was cut short, and the individuals around him fell to the ground. Jasper lifted his head, looking around in shock before turning to Finn.

"I've got skills," the Irishman said with a shrug.

Jasper slowly got to his feet and stared at the unconscious people on the ground. "Tell me you know what's going on."

"Maybe," Sabryn said as she came from around the vehicle. "We came from Emilie's. They busted through her doors and windows. Balladyn had to evacuate her. I think the afflicted realized that and made their way to you."

The door to the house opened, and Willa stepped out. "Why?"

"Afflicted?" Jasper asked with a frown.

"We were hoping you might be able to tell us more," Sabryn said.

Finn's lips twisted. "There's only one reason they'd go to Emilie."

"Ebony wood," Jasper guessed. "One of them mentioned something about that."

Finn nodded. "Sorry, mate, but it looks like word got out that you had success with Willa's problem."

"How?" Willa asked. "I don't understand any of this. There's no blood."

"There are no *wounds*," Jasper added.

Sabryn crossed her arms over her chest. "They're the same at Emilie's. We don't think this is some fluke. Someone did this on purpose."

Jasper's blood ran cold. The only people who could be responsible were the same ones who'd hurt Willa—George and Beth. There was no way anyone could know he'd agreed to spy for Rhona—nobody but her and the others in the group. None of them were spies. If they were, George wouldn't have needed to send him in. Which made him wonder why people had been afflicted—or believed they were. If George wanted to use this to get him further into the Skye Druids' good graces, she would've told him. No. This was something else. But what? He couldn't figure it out.

He squatted next to the man who'd originally banged on his door. Jasper remembered the location of his supposed wound. He put his hand over the man's chest and opened his magic to feel for ebony wood. It slammed into him almost instantly. It was a tiny sliver, no more than a splinter someone would get in their finger, but it was there. He turned to the next individual and searched her body. It didn't take him long to find the same type of splinter. He looked over the rest before standing, his stomach tight with dread.

Jasper looked up, his gaze meeting Willa's blue eyes first. Her brow was furrowed in question. He nodded before turning to Finn and Sabryn. "These people have ebony wood in them. The pieces are verra tiny, but they're there."

"Shit. I was afraid of that. Thanks for confirming," Sabryn said solemnly.

Willa padded barefoot, moving farther onto the walkway. "What now?"

"You three need to leave," Jasper said. He held Sabryn's gaze. If anyone would understand what he was about to do, it was her.

Finn swore under his breath.

"Are you sure?" Sabryn asked.

Far from it, but Jasper couldn't see another option. Besides, he had a lifetime of bad decisions and wrongdoings to make up for. This might erase some of the red in his ledger.

"Is he sure of what?" Willa demanded, looking between them.

Jasper turned to her, ready to explain.

There must have been something on his face because she shook her head. "You're coming with us."

"I can no', and I willna leave these people like this," Jasper stated.

Willa glanced around at the bodies. "You can't really mean to pull the ebony wood out of all of them."

"Someone has to."

"It doesn't have to be you."

"There's no one else," he pointed out.

Willa turned to Sabryn and Finn, but neither would meet her gaze. She swung back to Jasper. "The backlash will be massive. You got free with mine, but the odds of you escaping it this time are…"

"I know," he said when she didn't finish. "That's why you three need to leave. Whatever happens will happen only to me."

Finn grunted. "It shouldn't fall to only you."

"Take Willa and leave," Jasper told them. "Have Balladyn bring the other afflicted."

Sabryn's arms fell to her sides. "That's…a lot for you to do."

"I'm no' saying I'll get to everyone, but I'll do my best. It's time for you to go. I need to work while they're unconscious."

Willa took a step back. "This is insane. One person can't do what you're planning."

"Go," he urged her. He couldn't do anything until he knew she was far from him. Safe. Where she should've been all along.

Sabryn moved toward her. "Come on, Willa. We have to go."

"Jasper," she whispered.

He gave her a firm nod and a smile he didn't feel. "It'll be fine. I got yours out without incident."

When she didn't move, Sabryn walked to her and grabbed her arm. She led Willa past Jasper. He followed her with his gaze, their eyes locked. He wanted to apologize for everything again, to hold her against him one more time. Instead, he remained rooted to his spot. Finn stood with the back passenger door open. He closed it once Willa was inside. Sabryn saluted him and slid behind the wheel. Finn inclined his head before getting into the car, as well. Then, they drove away.

Jasper waited until the taillights faded into the night before searching the people's pockets until he found a lighter to burn the ebony wood. He put up the same protection spells as he had with Willa, but he wasn't sure how long they would hold. When the last one left his lips, he braced himself and reached for the nearest person.

His palm warmed when he hovered it over the sliver of ebony wood. He hated the twisted, wrong aura of the splinter as it brushed against him. Willa's had been coated in evil, but this was at an entirely new level. And these were only tiny flakes. Jasper didn't want to know what a large piece might do to someone.

It took an extreme amount of magic and concentration for him to extract the teeny shaving from the top layer of skin. Thankfully, it wasn't buried deep like Willa's had been. He held the sliver suspended above the woman and flicked the lighter. Fire flared, and Jasper dropped the splinter into it and watched it burn.

He wiped the sweat from his forehead with his arm and closed his eyes. The shaving might have burned, but the remnants of its evil energy still ran through him. He waited for as long as he could before shifting to the next person.

Jasper found the wood and focused on it. He tried to pull it out, but it wouldn't budge. He tugged harder with his magic. Gradually, it obeyed him. He quickly burned it. His stomach roiled at the nasty residual magic the ebony wood left behind. He jumped up and ran to the side, emptying his stomach until he was only dry heaving. When he could finally lift his head again, he stood with his hands on his knees, drenched in sweat.

"How many have you done?" asked a deep Irish voice behind him.

He glanced to the side to find Balladyn. "Two."

"It's pointless to bring the others then."

"Bring them."

Balladyn gave him a stern look. "We both know you'll never be able to help them all."

"I'll do what I can until I can no' do any more."

"You're barely on your feet now."

It took extreme effort for Jasper to straighten, but he did. Then he faced the Reaper. "Are you going to help me or no'?"

"You're killing yourself."

He held Balladyn's gaze. There was no need for a response. Jasper had to do this. And not just for himself.

"Dying won't fix things with Willa."

"Right now, I'm more concerned with helping those who have been hurt."

Balladyn shook his head, but he didn't argue more. "What do you need?"

"No one can help me."

"We know how the ebony wood affects humans. There's been nothing about it doing anything to Fae or Reapers."

"You really want to take that chance?"

"We do what we have to do."

Jasper ran a hand down his face. He needed to sit before his legs gave out. Balladyn wasn't just Rhona's mate, he was also the Warden of Skye. Jasper couldn't take the chance of anything happening to him. "I need everyone to stay unconscious. It's easier to work without their screams. Can you do that?"

"I can."

"Those two are free of the ebony wood," Jasper said, pointing to the ones he had worked on already. "It might be better if they're taken away."

"I'll see it done," Balladyn replied with a nod. "But that's not what I meant when I offered to support you."

It was getting harder to stay upright. Jasper did it with sheer will alone. "I'm aware."

"It's not a weakness to ask for help."

Jasper smiled wryly. "I agree, but this is about so much more. And you know that. I'm part of why this is happening. I don't know specifics yet, but the use of the ebony wood points in that direction."

"Don't shoulder the blame for someone using ebony wood. You had no part in that, and I suspect you never would have, even if they had told you about it."

The Reaper was right, but that didn't make Jasper feel any better. "Let me see how many more I can help."

"I'll return shortly," Balladyn said.

Jasper forced his feet to move and walked to the nearest person, a male teenager with unruly red hair and braces. He tried to kneel slowly but ended up falling hard to his knees. Jasper moved his hands over the teen and found a cluster of splinters in his left ankle. None he had found so far had been buried as deeply as Willa's, but all of these were infinitely more difficult to pull out. It was almost as if someone had added magic to make sure they remained in the bodies.

His magic answered quickly and easily. It pooled in his palms. However, he felt as drained and weak as a newborn. He didn't have time for that. Not when so many needed help. He shook his head and focused. It required a great deal of concentration to wrench the cluster free. Sweat ran down his face and into his eyes. The cold night air did nothing to cool the rising temperature in his body. It took him two tries to get the lighter to work and burn the wood. He had no energy to stand. So, Jasper crawled to the next victim.

The elderly woman had the splinter in the corner of her lip. One shaving should be easier than the cluster, yet it took much more effort. His arms and hands shook violently when he finally got it loose from her mouth. He blindly reached for the lighter when it suddenly flared in the dark.

"I got it," Balladyn said.

Jasper looked up as the Reaper brought the lighter to the tiny shard and burned it. There was no time to talk as Jasper went to the next person.

CHAPTER THIRTY-EIGHT

SKYE DRUIDS

Willa paced the library at Carwood Manor. It was her favorite room in the grand house, but nothing about the warm wood, comfy leather sofas, or the many shelves of stories could soothe her tonight.

She glanced out the window as the clock on the mantel continued to tick away time. Her thoughts returned to Jasper again and again. She, more than most, knew exactly what risk he was taking. And as angry as she was with him, she didn't want him to die.

As she turned for another lap in front of the fireplace, she caught movement out of the corner of her eye and glanced toward the doorway. She spotted Bronwyn. "We should be out there with the others helping. And I don't need a babysitter."

"Is that what you think I am?" Bronwyn asked with a chuckle. She shook her head of brunette locks that just grazed the tops of her shoulders. "The threat around Skye is growing, along with the danger on the isle. We've not figured out how so many were afflicted with ebony wood or even when. Is it connected to our growing list of enemies? We don't know, but we aren't taking any chances. I'm here to make sure nothing breaks through into our dimension from another. The manor is sentient. It was built with magic on magical land. I always knew that, but it wasn't until recently that it spoke to me. I'm not sure if it spoke to my father, but that isn't the point. My point is, the house is our refuge. It will protect us as long as I protect it from anything coming through a portal."

Willa plunked down on the sofa, her head in her hands. She felt like a child grumbling about not getting what she wanted. The reality was that she didn't appreciate Jasper sending her away or Finn and Sabryn agreeing with him. Or Scott ordering her to remain at the manor.

"Jasper shouldn't be out there on his own," she said as she lifted her head to look at the empty hearth.

Bronwyn walked to one of the chairs and sank into it. She leaned back and grabbed one of the thick pillows to hold against her chest. "He isn't. Balladyn is with him."

That should make Willa feel better. Why didn't it? She had passed out when he took the last bit of wood from her wound, so she had no idea how the process had affected him. It couldn't have been easy. Emilie had looked physically ill just talking about it. Yet Jasper hadn't hesitated to help her. He had risked his life, and while she didn't believe much he said now, she knew he hadn't been party to using the ebony wood on her or anyone else.

The look in his eyes had convinced her of that. It wasn't fear she saw. It was so much worse. Dread, panic, horror. His response had been that of someone who had suffered a trauma. He wouldn't have willingly gone along with using ebony wood. It was why he had gone to such lengths to make sure she was free of it.

Willa leaned back, sinking low in the cushions. No matter how hard she tried, she couldn't stop remembering how Jasper had kissed her. Held her. Brought her body to life. All she had to do was think about the delicious weight of him, or him pumping his hips as he filled her body again and again.

"It's okay."

She jerked at the sound of Bronwyn's voice. Willa bit back her anger at getting dragged away from her memories. "I'm sorry, what?"

"It's okay not to be angry at Jasper."

Willa pushed to her feet and began pacing once more. "I'm still furious."

"He told you about himself. That took guts."

Right after giving her a night she would never forget. "And?" Willa asked, sharper than she intended.

Bronwyn tucked one leg under her. "You felt something for him from the very beginning. That doesn't just go away."

"He's the enemy."

"Is he? Because I don't think an enemy would be out there saving those he was sent to destroy."

Tears suddenly burned Willa's eyes. "I can't forgive what he's done."

"Can't or won't?" Bronwyn blew out a breath. "Look, I'm not trying to push you in one direction or another, but he did what he thought was right. Just as you and Luke did by going after the book."

Willa halted, taken aback by Bronwyn's words. "We were in the right."

"Were you? We think Beth's doing wrong."

"She is," Willa said, rolling her eyes.

Bronwyn took a deep breath and slowly released it in an obvious effort to keep her voice even. "What I'm saying is that Beth thinks she's right. George believes she's on the correct course. And so do we. No one sees themselves as the villain when everyone deems themselves fighting for the best side."

Willa turned her face away. She didn't want to hear this.

"You shared what we've been fighting with Jasper, which helped him see another side. That, combined with the ebony wood attacks, convinced him he didn't want to help George or Beth anymore."

"Instead of helping us, he was leaving."

"He thought it was the best option."

Willa tried to inhale deeply, but her lungs wouldn't expand enough. She rubbed her chest. "Jasper was forced to help us."

"Rhona suggested it. He could've refused. Working both sides isn't exactly something that can be done without the person's consent. Actually," she amended, "it can't be done well unless they're on board with it. Which he is."

Willa took another deep breath, but this one failed to be big enough. It made her chest feel tight, not being able to get as much air as she felt she needed into her lungs. "You've forgiven Jasper then?"

"I didn't say that. I understand his position and why he was part of George's organization. But you can't deny that he changed on Skye. I think a lot of that has to do with you."

Willa snorted and shook her head as she resumed pacing. "He was sent to seduce me. Everything he did was done to reach that goal."

"Hmm. I'm not so sure."

Willa stopped once more and threw up her hands before letting them slap against her legs. "Why not?"

"You went to him. From the very beginning."

She was all too aware of that. "True. I all but threw myself at him. I'm the one who kissed him first. I'm the one who went to his house that night and refused to leave—even when he said I should."

Bronwyn sat up and set aside the pillow. "Exactly. He didn't want to take advantage of you."

"It could've been a ploy."

Bronwyn's brows rose as she held Willa's gaze. "Was it, though? Tell me, did any part of that night not seem genuine?"

In a second, Willa was back in his room, his body moving against hers, their gazes locked before they climaxed. "I can't say for certain. I know what I felt. I thought he felt it, too, but I can't trust my feelings."

"What if everything was real? Everything you felt, everything you experienced with him? What's the worst that could happen?"

Willa briefly closed her eyes. "It already has. My heart is broken."

"And the best-case scenario?"

She shrugged, unwilling to say the words.

Bronwyn smiled sadly. "Would it be so horrible if he had feelings for you? If he loved you?"

"He lied."

"We all lie, Willa. I'm not making light of what he did to you or any of us. I'm just laying out the facts. There's something between the two of you. Do you really want to let that go?"

Willa tucked a leg against her as she sank onto the sofa again. "What about his past? The money he's stolen from others?"

"There isn't really anything I can say to that. You heard why he did it. We're all raised by adults. Certain their way is what we're supposed to do. Now, he's old enough to know what he's done is wrong, yet he keeps doing it. Then again, it's all he's ever known."

"He could've tried something else."

"That could be said about anyone. Including you and me."

Willa frowned. "Me?"

Bronwyn shrugged in answer.

"My parents were amazing. Dad struggled some as a single parent, but he didn't lead me down an illegal path. He and Scott have always looked out for me."

Bronwyn nodded. "They have. The bonds of family are important."

"Then why do you make me feel like it isn't?"

"I didn't mean that." Bronwyn twisted her lips and changed the leg tucked beneath her. "I'm just saying that we generally do what our parents teach us. If a person is comfortable, they keep doing it. There are always those who refuse for whatever reason."

She swallowed as she realized Bronwyn was circling something she didn't want to say outright. "What do I always do?"

"Willa, that's not what I meant."

"It is. Tell me."

Bronwyn blew out a breath. "It isn't a bad thing."

"Tell me. Please."

"You follow directions."

For a second, Willa wasn't sure she'd heard that correctly. "And what's wrong with that?"

"Scott told me the other day that you've always wanted to leave Edinburgh."

"So?" Willa asked with a shrug.

"Why didn't you?"

She hesitated, not wanting to answer. Willa realized too late that she had walked right into the question. "We're a family. Dad wanted us all together."

"What about when Scott left?"

"It was to help George. He was supposed to return."

"And when he didn't?"

Willa glanced at the cushion, noting the creases and scuffs in the leather from years of use. The question hung in the air. "It was fine."

"So, why hadn't you left?"

"I don't know."

"You do. You just don't want to admit it to me. And that's fine," Bronwyn hurried to say. "It's good to love your family, but they should never hold you back."

Willa folded her arms across her chest. "I don't think following orders is wrong. There's a lot going on tonight, and…" She trailed off when it became clear there was no reason for her to be locked in the manor instead of helping, other than that's where her brother wanted her.

Everyone else had a duty. Everyone except her. She understood when she was injured because she couldn't do anything. But there was no reason for her to be held back now. She was on Skye to fight alongside everyone else. She had as much to give as anyone did.

Bronwyn blew out a breath. "I have great respect for Scott. He's one of us in this fight. You're his little sister, who needs to be protected. It's worse because of what happened to you in Edinburgh. He feels responsible for all of it."

Willa scoffed. "That's ridiculous."

"Maybe. But that's why he has such a tight hold on you. More so because we still haven't located your father."

"I have magic. I can fight with any of you."

"I said as much to him. I'm sticking my nose in business that isn't mine, and I apologize. But I've seen you pacing for the past few hours. You're smart and strong, Willa. You know what you can and can't do. No one should tell you that now but you. Take others' advice, but the choice should be yours alone."

Willa reached across and took Bronwyn's hand. "Thank you for being so honest."

"I had to learn the same lesson the hard way. Now, saying all of that, I'm not advocating you rushing out there tonight. There's too much going on, and we have no idea who started it or how to end it. Wait for the next round and put your foot down."

Willa grinned and nodded, even as she lied and said, "Oh, of course. I wouldn't be that reckless."

"Good." Bronwyn got to her feet. "How about some tea?"

"That sounds good."

Willa waited until she was alone before she began plotting her next move.

CHAPTER THIRTY-NINE

SKYE DRUIDS

There were only six more injured to help. But it felt like six hundred. Jasper rested while Balladyn took the most recent victim wherever it was the Reaper took them. Was it to their homes? Or maybe somewhere Rhona could talk to them. Jasper didn't even know if they were all Druids or just random people. And he didn't have the brainpower to think of any of that at the moment.

He blew out a breath and looked up at the sky. Inky black had faded to midnight blue, which was turning softer, getting lighter. Dawn would arrive soon. He wouldn't have gotten this far if not for the Reaper. Balladyn hadn't just kept the injured unconscious, he'd also ferried them away. But he had done even more. Jasper had argued to keep the Reaper from attempting to extract the ebony wood, and Balladyn had conceded.

Jasper should've realized the Fae wouldn't give up so easily. He found another to help in the form of Finn. Jasper had tried to refuse Finn's participation, but both Balladyn and the Druid had a ready answer. Balladyn had only brought Finn when Jasper grew too exhausted to continue. Finn would use his ability as a bleeder to siphon the weariness and bad energy from Jasper.

Balladyn found a container that Finn could use to dump everything he took from Jasper. He had no idea how Finn did it, and when Jasper asked what the container was, Balladyn wouldn't answer. After each session with Finn, Balladyn took the container away. Again, Jasper had no idea what he did with it or where he emptied it.

There was a slight change in the air, alerting Jasper that Balladyn had returned. He was getting better at noticing when the Reaper came and left. Jasper tried to turn his head but couldn't. His arm gave out, and he hit the ground hard with the side of his face and shoulder.

"Nearly done, mate," Finn said.

Jasper slid his gaze to the side to see the Druid squatting beside him. Even in the dim light, Jasper saw the dark circles under Finn's eyes, and the tightness of his lips. Jasper flinched away when the Knight reached out an arm. "It's affecting you."

"I can handle it," Finn told him. "It moves through me to that container thing, remember? It doesn't remain in me for nearly as long as it does you. Also, I've asked Balladyn what the container is again. I've not worn him down yet, but he'll tell us eventually."

Jasper managed a weak smile. He appreciated Finn's lighthearted banter. Lord knew they all needed it.

"Let Finn help," Balladyn said as he walked up.

Jasper wished he could refuse. He hated that he needed help to finish this because he worried that no matter how quickly it went through Finn and into the vessel, the residual ebony wood magic was still in Finn's body. No matter how often Finn bled Jasper of all the gunk, it was still there, coating him in its oily residue.

"I can no' get through as many as before," Jasper said.

Balladyn's lips flattened as he looked at the last six. "We've taken note. We've got things covered. You do what you do, and Finn and I will do what we do. It'll be over soon."

"Will it?" Jasper shook his head. "Have you found out who did this?"

Finn grunted. "Not yet. You'll be helping us with that, mate."

Jasper wasn't so sure he'd come out of this, but he didn't bother to say that. He had betrayed Balladyn, Finn, and the others, yet they were aiding him. Granted, it was because he could do what no one else could, but he knew where he stood with them.

"Here. Drink this," Finn said as he put a cold bottle of water in Jasper's hand.

He managed to turn onto his side and put the bottle to his lips. The first touch of the cool liquid made him sigh. He drank deeply, spilling more than he got into his mouth. When he finished, he handed the bottle back to Finn.

The Druid set it aside and rubbed his hands together as he dropped to his knees. Balladyn set down the vase-like, black container next to Finn. Finn put one hand on the vessel and the other on Jasper. He would never get used to the odd feeling of Finn's magic pulling the muck from him. It didn't happen all at once. It was a slow, gradual clearing of the fatigue and other crud, like tugging weeds from a garden so the sun could reach the plants.

Jasper's breathing started to regulate, and he was able to keep his eyes open. The minute Finn finished, Balladyn took him and the vessel away. Jasper didn't waste any time turning over and getting back to work. It took longer and longer with each of the injured. What had once taken maybe five minutes, now took over thirty. But he didn't give up. He would find a way to free everyone from the ebony wood. And then all he could hope for was that Rhona and the others found whoever was responsible and stopped them before they could do it again.

Some of the victims just had the one sliver, but others had multiple shards. Sometimes, they were clustered together. Other times, they were spread out. There didn't seem to be any rhyme or reason for any of it. He guessed Theo was doing what cops did, determining where the individuals were to find if the wounded happened to be in the same place or if there were multiple offenders.

By the time Jasper finished with the current victim, he could barely hold his head up. The sliver had been lodged in the woman's earlobe with her earring. That should've been easy to extract, but he was getting too weak. He crawled to the next person and searched for the ebony wood. He found it at the top of the man's bald head. Unfortunately, he had landed on it when he fell, pushing the shaving deeper.

Kirsi stood at her window and looked out into the night. Something had woken her just after midnight, and she couldn't go back to sleep. There was something in the air. She couldn't put her finger on what it was, but it wasn't right. Not necessarily evil, but not good, either.

She thought about going to her parents', but she didn't want to disturb them. They probably couldn't help anyway. She had started to call Rhona several times but decided against it when she couldn't even explain to herself what was going on. How would she tell Rhona?

If she made the call, the conversation would inevitably lead to the other things happening to her. Namely, hearing the being from The Grey and her fall down the mountain. She didn't want anyone else to know because it made her look daft, and she didn't want them to treat her differently. Which they would. Everyone would.

Well, everyone except Callum.

Kirsi hadn't seen him since the trail. He had gotten her home and up the stairs to the flat without her parents seeing, then helped her get situated in bed with her foot elevated and an ice pack. He had placed a drink and snacks nearby for when she wanted them, and after he'd taken care of her, he left.

She'd thought he might come by to check on her. That wasn't Callum, though. He was a loner. He kept his distance from most. Not that she blamed him. The only ones who seemed to want to be with him were women—young, old, and every age in between. They seemed drawn to him like moths to a flame. Everyone wanted the bad boy of Skye.

Kirsi tested her ankle. The swelling was gone, and it no longer hurt to put weight on it. She grabbed a cardigan and slipped her arms through it as she stepped outside in her pajamas and slippers. It bothered her not knowing what had woken her. She couldn't see anything in the sky like the mist, so what could it have been?

She made her way down the stairs and across the road. Then she walked the short distance to the shoreline. Dawn was coming, yet it wasn't chasing away whatever hung in the air. As soon as she thought the words, she knew they were an apt description.

Ferne had said something similar before, but now Kirsi sensed it herself. But there was nothing to see. Maybe if there were, it would be easier to digest what was going on. Being outside helped. She couldn't explain why, but it was as if she needed to be out in the fresh air.

Kirsi kept looking around, fully expecting to see or hear something. Had the creature from The Grey gotten loose? Was it another being? More mist? She rubbed her hands over her arms to try and shake off the chill, but it had settled into her bones. There was no getting rid of it now.

She suddenly halted. Her body went rigid before chills covered her, running from her head down her body. There was a new presence on the isle. Someone who hadn't been here before. No. Someone she hadn't *noticed* before.

She swallowed as terror gripped her. She shouldn't know these things. She never had before. Why now? More importantly, what was she supposed to do about it? Rhona wouldn't appreciate being called every five minutes with questions she most likely couldn't answer either. But Kirsi didn't want to do this on her own.

There was Ferne, but she hadn't known a lot to begin with. She could have gotten more answers, though. Kirsi reached for her mobile in her pocket only to realize she had left it in her flat. She turned to go and get it when the air flickered just as it had on the top of the mountain. She took a step back, her heart leaping into her throat. The creature was back.

But it wasn't the being she saw. Instead, it was a big black book. She could make out the tome in great detail. The marks on the leather cover, the dents in the corners from being set down too hard on a shelf. Even the crinkled page corners. She saw arms, like someone holding the book, but she couldn't see more than that.

As quickly as the image had appeared, it vanished as if it had never been there. She blinked and saw movement near the water. It was Callum, sitting on a squat boulder with something pressed against his face.

Kirsi wondered why she hadn't noticed him when she walked past. If she hadn't turned around and seen the...whatever it was, she wouldn't have seen him now. She stared at him. He glanced in her direction when she got halfway to him. That was when she noticed he held what was left of one shirt sleeve against the side of his bleeding face. She ran the rest of the way to him.

"What happened?" she asked breathlessly.

He waved away her words. "It's fine."

"It's far from fine. Come with me. I'll see to it."

"There's no need." He dodged her hand when she tried to grab him.

Kirsi walked to stand in front of him and looked into his amber eyes. He wouldn't meet her gaze, looking anywhere but directly at her. She wanted to smooth his hair away from his face. She wanted to tend to him as he had her. But he wouldn't let her.

Her gaze swept over him, noting his bare right arm where he had torn away the sleeve to hold against the left side of his face. No anger tightened his expression. Instead, she saw him as very few probably did—vulnerable. The need to comfort him was strong, but she wouldn't intrude if he didn't want her.

"Would you rather be alone?" she asked.

There was a long pause before he said, "Nay."

She didn't like the sight of the blood on his shirt or face. Had someone attacked him? Had he started it? Her stomach churned, thinking someone might have gone after Callum. People expected him to be like his father. They anticipated and assumed, but that wasn't Callum. No one gave him a chance to be his own person. He had shown her nothing but kindness.

He scooted to make room for her. Kirsi moved to his right side. She brushed against his bare arm as she sat. A shock ran through her, warm and electric, which had nothing to do with the numerous scars on his arm and everything to do with him.

She couldn't stop thinking about how he had followed her into The Grey and then driven her home. It had been Callum who'd stopped her descent down the mountain and then carried her to her car when she couldn't walk. And he'd never asked for anything in return. She wasn't sure they were friends, exactly, but he was the only one she could talk to about everything. If he wouldn't let her see to his injury, she would be here for him in other ways.

"Give me a name," she said.

He glanced at her, his brow furrowed. "Excuse me?"

"Who did this to you? Give me names, and I'll make sure never to serve them at the co-op. I can even *misplace* their mail," she said with a grin.

He stared at her for a long time before curving his lips into a smile. "You're full of shite."

"You think? Try me. Give me a name." Let him think she was teasing. She would do...something to whoever had hurt him. She didn't know what yet, but she'd think of something.

Callum chuckled and shook his head, looking back at the water. "You constantly surprise me."

"I look after my friends."

His head swung to her. His eyes were penetrating as he softly asked, "Is that what we are?"

"Of course."

"I doona have friends."

"You do now." She knocked her shoulder into his, needing to see his smile return.

Kirsi was able to breathe easier when she got what she wished for.

CHAPTER FORTY

SKYE DRUIDS

One by one, the entire team returned to the manor. Willa stayed out of the way and remained quiet as she listened to everyone. They were all dead on their feet, which made it easy to blend into the background. Scott barely paid attention to her after greeting her. It made it convenient to gather information without seeming too interested.

"Please, tell me someone got a lead on who did this," Sabryn said as she leaned her arms on the table.

Rhona was next to her, stifling a yawn. "Nothing yet. I have my suspicions."

"George," Scott muttered.

Bronwyn grunted. "It could be Beth."

"It might be both," Elias added.

Henry rubbed his eyes with the heels of his hands. "Then we go after them both."

"We don't know how far-reaching things were last night. Going after them now would be a mistake," Esther stated.

Carlyle nodded as he reclined in his chair, his legs stretched out before him and feet crossed at the ankles. "Agreed. We need proof, and then we have to make sure we can take them both. Otherwise, we could be going through this again."

"Getting the evidence we need won't be easy," Elodie said before covering her mouth on a yawn.

Theo stood with his arms crossed, leaning a shoulder against the wall. "I hope it's George or Beth who did this. Because if it's someone else—or some*thing* else—we'll end up as befuddled as we are now, trying to determine who created the mist."

"Or what's enveloping Skye," Ferne added.

Balladyn chose that moment to appear with Finn, who fell into a chair. Carlyle barely caught him before he toppled over. Willa instantly went on alert. No one had spoken about Jasper, and she was dying to know something, anything. The Reaper said nothing as he walked to Rhona and bent down to share a few quiet words with her. The waiting was excruciating. Willa had to bite her tongue not to demand that Balladyn tell her how Jasper was.

Finally, the Reaper straightened and looked around the room. Willa tensed when his gaze lingered for a heartbeat on her, but he didn't call her, which allowed her to remain unseen by the others.

"Jasper did it. He removed the ebony wood from all twenty-eight people," Balladyn announced.

Many in the room sighed with relief, but Willa knew there was so much more to it than merely getting the slivers out.

"How is he?" Nikolai asked.

Balladyn shrugged. "He'll need time to recover."

"I'm sorry I couldn't do more," Finn muttered, his eyes closed.

"There wasn't a need. Jasper is resting in his own bed."

Carlyle braced Finn. "Just as you should be."

Willa was shocked that no one was with Jasper. She glanced through the kitchen doorway toward the front door. She could slip out and be there in case he needed anything. Everyone in the room should be bending over backward for him now. She turned and found Balladyn's red-ringed silver eyes on her once more. He knew what she was thinking, but he said nothing.

"You should've brought Jasper here," Bronwyn said.

Willa silently thanked her.

"It was his idea to go home," Balladyn announced.

Shock reverberated through Willa. Her mind refused to accept Balladyn's words.

The Reaper continued, his gaze locked on Willa. "He suspects George or Beth,"—he stopped for a moment—"or *both* had a hand in all of this, especially since they recently used ebony wood."

Willa tried to sink into the wall as all eyes turned to her, but there was no escape.

"He thinks if George or Beth are on Skye, and he remains at his place, they might pay him a visit," Balladyn finished.

A grimace etched lines in Carlyle's face. "Fuck me."

"It could work," Elias said.

Elodie blew out a breath. "But at what cost?"

"He doesn't expect to live long," Finn stated as he opened his eyes. "He's doing what he can to help. Crazy bastard." Finn smiled sadly and shook his head.

Bronwyn got to her feet. "There's a reason Emilie refused to help those people last night. She was very clear there would be repercussions. Jasper risked everything to treat the afflicted. I, for one, don't like the idea of sitting by while who knows what happens to him for helping *our* people."

"We won't be sitting by doing nothing," Rhona replied.

Balladyn shook his head. "Nay, we will not."

"You trust him that much?" Scott demanded, his tone suggesting he thought them addled.

Finn turned his dark eyes to Scott. "I do. You weren't there. You didn't see what treating those people did to him."

"It could all be a ruse, something he planned from the beginning," Filip said.

Willa startled. She hadn't even realized he was there. It was the first time he had spoken. She shifted to see him standing near her brother, just a little behind him, hidden like she was.

"It could be," Rhona said with a halfhearted shrug.

Scott ran a hand down his face. "You have the entire isle to worry about. That's putting a lot of faith in someone who came here to betray us."

"Me," Willa whispered under her breath. Jasper had betrayed her, not any of them. At least, he hadn't gotten to them yet.

Rhona slowly got to her feet. "I trusted you and Filip. George sent both of you to convince Elodie to join her community. There isn't much difference in what you two did versus Jasper."

"I disagree," Filip replied. "We didna come to betray anyone."

Scott's lips twisted as he grimaced. "There could be an argument that we, in fact, did. George wanted Elodie because of her family's magic."

"And because of me," Elias interjected.

Elodie took Scott's hand in hers and looked up at him. "But you didn't. Neither did Filip. And neither has Jasper."

"Someone should be with Jasper," Bronwyn said into the silence that followed.

Willa glanced through the doorway again. She wanted to sneak out, but Scott kept looking her way. He would try to stop her, and she didn't have time for an argument.

"I'll know if someone enters his home," Balladyn replied.

Carlyle sat up in his chair, his hands on his thighs. "We're running on empty. We need rest before we face anything else."

"We don't even know what that could be," Henry said.

Ferne tucked her dark hair behind an ear. "Those injured are now safely back in their homes. That's a start."

"I need to interview them," Theo added.

Rhona nodded. "Emilie is sleeping upstairs. I suggest we get a few hours of rest, too. We don't know what's coming, and we need to be ready."

Willa waited as everyone filed out of the kitchen. Bronwyn nodded subtly. Willa returned the gesture. Thankfully, Scott and Elodie were too involved in their discussion to notice her. Filip seemed lost in thought. The room emptied until it was just her and Balladyn.

"Is Jasper really all right?" she asked.

Balladyn sighed as he tilted his head to the side. "That's a relative term. I'm not sure he'll ever be the same. I've known a lot of individuals in my long years of life, and I can say with all honesty, only a select few would've done what he did."

"You like him."

"Aye. I also understand him."

Willa bit her lip. "Meaning?"

"Meaning Jasper is doing the best he can."

"He lied."

Balladyn grinned softly as he stopped beside her. "You saw

something in him, something he didn't see in himself. He deserves a second chance."

"I'm not sure I can trust him."

Balladyn nodded and quietly walked away.

Willa remained in the kitchen. It seemed quieter in the manor now than earlier when it had just been her and Bronwyn with Emilie sleeping upstairs. She was confused about her feelings for Jasper, about wanting him to be safe and healthy, and about his motivations.

She wanted to believe everything between them had been real and that he'd meant every word and action. But doubt lingered. She didn't want to analyze every syllable that fell from his lips or scrutinize his every move. That wasn't any way for two people to live.

Despite her anger, she still had feelings for him.

She left the kitchen and meandered through the house. The rooms were vast. Many had only a few items within since Bronwyn was slowly restoring the grand manor. Willa couldn't shake the feeling that she needed to get to Jasper. She couldn't explain why, and the longer she tried to ignore it, the more it grew, becoming so urgent her stomach knotted and she became queasy.

Willa threw up her hands in defeat. She strode to her purse and dug a receipt from the bottom. She left a quick note for Scott and grabbed his keys. Then she made her way to the door. She unlocked it, but it wouldn't budge. She put her forehead against the wood. The house didn't want her to leave, but if she were going to get to Jasper, she would have to try and convince it to open the door.

"Please," she whispered. "I need to get to Jasper. I feel that he needs me. Maybe I'll find out he really can't be trusted. But I might learn he can be. I only know that I have to go to him." Willa tried the handle again. This time, the door opened. "Thank you."

She slipped from the manor, closing the door quietly behind her. There was a sound as the lock clicked into place. She ran to Scott's vehicle and climbed inside. For a moment, she thought someone might hear her starting the engine, but no one came rushing outside or looked out a window.

Willa backed up and went down the long drive to the road. The morning sun was blinding as she drove entirely too fast. The entire way to Jasper's, she kept trying to think what she would say. It might be better if she didn't talk at all. Just being there watching him was all she needed to do. That way, she wouldn't say something she might regret later.

As she neared his house, her stomach tightened nervously. Willa parked and walked to his door. She knocked, but no one answered. He could be sleeping. She tried the doorbell, but still, there was nothing. That was when she realized he might not be able to get out of bed. That only made her angry at Balladyn for leaving him.

She tried the door handle. It was locked, as she'd expected. Willa walked around the house to the back. That door was also secured. She tried the garage door, and the knob turned in her hand. Just as she was about to step over the threshold, she recalled that Balladyn had said he would know if someone entered Jasper's house. She shrugged and walked inside.

Willa glanced at his SUV as she hurried to the door that led inside. It should be locked. To her surprise, it wasn't. She paused for only a moment before continuing inside. Willa checked the downstairs to make sure he wasn't there before heading to the second floor.

She stopped outside his bedroom door. She'd only been inside once. Willa took a deep breath and softly turned the knob to peek inside. She didn't want to startle him. She looked through the small slit to find the bed empty.

Willa pushed open the door wider and rushed inside. One look showed that Jasper was gone.

CHAPTER FORTY-ONE

SKYE DRUIDS

Every muscle rebelled, the strain of standing too much to bear. But Jasper did it anyway. He didn't have a choice. He wasn't about to show his enemy his weaknesses. Though if his adversary didn't arrive soon, it might be out of his hands.

He tried to concentrate on the mountains rising behind him. This wasn't his first visit to the Fairy Pools, but it would probably be his last. Wind whipped around him, tugging his hair into his eyes as the roar of rushing water drowned out everything else. He had been in bed, attempting to sleep, when something yanked him away.

At first, he'd thought it was Balladyn, but the Reaper had gotten him to his room. There was no reason for him to come back. The next thing Jasper knew, he was standing beside the Fairy Pools. He assumed it was an enemy. Who else would do such a thing? More importantly, who had that kind of power? It certainly wasn't a Druid. Maybe a Dragon King.

Jasper swallowed, his throat tight. He'd already dry heaved

countless times, but his stomach clenched as if it were ready for more. Not knowing who had brought him to the pools caused serious apprehension, which didn't help his already overtaxed body.

"Show yourself," he demanded.

Jasper turned in a circle. It was odd visitors weren't meandering along the path beside the pools. The weather was nice, and while it was early, it was still one of the hottest spots for tourists.

Unease slid through him. He nearly called for Balladyn. The Reaper had helped him, but Jasper didn't want to test how far Balladyn would go for someone who had betrayed one of his friends. Besides, Jasper was used to doing things alone. He'd never had others watching his back, never had someone he could trust in a pinch. He'd done everything himself. Always. Even when his father was alive. He'd drilled it into Jasper's head that he couldn't count on anyone but himself.

Jasper had believed that his entire life. Until recently. It was an odd feeling knowing he could count on others. He'd always thought it would make him weak, but he'd just learned it had the opposite effect. Without Balladyn and Finn, Jasper wouldn't be standing here now. He owed them a large debt, one he feared he might never be able to repay.

He swayed, growing heated even as the wind brushed the exposed skin of his arms and face. He was getting so hot he was about to tear off his short-sleeved T-shirt. The fever had been trying to take hold for hours. It looked like it had finally succeeded.

"Come on! I doona have all day."

"You have all the time in the world."

Jasper's heart sank as he heard the feminine voice behind him

—one he would recognize anywhere. He turned and looked into pale brown eyes. "Beth."

"You look surprised," she said with a triumphant smile as the wind ruffled her short, light brown hair. "I bet you didn't know I could pull someone from their home."

He'd never liked Beth. There had always been something devious behind her eyes. And he should know since that was how he'd lived his life. Beth was different from the last time he had seen her. He'd never feared her before. He did now. If she had the ability to take him from his own home, what else could she do?

Beth's eyes glinted with amusement. "I can practically see the wheels turning in your head. You're trying to figure out how I did it."

"I know how."

"Oh?" she asked, her brows raised. "Do tell."

"The book."

She chuckled. "You are a smart one. The world is open to me. All I have to do is reach out and take it."

"You're the one who injured all those innocents with ebony wood."

"Guilty," she stated with a wide smile while batting her lashes. "And they were far from innocent."

"They're no' a part of your war."

Her smile vanished, replaced by anger that contorted her comely face into something heinous. "They're Skye Druids. That puts them front and center in this."

"Is it those on Skye you want to punish? Or is it Bronwyn."

"She'll get her comeuppance. Don't you worry. You should be more concerned about what I intend to do to you."

Magic filled his palms. He might get in a hit before she

retaliated, but he wouldn't cause much damage. He was too drained, and she was far too powerful. "You've come to the wrong person if you want someone to beg."

"I don't want you to beg, Jasper." Her smile was slow as it spread across her face.

He was so fucked. "What *do* you want?"

"Where do I start?" she mused, clasping her hands behind her back as she glanced at the sky. Then her gaze lowered to him. "I wonder if you would've been so cavalier with your trust if you knew the truth of who you are."

"I know who I am."

She laughed, shaking her head. "You don't have a clue. Your so-called friends know. Makes you wonder why they haven't told you."

"They had their reasons." She was trying to put a wedge between them, but Jasper wouldn't fall for it.

Beth twisted from side to side like a child, her glee evident. "George never would've sent you had she known. She's sure you won't turn on her, but we both know you already have. I'll love rubbing that in her face."

Jasper watched her. He wanted to slap Beth's smug expression away. He couldn't tell whether she had gone daft or was just goading him. It might be a wee bit of both. Which wasn't good any way he looked at it.

"You like it here," she continued. "It's about more than that glamorous house of yours or the horses. Even Willa. You have a connection to Skye."

"It's just an isle," he lied.

Beth chuckled. "You used to be better at deception. The truth,

Jasper, is much simpler. You like Skye, you feel at home here, because you were born here."

He wanted to deny it, but he couldn't. He didn't know where he'd been born. His father had never said, and Jasper had stopped asking. After a while, it hadn't mattered.

"Ooooh. If that one got you, I've got an even bigger announcement," Beth stated triumphantly.

"You didna bring me here to tell me made-up stories."

He barely got the last syllable out before something pummeled him in the chest. Shooting pain radiated from his abdomen to his brain and then flashed throughout his body. He looked down to see over a dozen pieces of ebony wood sticking out of him. His knees buckled. He slammed onto rock hard enough to crack bone before toppling sideways while struggling for breath.

Beth walked to him and pushed at his arm with the toe of her boot. She leaned over him, loathing and anger in her eyes. "You have no idea who you are or what you're capable of. Fortunately, you never will. I had to test you to make sure you were who I thought. You fell for it by helping all those worthless Druids. You saved them. Proving exactly who you are."

Jasper gasped for air. It was getting harder and harder to breathe. Beth's face was going in and out of focus.

"If only you had paid closer attention. You met your mother."

He tried to grab her leg, but his hand met nothing but air.

"Emilie realized you were her son the first time she saw you. You would've figured it out, too, had you paid closer attention to the pictures and noted the fact that you're the spitting image of her husband—your real father."

Jasper shook his head. None of it could be true. He never missed details like that. Then he recalled he'd been utterly focused on Willa and helping her. His mother. Emilie was his mother. Why hadn't she said anything?

Beth laughed, the sound echoing around him as the wind snatched it. "You should see your face. Your death will be long and very, very painful. I doubt you'll be able to keep the screams in for long."

He blinked and tried to focus. When he looked for Beth, she was gone. He stared at the morning sky with its sparse clouds and wished he could say his goodbyes to Willa and Emilie. It wasn't fair that he'd found the love of his life, only to lose her, and to come across his mother, without her telling him the truth.

"Jasper!"

The agony filling him was so intense he figured he was hallucinating Willa's voice. Even if she were here, he wouldn't be able to talk. He was having problems even stringing thoughts together.

"Jasper!"

He blinked and felt something wet slide onto his temple. The last time he had cried was when his father—no, the man who had raised him—had died. Jasper didn't want to die. He wanted time to make up for what he'd done to Willa. He wanted to prove he could live a better life and give up his old ways. He wanted to know his mother and find out about his father. He'd silently hungered for connections all his life. And they had been on Skye all along.

"Oh, God. Jasper!"

Willa's face was suddenly above him. She shoved her long, dark curls out of the way as tears fell down her cheeks. Her hands hovered above him as if she didn't know where to touch.

"Who did this to you? What can I do?" she cried and looked around helplessly.

Jasper managed to grasp her hand. "W-Wil-la."

"I'm here," she told him. "I'm here. I can remove these."

He stopped her and shook his head. It was too late for him. Nothing could help him now.

More tears fell down her cheeks. "You can't give up."

Jasper rubbed his thumb across the back of her hand. He wouldn't die alone. That had been one of his greatest fears, but he didn't have to worry about that now. Willa was with him. He had hurt her, but she had somehow found him. That thought stopped him cold. How had she found him? Had Beth brought her as she had him?

"B-B-Beth," he said, struggling with each syllable.

Willa sniffed, her eyelashes wet and spiky from crying. "Beth did this to you? I'll kill her myself."

"Dan...ger...ous."

"Let's focus on you. Hold on. I'm going to fix this. You'll be fine."

He worked his mouth, but words no longer came. Jasper held her hand as it became harder and harder to keep his eyes open. He heard Willa's voice talking fast. It sounded as if she were far away in a tunnel. He gripped her hand tighter. Scott and the others would protect her. Willa was a fighter. She would survive, he was sure of it. He just wouldn't be here to see it.

Jasper forced his eyes open one more time.

"Nay," she whispered. "Jasper, don't leave me. Don't give up. Hold on. Do you hear me? Hold on!"

If only he could.

CHAPTER FORTY-TWO

SKYE DRUIDS

Willa shook Jasper's shoulders, but he didn't open his eyes again. She looked around helplessly. No one was around, nobody near who could do anything. She looked at his chest and the numerous wounds the ebony wood had made, each projectile a different length and circumference.

And the blood. There was so much blood. It was everywhere. It had soaked Jasper's white shirt so completely that it ran onto the stones and the ground. Some even fell into the water.

Willa felt for a pulse. She couldn't find one but refused to believe that Jasper was gone. He was too strong, too determined to be felled—not after removing the wood from her and all the others the night before. He had survived all of that. He could make it through this, too.

Her eyes welled with fresh tears as she looked at the wreckage of his upper body. He hadn't hesitated to help her. She wouldn't falter in doing the same for him. She wrapped her fingers around a thick spike of ebony wood and tried to extract it. It was buried so deep that it wouldn't budge.

Willa utilized both hands and got to her feet for leverage. She used every ounce of strength she had, gritting her teeth while praying—and then cussing—to any higher power who would listen. The wood finally came free with a sucking noise. She fell to her back and released the wood before returning to Jasper, uncaring what might happen to her for touching it.

Blood gushed from the wound. She placed her hands over it to stanch the flow, but it didn't do much good. She couldn't do this alone. She needed help.

Willa fumbled for her mobile in her back pocket. With her hands slippery from Jasper's blood, she dropped it and watched impotently as it tumbled into the water and over a waterfall. Her mobile was a lifeline that easily connected her to family and friends. Now, it was gone. She nearly gave in to the urge to succumb to anguish, but she had one more card to play.

"Balladyn!" she screamed at the top of her lungs. One way or another, she would get the Reaper's attention.

She never took her gaze from Jasper's face. His eyes would open any second. He was a fighter. He wouldn't give up. But the truth was right before her. Breath no longer moved through his body. No amount of wishing or hoping could bring him back. Willa shut her eyes, dropped her forehead to her hands covering his injury, and sobbed.

If only she had heeded her intuition when it told her to get to Jasper hours earlier. She might have been able to do something. Maybe even save him. Instead, she had sat around and waited until she could sneak away so she didn't have to explain herself to anyone. Bronwyn had been right. Willa always did what people told her to do. Why hadn't she stood up to Scott? Why hadn't she followed her gut?

Because she didn't like to disappoint her family. And because it was easier than taking a stand. She loved her dad and Scott, but it was past time she stood on her own. No longer would she disappoint herself.

"I should've done it sooner," she whispered to Jasper. "You might still be alive. You didn't deserve this."

She sniffed and lifted her head, only to still. She was no longer outside. Instead, she was in a cave. Small lights hung near the arched ceiling, creating a soft, amber glow. The sound of water was quieter, too. The walls were smooth and covered in Celtic symbols.

Was this Beth's doing? Willa should get to her feet to prepare, but she couldn't leave Jasper. No way would Willa allow Beth to defile his body more than she already had. Willa didn't know the details of what Beth had done, but it didn't matter. The Druid was hers to track down.

There was still no sign of Balladyn. Surely, the Reaper could find her. Just in case, she called for him again, this time in a whisper. "Balladyn, please. I need your help."

Willa licked her lips and scanned the area in hopes of seeing Balladyn appear. But she was utterly alone. Each time she looked at Jasper, tears engulfed her. Her conversation with Bronwyn replayed in her head. Willa had been so horrible to him. She was hurt and had lashed out. Maybe she had been right to feel that way, but he had put aside his opinions and emotions to work with them. And had she done the same? No. She had licked her wounded pride and wallowed in misery.

There had been a spark of something between them from the moment she saw Jasper. She hadn't been able to get enough of him.

She'd even gone so far as to unexpectedly show up at his home just to be near him. He'd given her a night she would never forget. Willa had thought her future was stretched out before her with a man who would always be by her side.

When he laid out the truth for her, telling her things most people would go to great lengths to hide, she hadn't accepted him. She had turned her back on him. Justified or not, she had put her feelings before everyone else's and every*thing*, including locating her father. The hurt had gone that deep. It should've told her exactly how much she had fallen for Jasper.

"I'm sorry," she told him. "I should've stood with you. I should've asked questions and let you explain. But more than that, I should've told you I loved you."

She turned her head to her arm and wiped her cheek against her sleeve. It should alarm her that she didn't know where she was or how she would get out. Or that Balladyn hadn't answered. She liked to think he was the one who had moved them, but he would've shown himself. Which meant it was someone else. Yet she couldn't find it in her to be scared or worried when she had lost the person she loved most.

Willa glared at the ebony wood. The black material was beautiful and rare, but she would find each tree and burn it to the ground so no one else ever had to suffer again. She rose to her knees, her jeans squishing because of Jasper's blood. Then she began pulling more wood from his body. Some pieces were easier than others, but she didn't stop until every last bit lay in a pile beside her. Willa sat back on her haunches and sighed. When she lifted her gaze, she found a woman standing ten feet away.

"Hello," she said in an Irish accent.

Willa looked her over, taking in her chin-length black hair and too-gorgeous face before noticing the red, long-sleeved blouse tucked into bright yellow slacks with matching yellow heels. The woman was stunning. That alone clued her in to who she dealt with, but it was the silver eyes she could see even from the distance that told her it was a Light Fae. "Did you bring us here?"

"Nay," she said and shook her head. Then she nodded toward Jasper. "He did."

Willa looked at Jasper and placed her hand on his chest. "That's impossible."

"It isn't. But before I explain, let me introduce myself. I'm Alannah, and I'm a—"

"Light Fae," Willa finished for her. "I know. Where are we, and what do you want with us?"

Alannah clasped her hands before her. "Rhona once more invited a friendship between the Fae and the Skye Druids. You're in the real Fairy Pools, though not the tourist magnet that draws people from all over the realm."

"How do I get out? I need to bring Jasper to…" She trailed off. It would be pointless to take him to the hospital. The only place she could bring him was to the manor. Tears burned her eyes. Willa tried to hold them back, but she was drowning in sorrow for the love she had lost and the man she had been meant to spend her life with.

"I can take you anywhere you wish to go. Both of you," Alannah said.

Willa wiped at her wet cheeks. "What do you want in exchange?"

"Nothing. As I said, Jasper brought you here."

"How? You've not explained that part," Willa stated testily. She didn't trust the Light Fae.

Alannah's serene expression didn't change. "This section of the pools is closed to anyone who isn't Fae. It's only open to humans by invitation."

"You make it sound as if Jasper is a Fae."

"It sounds that way because he is. Well, he has Fae blood. It spilled above and seeped into the stones, the ground, and the water. All recognized him for what he is, one of us, no matter how little of our blood he might have."

Willa's throat clogged. "Does that mean you can help him?"

Alannah's shoulders lifted as she drew in a deep breath. "I don't know any Fae who can return someone from the dead."

"Then why are we here?" Willa asked angrily.

"Beth was returning for you. We offered you sanctuary."

Willa bent over and placed a kiss on Jasper's forehead. Then she got to her feet. "Take me back."

"You can't possibly think to face Beth."

"That's exactly what I plan to do."

"That would be suicide. Look what she did to Jasper."

Willa shrugged. "Someone needs to stop her. You could help."

"It isn't our fight."

"Of course, it isn't," she replied sarcastically.

Alannah took a step closer. "Stop and ask yourself why Beth is going to so much trouble."

"If you know something, just tell me. I don't have time for this."

"I don't know. She went out of her way to get Jasper alone."

Willa shrugged. "We all knew Beth would attack."

"I'm trying to help."

"Then bring Jasper back. Heal him," Willa demanded. "Do *something*."

Alannah's face tightened, and she glanced to the side. "I am. I'm talking to you."

"That's not good enough."

There was a long pause as the Fae stared at her. "It's all you're going to get."

Willa turned away as she struggled to keep her emotions in check. She knew she was being irrational and expecting too much, but she was grasping for something to cling to. "I can't lose Jasper."

"Sometimes, we don't get that choice."

She faced Alannah. "Please. There must be something…"

"Fate has already spoken," Alannah said before walking away.

CHAPTER FORTY-THREE

SKYE DRUIDS

"Where the fuck is Willa?" Scott shouted as he rushed from room to room.

He still didn't know what had woken him and made him check on his sister. As soon as he found her room empty, he began searching the manor.

Elias blocked his way in the hall. "Your vehicle is gone."

Scott shook his head, his chest tightening, making breathing difficult. This couldn't be happening. His dad was still missing, but by some miracle, Willa had been saved from the ebony wood. And by none other than Jasper. And now, his sister was gone. Unfortunately, he knew exactly where she had gone. "She's with that bastard."

"The bastard who saved twenty-eight people, as well as your sister?" Bronwyn asked as she walked up.

Scott had woken everyone with his shouts, and all had joined his search for Willa. That meant all of them were now gathered around to hear what was happening. "Aye. Him."

"Maybe she just needed to talk to him," Elodie said.

A surge of anger washed through Scott. "Then she should've told me."

"She's not a child," Carlyle stated. "She's an adult and can make her own decisions."

Theo quickly moved between Scott and Carlyle, holding up his hands to keep them in place. "All right. Easy, lads. Let's no' say anything we'll regret."

"Scott has every right to be upset. Willa is his sister, and she verra nearly died," Filip said.

Sabryn rolled her eyes. "So did Elodie. Elias didn't try to keep her under lock and key."

Scott jerked back, the words slamming into him like a punch to the kidneys. "Is that what you think I do?"

"I don't think it. I know it," Sabryn replied.

Bronwyn nodded. "So do I."

Scott looked around at the others. His gut clenched when Elodie wouldn't quite meet his eyes. "You, too?" he asked in disbelief.

"You're protective by nature, and she was hurt."

"But?" he pushed when she didn't continue.

Elodie glanced away. "You can try to keep pushing her away from Jasper, but she loves him. Her heart will always lead her back to him. All you'll do is put a wedge between you."

Scott leaned against the wall and ran a hand down his face. He hadn't thought he was overprotective of Willa, but apparently, he was. She was his sister, his blood. She meant the world to him. "Bloody hell."

"She'll come back," Ferne said.

Rhona strode up then. "I don't think she will."

"What?" Scott asked as he straightened.

Rhona's long, red hair was gathered atop her head. She looked as if she had dressed quickly, and her green eyes were locked on him. "Balladyn woke when Willa shouted his name."

"Where is she?" Scott had to get to her. All he needed was a location.

Rhona hesitated. "I don't know. And Balladyn hasn't been back since he left. That was an hour ago."

"And you're just now telling me?" Scott yelled.

Elodie smoothed a hand down his back and asked Rhona, "Have you called for him?"

"Of course," Rhona replied tightly.

Scott squeezed the bridge of his nose with his thumb and forefinger. "I have to get to Jasper's."

"I just came from his place. They're not there," Rhona told him.

Scott was at his wit's end. How could he help his sister if he didn't know where she was? And why hadn't Balladyn returned with her? "What do I do? I doona know what to do."

"We prepare," Elias said with a firm nod.

Filip snorted. "We doona even know what we're up against."

"It doesna matter," Theo said, walking past them to the stairs and going down a level to the second floor.

Scott quickly followed, along with everyone else. They gathered in their meeting room, where Theo wrote on the blank whiteboard.

He finished and faced them. "As I see it, we have multiple enemies. They could be connected, they could also be one entity, but our best bet is to assume they're individuals."

"We're so fekking screwed," Finn murmured.

Theo pointed to where he'd put Kerry's name and a question mark. "We know Kerry wasna working alone. We contained her, but she isna talking. That means whoever created the mist is still out there." He moved over and pointed to the next. "Second, we have the evil that brought Ferne to Skye." Theo directed everyone to the third spot. "And The Grey and the being there. At the moment, it's locked in its dimension. We doona need to worry about that."

"Unless it's part of the evil," Ferne said.

Theo nodded tightly. "Aye. Last, but no' least, we have George and Beth."

"We might want to consider them individually, too," Bronwyn pointed out.

Carlyle eyed the board with disdain. "That's a lot of enemies to consider."

"Aye. And any of them could have Willa," Scott said.

Rhona walked to the board and stared at it for a long moment. "Then we focus on the ones we can. Kerry, George, and Beth."

"You want us to go to Edinburgh to find George and Beth?" Finn asked.

Rhona turned to face them. "We'll do whatever we have to. I'm going to have a word with Kerry."

"I'll contact Beth and see if I can determine her location," Bronwyn said. "That is, if she speaks to me."

Scott blew out a breath. "I can try George."

"Give me a sec. Saber could save us a whole lot of time," Sabryn said as she pulled out her mobile and walked out.

Emilie walked into the room and looked around with wide eyes. "I didn't mean to overhear everything, but there was a lot of shouting. Does anyone know where Jasper and Willa are?"

"We're going to find them," Rhona said.

Emilie lifted her chin. "Not without me."

Willa was left with her thoughts, which was dangerous at the moment. Her gaze ran over Jasper, from his face to his mutilated chest and then down his arms. The hand farthest from her lay right at the water's edge. Being so consumed with his death, she hadn't noticed it before. The sight of all the blood covering him was too much. Whether Jasper left the cave on his own two feet or not, he would do it clean.

It took Willa four tries to stand. She had touched so much of the ebony wood she wasn't surprised that it was already affecting her. With each second, it was like she was being sucked into a dark pit, covered in tar. Each breath, each movement made more and more painful. But she wasn't finished cleaning Jasper, so she had to keep moving. She walked to his other side and knelt beside him in the water. She gently moved his hand into the pool, tenderly wiping him free of blood and grime. She remembered how he had held her with that hand. New tears gathered, but she didn't try to stop them. She worked her way up his arm as she softly cried.

She saw something move out of the corner of her eye. She jerked her head to the side and found Balladyn. The Reaper met her gaze with a grave look. "Where were you?"

"I got to you right before you and Jasper were brought down here." He walked to squat near Jasper's head. "I've remained veiled since. The Fae can't know about me."

"Is there something that can bring Jasper back?"

Balladyn stared for a long moment before taking a deep breath. "What do you know about Skye?"

"Can it help Jasper?"

"Maybe."

She swallowed and glanced his way as she went back to cleaning Jasper. "Not much. Just that it's home to powerful Druids."

"Until recently, I never gave it much thought. I didn't know there was more to this isle. Like you, I believed it was just a place where Druids gathered. The heart of all magic on Earth is on Dreagan with the Dragon Kings, but magic can be felt everywhere on the realm. But there's more here on Skye than others. It's second only to Dreagan."

Willa didn't want the history lesson, but she hoped the Reaper had a point. So, she let him continue uninterrupted.

"It isn't the magic that makes the Skye Druids formidable. Nor is it Druids who make the isle powerful. It's a symbiotic relationship. The magic of the Druids feeds into the magic of Skye. It's why the Fae are drawn here. And why they acknowledged the Skye Druids and no others."

Willa tried to tear Jasper's shirt. One minute, it was there, and the next, it was gone. She nodded her thanks to Balladyn. He then made a small towel appear in her hand. She wet it in the flowing water and wrung it out before diligently cleaning Jasper's chest.

Balladyn shoved his long, silver-and-black hair away from his face. "Do you know why so many flock to the Fairy Pools?"

She shook her head.

"There was once a rumor that it had healing powers."

Willa paused and lifted her gaze to his. "Does it?"

"Do you really believe Druids would allow anyone to swim in them if they did?" he asked with a slight curve of his lips.

"Nay. Of course, they wouldn't."

"Because those aren't the healing waters of legend. These are."

"What?" she asked breathlessly.

Balladyn's smile was sad. "The Fae aren't allowed to share that with anyone, but we won't stop someone from getting into them, either. Alannah tried to tell you."

Willa gave him a dark look. "She did not."

"If you hadn't been so distraught, you would've noticed that she looked at the water several times."

Had she? Willa couldn't be sure. "Then…is what I'm doing enough? Jasper is…"

"I don't know. He has Druid and Fae blood running through his veins. But there's the ebony wood, too."

"It'll work." It had to.

Balladyn nodded. "Aye. It will."

He was humoring her, but Willa didn't care. "Is what I've done enough? Does he need more?"

"I wouldn't take any chances."

"Then I need to get him into the water."

"I cannot help."

She tossed aside the rag and forced herself to her knees. Jasper was tall and muscular. Moving him wouldn't be easy, but he was already near the water. All she had to do was roll him into it.

Willa shifted to his other side and dug her toes against the rocky floor as she attempted to roll Jasper over. Her shoes slipped time and again, her body wracked with its own pain. She tried different locations until she finally got a good hold. Eventually, she managed to get one hand under his shoulder and the other on his hip. Then she pushed.

Jasper's body was half-turned. Her muscles screamed with the exertion, but she had come this far. She couldn't start all over again. Willa clenched her teeth and put everything she had into it. Finally, he rolled to his stomach.

"Just a little more," Balladyn urged.

She hurried into the water. It lapped at Jasper's face. Since his feet and legs were already halfway in, she wound her arms around each limb and tugged him deeper. She only moved him an inch or two. Then she went back to his upper body. Willa tucked his arm against him before pulling his shoulder toward her. Her already taxed muscles screamed in protest, but she didn't relent.

Happiness filled her when she flipped him onto his back again. It only took a little more tugging before he floated in the water. She backed up, supporting him until her feet no longer touched. She treaded water, her face near his. For a moment, she closed her eyes as the water inched up her face. It felt so good. Then she remembered why she was in the water to begin with. She kicked her legs harder to keep her head above the surface.

"This is going to work. You're going to be healed," she whispered.

Balladyn beckoned to her. "Time to get out, Willa. Hurry."

CHAPTER FORTY-FOUR

SKYE DRUIDS

Willa didn't want to let go of Jasper, but something in Balladyn's voice told her she didn't have a choice. She kissed Jasper on the cheek and swam to shore. A loud crack and hiss sounded behind her. She turned to look, only to have Balladyn haul her onto dry land.

She stumbled against him as currents snapped over the top of the water, surrounding Jasper in brilliant white and violet streaks. This couldn't be good for him. She needed to get him out.

"Nay. You must stay," Balladyn cautioned as he held her.

Willa could only stare as the energy streams grew more rapid. The air sizzled with power she had never felt before. She was so gripped by what happened atop the water that she didn't notice the other lights at first. Once she did, she was shocked to see them coming from everywhere. The walls, the floor, the ceiling. They wove around her and Balladyn like misty ribbons before heading for Jasper. The air crackled, but not once did she feel threatened. Instead, she felt cocooned, safe.

The currents lit Jasper's body as it floated farther from her. Willa strained to keep him in sight. She couldn't tell how big the body of water was in the dim light. It could be a large pool, or it could be a stream.

A gasp tore from her when the first bolt of light pierced Jasper's chest. He jerked. Then more of the energy impaled him. It used the wounds from the ebony wood to penetrate him. The currents atop the water grew brighter, matching the light ribbons. All of them pierced Jasper until he was ablaze with light. It became so dazzlingly intense Willa had to shield her eyes with her arm.

Then, just as quickly as it had begun, the light was gone.

And so was Jasper.

"Where is he?" she asked, too shocked to move.

Balladyn walked around her to the water's edge and shook his head. "I don't know. This is the first time I've ever witnessed this."

"Did you know about the light?"

He glanced at her. "Aye."

"Surely, someone told you what happens next."

The Reaper shrugged. "The person was healed."

"All of them? Everyone who goes into the water comes out whole?"

"I didn't say that."

She walked around him so he had to look at her. "I need facts."

"Most are restored."

"Most?"

His lips flattened briefly. "I did warn you about the ebony wood. Jasper was already also gone from this world."

She lifted her chin, refusing to give up. "I need to find him. Someone, somewhere, knows something."

"You got him as far as he could go. The rest is up to Fate."

"I don't believe that. I can't."

Balladyn sighed. "Stay here. Let me see what I can discover."

She blinked, and he was gone. Willa didn't know if he was veiled or if he had teleported away. Or both. It didn't matter. Balladyn would help her. But she had a troubling thought. What if Jasper really *was* gone?

Willa slowly paced the area, because if she sat down, she might never get up. It was larger than she'd first thought, most of it taken up by water. Had their entry brought them to the water's edge on purpose? Balladyn and Alannah might have guided them here to make things easier. Or maybe she was only making those connections in her brain because it made things easier to digest.

She wanted to turn up the lights to see more, but there wasn't a switch. There were also no wires. Fae magic, then. But what else would it be in the real Fairy Pools? She'd never look at the others the same again. As beautiful as they were, she would always think of these. Hopefully, the waters here would be potent enough to return Jasper to her. She'd learned of her love for him too late. Restoring what was gone bent the rules of the universe, but she had to try.

For Jasper. For the love she had tried to deny.

Willa drew in a shaky breath. Just when she thought she had no more tears to shed, they fell onto her cheeks once again. She glanced at the water, to the last place she had seen Jasper. Her heart ached at the thought of the pain he had endured. There was guilt there, as well. She'd never let him explain. Had shut him out completely. She had only thought about herself and her pain. Why hadn't she considered that he hadn't named the horses? That admission told her so very much about him, but she hadn't realized it then. She only did now, when she had held his breathless body, and once he was gone.

She turned away from the water to look at the Celtic symbols. She walked to the wall to take a closer look. Soon, she turned her attention to the water again. Willa's impatience was growing. She paced in a circle as memories of her time with Jasper drifted through her mind.

The squishing of her wet socks in her boots became too much. Willa stopped and removed both. The rock was cold beneath her feet, but it was better than being soaked and icy. She wished she could do something about her saturated clothing. The cool air caused her to shiver. She wound her arms around herself to keep as much heat as possible against her as she paced. At least she was moving easier now.

"I can't find him."

Willa jumped in surprise, barely containing her shriek at the sound of Balladyn's voice behind her. She whirled around and searched the Reaper's face. "What does that mean?"

"It means he isn't here. I should return you to the manor. They'll be waking soon."

She started shaking her head midway through his words. "I'm not leaving until I find Jasper."

"The Fae allowed you here because of him. I don't know if they'll let you remain."

"Allow? *Let*? I dare them to make me leave." Even as she made the declaration, she knew it was a false threat. She couldn't do anything against a Fae. They were more powerful than the Druids.

Balladyn briefly lowered his gaze to the ground and blew out a breath. "You're chilled."

"You can remedy that."

"I can," he stated flatly. "Willa, there's determination, and then there's stubbornness."

She lifted her chin. "If you were in my place and looking for Rhona, would you leave?"

"You know I wouldn't. That doesn't change the fact that we should return to the manor."

"Then you go. Tell Rhona and everyone what happened. But I'm not leaving." Willa knew Balladyn could force her, but she really hoped he wouldn't. Tears blurred her vision. "I can't."

Balladyn ran a hand over his jaw, and her wet clothes suddenly dried. "I'm going to regret this. I'll return soon."

He was gone before she could reply. She stared at the spot he'd been for a moment, then went to a wall and slid down it to the ground. She pulled her knees up to her chest and rested her head against the wall. Tears welled in her eyes and fell onto her cheeks. It seemed she let someone down no matter what she did.

Her father, Scott, the group, Jasper, and even herself. All these years, she'd thought she knew herself and what she wanted, but she hadn't known anything. Not until she came to Skye. Not until she'd met Jasper.

Not until she'd fallen in love and saw the world in a new light.

Saw *herself* differently.

Yet she hadn't really noticed anything until Bronwyn put it to her in black and white. Willa had a clear picture of who she wanted to be and what she wanted. And that included Jasper. If he would have her. They'd have to work through some things, but she would do it. She had her own stuff to sort through regarding her family.

Her face crumpled when she realized she hadn't thought about her missing father in hours. She hadn't thought about Scott or anyone else, either. The world had simply stopped when she arrived at the Fairy Pools and saw Jasper on the ground. She had run as fast as she could, but it hadn't been quick enough.

Balladyn reappeared before her. He blew out a breath, his lips tight. "Your brother is intense."

She smiled despite the situation. "He's like that with those he loves."

"I've calmed him for the moment, but he won't rest until he talks to you."

Willa started to reply when everything blurred for a heartbeat. It felt as if someone had grabbed her shoulder and tugged, but nothing and no one was there.

"Fek," Balladyn said, taking hold of her arm.

It lasted another few moments before it finally relented. She looked up at the Reaper. "What was that?"

"I suspect Beth." Balladyn's jaw clenched as he released her. "You faded, Willa. If I'm not mistaken, she was trying to pull you to her."

"But…how can she do that?"

"That damn book. There's more to it than teachings or spells. She shouldn't be able to pull anyone to her. Reapers can't even do that. I'm not sure a Dragon King could swing it. Only one person can."

Willa raised her brows. "Who?"

"Erith. I mean, Death."

She'd been afraid he would say that. "Death is a Fae, right?"

"She's a goddess."

Willa's eyes widened. "Shite."

"Exactly. If Beth has gained that kind of power, then the book is as dangerous as I feared."

Beth got to her feet and shimmied her shoulders. She hoped it would shake off whatever Beth had tried. "Meaning?"

"Beth is *drough* now. But nothing like Bronwyn. The book gave Beth abilities, but it has also taken from her. She's lost her soul. A *drough* is dangerous because of the added magic they get by turning, but she's something more now. Much more."

The knot of anxiety in Willa's stomach grew. "You need to warn the others."

"She shouldn't be able to get to you here. It's probably the safest place for you to be. Still, I'm not wild about leaving you."

"The others need to know. Go. Please."

He nodded and vanished once more. Less than a minute later, Beth tried to pull Willa again. She was nearly yanked off her feet. She clung to the wall and fought against the magic until it finally yielded. The Fairy Pools had kept Willa safe, but she wouldn't be able to stay here forever.

Willa had a decent amount of magic, but it wasn't enough to go up against a *drough*, much less Beth. Not if Beth had the power of a goddess. What about Jasper had made Beth target him first? Why not Bronwyn?

Beth was doubtless the culprit for the ebony wood victims. She was also the most likely to have ordered it used on Willa. Yet that didn't explain why Beth had used it on so many on Skye. Unless… she was searching for something. Like a person who could remove it. Willa closed her eyes as the puzzle pieces started falling into place. Jasper had been trying to help, but all he'd done was seal his fate.

Willa gasped when she felt the tug again, like someone had gripped her soul and pulled. She planted her feet and refused to budge. Beth didn't give up easily this time. She yanked hard, causing Willa to grip the wall once more. Willa cried out when the power moved her back from the wall a few inches.

"She willna take you."

Willa's head snapped up, and she found herself looking into familiar dark eyes. Jasper cut his hand through the air between them. Instantly, the yanking ceased. She couldn't believe Jasper was here.

She touched his arm, afraid he was only a hallucination. She ran her gaze over his bare chest, seeing that every wound had vanished. "Is it really you?"

"It's me."

Willa threw her arms around him. His skin was warm, his body firm. Everything she wanted to say, everything she *planned* to say locked in her throat, clogged it with emotion. For the moment, it was enough that she could hold him.

CHAPTER FORTY-FIVE

SKYE DRUIDS

Jasper closed his eyes and gave himself over to the feel of Willa's soft body against his. He had never thought to hold her again. She felt so good, he never wanted to let her go. He allowed himself a few seconds to just be, a moment where his past and the pain he had caused her didn't matter.

Eventually, he opened his eyes and forced his arms to loosen. He leaned back to look into her blue eyes. His heart clutched at the sight of her wet cheeks and spiky lashes. Many had cried because of him, but none had cried *for* him. Until Willa.

"It worked," she whispered in awe as she ran her hands over his chest.

He wiped away a tear with his thumb.

"I have so many questions."

"I know," he replied.

She stared into his eyes. "Jasper, there are things I need to say."

"Later," he said over her before she could say more.

A brief frown furrowed her brow. "I've waited long enough."

"Beth willna stop trying to get you. I need to stop her."

"Can you?"

He couldn't, but he would give it all he had. "Maybe."

"Then use me as bait."

"Absolutely no'."

"It could work," Balladyn said from behind her. "It would take all of us, though."

Jasper shook his head and looked at the Reaper. "I can no' take that chance."

"It isn't your decision," Willa stated. "It's mine."

Jasper knew it was pointless to argue because it was her choice. That didn't mean he wouldn't try to talk her out of it. "Please. Doona do it."

"She won't be alone," Balladyn said.

Willa stepped to the side so she could see the Reaper. Jasper fisted his hands, his palms tingling from holding her. Being this close to her made it hard not to have her against him. It made it nearly impossible not to taste her lips one more time.

When he woke near the water, he should've gone straight to find Beth. He didn't know how he was alive, much less healed, but only one person had been in his thoughts—Willa. Something had led him straight to her. He hadn't been able to get to her quickly enough, especially when he realized Beth was trying to pull Willa to her.

At one time, Jasper had wanted to go back and change the past, but if he'd done that, he wouldn't have met Willa. Even if she could never be his, he didn't want the little time he'd had with her erased. He would hold on to that forever.

But there was something he *could* do. He could confront Beth.

Balladyn's gaze narrowed on him as if he were reading Jasper's mind. "You won't stand a chance against Beth on your own."

"No one will. She's too powerful," he answered.

Willa swung her head to Balladyn. "Did you warn the others?"

"Aye. They're all at the manor."

Jasper motioned to Willa. "Take her to them."

"I'm not leaving you," she stated. "Not after everything that just transpired."

Jasper glanced at the ground and took a deep breath. "You have a chance at a life, Willa. I doona. No' like you."

"You could. If you wanted."

He wanted. More than she would ever know. "Beth will come for me again. She needs me dead."

"Why is that?" Balladyn asked.

Willa nodded as she looked from the Reaper to him. "Aye. Why?"

"Because of my mother."

Balladyn held his gaze. "How did Beth find out?"

"You know his mother?" Willa asked Balladyn.

Jasper didn't look away from the Reaper. "They all do."

Shock softened Willa's face as she swung her head back to Balladyn. "Why didn't anyone tell Jasper?"

"We planned to," Balladyn replied.

Jasper ran a hand over his jaw. "Beth infected the Druids with ebony wood. She wanted to see if I was Emilie's son."

"Emi...? Dear God," Willa murmured in shock.

Balladyn's jaw tightened. "A test you passed."

"Wait. Just...wait," Willa said tightly, holding her hands up before her. "Why did Beth need to know if Jasper was Emilie's son?"

Jasper flexed his hands to leash his frustration. "She didna say. My guess is she has something planned."

"And you stood in the way," Balladyn added with a nod.

Willa's brow furrowed deeply. "That doesn't explain why Beth is after me."

"Maybe she's just a bitch."

Balladyn crossed his arms over his chest. "Maybe. But you two are bound together. Look how far you went to heal Jasper, Willa. And, Jasper, I don't need to remind you of the lengths you went to in order to remove the last bit of ebony wood from Willa."

"That's all true, but it still doesn't explain Beth's focus on me," Willa stated.

Jasper briefly closed his eyes as a thought took root. "Maybe it has nothing to do with you. What if she planned to use Willa to draw everyone else out?"

"Then I'm the perfect bait," Willa replied.

Balladyn grunted. "Not if Beth takes you somewhere."

"Then we don't let her." Willa shrugged as if it were no big deal. "We bring her to us."

Balladyn grinned. "It's likely Beth is still on Skye. We can do this."

"One less enemy is always good," Willa said.

So many things could go wrong, even with Balladyn on their side. But if Jasper's intent was to end Beth, it was the only plan. "All right. But Willa doesna leave here until everything is set."

"I'm right here," Beth said in a flat tone.

Balladyn nodded. "Agreed. I need to fill the others in."

"One more thing." Jasper stopped the Reaper before he could teleport away. "I need to speak to Emilie."

Balladyn nodded. He closed the distance between them and

touched Jasper's shoulder just as Willa shouted, "*Wait!*" But it was too late. They were already at Carwood Manor. Balladyn deposited him in the library and walked out. Jasper faced the hearth and the fire that crackled to drive off the chill in the air. He stared into the dancing flames and waited for his mother to arrive. The soft click of the door closing alerted him that he was no longer alone.

"Why did you no' tell me?" he asked as he turned around.

Emilie sighed and wrapped her arms around her middle. "How do you think that would've gone? '*Hi. I'm your mother. You were stolen from me. Oh, and by the way, I named you Travis.*'"

He tilted his head and shrugged. "I doubt I would've listened."

"Exactly. So, I kept my mouth shut."

"You had a second chance when I returned. You could've shown me pictures of my father."

She dropped her arms and came farther into the room, walking between the sofa and a chair. "You have no idea how much I wanted to do just that. I held my tongue because if you were to help Willa, you had to be completely focused on that. If you weren't, you could've killed both of you."

"Did you ever intend to tell me?"

"Aye."

He briefly looked away. "My name is Travis?"

Her lips curved into a relieved smile. "Travis Gregor Wilson. After my father and yours." She paused. "Did…the man who took you…was he good to you?"

Far from it, but Jasper wouldn't give her those details. It would only cause her more pain, and it was time for healing. "He was a hard man, but he wasn't abusive."

"I suppose I can be thankful for that." She licked her lips. "I didn't know until Theo showed me his picture yesterday that he was the man I healed from the ebony wood."

Anger and sorrow cut through Jasper. "And he repaid you by taking me."

"I looked everywhere for you. I hired so many people. I never gave up. Never. I want you to know that."

"I do. And it wouldn't have mattered who you sent looking for us, they never would've found me. Albie was good at hiding us. We lived under different names from week to week."

Emilie dashed away a tear. "I know you have a life, but I would very much like to get to know you."

"I'd like that, too." If he made it through the upcoming battle.

"Can I hug you?"

Jasper closed the short distance separating them and wrapped his arms around his mother for the first time. She was tiny, barely reaching his chest, but she had a firm grip. His eyes burned when he felt her shoulders shaking and heard her sobs. He couldn't imagine what she had suffered all these years because of doing what she believed in. How different would things have been if she'd let Albie die that long-ago night? He never would've taken Jasper. And Jasper would've known his parents and had a younger brother or sister.

"Forgive me," Emilie said and turned away, wiping her eyes.

"There's nothing to forgive."

She faced him again, her back straight and shoulders squared. "There's a lot I need to share in a short time. I assume you're going after Beth."

"I am."

"Then you need to know who your family is and why Beth targeted you."

"She already killed me once."

Emilie's expression hardened. "She caught you unawares. And Willa has my eternal gratitude for getting you into the healing waters. Now. Let's start at the beginning."

"It's fucking insane," Scott said.

Rhona agreed, but they didn't have any other option. Beth had her sights set on Willa, and with Jasper alive, they could triumph. However, even with all of them, it was still a huge chance.

Beth's power had grown significantly. Balladyn was troubled, and if *he* was concerned, she certainly was. They needed a win. But could they get it? Each in the group had willingly agreed to the plan, but that didn't mean she should give it the go-ahead. Not if it would decimate them. Because she would need all of them to face their other foes.

"Willa is strong. She can do this," Filip said.

Scott shook his head. "She shouldna have to."

"She's the one Beth is after," Balladyn pointed out.

Rhona listened to more of the same argument with half an ear. What would Corann do if he were still around? She tried to imagine the previous leader of the Skye Druids there and what he might say, but she could only guess. Would there ever come a time when she didn't wonder if she was making the right decision?

They were at war. It might not be playing out in the news, but that didn't mean it was any less dangerous or alarming. In many ways, it was much worse. She wanted to make sure none of her friends got injured or killed, but she couldn't ensure that. Nothing she did would get them all home every time. She and Balladyn talked about that at length. Often. He always tried to caution her on what could happen. They had been lucky so far. How long would that last?

She looked at every person in the room. Her gaze paused when she came to Esther and Henry. The siblings had an important role to play as TruthSeeker and JusticeBringer. Those responsibilities had led Esther to Skye in the first place. Rhona didn't worry about Esther. Being mated to a Dragon King made her all but immortal. She would live for as long as Nikolai did, and since only a Dragon King could kill another King, it meant they would likely live far into the future.

Their group would be going up against Beth with a Reaper and a Dragon King. That should calm her anxiety, but it didn't. And maybe that was how it would always be. She didn't want to be the kind of leader who didn't question her choices. She had to look at every angle to make sure she could make an informed decision.

She had an amazing group of warriors around her. Some who chose the life, and others who'd stumbled upon it. They had earned each other's trust through past trials. She and Balladyn had helped defeat the Fae Others when all seemed lost. She would defend Skye with her dying breath, and she knew Balladyn would, too. It might very well come down to the two of them in the end.

Her mate moved to stand before her. She tilted up her head to look into his beautiful eyes.

"You have doubts?" he asked in a soft voice no one else could hear.

"You know I do."

He took her hands in his. "There's a risk with every battle— some more than others."

"You said it yourself. She's powerful."

"Then we find out just how strong. Willa will do this with or without us. We need to take this chance. We may not defeat Beth this time, but we'll get a peek at her magic."

Rhona knew what she had to do. Balladyn moved to resume his position beside her. The door opened, welcoming Emilie and Jasper. Jasper looked different somehow. Not necessarily a physical change, but something…deeper. He inclined his head in her direction, and she responded in kind.

Rhona took a deep breath and said to the room, "You've all heard the plan. You know the risks. It's up to each of you whether you join this battle or not."

Sabryn shot her a grin. "I'm in. Always."

"Me, too," Carlyle said.

Finn snorted. "Do you really need to ask?"

One by one, they all agreed, including Emilie, which surprised Rhona. But maybe it shouldn't have.

Rhona nodded. "We have a good plan. You all know what to do. Good luck."

CHAPTER FORTY-SIX

SKYE DRUIDS

Getting out of the Fairy Pools was as disorienting as getting into them. However, that wasn't exactly true since Willa hadn't realized what was happening when she and Jasper arrived in them. But she knew when Balladyn teleported her away.

The next thing Willa knew, she stood alone in the open, waiting for Beth. Balladyn had given her a quick rundown of the plan before jumping her to where Beth had killed Jasper. It seemed simple enough. All Willa had to do was stand there.

Except, demanding to be used for bait was a lot easier when she wasn't about to face a Druid who had killed Jasper. Willa's stomach churned with fear and apprehension. Balladyn had told her to act distraught. She didn't have to pretend. That reaction had been on the fringes since she'd watched Jasper crumple to the ground hours earlier. Now, it swallowed her whole.

She might look as if she were alone, but she wasn't. Balladyn was near her, veiled. Jasper and the others were hiding, but much farther away. The pools had a few places to hide near them, but not many. Which meant they had to take cover some distance away. They had a plan. And they had several contingencies. Each of them began with her exactly where she was.

Willa hadn't had a chance to talk privately with Jasper. It hurt that he hadn't wanted to hear what she had to say. Maybe dying and being brought back had changed him. Willa shook her head. He had held her as tightly as she had him. She loved Jasper, and she would tell him as soon as she could. They could have something together. She felt their connection. It had been tangible and real, something that didn't come along every day. Something she would be a fool to walk away from.

Jasper wasn't the only one she hadn't gotten to speak with. There was also her brother. She was surprised that Scott hadn't tried to keep her from doing this. She wished she could've had a few moments to tell him how much she loved him and ask about their father. She would have time after. It was good to stay optimistic about an outcome.

The breeze was chilly. Willa shivered as she stared at the flowing water. Would Beth come to her? Or would the *drough* pull Willa away? It was hard not to think about whether Balladyn could follow wherever Beth pulled her because Willa wasn't convinced Beth would return to the same location. Balladyn would have seconds to return and grab the others so they could attack Beth. It was a crazy plan. But sometimes outrageous worked.

Willa's breath stalled as she felt a tug on her body. This time, it was like someone had reached inside her and grabbed her bones. Something yanked her away, cutting off her shriek. Willa tumbled to her knees onto pebbles and sand, water washing over her hands and arms up to her elbows and soaking her jeans.

"How utterly pathetic," said a voice behind her.

So, it had begun. Everything rested with her friends. Willa trusted them to find her before Beth could do whatever she planned. She swallowed and tamped down the rising fear. She tried to stand as the waves continued to roll against her. The rocks and sand beneath her feet were slippery, but she stood without falling. Then she turned to Beth.

Fear took a back seat as she gazed at Jasper's killer.

"Oooh," Beth said with a fake shudder. "Am I supposed to be put in my place by your glower?"

"You murdered Jasper."

"I sure did," Beth replied with a smile. "Idiot never saw it coming."

"Why?"

Beth rolled her eyes. "Why does anyone take another's life? He was in my way. In case you haven't figured it out, George sent him to seduce you."

"Why should I believe you?" Willa remembered at the last minute to play her part. But it was hard. Especially when she fought against the need for revenge.

"I couldn't care less. The bottom line is that Jasper was so much more than any of you knew. If you had known, you would've worked harder to get him on your side." Beth tilted her head, her brows drawing together. "Or maybe you already did. No matter."

Willa's rage grew to new heights, making it difficult for her not to lash out. "So, you want me now? Am I more than anyone knows, too?"

Beth threw back her head and laughed. "You're an insignificant ant. I'm going to take your life because I can. Jasper's death was just the beginning. I'm going to kill each and every one of you when you least expect it. And there's nothing you can do about it."

"Come on, then. Give me what you've got," Willa taunted, spreading her arms.

"If you insist."

The blast of magic came at Willa fast. She didn't even have time to comprehend it before it slammed into her like a giant fist to the gut. The force sent her flying backward. When she landed, the shock of the frigid water made her forget about the pain rolling through her body. She gasped as her head cleared the surface. Everything hurt. She gasped again, urging her lungs to expand so she could breathe.

All Willa wanted to do was curl into a tight ball. But she made herself move her arms and legs. She pushed away the pain. There would be time for that later. Now, she faced a threat that intended to take more lives. Willa just had to get to her feet and stay there until Balladyn and the others arrived.

Somehow, she maneuvered herself into a sitting position. The waves helped. Her legs crumpled on her first attempt to stand, but she pulled herself to her feet. The hard part would be walking out of the water. The waves buffeted her hips, helping to keep her upright while pushing her toward the shore.

"You should be dead," Beth said.

Willa almost laughed at Beth's confusion, but it took a lot for her to stay on her feet. Water sloshed and ran down her body as she reached the shallow water. She began shaking uncontrollably. Her teeth chattered from the chill. She spotted a figure behind Beth and grinned when she saw it was Jasper.

"Sorry to burst your bubble," Willa said as she walked from the sea, "but I'm very much alive. And I'm not the only one."

Beth whirled around and let out a furious shriek when she saw Jasper. "There's no way. I made sure you'd die."

"You're no' as powerful as you think," Jasper said, advancing on her.

Willa shouted a warning when she saw Beth throw magic. Jasper ducked, and it flew past him to slam into a small boulder, which exploded on impact. Willa gathered her power and readied to heave it at Beth when the rest of the team appeared. They circled Beth, putting the sea at the *drough's* back. Everyone was ready to pummel her with magic, but they waited. As Rhona had ordered. She intended to take Beth to the Red Hills and imprison her with Kerry. They really were going to win this. Willa had been so scared, but this was over quickly and easily. She couldn't wait to take a hot shower.

"It's over, Beth," Bronwyn stated.

Beth laughed. Willa watched the *drough*, wondering why she didn't seem at all concerned that they surrounded her.

"Oh, dear cousin, it's only beginning," Beth replied.

"Nay. It isn't," Rhona said and took a step toward Beth. "This ends today."

Beth glared at Rhona. "It ends when *I* say it does. You have no power over me. Enjoy your life while you have it because it'll be over soon."

"Behind you!" Jasper shouted.

Willa was in the middle of turning when magic smashed into her back. She went down hard, her head slamming against a rock. Despite the rush of water against an ear, Willa heard shouts. She fought against the blackness that dotted her vision. She wasn't sure she would make it to her feet this time. Suddenly, someone was there to help her up.

"Are you okay? Willa? Answer me," Scott yelled over the deafening sounds of battle.

She nodded and lied through her teeth. "I'm good."

He yanked her to her feet and spun around to fight one of Beth's guards. How could they have forgotten about them? Willa staggered on shaky legs and looked around at the utter chaos. At least a dozen Druids fought her friends. She gathered her magic and shoved a blast at a woman coming up behind Filip as he battled someone else.

Willa spotted a figure approaching out of the corner of her eye. She tried to get off a blast of magic, but the man was on her too quickly. He wrapped his large hand around her neck and squeezed, lifting her off her feet.

"Remember me?" he said through clenched teeth.

She gaped at the blackened eye socket where his eye used to be. Other parts of his face were blackened as if decaying, as well. When she saw him in Edinburgh, he hadn't been so infected. At least she knew who had used the ebony wood on her.

"I willna use magic to take your life this time. It'll be my bare hands. I want to feel the breath leaving your body," he said, bringing his face close to hers.

Willa kicked out, connecting with his leg as she clawed at his hand. She heard someone shout her name and looked over her attacker's head to see Jasper knocking aside anyone who tried to stop him from getting to her. One look at the determination on his face allowed calm to settle over her.

Willa's magic surged into her hands. She put her palms against her attacker's face and released it. He screamed and loosened his hold, so she dropped to the ground. She found herself in the water once more. She looked up to see him tearing at his face as flames erupted, covering his entire head. He was dead before his knees hit the earth.

She dragged in gulps of air between coughs. Then Jasper was there. He slid to one knee and went to touch her but hesitated as if he weren't sure where to put his hands. All she wanted was to fall into his arms, but two more of Beth's guards had turned their attention on them. She tried to warn Jasper, but the words didn't make it past her injured throat. She pointed instead.

He tugged her to his side and rolled them out of the way. He sat them up, and they released a volley of magic together. One of the guards dropped like a stone, but the magic only grazed the other, and he ran, hoping to escape.

Jasper jumped to his feet to fight. Willa looked around to see who would come at her next. But there were no other attackers. Somehow, the battle was over. She didn't lower her hands for several minutes, just to be sure. Seven of Beth's people had died on the beach, but Willa saw no sign of Beth herself.

"It was a diversion," Jasper stated, shaking his head.

Elias clenched his hands into fists and let out a bellow of frustration.

"She fucking planned for something like this," Sabryn said, sounding winded.

Theo was breathing heavily as he motioned to the mess. "We need to see to our wounded and get this cleaned up."

Jasper was beside Willa once more. "Where does it hurt?"

"Everywhere," she whispered, suddenly so tired that words were difficult.

"I've got you."

He gathered Willa into his arms, and she bit back a groan of pain. Then he was on his feet. She put her head on his shoulder.

"Gather together," Balladyn called.

Once everyone made their way into a tight group, touching someone near them, Balladyn jumped them all to Carwood Manor. Then, he immediately returned with Nikolai to handle the bodies on the beach.

Jasper carefully set Willa in a chair, promising to return soon. Bronwyn and Elodie issued orders to those not wounded. There was plenty of first aid, and the injuries were seen to in a timely manner, proving this wasn't their first go-round with battle. Willa knew that, of course, but hearing the stories was different than being caught up in the middle of it.

"You were amazing," Scott said with a smile.

Willa watched Elodie bandage his left shoulder before moving on to a gash on his right thigh. "I was angry." She winced at the pain in her throat.

"But effective," Carlyle said.

Finn lifted a bottle of whiskey as Bronwyn saw to his back. "Hear. Hear."

Willa turned her head to look for Jasper but saw he had left her to speak to Emilie. The Healer had a cut on her forehead that Jasper finished tending to. Willa smiled at the sight of them. They had lost so many years but would have a chance to catch up. Beth had nearly taken that away. Had she tried to kill Jasper anywhere else, he would likely be dead.

Every breath hurt. She fought to stay awake because she needed to talk to Jasper. She closed her eyes for a second. When she reopened them, Jasper was beside her, concern clouding his dark eyes.

"Stay with me, Willa," he urged.

She nodded. If only the pain would stop long enough for her to tell him she loved him, but it only seemed to grow.

"Where does it hurt?" he asked again.

It took two tries before she could whisper what she had said before, "Everywhere."

"There's no blood," Scott said worriedly.

Willa frowned and tried to look at her brother, but everyone was hazy.

"We got this," Elias announced as he hobbled to her with the other Knights.

Rhona stood on Willa's other side. "We all do. We need every Druid."

"Fight," Jasper whispered.

Willa tried to nod as they all linked hands around her. She didn't know what was happening, but the pain was unbearable. She fell into blessed oblivion.

CHAPTER FORTY-SEVEN

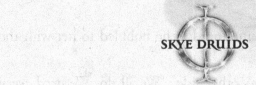

SKYE DRUIDS

"Go to her," Emilie said from beside him in the hallway.

Jasper pulled his gaze from Willa. They had healed her using a chant Elias had learned from the MacLeod Druids. Willa had yet to wake, though, and each minute that passed was excruciating. "I will."

Emilie covered his hands with hers and gave him a soft smile. "Be there when she wakes. You need to talk to her."

"I'm no' sure she'll want to hear what I have to say."

"Of course, she will. She loves you."

Jasper frowned. "How do you know?"

"I see how she looks at you, but it's more than that. It's what she did to bring you back."

"She would've done that for anyone. She's a good person."

Emilie gave him a stern look. "You have nothing to be afraid of."

"I'm no' a good person."

"Everyone makes mistakes. We're meant to learn from the past.

You've shown everyone—including yourself—what you're really made of these past days. That outshines any darkness."

Jasper turned his hands around to hold hers. "You say that because I'm your son."

"I say that because it's true. Go to her. Willa needs you just as you need her."

He hesitated, and Emilie gave him a little shove. "All right, all right," he said with a chuckle.

"I'll be here. Promise," she said.

Jasper enfolded her in his arms. He gave her a soft kiss on the cheek before pulling back. He saw her eyes glistening as he turned away, but then again, his were, too. Jasper cleared his throat and made his way to Willa.

Scott rose from the chair beside the bed when he noticed Jasper. He inclined his head before walking out. Jasper was glad that Scott didn't act as if he wanted to take his head off anymore. As he made his way to the chair, Jasper saw a fluffy white cat with gray markings on its ears, nose, paws, and tail jump onto the bed. He had no idea where the feline had come from. The cat curled up between Willa and the edge of the bed. Jasper sank into the chair with a sigh. Things could've gone so very wrong today. Not only had Willa been in danger, his mother had, too. It felt odd thinking that, much less saying it. *Mother*. All the years of believing he didn't have one when she had been on Skye all along.

It would take him a long time to forgive Albie for taking him from his mum and forcing him to live the life he had for so long. But like Emilie had said, the past was the past. He would learn from it so he didn't repeat his mistakes.

He leaned forward and smoothed back Willa's long, brunette hair. He hadn't been ready to hear what she'd had to say earlier because he feared what it might be. He still wasn't sure. Emilie thought Willa loved him. But was it enough after his betrayal? Would she give him time to prove he wasn't that man anymore?

Jasper felt something cold and wet on his finger. He looked over to find the cat sniffing him before the feline lifted its big blue eyes to him. Jasper petted him. He smiled when the animal purred loudly. The more Jasper stroked, the happier the cat seemed.

Something about petting the soft fur and hearing the purrs relaxed him. The worries of tomorrow fell away. No one in their group had been killed. The fight was far from over with Beth—and George—but he and the others would be ready for the next battle that came their way.

Willa slept for hours. Eventually, Jasper relinquished his chair to Scott and took the time to eat, shower, and change. When he returned, Willa was on the bed brushing her wet hair and laughing at something Scott said, the cat in her lap.

Scott cleared his throat. "I…um…I'm going to go."

Jasper stepped aside to let Scott leave.

Willa set down the brush and smiled at him. "I've been waiting for you."

"Someone should've told me you were awake."

"I asked them to let you have some time to yourself."

Jasper took a couple of steps toward her. "How do you feel?"

"Like I was in battle. But I'm okay, thanks to everyone," she said with a grin.

"Good. That's good." Damn, he was nervous.

She motioned him forward. "Sit, please."

Jasper eyed the bed but chose the chair so he could look at her.

"How are you?" she asked.

"Bruised. I'll be sore tomorrow. Otherwise, I'm okay."

"Will you tell me what happened at the Fairy Pools?"

He ran a hand over his jaw. "I'm no' sure. Besides the pain, the last thing I remember was you asking me no' to go. I remember thinking that I didna want to, but I couldna stop it. After that, nothing."

"Nothing?" she repeated, brows raised.

"Nothing. I woke up on the ground near the water. I had no idea where I was, but I had a sense of the direction I needed to go. I followed the water, and it led me to you. Why? What did you see?"

Her throat bobbed as she swallowed. He listened in shock and awe as she described the light and voltage that went through him multiple times before he disappeared.

"Bloody hell," he murmured. "I vanished? I doona recall any of that."

"No voices? Faces?"

Jasper blew out a breath. "Nothing. Fae blood, huh? I'll have to tell Emilie. I doona think she knows."

"That Fae blood saved you."

"Nay," he said and looked into her eyes. "You did. You got me into the water."

Willa shrugged and sank her fingers into the cat's fur. "I couldn't let you die."

"What I did to you—"

"Was done because you thought it was the right thing to do," she spoke over him. She shrugged one shoulder. "You changed your mind about all of it, and you told me the truth. That took courage. You could've left without saying anything, but you didn't. You held nothing back."

He studied her face for a silent moment. He'd never seen

anyone so beautiful. He loved her and wanted to spend his life by her side. "I wasna a good man."

"You've proven to me the type of man you are. That's what matters."

"And my past? The way I've lived?" He had to know where she stood before he got his hopes up.

She inhaled and then slowly released the breath. "Do you intend to keep conning people?"

"Nay. I didna lie before. I'm done with that."

"Then it's in the past. Everyone deserves a second chance. Especially you, after what you've done for everyone on Skye."

He sat forward, his heart racing. "Willa."

"Shh," she said and shook her head. "I've been trying to tell you something since you came back from the dead." She gently removed the cat from her lap and scooted toward him. "I love you. I loved you before I knew I did."

Jasper could hardly believe the words.

"We had a rocky start, but I want to see where this goes. I want you."

He stood and gazed down at her. He cupped a cheek in one hand and rested the other on her side. "For the first time in my life, I can be myself with someone. I've worn so many masks over the years that I forgot who I was until I met you. I've hidden nothing from you. I couldna. You bring out my true self. You make me want to be a better man. I like who I've become here, and I want a life on Skye. With you. I doona deserve you, but I love you, Willa. More than all the stars in the universe."

Her smile was blinding. "You deserve every good thing that comes to you. Me included."

"I willna argue with that," he whispered before lowering his head for a kiss.

He tangled his hand in her wet hair and tugged her so they both lay on the bed. They forgot the rest of the world as passion swept them into a wild, frenzied dance. They ripped away clothes until they were skin to skin. He sighed when he thrust into her body. This was where he belonged. He had found his past and his future on Skye. But more than that, he had found himself and the love of his life.

EPILOGUE

SKYE DRUIDS

Three days later…

Willa scratched her head and looked at Jasper across the sofa. They had returned to his house two days earlier. "So, let me get this straight. The Fae blood comes from your dad's side, and he never knew?"

"Apparently, no'," he said, rubbing her feet. "Mum can explain it better."

She loved that he already called Emilie his *mum*. "I want you to tell me."

"The way Mum explained it, he and his family used to joke about it because his great-grandfather used to say they had Fae blood. It turns out he was right."

"Wow," she said with a shake of her head. "And the ebony wood comes from her side."

"Right. She was correct that anyone who's experienced it can detect it."

"Meaning me."

He grinned. "Meaning you."

Willa propped an elbow on the back of the couch. "The guy who used it on me in Edinburgh had black marks on his face."

"The backlash. It affects people in different ways."

"Have you felt anything since helping me and the others?"

Jasper shook his head. "I took precautions, remember?"

It would be enough. She would will it so. Everything he had done had been to help others. Then again, the same could be said about Emilie, and she had lost everyone.

"How about you? You touched quite a few shards of the ebony wood," he said.

"Balladyn thinks the Fairy Pools must have healed whatever damage the wood did when I got in the water with you."

Jasper nodded slowly, his gaze piercing. "Balladyn said the same to me. You'll tell me if anything changes."

Willa grinned. "Promise."

A horn honked outside. Jasper frowned and rose to his feet. Willa couldn't hide her smile as she jumped up and shoved her feet into her slippers. She watched as Jasper walked to a window and looked out. His frown vanished, replaced by disbelief and then utter joy.

"What did you do?" he asked as he slid his gaze to her.

"Returned what you never should've given away. Shall we go outside and greet Bay, White, Gray, and Sorrel?"

He yanked her against him and gave her a long, lingering kiss. "Nay. We're going to greet our horses and name them properly. I didna give any of them names because I didna have roots. Now, I do. And they deserve names."

"That they do." She beamed.

Hand in hand, they walked outside just as the horses were being unloaded and led into the pasture. Willa stayed at the fence and watched as they rushed to greet Jasper. She wasn't sure who was more excited, but it didn't matter. Things had fallen just where they were supposed to, even though others had fought to change that.

There was more ahead, but Willa had faith in love and Jasper. She trusted in her family and the group of friends he would risk everything for. The only thing missing was her father.

Beth stood next to the bed as Sydney moaned from withdrawal. She had moved up her timeline to bring him home because she was tired of going to the hospital to see him. Besides, she needed facts from him about his last battle with Bronwyn.

Walking from the room, she nodded at the nurses who looked after him. They would keep her updated until she returned. Her thoughts were no longer on Sydney, however. They were on Skye. She'd gotten a look at those she would be battling, and it had been worth the cost of a few of her people. Rhona's group hadn't used the full force of their magic, but neither had she.

Beth had known something was up the first time she couldn't call Willa to her. That was when she made new plans. Everything had worked out perfectly, except for the fact that neither Jasper nor Willa was dead. But the book would fix that next time.

She made her way to the room she had converted into her office. Madeline stood at the door in all black, her black hair back in a severe bun. "George has requested you ring her."

Beth snorted and walked around to sit behind her desk. "She's becoming a nuisance."

"Is it time to get her out of the way?"

Beth stopped looking through her mail and paused. "I had thought so, but I think I still have a use for her."

Edie stared out the window. She hadn't slept since hearing the voice in her head. She had tried not to think about it, but it was difficult not to. She didn't know if she was going daft or not. She heard it at least once a day now, but she continued to ignore it.

"You can't ignore me."

She shut her eyes tightly. If Trevor found out, he would take the kids away.

"You're not losing your mind, Edie. It's rare for a Druid not to be happy about the Ancients speaking to them."

Her eyes flew open. "Ancients? Why didn't you tell me before?"

"We're not used to being ignored."

"I thought you were supposed to be many voices."

"Only the truly special hear only one."

"I'm...special?"

"More than you know. It's time, Edie."

"Time for what?"

"For you to become who you were meant to be."

Carlyle reclined in the hot tub with his eyes closed, trying to ease the aches of battle from his body. His mobile rang. He answered without looking at the screen. "Yeah?"

"About bloody time you answered my call."

Carlyle's eyes popped open, and he sat up. "Mason."

"That's right, *old friend*."

Carlyle laughed as he turned off the jets so the water quieted. "What do you want, Mason?"

"Information on Ferne."

"If you want to know about your sister, then call *her*."

Silence met his statement. Carlyle frowned and wished he could see Mason's face. "What is it?"

"Don't forget you have a family."

The threat was clear. "You're sinking to a new low."

"You and Ferne made your choice."

Thank you for reading **ENDLESS SKYE**. I hope you enjoyed the story! I love the Skye Druid world, and it's always so much fun to return to it.

If you want more Skye Druid stories, than be sure and grab the next book in the series, **STILL OF THE NIGHT**.

BUY STILL OF THE NIGHT NOW
at www.DonnaGrant.com

* * *

To find out when new books release
SIGN UP FOR MY NEWSLETTER today at
https://www.tinyurl.com/DonnaGrantNews

Join my Facebook group, Donna Grant Groupies, for exclusive
giveaways and sneak peeks of future books.
https://www.facebook.com/groups/DGGroupies

* * *

Keep reading for a peek of STILL OF THE NIGHT...

STILL OF THE NIGHT EXCERPT

SKYE DRUIDS

Killian adjusted his grip on the steering wheel as he drove off the ferry onto Skye as it began to rain. He swallowed heavily and followed the vehicle in front of him. After merging onto the road, Killian took the curves around the isle.

Nothing had changed.

And yet, so much had changed.

It felt like a lifetime since the last time he had been on the isle. In many ways, it had been exactly that. The last time he had driven the roads, he'd been on top of the world. It had been the best summer of his life. There hadn't been a care in the world. No worries, no doubts. No fears. How naïve they had been, *he* had been.

The windscreen wipers diligently kept the glass clear as the drops beat fiercely upon his car. It kept him from catching a glimpse of buildings and landscape, but he knew from his memories how deep a blue the water was, how vibrant the green of the grass.

Killian kept to the roads along the coast instead of heading straight to his destination. Mostly because he was a coward. His nose wrinkled at that. His father would've denied such a thing, but it was true. He was scared. More frightened than he had ever been for anything, including standing in court in defense of his clients with their lives in his hands.

He found an area to pull off the road to stare through the rain-drenched windscreen to the brooding Cuillin Mountains. Locals called this range the Black Cuillins because of the dark color of the rock. Killian dropped his gaze. His mood matched that of the weather. Maybe it was a sign that it had begun to rain the moment he drove onto the isle. Or maybe he was being superstitious. There was no way the weather cared about mood, much less one person in billions. Killian gave a shake of his head and pulled back onto the road.

His drive took him through one village and then another. He passed cottages dotting the landscape. Some near the coast, some higher up in the hills. He drove around lochs and past waterfalls. It was the same, and yet different. Each time he attempted to drive toward his destination, something held him back. Finally, he gave up and made his way to the B&B where he had rented rooms.

His mobile rang with a call. Killian ignored it, not even bothering to look down. He knew it was his father. He wanted something he couldn't have. Yet, there was a last teensy bit of hope that had sent him toward Skye the night before. One way or another, he would know the answer to the question he didn't dare speak aloud—not even to himself.

The ringing finally stopped, only to start again a moment later. Killian reached over and turned off the ringer. His father had a very narrow view of the world, and few things could alter it.

Killian didn't want to waste his time explaining—for a third time —only to end in another argument. His father could wait.

Everyone could wait.

For the first time, Killian was doing what *he* wanted.

That thought brought a flood of memories from that summer, and with them the soft, Scottish words, *"It's your life. You get to make your own decisions."*

He had brushed off her words then. If only he would've listened. How different the last seven years would've been. The only time he had done what he wanted was that summer. For as long as he could remember, everything had been planned for him. Where he went to school, university, his job, and even when he was expected to marry, along with who he was expected to take as his bride.

The tires of his vehicle crunched over the pebble lined drive to the B&B. The house was as charming as one would expect from such a location, but he didn't care about that. It was the first one that came up on his search, and he had booked it without looking at any others. Plus, it was close to the reason he had really come to the isle.

Killian climbed out and walked to the door, pulling the collar of his coat up to keep most of the rain out. He shook himself off under the awning before entering. It was the off season for visitors, which meant there was no waiting for him to get checked in. Once he had the key to his room, he got his luggage from the back of the vehicle.

Then, he was in the second-floor room staring out the window of rain-soaked Skye. The sun and blue skies were hidden by melancholy gray clouds that covered the sky from every direction. Killian quite liked the weather. He always had an affinity for storms, especially those that involved thunder and lightning. But any storm would do.

He sank onto the bench at the foot of the bed and continued his perusal of the landscape he could see through the window. There was a small sliver of blue from one of the lochs he had driven passed. Had he swam in those waters? Maybe. It seemed they had always been swimming that summer. Swimming and loving, laughing and talking.

The sun had never been brighter, the storms never so fierce. Life never so vibrant and beautiful.

Killian blew out a breath as he stood and pulled out his laptop. He set it aside, searching for the stack of papers that he had put with it. He found the papers and carefully folded them to stuff into the inside pocket of his coat. He paused, trying to decide if he wanted to remain in the room with his memories, or if he dared to face the past.

BUY STILL OF THE NIGHT NOW
at www.DonnaGrant.com

ABOUT THE AUTHOR

New York Times and *USA Today* bestselling author Donna Grant® has been praised for her "totally addictive" and "unique and sensual" stories.

She's written more than one hundred novels spanning multiple genres of romance including the bestselling Dragon Kings® series that features a thrilling combination of Druids, Fae, and immortal Highlanders who are dark, dangerous, and irresistible. She lives in Texas with her dog and a cat.

www.DonnaGrant.com
www.MotherofDragonsBooks.com

f facebook.com/AuthorDonnaGrant
⊙ instagram.com/dgauthor
BB bookbub.com/authors/donna-grant
g goodreads.com/donna_grant
℗ pinterest.com/donnagrant1